Millionaires

are a girl's best friend

Millionaires
are a girl's best friend

JACQUI
BRODERICK

POOLBEG

315478

Published 2006
by Poolbeg Press Ltd
123 Grange Hill, Baldoyle
Dublin 13, Ireland
E-mail: poolbeg@poolbeg.com

© Jacqui Broderick 2006

The moral right of the author has been asserted.

Typesetting, layout, design © Poolbeg Press Ltd

1 3 5 7 9 10 8 6 4 2

A catalogue record for this book is available from the British Library.

ISBN 1-84223-226-6
ISBN 978 1-84223-226-2 (From January 2007)

Typeset by Type Design in Palatino 10/13.8pt
Printed by Litografia S.A, Spain

www.poolbeg.com

About the Author

Jacqui Broderick was born in England. She moved to Ireland in 1997 and now lives in Galway with her three children and numerous horses, ponies, dogs and cats.

She is the author of three books; *The Shane Broderick Story*, a biography, was published in 1999. Her novels are *Trainers* and *Winners*. She has been involved with horses all of her life. When not writing, she divides her time between Connemara where she works as a guide bringing groups of horse-riders through the Connemara wilderness, and Galway, where she trains young ponies.

Acknowledgements

I'd like to thank the following people:

My wonderful mum, as always, for providing an excellent children's taxi service and for being brave enough to come into my office with cups of tea.

Everyone at Poolbeg for their wonderful support and the fantastic job that they do in turning a manuscript into the book that every writer dreams of.

Gaye Shortland, my superb editor, whose healing hands have worked yet again!

My children who daily fill my life with love and happiness and who daily make me so proud and amazed that I could have had any part in creating such wonderful characters and who keep me supplied with cuddles and tea.

My dad, who listens to my moans and gripes – at least I think that he is listening.

Stephanie, for her support and friendship from the other side of the pond.

Emma, brilliant agent, and my dear friend, for her valuable careers advice and guidance.

Astrid and all of the Day family for their wonderful friendship and for the peace and happiness that we have found at their home.

Rebecca and her Angels, who came along at just the right moment in my life to let me know that everything was going to be OK.

And, of course, special thanks to my special friend for love, friendship and guidance.

Cancer touches so many lives, young and old. Just after I had completed this book, a good friend found out that she had cancer. Hopefully now she is on the road to recovery. The Irish Cancer Society were a tremendous help to me in providing information while I was working on this book. They have a hugely informative website and great telephone helpline. Nothing was too much trouble, no question too stupid, even though they must have had a wealth of other work to do, rather than listening to the ravings of an author. A huge vote of thanks to everyone connected with the Society and to all of the doctors, nurses and scientists who deal with this disease on a daily basis. And one word of advice to everyone. Don't be a hero. If you have any doubts go and get checked out.

To Kelly, James and India, with love

1

The worst thing of all was that Rory laughed. And it wasn't as if it was a sympathetic oh-what-a-dreadful-thing-to-happen kind of embarrassed chuckle. No – this was a full-blown what-a-fool-you-have-made-of-yourself kind of guffaw.

At first Stella hadn't realised that there was anything wrong.

"This is my horse," Rory had announced proudly as an enormous prancing mass of muscle and flailing hooves was led across the parade ring towards them. "And my trainer, Henry Murphy," he added, shaking hands with the tall man who had walked alongside the horse across the damp turf to join them. "Henry, this is Stella O'Rourke."

Stella had done a double-take. Henry Murphy was gorgeous. She dragged her eyes away from him to look at the nondescript-looking owners and trainers who were standing in the parade ring. Then she chanced a look back at him. Yes. He was definitely gorgeous.

"Move Out looks very well!" Rory yelled above the roar of the spectators as the horse halted beside them. Move Out's black coat shone with sweat and his white teeth champed frenziedly at his bit, sending showers of foam into the air as he tossed his elegant head, while his sour-looking girl groom, red-faced from exertion, clung to his bridle, her knuckles white with the effort.

Henry grinned, gazing lovingly at the horse. Then, to Stella's alarm, he grabbed the bridle and pulled the huge animal even closer to where she stood. "He should do well in this next ra–"

And that was when Stella realised that something was wrong. Amid the cacophony of noise from the racecourse there was a stunned silence from the group surrounding them. And everyone was staring at *her*. Stella felt a cold shiver of horror run down her spine, sending icy tendrils over her limbs, as if a bucket of cold water had been thrown over her. She gazed at the wide-eyed, shocked expressions around her.

And that was when Rory started to laugh.

Stella looked down at the beautiful cream jacket she had bought especially for the day. A huge blob of dirty greenish-brown foam from the horse's mouth had landed on the front of her jacket, and had dripped slowly downwards leaving a stain in its wake while small splatters of foam covered one arm. Slowly Stella raised her head and glared at the man who had ruined her first date with Rory . . . and in his eyes she read . . . *amusement*!

"Excuse me, I need to go to the ladies' to get cleaned up," she said, husky with embarrassment, before turning away and walking with as much dignity as she could muster across the grass of the parade ring.

The cruel laughter of those who had witnessed her disgrace rang in her ears.

The racehorses were being led around the concrete path that circled the parade ring, intense grooms clinging to their bridles as their nervous charges pranced in anticipation of the coming race. The way out of the parade ring was barred by the horses. Stella waited fretfully, aware of the curious stares of the spectators. An enormous grey horse, scared by a sudden gust of autumn wind that lifted his brightly coloured rug, jumped sideways towards her. Panic-stricken, she darted out of the way of his flailing hooves and enormous grey body, feeling her high heels sinking into the damp grass. She wobbled and crashed into an elderly horse-faced woman who tutted as Stella stammered an apology. Then, seeing a gap in the line of horses, Stella made a dash for the edge of the ring.

She ducked under the white guardrail at the edge of the parade ring, the line of spectators who had been leaning on the rail moving out of the way. She was aware of their looks of amusement and sympathy as they noticed her ruined jacket and she was painfully aware of her face, burning crimson with embarrassment. Only pride kept her from crying aloud as she walked towards a sign for the toilets positioned high above the racecourse with an arrow pointing to a dingy red-brick building. After what felt like an eternity she reached the open door of the ladies' and plunged thankfully into the dim, tiled interior that reeked of disinfectant and cheap air freshener. Two smartly dressed ladies, preening themselves in front of a smeared mirror, glanced at her reflection. She saw one nudge the other and look at her with a grimace of distaste, then look away quickly as Stella met her glance with cold, angry eyes. "Come on, Maeve," said the woman, gathering up her handbag from beside the washbasin and flashing Stella a sympathetic smile before she sashayed out of the toilets. Her companion, dabbing hard at a blob of mascara that had smeared beneath her eyelids, was slower to move. She glanced at Stella as she turned and, as the stained jacket caught her eye, looked so hard that she missed the exit and lurched straight into the wall. Stella was too busy looking in the mirror at that point to be amused at the other woman's misfortune. She stopped dead, frozen in horror, staring at her reflection. Bitter tears of disappointment trickled unchecked down her cheeks, smudging her mascara and leaving a dark trail through the foundation that she had so carefully applied that morning. The smeared, pitted glass couldn't disguise the dreadful mess the horse had made of her jacket, the jacket that she had chosen so carefully for this so, so special occasion. The day that she had so, so looked forward to.

*　　*　　*

Stella had wanted Rory even before she had met him. Her boss, Kevin O'Meara, had ordered a brainstorming session for a special Valentine's edition of the magazine she worked for, *MiMi*. He wanted to do a special feature on Ireland's most eligible bachelors and 'chicks-about-town'. 'Eligible spinsters', he had decided, was really not the kind of term that should be used to describe the unmarried, wealthy female readership of the magazine.

And so, all of the editorial staff had found themselves sitting around the vast expanse of the boardroom table early one Monday morning, sipping strong black coffee, nibbling croissants and nursing hangovers while they racked their brains for names of wealthy singletons of a certain age. Kevin had suggested Rory McFadden. Born into a wealthy land-owning family, he had made his millions running his own property development company. Sorcha, Stella's stroppy assistant, had even found a photograph of him in an old copy of *Hello* magazine. He made an imposing figure, lolling against the bonnet of his sports car.

Perfect, Stella had decided on the spot. He was just the kind of man she wanted to marry. None of the other eligible bachelors interested her – they were all too young, too old, or too involved. Either that or the other members of staff had dreadful tales about their sexual preferences or debauched styles of living. And that wasn't what she wanted. No, when a girl got to be twenty-six she was looking to settle down. To get married, have a few children, live the kind of existence that Stella constantly read about in her glossy magazines.

Securing an opportunity to meet Rory hadn't been easy. It just wasn't possible to go into Kevin's office and lean across the desk and demand to be sent to interview him. "By the way, boss, I'd like to marry Rory McFadden. I think he is *just* the kind of man that I've had on my wish list for all these years."

No, it all took time. Had to be done slowly, subtly, with patience and planning.

And then finally her chance came. The guest list for an art gallery opening landed on her desk.

"Organise a photographer for this, can you? I want to cover it for the social diary," Kevin had said as he hurried past.

Stella propped the list against her in-tray to remind her to make the call and then a name leapt off the page at her. Rory McFadden! Her big chance! She went along to the gallery opening to 'help' the photographer and within half an hour of walking through the doors had managed to get herself introduced to Rory.

He had been just what she had hoped for. Tallish – thankfully she wasn't wearing her highest heels – and rather than just drop-dead gorgeous, he was a majestic figure and immaculately dressed (expensively, too, of course – Stella knew all about these things). By the end of the evening she had secured herself an invitation to the races to watch one of his horses running. That was the first hurdle over. Now all she had to do was to get Rory to fall in love with her – and hopefully fall in love with him in the process. First step, knock him dead with her beauty, charm and wit on their first date. Well, she had done that all right. Her new cream suit had cost a week's wages, the handbag and shoes a similar amount. She had never paid so much before at the hairdresser's, but it had been worth every penny when she saw the glorious golden blonde colour and the sleek stylish cut that flattered her high cheekbones.

Rory's mouth had dropped open when he had picked her up before the races. "You look fantastic," he grinned, opening the passenger door of his new Mercedes for her. Stella had settled herself into the seat with a smile of satisfaction. All of the trouble and expense she had gone to for this first date had been worth it.

* * *

And now it was all ruined. Ruined because bloody Henry Murphy couldn't control a bloody horse! Rory had laughed at her. He obviously thought she was an idiot, not knowing enough about horses to stay well out of their way. She'd made a total fool of herself, her much-dreamed-of fledgling relationship with Rory over before it had even had the chance to begin.

A noise made her start and turn.

"Erm . . ." Rory stood uncertainly in the doorway, holding out the long black coat that he had been wearing. "Not sure if I should come into the ladies' toilet, but I thought that you might need this." He shoved the coat in Stella's direction. "It will probably be enormous on you, but it will hide the worst of the stain on your jacket."

Stella looked at him gratefully, hoping that crying hadn't done too much damage to her make-up. She took the coat. "Thank you."

"Right then," Rory said, backing rapidly out of the toilets as if he expected to be yelled at by some prudish old lady.

Stella put on the coat and checked her reflection in the mirror. The coat was enormous, but once she had turned up the collar and rolled up the sleeves it looked quite stylish, the great dark swathes of fabric making her look delicate and waif-like. Then dabbing a small smear of mascara from the corner of one eye, she turned away and taking a deep breath went back outside into the bustle of the race meeting. Rory obviously cared enough to come and find her and help with her dreadful predicament. Perhaps the date wasn't going to be such a disaster after all.

Rory was still in the parade ring with Henry Murphy when Stella returned. The horse was saddled and being led around by his groom. Stella glared at the enormous black horse which was still tossing its head and dancing as if the ground were red-hot beneath its delicate hooves. How anyone could actually like those bloody-minded creatures was beyond her.

Henry smiled as she went towards them, but Stella ignored him completely and flashed a wide smile at Rory.

"My coat suits you," Rory beamed, holding her by

the shoulders at arm's length to study her. "Now, Henry, look after Stella while I go and put my bets on. And *try* not to let another horse damage her!"

Henry grinned. "No guarantees!"

Sheila flushed with fresh annoyance. It was *not* a joke!

"He'll have to be quick," mused Henry, watching Rory sprint lightly across the parade ring. "The horses will be going out onto the course in a few minutes."

Stella stared fixedly at the horses – anything to avoid having to talk to Henry. He really was the most annoying man that she had ever met and her fingers itched to slap his cheek to remove his inane grin.

"Are you OK?" he asked, coming to stand right beside Stella.

"Well, obviously bloody not," she said tightly. "Your horse just ruined my jacket."

"It's only a few speckles of horse spit!" Henry gave a barely disguised snort of laughter, which, seeing the look of anger on Stella's face, he rapidly turned into cough. "I could hardly stop the horse tossing his head, could I?" he said, tilting his head to one side to look at her quizzically.

Stella met his eyes for the first time and felt her stomach lurch uncomfortably. Henry had gorgeous eyes, deep green, surrounded by the longest thickest lashes that she had ever seen. She looked away abruptly. "I thought that you were his trainer. You can't be doing a very good job if you can't even teach him to stand still."

This time Henry didn't even bother to disguise his howl of laughter. "I train him to race, not to stand to attention! He's a racehorse, not some circus performer!"

* * *

"So," Henry said smoothly, a short time later, as they stood in the Owners' and Trainers' Bar toasting Move Out's brilliant win. "Am I still a bad trainer?"

Stella shrugged and took a long swig of her champagne. "I neither know nor care," she said airily, looking across the bar towards Rory who was drinking his champagne out of the enormous cutglass vase that he had been awarded as the winning owner. "I just hope that I never have to see you or that bloody horse again."

"I'm sure that you'll see plenty of me, if you carry on seeing Rory," Henry grinned, fixing his beautiful eyes on her.

"Not if I can help it," Stella snapped back, dragging her own eyes reluctantly away from his. She turned away quickly before her eyes, which were acting as if they had a life of their own, made contact with Henry's again. She reached Rory who merrily offered her a swig of champagne out of the cutglass vase.

"You've brought me luck today," he said enthusiastically as he put his arm around her shoulders. "I've really enjoyed having you with me. And I'm sure that your jacket will clean up." He moved his black coat aside to look at the stain with a grimace of concern.

Stella pulled the coat shut again quickly – she didn't want reminding about Henry and the bloody horse.

"Will you come out with me again?" asked Rory with a smile as she handed the champagne back to him, raising his eyebrows quizzically.

Stella felt her heart leap with delight. The day hadn't been a disaster after all. Rory was going to take her out again. And this time there would be no mistakes. No horses to ruin everything.

"I'd love to," she nodded gratefully.

"Great," Rory said, giving her arm a playful squeeze. "We'll go for some lunch on Sunday and then we can drive over to Henry's to look at a horse he thinks I should buy."

2

Gingerly Amber turned the door handle and crept stealthily into the bedroom, her bare feet padding lightly on the carpet. Then taking a deep breath she snapped on the switch, flooding the room with light. She expelled the breath, feeling her heart pounding against her ribcage. This was ridiculous. Stella was out for the evening. It wasn't as if she was going to come back and find Amber rifling through her wardrobe. Was it? And if she did, then it wasn't likely that she would be very upset. Well . . . not very. It wasn't as if Amber made a habit of going through her flatmate's belongings, but this was an emergency.

If only her credit card hadn't been rejected at the checkout of a really trendy shop, with half of Dublin standing in the queue behind her gawping and sniggering at her embarrassment. The shop assistant had lovingly folded up the wispy slip-of-a-dress. Its dark satin fabric shimmering in the shop lights and the tiny embroidered flowers with the tiny dots of shining beads glittering and winking with delight at being taken out of the shop on an adventure. The assistant had swiped Amber's credit card through the machine and then stood drumming her long red talons on the counter as the machine remained silent.

Amber glared at the machine, willing it to spew out the payment slip, but nothing happened. Finally the assistant shifted her position, sighing as if the weight of the world were on her shoulders, and peering at the card tapped the number into the machine, her long nails clattering on the keyboard. Then finally the machine whirred into life.

The assistant raised her eyebrows and pulled a wry face at Amber. "Rejected!" she snapped, almost throwing the card back at Amber and, lips pursed with annoyance, she snatched the gorgeous dress back out of its bag and threw it onto a rail behind her. Amber could almost hear the dress scream in protest – how it had really wanted to belong to her!

How could her card be rejected? There must be some mistake. She was sure she had put some money into her account this month. But maybe she had used it to buy that gorgeous pair of shoes last week? And, now that she came to think of it, hadn't there been a letter about a cheque and insufficient funds? The bank manager certainly was no friend of hers. Life seemed to be a constant battle to afford the things that she really *had* to have – a constant juggle of credit card against pay cheque, with the pay cheque usually losing out.

In any case, that was the end of the wonderful dress. And she hadn't a thing that was suitable for such an auspicious date. And so she had been *forced* into the raid on Stella's wardrobe.

It wasn't every day that Amber was asked out by a gorgeous super-cool guy. Usually it was ugly dorks with spots and nerdy haircuts – for some reason she seemed to attract *them* like a magnet. But this guy was different. This was the guy in the pub casually playing pool that all of the girls from work had surreptitiously been looking at – watching the way he ran a hand through a lock of hair that kept flopping over his forehead, watching the tight curve of his bottom as he leant across the table to take a shot. They had all been eyeing him as they stood there at the bar. Even those who were old enough to know better, or who had men of their own waiting at home. Miraculously though, it was Amber that he winked at when he looked up and saw all of the factory girls drooling over him. And when he finally drained his pint and left the pool table, it was Amber that he grinned at. She had felt her mouth drop open as one of the girls nudged her in the ribs and hissed, "He fancies you!". No one *that* gorgeous ever fancied her. He had a nice haircut and not a spot in sight.

Then the girls parted like the Red Sea as he walked towards Amber. They stood, staring enviously, as he boldly walked straight up to her and asked what she wanted to drink. When she opened her mouth nothing came out and she stood for what seemed like minutes dumbstruck, until Jules, one of the factory girls said loudly, "A pint of Carlsberg. She drinks pints."

"Thanks, girls," he said dismissively and as if obeying an unheard command they all backed away from the bar, leaving Amber standing alone with him.

A pint appeared on the bar beside her. "Thank you," Amber managed to say, but her voice came out like a strangled squawk. Over his shoulder she was aware of the stares of naked envy from the factory girls. She picked up the glass, watching some of the golden liquid slop over the side as her hand trembled. She cursed herself for acting like a silly nervous teenager overawed by the presence of such raw testosterone.

"I'm Luke," said Mr Raw Testosterone, clinking his glass against hers.

"Amber," she replied, taking a long swig of her drink to steady her nerves. Even his name was cool. Why couldn't he have had a nerdy name? Anything to make him seem ordinary.

Once she was halfway down her pint Amber began to relax. Luke was nice, really nice. He made her laugh. She glowed beneath the full spotlight of his considerable charm. He made her feel as if she were the only woman in the room. And then far too quickly he was telling her that he had to go – he and his friends were meeting people in another pub – it was someone's birthday. He was terribly disappointed when he had just met her. He would have loved to have stayed with her all night. There was a strong emphasis on *all night*. He would meet her outside the pub on Saturday night at nine and they would have more time to get to know each other. They exchanged phone numbers and then he was gone, leaving Amber feeling breathless and bewildered.

And it was all because of Luke that she was having to raid Stella's wardrobe. That and a credit card which wouldn't come out to play. Stella's room was immaculate. Her double bed was covered in a cream duvet, with a bright wine satin throw tastefully arranged over the end, which coordinated with the silky cushions that she had arranged around the curve of the pillow. Yet it was a room devoid of personality – too tidy. No photographs littered the bedside table which was artfully arranged with a vase of roses and a few books. There was nothing to tell anyone of the person who spent her time in the room – it was like an expensive hotel room. Amber opened the wardrobe. Stella's clothes were arranged in a regimented row: skirts at one end, next to blouses, dresses and then coats. Beneath the clothes, Stella's shoes stood in regimented lines, with a row of handbags beside them. Amber ran her hand along the rail of clothes, looking at the expensive labels. Stella was going to have to find herself a wealthy husband to support her in the manner she so obviously wanted to become accustomed to. Slowly Amber shifted through the line of dresses until she found the one that she wanted. It was gorgeous. Bright red and clingy in a tasteful kind of way. Stella didn't *do* tarty. This dress showed off the body's curves without flaunting them. Gingerly Amber took the dress off the rail, feeling like a thief. Stella would probably kill her if she knew what she was doing. But this really was an emergency. She pulled the dress off its hanger and held it against her body, savouring the luxurious feel of the fabric. She looked in the full-length mirror that hung on the wall beside the wardrobe. The dress looked wonderful against her skin – the red colour highlighted her dark colouring. It was perfect. She shot out of the room before she lost her courage and put the dress back.

*　　*　　*

Amber felt fantastic as she emerged from a taxi outside the pub. All her preparations for the evening had gone perfectly. Even her hair had co-operated and now hung in a soft dark cloud around her face, unlike the wiry frizz that it normally seemed to prefer. Beneath her best black coat, the red dress looked perfect. She had finally gone for broke and borrowed Stella's black killer heels to go with the dress. In for a penny, in for a pound – she might as well be hanged for a sheep as a lamb. In any case, she would make sure the dress and shoes were back in the wardrobe before Stella arrived home.

She glanced at her watch. She was ten minutes late. But it was good not to appear too eager. She crossed the pavement and went around the corner to the front of the pub, feeling her heart sink as she saw the entrance was Luke-less. Relief that he wasn't there, pacing impatiently, waiting for her, mingled with a nagging concern that maybe he had changed his mind. Feeling terribly conspicuous, she walked to the pub door and stood beside it. From across the street someone wolf-whistled. She looked up expectantly, hoping that it would be Luke dashing towards her, but it was only a group of young lads clustered on the street corner opposite, laughing and giggling.

A man came around the corner. Amber felt her heart lurch with excitement which rapidly cooled to bitter disappointment. It wasn't Luke.

"All on your own, darlin'?" he slurred drunkenly, leaning too close to her and giving her the full benefit of his whiskey-laden breath.

"No!" she snarled, glaring at the man, who thought better of chatting her up and lurched into the pub.

Where could Luke be? He had been so definite about their arrangement to meet here, outside the pub. She checked her phone. Maybe he had called and she hadn't heard the phone ring. The smiley face on the phone grinned inanely at her. No missed calls. Maybe he was waiting inside, she thought hopefully. She shoved her phone back into her bag and pulled open the pub door.

Taking a deep breath, she plunged into the mass of people inside and began to search for Luke, trying to appear nonchalant.

"Lost your boyfriend?" some wit yelled from across the pub.

Amber smiled tightly. Where the hell *was* Luke? She moved through the pub, trying to ignore the nasty little voice inside her that laughed over the hum of conversation, sniggering, "You've been stood up *again!*".

She scanned the crowded pub again. It was hard to see over the tall heads of the men – everyone was so much taller than she was. Self-consciously, she circled the pub again. Two minutes later she had to admit the obvious: Luke wasn't there. He had stood her up. Built her up with all the bullshit chat-up lines, all the mega-watt attention, and then just not turned up.

"Look where you're go . . . ing!"

Amber, her head turned to look around the bar, had walked straight into the protruding beer belly of an enormous man. Cold beer from one of the glasses he was carrying at head height cascaded down her front. She jumped back, gasping as the icy liquid poured over her coat and soaked through the front of the dress.

"Stupid cow!" the man growled, looking in annoyance at the half-empty beer glass. Amber turned and fled, her killer heels skidding on the soaking floor.

Outside a couple were just getting out of a taxi. Barging past the man, who was paying the driver, Amber darted into the back seat, biting her lip to stop herself crying. She gave the driver the address and sat back feeling the beer sticky against her skin, clinging to the fabric of the ruined dress. She watched the darkened streets slide by as the driver crossed the city . . . couples out walking, enjoying the night . . . together. While she headed home – alone. As always.

How could she have been so stupid as to expect him to turn up? He had just been messing with her. But she had believed him. She had really thought that he had wanted to see her again. How the girls at work would laugh when she told them that she'd been stood up!

The driver drew to a stop outside the apartment block. Amber looked up at the darkened windows. Stella wasn't home – that was something. Numbly she paid the driver and walked slowly up the stone steps to the front door. How different this evening should have been! She'd thought that now she would be laughing somewhere with Luke, bathing in the spotlight of his megawatt charm.

She let herself into the apartment that she'd shared with Stella for the past two years. She pulled off Stella's shoes and, in a sudden burst of temper, threw them across the room. They hit the wall and then lay abandoned in a heap on the carpet. Grim realisation of her situation slowly seeped over her. Not only had she been stood up, but she had ruined Stella's dress in the process. Hardly daring to look, she stood in front of the living-room mirror and pulled off her coat. A dark wet streak marred the immaculate fabric of the dress from top to bottom.

"Oh fuck!" Amber whispered bleakly.

She went into the chaos that was her own room and unearthed her nightdress and a dressing-gown from beneath the pile of clothes that she had tried on earlier in the evening. She took off the dress, the drying fabric sticking to her skin, leaving a damp, itchy streak on her flesh. Maybe the beer would sponge out of the dress? Then she could get it back in Stella's wardrobe and she would never know. How could she have been so stupid as to borrow the bloody dress in the first place? She should have realised that Luke wasn't going to turn up. It was all too good to be true. She got a hanger and put the dress on it, ran warm water from the tap into the washbasin and began to dab ineffectively at the stain with a sponge. The water spread further across the fabric, making it worse than before. She was going to have to hide the dress, bring it to the dry-cleaner's and then get it back into Stella's wardrobe. Somehow. Amber stifled a sob. Crying wasn't going to change anything. She shouldn't have been so stupid in the first place.

Above the noise of the water running came the shrill note of the phone ringing. Amber threw the sponge into the washbasin and ran into the living room. Luke was ringing to apologise for standing her up! Something had delayed him. He really did want to see her. Cursing her fumbling fingers, Amber rummaged in her handbag, desperately searching for the mobile phone. Finally she found it, dragged it out and pressed the receive button.

"Hello!" she trilled into the receiver.

"Amber – sweetheart," her mother's voice whined, its tone wheedling like a small child who is pleading for a new toy, "something's come up. Can you come over tomorrow? I've got a terrible problem – left my purse on the bus . . ." Her voice trailed away as if she were searching for an excuse.

Amber knew that she was lying.

"I need to borrow fifty euros from you."

3

The odour of Lavender Garden at Midnight gradually covered the all-pervading odour of stale beer. Stella gave the spray-can a final squirt up into the air and shut the bathroom door. It was strange that the whole flat, and especially the bathroom, absolutely stank like a pub. As soon as Amber had gone out on some mercy dash to see her mother, Stella had gone around with the air freshener to get rid of the smell. She had also checked all of the rooms and cupboards to see if Amber had been sick somewhere or if there was some drunken man secreted in one of the rooms. But there was nothing. It was all very strange, especially when Amber had told her very sincerely, when she had come about the advert for a room-mate, that she never drank much. Stella had been a bit sceptical then, but Amber had been the best choice out of some very dodgy applicants wanting to share the apartment with her. The choice had been limited to a rather large woman (who kept sniffing into a grubby handkerchief, saying that her husband had just moved his much younger mistress into the house and that she didn't want to do *her* washing as well as his) and a waif-like hippy with rings everywhere and hair that looked as if it hadn't been washed or combed since she was about ten years old. Amber at least had looked fairly normal.

Except for today when she had gone out at the crack of dawn clutching a carry-bag, mumbling something about having to go and give her mother some money and looking guilty as hell. Of course, she knew Stella disapproved of the way she could never say no to her mother.

Stella had spent the morning in a frenzy of cleaning – she was such a bundle of nerves thinking about her lunch date with Rory. She couldn't afford anything to go wrong *this* time. Amber stomped back into the apartment a few hours later, clutching the newspaper and a huge box from the cake shop which she dumped on the table.

"Comfort eating," she explained, tearing at the string that tied the box closed. She finally succeeded in getting the box open and shoved the cakes onto a plate.

"Would you like one?" she asked, shoving the box under Stella's nose.

"No, thanks, I've just eaten," said Stella, looking at the cakes as if she thought that they were going to bite her. "Why are you comfort eating?" The very thought of sinking her teeth into one of those spongy cream-oozing creations was making Stella feel quite nauseous. Amber slumped down on the sofa and took a huge bite out of one of her cakes.

"I got stood up," she sighed miserably.

"What? By Mr Testosterone himself?" Stella winced as a blob of cream slid out of the cake that Amber was eating and landed perilously near the edge of her plate. She fought the urge to leap up and get a cloth to give to Amber in case the cream slid off her plate and landed on her expensive sofa.

"I waited for ages outside the pub and then I went in to see if he was there . . ." Amber's voice trailed off to a whisper as she miserably remembered the previous evening. She didn't dare mention the accident with the dress. Even if she pretended it had been one of her own dresses Stella would have wanted to help sort it out and then it would have all come out.

"And he didn't even call to say he wasn't coming?"

Amber bit into her cake and chewed it hard, concentrating on the taste of the cake rather than letting herself remember the awful evening.

"I did get a call," Amber took the cake from her mouth, ran her finger along one edge of it and slurped the whipped cream up from her finger, "but that was from my mum wanting to borrow money."

Stella took a sip of her mineral water. Sometimes Amber really annoyed her. She just let her rotten family walk all over her. They took all of her money and only had to snap their grasping little fingers and Amber dropped everything to go and help them.

"You should be tougher," she told Amber.

Amber, ignoring the fact that Stella probably meant be tougher with her mother and not lend her money, replied, "I always pick men who are rotten bastards. They always hurt me."

Stella shook her head, annoyed at Amber's self-pity. She always picked the wrong men because she was always so eager to please. She should be far more selective, wait until the right man came along rather than being grateful for any attention that any man paid to her. There was no wonder she was always ending up with total bastards and getting hurt. She wished that she could protect Amber. She was so kind, so gentle and so vulnerable. If only she would toughen up and be less sensitive. If only she could decide what kind of man she wanted and wait until *he* came along.

Stella, on the other hand, had a master plan and she was *very* selective about the type of man she had anything to do with. To get anywhere with her they had to be obviously wealthy, unmarried, with a good job and good prospects. There was no point in messing around with anything less. She wasn't going to marry just for love and end up with some pauper, living from hand to mouth. Like her mother had done.

No wasting time with unsuitable men for her.

"Henry." Stella spoke without being aware that his name had slipped from her lips. Just the thought of unsuitable men had brought him clearly to mind.

"What?" Amber frowned quizzically over the top of her cream sponge.

"Nothing," Stella sighed, curling her lip in annoyance at the very thought of Henry Murphy. She pictured her ruined jacket, hanging forlornly over the back of a chair in her bedroom. She must take it to the dry cleaner's to see if they could do anything to remove the stain. And then she pictured Henry, his gorgeous eyes dancing with amusement, and that lovely, lovely smile. Her stomach fluttered suddenly with butterflies.

"You said 'Henry'," Amber persisted.

"Oh, he sprang to mind when we were talking about unsuitable men," Stella said airily, quickly getting up from the sofa and putting her empty plate on the table, hoping that Amber wouldn't notice the flush that was flooding her cheeks. "He ruined my jacket."

"Not personally he didn't," muttered Amber. "It was Rory's horse did that."

"I hope that the dry cleaner's can get the stain out," said Stella petulantly, wondering why Amber suddenly looked flushed herself.

"Surely he's not that bad?" Amber finished the last cake and dabbed at the remaining crumbs with a fingertip.

"Well, he . . ." Stella fought to think of a word to describe Henry. How could she explain how awful he was, how much he had irritated her and yet how attractive she had found him?

Amber let out a snort of laughter. "I think that you rather fancy him,"

"Most definitely not. He's the most annoying man that I have ever met," Stella said huffily. "Anyway, I've got Rory now. He's perfect for me."

"Really?" asked Amber, with more than a hint of sarcasm in her voice.

Stella stood up and went to get her coat. Rory would be here any minute. *She* would never be stood up. She wished that she could go and stand outside and wait for his arrival as she couldn't stand Amber's stupid teasing.

She breathed a sigh of relief when she saw Rory's car glide graciously down the street.

"See you later!"

She dashed out of the apartment and down the stairs. Then, reaching the entrance hall, she waited. It wouldn't do to appear to be too eager. She would keep Rory waiting, just for a few moments.

Stella pulled open the front door and walked slowly down the steps to the waiting car.

"You look great," Rory said as she settled herself into the leather front seat. "And that colour won't show up any horse spit!"

Stella forced herself to laugh airily.

"Lunch first, I think, and then we'll head off to the stables. I want to take a look at that horse Henry thinks I should buy." Rory accelerated away, oblivious to the other drivers who courteously pulled into the side to let him down the narrow street.

* * *

"How many horses do you have?" Stella asked when they were finally settled into a corner table of the restaurant.

"Four," Rory replied, not bothering to look at her over the top of the wine list.

"Are they flat horses or jumpers?" Stella persisted, eager to show off her new-found knowledge about racehorses. She had spent the last few days reading the racing section of every newspaper that she could get her hands on, in order to have something to discuss with Rory and to make him think that she was interested in his hobby.

"Chasers." Rory snapped his fingers a nearby waitress. "A bottle of number twenty-seven!"

The flustered waitress glanced in his direction and muttered under her breath.

"I prefer chasing to anything," Stella told him. At least she knew the difference between flat racing, hurdles and chases.

"I like to do a bit of chasing myself." Rory shoved his hot and clammy hand on her leg beneath the table and ran it up her thigh.

Stella smiled gratefully when the waitress arrived a moment later and slammed the bottle of wine and two glasses down on the table. Rory reluctantly withdrew his hand, grasped the wineglass and sampled the dark-red liquid that the waitress poured for him.

Stella felt her eyes widen in disbelief as he began to churn the wine around in his mouth, making a noise like a washing machine that was about to explode. "That will do, I suppose," he declared, having swallowed the wine.

The waitress looked as if she would love to hit him

over the head with the bottle.

An hour later Rory had drunk most of the bottle of wine and eaten the most enormous meal that Stella had ever seen, while she had nibbled on hers.

Rory called for the bill and the waitress brought it to the table.

"One hundred and thirty-seven euros and seventy-five cents." Rory read and slapped down some notes. "Right then, let's go and take a look at this horse.

"Thanks, call again," snapped the waitress, wryly looking at the tip-less payment.

* * *

Thornhill Stables, Henry's home, was a mile off the main road, down a rutted track. Stella grimaced when she saw the ramshackle sprawl of grey stone buildings. Rory drove beneath a soaring arch into the stable yard and parked the car on a stretch of weed-encrusted concrete.

Henry appeared from a cottage at the far end of the yard which looked as if it would fall down if a puff of wind blew.

"Nice jacket!" grinned Henry as Stella eased herself gingerly out of the car, looking tentatively at the ground in case she trod in the end-product of racehorse.

"Thank you," she smiled tightly. The joke about her jacket was going to run and run. She risked a glance at Henry and then looked away quickly as she saw his eyes on hers.

"Let's have a look at this horse then!" Rory slammed the car door loudly, making Stella fear for the safety of the buildings.

She followed the men as they walked across the yard. What a dreadfully run-down place this was! The buildings formed a square around a tangle of grass in the centre. Three of the sides of the square were taken up with stables. Doors with chipped and peeling paint hung drunkenly from broken hinges. But those that shut properly had elegant horses' heads looking out of them. Above the stable yard the slate roof sagged dangerously in the middle and there were gaping holes where the slates were missing and the bare wood of the trusses showed through. Henry must be absolutely penniless, thought Stella, as she followed Rory into the dim interior of one of the stables. Inside, the old building retained its once beautiful features, the cobbled floor was immaculately swept and the wood panelling was freshly painted.

"This is Monday Man," said Henry proudly, sweeping the rug off an enormous grey horse. "I think he would be perfect for you, Rory. This horse could win you your Galway Plate."

Shortly afterwards, the deal was done.

"Let me show you my own Grand National horse, The Entertainer, " Henry said once Rory had finished writing what Stella thought was an alarmingly large cheque for Monday Man.

Henry led the way across the yard to another stable. Inside stood a tall, scrawny-looking horse, with ears that even Stella could see would have looked more suitable on a donkey.

"He's not done much yet," Henry said, proudly patting the horse's skinny neck, "but I think he will eventually."

*   *   *

"My new horse looks a good one, but Henry's Entertainer looks pretty useless," Rory said scathingly as he turned his car off the rutted driveway onto the main road, the engine roaring into life as he shoved his foot hard on the accelerator. Stella grinned as the thrust from the car pushed her back into the leather seat.

"Look – down there – Thornhill House." Rory swerved the car to the wrong side of the road, swung into a small lay-by and jerked to a halt. Stella looked in the direction that he was pointing. There, peering through a gap in the trees across fields and parkland she saw a sprawling old mansion, standing proudly amidst gardens that were a riot of autumn colour. The enormous house was built of old stone, faded to myriad shades of grey beneath a dark slate roof. A long driveway wound through trees and shrubs to the front of the house.

Stella gave a gasp of pure delight. "Oh, Rory," she breathed, "what a gorgeous house!"

"Yes," Rory replied with a snort. "Bet Henry rather thinks so too."

4

"Just look at this! Come over here to the light!" exclaimed Stella, startling Amber who was painting her toenails on the sofa while watching a video of her favourite movie, *Love Actually*. Amber paused the movie and got regretfully off the sofa. What did Stella want her to look at that could possibly be more important than admiring Hugh Grant's dance scene? Across the room Stella was removing the plastic wrapping from the cream jacket that she had just brought back from the dry cleaner's. Amber walked slowly across the room, severely hampered by the wedges of cotton wool that she had stuffed between her toes to keep them apart while she painted them ruby red. Heaven knows why, it wasn't as if anyone was going to see them, but somehow watching a 'happy-ever-after' movie gave her the hope that just maybe someone soon would be looking at her toes, and hopefully the rest of her body, so it paid to be prepared. Stella, of course, had proper separators for when she painted her toenails, but then someone *was* looking at *her* toes, or presumably soon would. Even if it *was* the arrogant jerk that she had come home with last weekend.

Amber shoved her way past carrier bags bearing the names of some pretty exclusive dress shops, fighting the urge to drop a sly kick at some of them. *She* didn't dare even venture into Chez Penney's, let alone Chez Vogue – the snooty shop-girls in there would be able to tell at twenty paces that Amber's credit card was dead on its feet.

Stella pulled off the remaining plastic wrapper and laid the jacket reverently on the table. "Look at that," she whispered, shaking her head in disbelief at the immaculate expanse of cream fabric. Amber looked. The jacket that the last time she had seen it had been liberally splattered in greenish-brown splodges was now pristine again. Amber looked enviously at the obviously expensive and very beautifully cut jacket. "Well, at least you'll be able to forgive Henry now," she mocked lightly, jealousy making her feel malicious.

"Henry!" spat Stella. "I'll forgive him when hell freezes over!"

Amber stifled a smile. *The lady doth protest too much, methinks,* she mused, slowly waddling back to the sofa to continue painting her nails.

"Funny thing," Stella said, sliding the plastic back over the jacket, "I saw a red dress just like mine in the dry cleaner's."

Amber swallowed hard and was very glad that her back was to Stella, so that she couldn't see the hot flush that was spreading rapidly up from her neck. "Oh?" she gulped.

"The girl in the Tamara Pierce shop where I bought it told me that the dress was unique, that only one like it had been made," Stella was saying.

Amber could hear her heading towards her bedroom. At any moment she would find that her dress was missing and then she would know that Amber had 'borrowed' it – and probably ruined it. The woman in the dry cleaners was very doubtful that the beer stains would come out without leaving a permanent mark. Amber stole a glance over her shoulder.

Stella had gone into her bedroom and laid the jacket on the bed. "I'll have it out with that girl in Tamara Pierce the next time I go in there!"

"Yes, you should." Amber fought to keep the panic out of her voice. Stella was going to open the wardrobe and start looking for her red dress. With her organised wardrobe it wouldn't take her long to discover that the dress was missing. And she would be *so* angry. The wardrobe door creaked open. Amber's neck began to ache with keeping it craned at such an odd angle and with the tension that she could feel tightening every muscle in her body.

"I must find that dress," Stella was saying, her voice muffled by the wardrobe door. "I want to see if it really is the same as that one in the dry cleaner's."

"I've got to go out!" Amber yelled, leaping off the sofa, scattering the wedges of cotton wool in all directions.

"Where are you going?"

"Oh, I forgot that Mum is expecting me at lunch time!" Amber lied.

"I thought that you usually went to your mum's in the afternoon." Stella emerged from the wardrobe and came to stand in her bedroom doorway.

"She wanted to make me lunch," Amber lied again, feeling her voice rise in panic.

"Make you lunch?" Stella said doubtfully.

"That's right." Amber nodded her head pointedly. Stella must know she was lying. Her mother very rarely even offered her a cup of tea, let alone made lunch for her.

"That's lovely. Have a great time," Stella said enthusiastically.

Amber pulled on her socks over the tacky nail varnish, feeling the woollen fabric sticking to the ruby-red paint. She had ruined her toes in her panic. Ah well, it wasn't as if anyone was going to see them. She shoved her feet into her shoes and grabbed her jacket from her bedroom.

"See you later!" Stella had settled herself down on the sofa, rewound the video and opened a glossy homes and gardens magazine. "I'm going to start planning for the future," she mused dreamily.

* * *

Amber walked along the pavement, already strewn with damp rust-coloured leaves, blown by the autumn gales. A few dates with Rory and Stella was already re-decorating a country estate and planning a dinner menu for twenty. Amber scuffed through a pile of damp leaves. Stella seemed to think that love should come on demand, should be something that you order, like a pizza. 'I'd like a handsome rich man with a swanky car on the side, please. Deliver to Stella O'Rourke immediately!' She was determined that the person she was going to marry had to be wealthy. But love didn't come like that. Nothing could determine who you fell in love with. It all had to do with chemistry. Fate. It was written in the stars. Then when you fell in love you went through life together, taking whatever came at you, like a team. You couldn't just decide that you would only fall in love with someone who had a certain bank balance, or who lived in a certain neighbourhood, or who did a certain job. Love was something that no one had any control over. If love was something that you could control then she wouldn't be walking miserably through the streets alone on a Saturday morning. A couple walked towards Amber, heads together, sharing their own secret world. Amber sighed as they passed her. If love was something that could be controlled, she would have someone with her, someone who would love and cherish her forever. But it wasn't something controllable. Love was wild and unruly. That was why she kept falling for utter, utter, absolute bastards who kept breaking her heart. If Stella was attracted to rich men, then Amber was very definitely attracted to scumbags. And they never usually had fat wallets either. A pretty face and charm in buckets and the morals of an alley-cat – that was the type of man that Amber was usually attracted to.

She passed a shop window and glanced at her reflection. There was nothing unusual about her. She was pretty but not in an exceptional way. Her mass of dark wavy hair, now beginning to frizz with the damp air, was definitely a good feature. But there was nothing about her that said: 'I'm a sucker for a bastard. Come and hurt me!'

Amber reached the bus stop and ducked into the shelter, out of the wind. A tall, good-looking guy grinned in greeting.

"Cold out there," he shivered dramatically.

Amber nodded and then ignored him. Too good-looking. He was bound to be a bastard of the first degree. Surreptitiously she reached into her handbag and pulled out her purse. It felt worryingly light – she jingled it hopefully. Unless some miracle had happened and fresh air had been turned into money, she was virtually penniless. Shit. She rummaged in the zipper pockets of her handbag, fumbling into the furthest recesses, looking for loose change that might have been abandoned there. Amongst screwed-up bus tickets and sticky sweet wrappers she found enough change for a bus ticket, provided the driver didn't check the one-cent coins too hard.

At least when she got to her mum's she would get

the fifty euros back that she had lent her. That would last her for the rest of the week. Until payday. She resented the absence of the money – that had been her last fifty euros. She hadn't dared visit the hole in the wall. Her card would have melted if she had put it into the machine. Thank goodness money for the rent on the apartment was deducted from her wages as soon as they were paid into the bank. And she had to give money to Stella as soon as she was paid, for food for the month – otherwise she would never be able to eat. The money would just go. And it was never any good trying to borrow some from her mother. Cash flowed only one way there. Towards her mother. And it only came back when Amber asked for it, and then only if she did that very firmly.

The bus arrived. The tall man stood back with a courteous smile to let her on first. Amber stuck her nose in the air and ignored him. The creep needn't think that he could get around her that way. She plonked herself down on a seat and watched the cityscape slide by the window until it was her stop.

The Swiftbrook Estate was a world away from the fancy world that Stella was dreaming up for herself, thought Amber, as she got off the bus. Even though she had grown up in the neighbourhood, the atmosphere was still oppressive. Squat tower blocks, festooned with washing draped over concrete balconies, were crudely decorated with spray-can graffiti. Wispy grass grew listlessly in what some architect had once imagined would be play areas in between the cold concrete structures. She walked past Block Four. There, high above the pavement looking out over the city rooftops, was the flat where she had grown up. That was where she had spent the first sixteen years of her life and where she had last seen her father, shouting abuse at her mother as he walked away with a bag slung over his shoulder. Amber turned a corner at the end of the tower blocks and began to walk through narrow streets of terraced houses. Here the atmosphere changed – even the air seemed lighter and the grass grew more hopefully.

Her mother's house was set at the end of one of the rows of terraced houses. Ruby Casey had moved to the house when her husband left. Her married lover, Kenny, wanted a place where he could stay away from the claustrophobic atmosphere of Tower Block Number Four, with the prying nosy neighbours and the memories of John, her first husband. Now, Kenny and Ruby had established a new life. Amber had moved out when her mother had left the tower block. It was patently obvious that she wasn't welcome at the new house. Ronnie and Georgina stayed with Ruby. They were Amber's younger siblings – who she had eventually discovered were Kenny's children, brought up with her until Amber's father discovered that he had been duped into bringing up another man's children and left. Kenny split his time between his two homes, slithering craftily between a wife in Ballsbridge, who had no knowledge of her husband's other family – and Ruby.

Amber turned into the small, neat front garden of the terraced house. What a different life her mother lived now! This was a world away from the tower block with its constant noise and all-pervading smell of urine. The front door was painted green and had a polished brass knocker in the shape of a lion's head in the middle of it. Amber banged the knocker and a few moments later Ronnie, her younger brother, swung open the door.

"Oh, it's you," he said with all the grace and charm of his surly nineteen years.

Amber walked past him into the lounge. Georgina, her eighteen-year-old sister, sprawled on the squashy fake-fur sofa, plump legs stretching the stitching on her leggings. She barely glanced up from the television that blared out some repetitive pop music. Kenny sat in a vast leather armchair beside the gas fire. He glanced at Amber over the top of his newspaper.

"All righ' then?" he asked brusquely. He had never lost his rough Dublin accent as he accumulated his money. Amber looked at the cosy family scene and wondered where his wife thought he was. You could bet that it would never occur to her that he was sitting with another family in a Dublin back street. She probably thought that he was off on yet another of his business trips.

Ruby emerged from the kitchen. She had changed in the years since she had left the tower block from a haggard nervy woman to one who was trim and trendily dressed. She obviously thrived on Kenny's money and attention. But something remained of the woman that Amber remembered from the tower block days – her eyes were still watchful and wary.

"Oh, it's you," she said. There was an accusing tone to her voice as if Amber had come on an unexpected visit at a very inconvenient time.

"Just me," Amber replied with a sigh, wondering why she made the weekly trip, when she was so obviously unwelcome in their family set-up. She stood uncertainly in the doorway.

Ruby looked at her nervously. She was probably terrified that Amber was going to ask her to return the money that she had borrowed. The last thing she would want Kenny to hear was that she was scrounging money – presumably he didn't know anything about Ruby's little trips to the amusement arcades.

"Well, we're just going out." Ruby glanced at her reflection in the mirror that hung over the gas fire.

Kenny lurched to his feet. "Come on, you lot!" He poked at Ronnie with his foot. Amber followed them outside.

"Call sometime next week," Ruby said, sliding into the front seat of Kenny's car. She waved cheerily as the car pulled away from the kerb, leaving Amber watching, desolate and penniless.

5

Driving out to Henry Murphy's ramshackle racing stables *again* really was a sign of how far she was prepared to go to show Rory what a wonderful girlfriend she was. To set foot in that dreadful place and have to tolerate its aggravating owner was beyond the call of duty for any prospective wife. But it was lovely to go out with Rory again – he seemed to have become really fond of her, really quickly. Since their first couple of dates he had phoned once or twice every day wondering where she was and what she was doing. It was lovely to have such a devoted boyfriend – he made her feel really protected and cherished. Stella wished though that Rory had another interest rather than his bloody racehorses. It was too much really, having to stand in cold miserable racecourses watching his horses hurtle around a muddy track. Since the incident that had almost ruined her jacket, she had made sure that she had stayed well away from any of the horses. And she certainly didn't want to spend any time near Henry Murphy. It was strange though, considering how much he annoyed her, how often her thoughts strayed to him. She would often find herself prickling with annoyance at the thought of how his eyes danced with amusement when they saw her.

Admittedly, however, he was attractive.

It certainly wasn't Stella's idea of fun, to head out to the racing stables on a miserable cold winter afternoon, but if that was what Rory wanted, then she would go along with him. At least she could enjoy sitting in his lovely car, luxuriating against the squashy leather seats and watching the envious glances of the passers-by as they glided along the road.

Now though, Stella sat up, peering hard through the bare winter branches. They were near the racing stables so now she would be able to get a glimpse of the beautiful Thornhill House. As she spotted the grey stone house in the distance, something rust-coloured near at hand caught her eye. A slight movement at the side of the road amongst the foliage.

"Rory, stop!" she cried, putting a hand on Rory's arm.

"What on earth's the matter?" Rory snapped impatiently, stepping hard on the brakes to bring the powerful car to a halt.

"There was something just back there, an injured cat or fox or something!" Stella reached for the door handle.

"Oh, for heaven's sake," sighed Rory, peevishly. "Can't you just leave it? A fox? So what?"

But Stella was already out of the car and jogging back up the road as fast as she could in her high heels. Then she began to slow her pace – maybe she had imagined it – it was probably just a piece of cloth, or some rubbish. She looked out through the trees to Thornhill House – what a wonderful place that would be to live in! Maybe Rory could buy something like that when they were married. She was sure that he was fond enough of her to want to marry her – not now though, maybe in a year's time, when she had proved to him what a suitable wife she would be.

Then she saw what had caught her eye in the first place. Lying on the side of the road was a rust-coloured terrier puppy.

The little puppy raised its head when it saw Stella and the very end of its tail thumped faintly against the damp earth.

"Oh, you poor little thing!" Stella winced in sympathy as she crouched beside the little form. Growing up on a farm in the West of Ireland had made her used to dealing with injured animals. The kitchen at home had been constantly full of rescued animals and birds that they had found in the fields or on the beaches and brought home to nurse back to health, sometimes successfully, but more often than not the creatures, weak and terrified when they were found, died in spite of their ministrations. She ran a gentle hand over the puppy's harsh coat. There were no obvious signs of injury – the pup had probably just been abandoned and had been wandering for days until it had collapsed through exhaustion and hunger.

"You poor little thing!" She slipped her jumper over her head, lifted the puppy into the warm fabric and then stood up.

"What is it?" Rory said peevishly. He had parked the car and walked back up the road to her.

"A puppy – I think he's been abandoned." Stella moved her jumper away from the pup to show it to Rory, who made an impatient tutting noise.

"Leave the bloody thing here – it will probably die anyway," he said sullenly.

"Rory, I can't! That would be cruel!" Stella smiled warmly at him, trying to melt his coldness. She had to take the puppy with her and help it.

"I think you're bloody mad!" he snapped sulkily, then spun around on his heel and marched back to the car, his shoulders hunched petulantly.

Stella followed him. She couldn't just abandon the pup at the side of the road. Surely Rory could see that.

Rory climbed into the car and slammed the door. Stella opened the passenger door and slid into the seat.

Then Rory turned to her as she cradled the puppy on her lap. "Well, it's a cute little thing. I hope that it lives. The rescue centre will be able to find a good home for it."

Stella shot a quizzical look at him. At least he had accepted that she had to bring the puppy with them now, but she certainly couldn't imagine taking it to the dog pound. Though the last thing that she had ever wanted was to get stuck with another dog – there had been enough of them when she was growing up . . .

A few moments later Rory turned off the main road and the car bumped down the long track to Thornhill Stables.

"What have you got there?" Henry asked, coming across the yard to greet them.

"A puppy – I found it on the road – it's sick," Stella said, showing Henry the contents of her bundle.

"We'll take it inside – it will be warm by the Aga and I'll get it some milk," Henry said, gently rubbing the top of the puppy's head. "It's a male. He's like a little teddy bear."

Henry led the way across the yard to the cottage. Rory followed for a few strides and then turned and walked towards the stables.

"Rory?" Stella asked quizzically but Rory had already gone.

The front door of the cottage was warped and Henry had to shove his shoulder against it to push it open – it shrieked in protest as the wood caught on the worn sandstone floor.

"Come in!" Henry led the way along a short sandstone corridor lined with photographs of him and horses at various race meetings.

At the end of the corridor was a cavernous kitchen, dominated by a large cream-coloured Aga and an enormous pine table, one leg of which was held up with a pile of books.

Quickly Henry poured some milk into a cup and shoved it into the microwave. Seconds later the milk was tepid and he spooned some of it into the puppy's mouth. Then he dragged a towel off the drying rail above the Aga, gently wrapped the puppy in it and handed Stella her jumper back.

"Now, leave him here and we'll see if he's any better in a while," he said, taking the pup off her and laying it gently beside the warmth of the Aga.

Stella began to put her jumper back on, but as she lifted it over her head the musty doggy smell made her wrinkle her nose in distaste. "I don't think I need this on." She bundled the jumper under her arm and, giving the puppy's head a gentle rub, followed Henry outside.

"I've come to look at Lover Boy, my horse, not tend to some bloody puppy!" snapped Rory, stomping across the straw-strewn yard towards them.

"Right then," Henry said in a voice that could have been used to pacify a sulking toddler. Then he yelled for the stable lad: "Tim!"

When Tim appeared, Henry told him to saddle Rory's horse and bring it up onto the gallops.

"Do you want to walk to the gallops, Rory, or come in my Jeep?" he asked as the horse was led out into the yard.

"Walk," Rory said shortly and began to head off across the yard to the field behind the stables that Henry used as a gallop. Stella jogged to catch up with Rory and shoved her arm in his.

"Oh, you've torn yourself away from the mutt, have you?" Rory said sarcastically.

Stella bit her lip. Surely Rory wasn't sulking because

of the puppy? He hurried across the grass, paying no heed to the fact that she had to jog to keep up with him, her heels sinking into the soft grass making it hard to walk. Then he stood, impassive, as the horse galloped around the field.

"He's magnificent," Stella breathed, caught all of a sudden by the bug that afflicts thousands with a love for the horse. Lover Boy powered along the field, following a high stone wall, behind which Stella could see the grey stone of the gorgeous Thornhill House, beautiful also from this different angle. From here she could see the side of the house, with its sloping roof and tall windows.

"Magnificent," Henry agreed, coming to stand beside her. Stella wasn't sure if he was talking about Lover Boy or the house.

"That's enough," Rory growled and, turning on his heel, headed back to the yard. "Come on, we're going."

"I'll just get the puppy." Stella hurried to the cottage before Rory had the chance to stop her.

It was warm inside the kitchen. The puppy was curled beside the Aga, still wrapped in his towel. He was sleeping and whimpered and stirred as she picked him up.

"Keep the towel," Henry said, appearing in the doorway. "You'd better go – Rory wants to leave now." He moved out of the doorway to let her pass. "And when Rory wants something he usually gets it."

He said the last bit so quietly that she wondered if she had imagined hearing him speak.

Stella ran out into the yard. Rory had already turned the car around and was revving the engine.

"Don't let that fucking dog pee on my seat!" he snapped without taking his eyes from the windscreen.

"He's wrapped in a towel that Henry gave me," Stella told him, adjusting the puppy on her lap.

"Nice of him," sneered Rory, shoving the car into gear and lurching out of the yard. Stella stared miserably out of the window, watching the countryside slide by as the car hurtled back towards the city. What on earth was the matter with Rory? How could he be that angry just because she had picked up the pup?

"I'm sorry for picking up this dog," she stammered, wanting to put right the dreadful atmosphere that existed in the car.

"I don't give a damn about the dog," he said tightly.

Stella sighed. What on earth had gone wrong with the day? Why had Rory changed so suddenly? He had been so nice up until today.

The countryside changed abruptly as the fields gave way to the urban sprawl of the city. Rory slowed the car as the traffic built up. Stella longed to be home, to get out of the car and try to talk to Rory properly to see what was wrong with him. At least Amber was out for the day and so they could have the apartment to themselves to try to put this dreadful atmosphere right.

At last they arrived outside the apartment and sat in silence as the final notes of the car engine died away.

"Do you want to come in?" Stella asked.

Rory shrugged. "I suppose so," he sighed, as if she

had asked him an almighty favour. Stella could have wept with relief – at least he wasn't going to drive off in a temper without her knowing what was the matter with him. Whatever it was that had upset him, she would make it right. The last thing she wanted was to lose Rory.

Stella led the way into the apartment, the puppy cradled in her arms. She put it, still wrapped in its towel, in a corner of the living room, beside the radiator. She wished with all of her heart that she had never seen the damn thing. Whatever had happened, the puppy was the start of everything going wrong with her relationship.

Thankfully the apartment looked tidy. Amber had gone to work. A rotten way to spend a Sunday, but she was probably short of money – again.

Rory prowled around the apartment, his face tight, lips white where he pressed them into a taut line.

"Coffee?" Stella asked, trying to ignore the obvious anger in him. Maybe if she pretended that everything was normal he might forget his temper and everything would be OK again.

"No."

"Are you all right?" It was patently obvious that he wasn't. In fact, far from all right.

"Why did you come back with me?" he snapped suddenly.

"What?" What on earth was he on about? A cold panic was sinking into the pit of her stomach. Rory was very angry. At her. Their relationship was in grave danger –

she had to put things right between them. *Had* to.

"Well, it was obvious to me that you wanted to be with Henry. You couldn't wait to get into that cottage with him."

"Rory, I went in to keep the puppy warm and to get some milk for it."

"I won't be made a fool of while you play around with Henry Murphy. I can see how he looks at you."

"I'm not interested in Henry, far from it!" Stella exploded, filled with self-righteous indignation. "I can't stand the sight of Henry!"

"It doesn't look like that to *me*," Rory growled. "And don't start crying – you won't get around me like that."

Stella stifled a sob of frustration. "Rory, honestly, I'm not interested in Henry. I'm sorry if you thought that. Look, I won't even talk to him in the future if you're worried."

Rory glared at her for a moment and then sank tiredly down on the sofa. "It's just that you're so attractive. All the men want to be with you. I can see them looking at you. They look like thirsty dogs looking at a water bowl."

"I can't help how they look at me," Stella scowled. "I'm not interested in them. Only you."

Rory held out his hand and Stella grabbed it thankfully, "It's just that I care about you so much," he said, clutching her hand.

Stella felt the tension slide out of her body. The crisis was over.

6

Stella glanced at her watch and gave a groan of frustration. Time was getting short and she still hadn't decided what to wear to go out with Rory. Behind her the bed was littered with outfits that she had discarded. The knot of tension in her stomach gripped tighter. Going out for an evening didn't usually cause such chaos and confusion, but this date was *very* important. Thankfully, their fledgling relationship had survived The First Row. Hopefully there wouldn't be any others. But it was obvious she was going to have to be careful not to make Rory jealous again, which made choosing an outfit rather difficult. She wanted to wear something elegant, but not too plain, feminine without being sexy. But sexy enough for him to fancy her. Rory's reaction to Henry helping her with the puppy had made her feel very wary. The last thing she needed tonight was for him to start to feel jealous of a waiter peering down her chest if she wore a top that was too revealing.

The pile of clothes on the bed grew steadily higher and she grew steadily more flustered.

"Maybe . . ." she wondered out loud, reaching into the wardrobe and pulling out The Red Dress. Since she had seen what looked like an identical red dress in the dry cleaner's Stella had rather gone off her much-loved dress. What was the good of paying a fortune for a dress and then having someone else walking around in one exactly the same? She really must have words with the girl who had sold it to her. But for the moment this was an outfit crisis. She slid off her dressing-gown, yet again, and pulled the dress over her head. The red dress was perfect: elegant and sexy, yet demure.

"So? What do you think?" Stella asked, closing her bedroom door on the chaos that littered the bed. She would deal with all the mess when she got home.

Amber was sitting on the floor in front of the gas fire, cradling the puppy in her arms like a baby.

"Yep, lovely." Amber glanced quickly in Stella's direction, with something that looked strangely like alarm in her eyes, before turning her attention to the puppy again.

"Thanks for your vote of confidence," muttered Stella crossly, twisting her arm around to her neck as something prickled her. She had needed Amber to tell her that she looked nice, but she was too busy with the puppy. Since the puppy had appeared Amber had spent every moment cuddling and playing with it. Stella's grasping fingers found what had been prickling her – a laundry ticket, pinned into the label at the back of the dress. That was odd – she must have forgotten to remove it the last time that she had the dress cleaned. Deftly she unpinned the label and shoved it into the bin. Now that really was odd. An enormous piece of clear plastic wrapper had been shoved into the bin. Like the stuff they used to wrap dry cleaning. Amber was too grungy to use the dry cleaners very often – maybe living with Stella was finally smartening her up.

"Did you get some dry cleaning done?" she asked.

"Erm … yes." Amber's voice rose a tone higher.

"Ahh," Stella replied. Amber was obviously too embarrassed to admit that she was finally cleaning up her act.

A car horn blared loudly outside.

"I think your date has arrived," Amber said, holding up the puppy and waving its paw in Stella's direction. "Can't be bothered getting out of his car and walking all the way up here to get you?" Her voice was tinged with sarcasm.

Stella clamped her lips together, unable to think of a smart reply. "Don't wait up. I may be late," she told Amber, pulling a black jacket on over the red dress.

"You hope!" retorted Amber. "Hey, this puppy is just like a teddy bear – how about we call him Teddy?" She followed Stella to the door with the puppy draped over her shoulder.

"I like that," Stella smiled, rubbing the puppy's soft furry hair.

Rory sat in his flashy sports car, revving the engine.

"Come on, I've got a table booked for 8.30," he told Stella impatiently as she got into the car, barely glancing in her direction. He shoved his foot on the accelerator and powered the car away from the pavement before she had even shut the door properly. Stella hurriedly fastened the seat belt.

"Where are we eating?" she asked, glancing out of the windows and seeing the envious gazes of people on the pavements as the flashy car whisked by.

"Farley's. It's a new restaurant. Very exclusive," Rory said, honking his horn aggressively at a car in front of him which was slow to pull away from a set of traffic lights.

A short time later he turned the car off the main road onto a sleek tarmac drive that ran through a broad avenue of trees.

"Hmmm, nice job they've made of converting the farm buildings." Rory guided the car into a space between a Rolls-Royce and a Ferrari. He nodded approvingly, gazing out of the car windscreen at the old stone buildings. Bright lights set into the grass at the edge of the carpark shone upwards, making the stone shine a burnished gold in the yellow glow. Inside, through enormous arched windows, Stella could see that the restaurant was full of people.

"This was a derelict farm a year ago," Rory told her, as they walked across the carpark. "Some friends of mine converted it into a restaurant and some *rather* exclusive art galleries and shops." He opened the door and marched in. "There's Kian O'Sullivan!"

He strode across the crowded restaurant, Stella just managing to grab the door and push it open before it banged shut behind him.

"Kian, wonderful to see you!" Rory pumped the hand of a large red-faced man who was sitting at a table in the centre of the restaurant, surrounded by a horde of very young-looking girls. "The place looks fantastic!"

Stella crossed the restaurant in his wake and then stood uncertainly on the edge of the conversation. Kian glanced at her briefly and the girls by his side glared at her and then, deciding that she was of no consequence, went back to their giggling conversation.

"This is Stella," Rory introduced her finally, then continued his conversation with Kian.

A flustered-looking waiter bustled through the crowded restaurant. "Your table is ready, sir," he told Rory, guiding them across the room to a window table. He pulled out the seat for Stella and made a huge show of arranging the napkin on her lap. Stella looked nervously at the huge array of cutlery and glasses that were crammed onto the table. It would be awful if she used the wrong knife, just when she was trying to impress Rory.

"The guinea fowl is supposed to be rather nice," Rory said as another waiter handed them menus.

"I think that I might just have the special salad – it sounds so nice and healthy," Stella laid down her menu. "I've been eating far too much this week," she lied.

Halfway through the meal Stella began to relax. Rory, after downing half a bottle of red wine, was in fine form. Stella stopped concentrating on cutting up her lettuce and transferring each morsel carefully to her mouth and glanced around the room. The restaurant was gorgeous, all wooden floors and bare stone walls set off with beautiful, opulent furniture which formed the perfect backdrop for the obviously wealthy crowd that had gathered there to eat. This, she decided, was really the way to live. Mingling with wealthy people, in the finest restaurant, with an expensive car sitting outside in the carpark for the trip home.

The waiter had just cleared their dinner plates away and brought them their coffee when suddenly there was a shriek of recognition from across the room.

"Rory!" yelled three high-pitched and very posh voices.

Stella looked across the room to see three scantily clad girls in various shades of blonde descending rapidly on them. With barely a glance in her direction the three girls launched themselves at Rory, covering him in kisses before dragging vacant chairs from adjoining tables and plonking themselves down close to him.

"This is Tiger, Olympia and Noki," Rory introduced the three. "Stella, a friend of mine."

The girls looked at Stella with uninterested eyes. Once she had been dismissed as a mere friend the three girls, assuming that she wasn't worth bothering with, turned their attention to Rory, swigging wine out of his glass and chattering loudly, all flirting outrageously with him.

Stella took a long swig of her red wine, downing half of the glass as if it were lemonade on a hot summer's day. She couldn't bear the three young women. How dare they muscle in on her date and completely monopolise Rory's attention!

"Rory, I think I need to get home," Stella said quickly when there was a momentary lapse in the clamour of conversation.

"Oh," said Dark Blonde, who Stella guessed was called Noki. She looked across the table at Stella as if she had announced that she was going to dance naked on the table.

"Isn't it a bit early?" Middle Blonde scowled at Rory.

"I have to get up early for work," snapped Stella. The girls were really getting on her nerves. She just wished that they'd clear off and leave her with Rory – they were ruining her evening.

"Work?" said Pale Blonde, as if she had never heard the word before. "Oh, how awful! Ring me, Rory darling, won't you?" She smacked a lingering kiss on Rory's lips and, shooting Stella a triumphant look, led the way back across the restaurant with the other blondes trailing regretfully in her wake.

Rory let out an audible sigh of regret as he watched the girls sashay their way through the tables. "Lovely girls," he breathed, turning his attention slowly back to Stella. "Better get the worker home then."

Stella stalked out of the restaurant. The blondes had ruined her evening. She had hoped that for once she would be able to sit and talk to Rory away from those awful racehorses of his, without the distraction of the racecourse. Her first real chance to show him what a lovely person she was and how he would be foolish not to consider her as a future wife.

"Nice restaurant," Rory commented, as he gunned the car engine into life.

"Yes," Stella said shortly. She just wanted to go home to cool off the ferocious temper that was boiling within her.

"Didn't you enjoy yourself?" asked Rory, when she had sat silently for some time.

"Yes, but ..." She stopped lamely, before bravely ploughing on, "those girls ... chatting you up ... all over you . . ."

Rory let out a guffaw of laughter. "They're just friends."

"Yes, but they were so obviously chatting you up."

Rory sighed. "Look, if you don't like me having friends then there's no point in continuing with this. Is there?"

Stella was silent, listening to the purr of the car engine, watching the array of lights on the dashboard, seeing a man nudging his companion to look as the car glided by. In the semi-darkness she looked at Rory, with his expensive clothes, his gold watch glinting in the light from lampposts. She didn't want to give this up.

"I'm sorry," she whispered quietly.

"That's better." Rory ran a hot hand up the length of her thigh. "Now, do you fancy coming back to my place for a nightcap?"

*　　*　　*

Stella woke with a jolt. Bright light flooded into the bedroom, streaming in through the open curtains.

"Oh my God!" she gasped, shoving back the bedclothes. She was going to be late for work.

"What the hell!" roared Rory, as a blast of cold air hit his warm skin.

Shit, shit, shit! How could she have been so stupid as to oversleep? Stella lurched across the bedroom to find her clothes. Damn, she couldn't go into work wearing her red dress. That would be just too obvious. Everyone would know that she hadn't been home all night. Stella pulled on her underwear and slid the red dress over her head,

"Where are you going?" Rory propped himself up on one arm and grinned at her wolfishly, as she fastened her shoes.

"I must get home – I've got to change and shower and get to work. I'm going to be *so* late!"

"Oh, for heaven's sake, relax," Rory yawned. "Ring up and tell them you aren't coming in." He picked up his mobile phone from the bedside table and held it out to her.

Stella shook her head. "I can't. I need to get to work – they're relying on me."

Rory slammed the phone back down peevishly. "What's so fucking important at work? Why are you in such a hurry to get there? You must be shagging the boss or something."

"No! Of course not!" Stella retorted. How could he say such a thing? She had a responsible job. She had taken a long time to climb up the ladder at work, and she was damned if she was going to let them down on a whim.

"Must be. Otherwise why wouldn't you want to spend the day here with me?" Rory turned away and pulled the bedclothes up around his neck, his whole body rigid with tension.

"I can't take days off just like that," Stella whispered, tears threatening to spill down her cheeks. How could Rory make accusations like that? She loved her job but certainly wasn't in love with her boss as he was implying. Nothing could have been further from the truth. Kevin O'Meara, her boss, was a horrible creep, but apart from him she did enjoy every bit of her job.

"You could if you cared anything for me," Rory said in a wheedling little voice. "You must have someone else there. Go on! Go off to your boss!"

Stella crossed the room, sat on the edge of the bed and gingerly touched Rory's shoulder.

He shrugged off her hand with a jerk.

"There's nothing between me and my boss," she said quietly, bewildered by the sudden twist in his mood. "Please believe me."

Rory was silent.

Stella put her hand slowly back onto his shoulder

with a sigh of frustration and looked around the gorgeous room. This was the kind of place that she would love to live in. She had adored Rory's apartment from the moment she had walked in the previous evening. Every inch of it had a deliciously expensive air about it, from the acres of pale carpet to the opulent furniture and bright modern paintings that adorned the walls. And now she would never be able to spend time here. Rory was dismissing her as curtly as a waiter who had given bad service, just because he had suddenly assumed that she was having an affair with her boss. The injustice of it rankled terribly.

"Stay if you want to," said Rory sullenly, breaking the tense silence. "Ring up and say you aren't coming and then get back into bed."

He was giving her a reprieve. Stella snatched up the mobile phone and began to punch in her work number.

7

Amber shook her head slowly in disbelief. "So you just phoned work and said that you were sick?"

She glared across the room at Stella who pushed her hair behind her ears and then shrugged in a helpless gesture before hesitantly saying, "Yes."

"And your boss believed you?" Amber finished mopping up the puddle of puppy wee that Teddy had just done. She got to her feet, tucking the small rust-coloured puppy under her arm. Teddy wriggled furiously, his short legs working in an effort to free himself from her grasp. Amber crouched down and let him go. He scampered away with his curious uncoordinated gait, growling furiously at a rubber ball that the girls had bought him to play with.

"He must have known that you were lying! You have never had a day off sick. Ever!"

"I know." Stella tapped Teddy's rubber ball with the

toe of her kitten-heeled mules, sending it rolling across the carpet. The puppy dashed after it, small black-tipped ears flapping. "But Rory . . ." her words ground to a halt. She sighed, trying to gather her thoughts and frame the words to explain that she hadn't gone to work because Rory had accused her of having an affair and because she had been feeble enough to let him manipulate her into staying with him for the day. It had been a nice day. They had spent the morning lolling around his apartment, and then had lunch in a lovely restaurant and in the afternoon he had taken her shopping. She had come home with carrier bags filled with expensive underwear and clothes. But the trip had been spoilt by the nagging sensation of guilt that she had let them down at work. She loved her job and had spent years working her way up from humble Girl Friday to editor of the beauty page, at *MiMi Magazine*. And she had done that by making herself indispensable to everyone – and never missing a day's work.

"Bloody hell!" Amber crawled across the floor to retrieve the ball from Teddy's needle-sharp tiny teeth. "Was he so wonderful that you couldn't tear yourself away?" She sat on her heels and grinned at Stella.

"Not exactly," Stella answered, wryly. "He didn't want me to go."

The pup, tiring of playing with the ball, capered across the room and began to gnaw at the heels of Stella's shoes. She reached down and pulled him onto her lap, tilting her face down so that Amber wouldn't be able to read her expression, as she recalled Rory's hasty and very inadequate lovemaking – if it could be called that. Climbing on top of her and banging away for a few moments hardly warranted the grand title of lovemaking.

Amber gave a snort of annoyance. "But surely you couldn't not go to work just because he wanted you to stay with him? You have responsibilities."

"He accused me of having an affair with my boss."

This time the snort was one of amusement that turned rapidly to amazement as the impact of Stella's words sank in.

"What!" Amber said incredulously.

"His apartment was gorgeous." Stella changed the subject abruptly. She didn't want to discuss the pathetic way she had let Rory manipulate her.

Amber watched her friend as myriad emotions flickered across her beautiful face. Stella jumped to her feet, wanting to stop the discussion. "I think we need puppy food. Do you want to come? We could get a drink on the way back."

Then, seeing the startled look of horror on Amber's face and realising that yet again she had no money, Stella added, "My treat."

They walked to the shop, bought the dog food and then went to a pub crowded with early evening drinkers relaxing before making the journey home. Amber took her pint glass from Stella with a guilty smile. She still hadn't had the money back that she had lent her mother, and this month the repayments on her credit-card bills had cleaned out her salary. And still had hardly made a dent in the balance figure.

Now Christmas wasn't that far off and she dreaded to think how she would cope with that – the thought of it made her feel ill.

Just then a familiar face caught her eye. Amber looked, transfixed, over Stella's left shoulder, unable to hear the words her friend was saying. She was just aware of her mouth opening and closing while all the time Luke was coming towards them, a huge grin splitting his face.

"Hey . . . babe," said Luke, obviously struggling to think of her name and failing. He squeezed past Stella and enfolded Amber in a bear hug. He smelt of beer and smoke.

"Where were you the other night?" Amber yelped, and saw Stella raise her eyes skywards. OK, so it was completely uncool to be so naked in her demanding to know why she had been stood up. Of course she should have immediately apologised for standing *him* up, make him feel that she didn't give a damn about him. Amber could almost hear Stella lecturing her about how to make a man weak with desire. But how could *she* talk? Ms Stand-By-Your-Man-And-Don't-Go-To-Work-Just-Cos-He-Says-So.

"Oh!" groaned Mr Super Cool, slapping a long-fingered hand to his forehead. "I had some urgent business that I had to sort out – and I hadn't got your phone number with me. I felt terrible letting you down like that."

Amber caught Stella's eye and ignored the glare of

disbelief she was giving her. OK, so it did sound like a feeble excuse. But it *might* be true. And he really had the nicest smile.

"Let me make it up to you. *Please* come out with me tonight!" He fixed his beautiful brown eyes on her, reminding her of Teddy when he was hungry or wanted playing with.

"OK," she said, shooting a defiant glance at Stella, who shook her head imperceptibly in disbelief.

*   *   *

"He's really nice, don't you think?" Amber swung the shopping bag gaily as they walked home.

"He's a total slimeball," declared Stella tonelessly.

"He said that he couldn't get hold of me to tell me that he wasn't coming," Amber replied huffily. She stopped swinging the bag and walked silently beside Stella.

"That's total rubbish," said Stella. "The oldest line in the book."

"Well, I believe him," Amber snapped, clamping her mouth shut into a tight line. Sometimes she really hated Stella; she was such a know-it-all. She was hardly any great expert on how to deal with men. Look at the jerk she had landed herself with! Just because he was rich.

"What shall I wear?" Amber asked eventually, desperate to break the uncomfortable silence that had fallen between them.

"I don't know," Stella replied shortly, then softening

to one of her favourite subjects – clothes – she added, "How about that nice pink top with your black trousers?"

Teddy began to yap loudly as Stella put the key in the lock.

"He's going to be a good guard dog," grinned Amber. She pushed open the door, shoved the bag of dog-food down on the kitchen worktop and headed into her bedroom.

Stella followed her. If her friend was going to make a fool of herself over some cold-hearted lying cheat, then she might as well make sure that she looked nice doing it.

Amber wrenched open the wardrobe door and sighed. Every inch of space was crammed with the results of her shopping forays, and yet there still wasn't anything to wear. None of the articles of clothing that she bought ever went with anything else. And something that had looked like a bargain in the shop had become rather less so when she got it home and realised that it really didn't suit her or go with anything else in the wardrobe.

"What about this?" Stella reached into the mass of colour and texture and pulled out a T-shirt. Amber saw a look of distaste flicker over her face before she managed to assume a polite expression. "Perhaps not." She folded the hideous creation solicitously before shoving it back.

Amber felt the familiar knot of tension grip her stomach as it always did when she was faced with the decision of what to wear for an important date. If only Stella had gone out! She could have raided her wardrobe. Again.

"Maybe we should have a look at what's in my wardrobe." Stella shut Amber's wardrobe door and headed into her own room with Amber trotting thankfully behind her. She flung open the door and immediately pulled out a beige dress. "Here!"

Amber took the dress, held it up against herself and gazed in the mirror. The long, plain dress had tiny buttons all the way down the front and a pretty scooped neck. It looked gorgeous against her dark colouring, highlighting her dark hair and green eyes.

"You may as well look pretty while you make a fool of yourself," said Stella.

A short time later Amber had showered and blow-dried her hair – and even found enough change in the side pocket of a discarded handbag for a taxi.

"Have a good time!" said Stella.

*   *   *

As the taxi got closer to the pub Amber clamped her knees tightly together to stop them quivering. This was ridiculous – she was behaving like a schoolgirl on a first date. Just because Luke was gorgeous she had gone to pieces. She must keep control of her feelings. Maybe he wouldn't turn up again and then she would have to go home looking like a total idiot and Stella would take great pleasure in saying 'I told you so'. Then, as the taxi swooped around the corner Amber's heart lurched in her chest. He was there. Luke was actually standing outside the pub waiting for *her!* She fumbled in her purse for the money to pay for the taxi and then succeeded in dropping the small change that she had so carefully counted out all over the front seat of the cab.

"Oh, go on!" snapped the taxi driver impatiently, lurching to a stop outside the pub. He shook his head wryly as Amber fumbled with the door handle and then half fell out of the cab in her haste.

"You look great!" Luke planted a kiss on her cheek and grinned disarmingly.

Amber fought the urge to stand on the pavement and gaze at him with her mouth open in sheer wonderment.

"Come on, let's get a drink. I think I've got a lot of making up to do for letting you down the other evening."

"OK." Amber wished that she could think of something witty to say as he took her arm and guided her into the pub. Or actually, just anything to say at all.

"Pint of Carlsberg, is it?"

Amber nodded and Luke shoved his way to the bar. The barmaid almost fell over her high heels in her rush to get to him. "Pint, Luke?" she breathed and Amber saw her face fall as she realised that Luke was with someone. A grin of triumph split Amber's face. This trophy man who everyone seemed to fancy was actually with *her!*

"We'll sit over here." Luke handed Amber her pint

and led the way across the bar to a crowded table. "Shove over, Max!"

Luke perched on the edge of the bench seat and shoved the lads who were at the table over to make room for him and Amber. "These are the Party Boys," he grinned, naming all of the lads who were at the table one by one. Then chinking his glass against Amber's he said, "Drink up now and we'll have a grand time!"

* * *

Amber weaved her way slowly back to the table after yet another trip to the Ladies'. "Shorry," she slurred, cannoning off a man who was standing at the bar. Three pints was one too many.

"Got another pint for you!" Luke roared, pushing the tall glass across the table towards her. Amber felt her stomach heave at the thought. She shouldn't have drunk so much, but nerves and the sheer delight at having hooked such a prize as Luke had made her gulp the first couple of pints as if they were lemonade. And now she was paying the price. Luke's friends had gone. Amber couldn't remember them leaving. Luke put his arm around her. Amber struggled to focus as his face moved closer and closer. And then his lips closed onto hers and she felt herself turn to liquid inside . . . he was *sooooooooo* delicious, she wanted to stay kissing him forever.

A taxi took them to a party. Amber was aware of thumping music, and Luke kissing her in the most delicious way, slowly, his lips soft, pliable against hers, his hands roving over her body, awakening sensations that made her shiver with longing.

"Do you want to come upstairs?" he whispered, his voice hoarse in her ear.

She felt her hair move as he breathed against her skin. She nodded, enthralled. This gorgeous man, who everyone had fancied, actually wanted *her*.

He took her hand and led her upstairs past couples entwined together and two girls by the front door who were arguing, shrieking at each other in high-pitched voices.

Amber heard herself giggling as Luke threw a man, who had been sprawled fully clothed on the bed, out of the bedroom and locked the door.

Luke lay her down.

She gave a sigh of infinite pleasure as he undid the buttons on Stella's beige dress and finally moved his warm hands over her body.

Afterwards she felt more sober, the vigorous exercise working the alcohol out of her system. She lay in Luke's arms and gave a sigh of sheer delight. This was truly wonderful. She was very lucky to have found such a lovely man who obviously wanted her so much. Stella had been wrong about him.

"Come on, babe. I'll get you a taxi." Luke rolled out of bed and started to pull on his jeans.

Amber slid reluctantly out of the warmth of the bed and began to button Stella's dress. Damn, some of the buttons were missing! She didn't remember losing them, although there was a vague and uncomfortable memory of Luke pulling at the buttons in frustration when he couldn't undo them fast enough in his haste to get her undressed. Luke punched some numbers on his mobile and ordered a taxi.

"It'll be about ten minutes. I'll get you a coffee," he told her, snapping off the phone.

"When will I see you again?" Amber asked, sipping the bitter coffee. Stella would be horrified if she could see how un-cool she was being. Never be too eager, she would say scornfully. But Amber couldn't bear the thought of not knowing when she would see Luke again – and obviously he had forgotten to take her phone number.

"I'm not sure, I'm a bit busy for the next week – or so, but I'll see you around, I'm sure."

Amber stared hard at the dregs of her coffee, feeling sick. He was giving her the brush-off.

Stella had been right all along. He was worse than even Stella had thought. He had taken her out and she had let him use her for sex. What a cheap fool she had been to fall for him!

Luke pulled back the curtains and peered along the darkened street. "Here's the taxi." He walked her outside, gave the taxi driver money and told him to take her home. Then, dropping a perfunctory kiss on her cheek, he went back inside the house without a backwards glance.

Amber sat in the back of the taxi and gazed numbly at the houses they passed, all in darkness, the orange street lights casting an eerie glow over the gardens.

"Night, love," the driver said cheerily as he dropped her off at the entrance to the apartment.

Amber let herself in, barely aware of Teddy scrabbling against her legs with his sharp claws, desperate for attention. How could she have been such a fool? Getting drunk and being used for sex!

"Had a good time?" Stella emerged from her bedroom.

"No!" gasped Amber, clamping her hand to her mouth and dashing to the toilet where she was violently sick.

8

Amber glared at her supervisor's back as she stalked away down the production line. "That bloody Dymphna's turned into a right cow since she's been promoted to supervisor," complained Mel, the girl beside her, slamming a handful of chocolates into a box.

"Jumped-up bitch!" snapped Jules. She reached across the production line, grabbed one of the decorative sweets and shoved it defiantly into her mouth.

Amber nodded, bleakly. She would have liked to have joined in the conversation, but her hangover was so bad that she hardly dare open her mouth. A sharp pain banged behind her eyes and every movement caused waves of stomach-churning nausea.

"Dymphna really had it in for you," Jules muttered sympathetically, darting a look to see where the supervisor had gone to.

Amber moved her head slowly up and down. She dare not move too quickly, it was too painful. She wished that she could have had the day off. She would have loved to have rung in sick, but she couldn't afford it. Every penny was needed, to pay off those dreadful credit-card bills. At least being at work stopped her from thinking too much and feeling sorry for herself about the way that she had got drunk the night before and let Luke use her in the most sordid and base way. Coming to work with a killer hangover was a punishment, to make sure that she never did anything so stupid again.

It had been rather unfortunate that Dymphna, newly promoted and eager to prove herself to her boss, the sleazy Tony Moran, who just happened to be her boyfriend, had caught Amber sneaking into work late. It made it even worse that someone had already clocked her in, but Dymphna could never prove who that was. Amber struggled to bite her tongue as Dymphna launched into a tirade of abuse about Amber's timekeeping and her general lack of team spirit, as she followed her through the factory to her place on the production line.

"She's coming back!" Mel hissed, hastily grabbing another handful of chocolates and shoving them into a box.

Dymphna slowly made her way down the production line, arms folded aggressively across her bony chest, stopping here and there to chastise any worker who wasn't up to scratch.

"A bit slow today, aren't we, Amber?" Dymphna peered at the boxes that Amber had filled.

"Sorry," Amber whispered, trying hard not to stare at Dymphna's long pointed nose, which wriggled at the end as she spoke.

"How long are you here now?" She glared at Amber with her curious protruding eyes, then without waiting for a reply continued, "You had better quicken up." Then, solicitously straightening a bow on one of the chocolate boxes, she turned on her heel and stalked away.

"Take no notice," Jules hissed at Amber, defiantly shoving her finger into one of the chocolates before she shoved it into the box, "She was slower than everyone! She only got promoted because she shagged Tony. Everyone knows that's the quickest way up the career ladder!"

"I wonder if she licks the melted chocolate that we use in the production room off his belly?" mused Mel and they all groaned at the thought of their two pale-skinned bodies writhing together.

Amber jumped as her phone began to vibrate in the pocket of her overalls, telling her that there was a call. Phones were strictly forbidden on the factory floor, but everyone carried them anyway, just turning off the ring tone and hoping that they wouldn't be caught if they answered any calls that came through. Dymphna took great delight in being able to reprimand any of her staff who were found disobeying the petty company rules and regulations. Someone had once likened her to a child who loves to torture small insects, slowly pulling off the legs one by one just to see how long she could spin out the slow death.

Thankfully, Dymphna was nowhere to be seen. Amber dragged her phone out of her pocket, hampered by the white skin-tight rubber gloves that everyone had to wear. "Hello!" she hissed into the mouthpiece, casting furtive looks around the factory floor to see if Dymphna was stalking along the production line, or skulking behind stacked boxes of chocolates. The coast seemed to be clear.

"Amber?" whined her mother's voice into the earpiece. "You'll have to come over – I've got terrible problems with Georgina. Your sister has totally gone off the rails this time. You'll have to come and sort her out."

Amber sighed. It was incredible how her mother wanted her to go around when there were problems. When things were going well she didn't want anything to do with Amber – she was too busy looking after someone else's husband. Mel shot Amber a look, to warn her that Dymphna was approaching.

"I can't talk to you now," she whispered, crouching down as if she had dropped something. "I'll ring you later." She snapped off the phone and shoved it into her pocket, then scrambled back to her feet.

"Not using the phone under that table, are you, Amber?" asked Dymphna, her pale shark's eyes glittering maliciously with the anticipated delight of being able to bully someone again.

"A chocolate fell off the production line. I bent to

pick it up, that's all." Amber forced her face to assume a look of total innocence.

"Where is it then?" Dymphna raised eyebrows plucked almost into extinction and held out her hand for the imaginary piece of chocolate. Amber was sure that Dymphna could hear the gulp of horror that she gave – now she was really trapped.

"Here it is!" yelled Jules, shoving a fluff-covered chocolate into Dymphna's hand. "It rolled all the way over to me. Wasn't Amber great to try to get it back? Just *imagine* it rolling all the way across the floor!" She smiled innocently at Dymphna who, knowing that she was beaten, glared at the women and then stalked away, her rubber-soled shoes squeaking in the silence.

Amber sank thankfully down onto her stool. "Thanks, I owe you one," she said, grinning across the table at Jules and Mel.

The clock above the factory door eventually ground around to lunch-time. Everyone was convinced that it was a special clock that went slower than any other in the world. Time seemed to stand still when they were at work. Finally they were all able to escape the sterile atmosphere of the factory floor and head out into the locker room. "Here, love." Lily, one of the older women, shoved a couple of tablets into Amber's hand. "These are brilliant for hangovers." Lily's face was yellow and etched in deep lines from a lifetime of hard drinking and heavy smoking. She recognised the symptoms of a killer hangover when she saw one and felt sympathy for a fellow sufferer.

"Cheers, Lily!" Amber shoved the tablets gingerly into her mouth – any sudden movement would make her retch again. She pulled off her hairnet. "Anyone coming into town?" she asked, unbuttoning her overall and shoving the hated rubber gloves into the bin.

"Nah," grinned Mel. "We'll be having a long lunch hour – Dymphna always goes for her *production meeting* with Tony today. She'll be gone all afternoon, so we're heading for the pub – Sarah will clock us all in as usual."

"Funny how Dymphna's *production meetings* always take place at a hotel out of town," giggled Jules.

The girls left the changing room and Amber punched in her mother's phone number.

"Now, tell me what the matter is with Georgina?" she asked, when her mother eventually answered the phone.

"Ohh," Ruby sighed dramatically. "Georgina's wearing me out. She's always so moody. She keeps staying out late at night, not coming home sometimes. You'll have to come and sort her out. I can't cope with her."

"I'll come over tonight," Amber said wearily. She had enough problems of her own without having to make the journey all the way across town to sort out their arguments.

She headed out of the factory and towards the shops. Festive garlands hung across the streets and tinsel and bright lights glittered in the shop windows. Amber sighed, feeling the familiar tension gripping her stomach. Christmas was coming rapidly and she had no money to buy gifts for anyone, and they would all be expecting her to produce goodies for them. Her credit cards were at the limit, and this month's salary had all been magically transferred into Stella's account to pay for the rent on the flat and her contribution towards the food and utilities. She had enough left for bus fares and maybe a night out, but that was all. Wearily she mooched down the street, gazing bleakly at the shop windows crammed with inviting goodies all screeching *'Buy Me!'*.

Amber wandered into one of the big shops and was immediately warmed by a blast of hot air from the blowers in the doorway. She undid her coat and drifted slowly down the aisle, letting the piped music wash over her, lulling her into a delicious sense of relaxation. At every side of the aisle, shoppers heaved overflowing trolleys and hauled bulging shopping bags through the shop floor, jostling with each other to grab overpriced and overpackaged boxes of toiletries as if they would never be available again.

If only Christmas was a month later, her bank balance would surely be a little bit healthier by then and she would be able to afford to buy presents. And then suddenly Amber saw the answer to her problems. Over by the Customer Service desk a huge sign, with flashing lights, attracted her attention.

'Buy Now. Pay nothing until February. Instant Credit.'

The answer to all of her problems. Amber lurched across the crowded store, elbowing blank-eyed shoppers out of the way in her haste to get to the desk.

An hour later she was cramming heavy shopping bags into her locker at work, with a sinking heart. It had all been so easy. She merely had to fill in a form, answer a few questions about her income and where she lived. The Customer Services Assistant had keyed her answers into a computer, her long red talons flying over the keys, and a few moments later a plastic card had been handed across the desk into Amber's clammy hand. And then, short of breath and flushed with excitement, Amber had begun a trolley dash around the store, shoving expensive goodies into the most co-operative trolley that she had ever pushed. The trolley seemed to guide her, as if by its own volition, towards the beauty counter, where her arms, weak with relief at having so much money, hauled gorgeous cellophane-wrapped creations into its shiny wire recesses. And then the trolley set off across the store to the men's department, bypassing the cheap clothes until it came to rest beside the gorgeous cashmere sweaters that seemed to melt into her fingers as she hauled them off the shelves and threw them gaily in amongst her other treasures. With a final flourish, the trolley whisked her back across the store to the ladies' department, where a whisper-thin silk-and-lace wrap that would look gorgeous on Stella flew from the rail and nestled in amongst the cashmere sweaters.

Even visiting the checkout was like magic. A grinning assistant skimmed her card through a machine and reverently packaged her goodies, shoving the till receipt into one of the bags and handing Amber a slip to sign. Gaily she signed her name beneath the rather large bill, adding a flourishing swirl of delight to the end of her signature. And then she was outside, fingers clamped around the string handles of her bags, feeling the cold air seeping into her bones again as the full horror of what she had just done washed over her.

Now the metal door would barely shut, with all of the shopping bags crammed into her locker. Amber finally shoved it shut and leant on it to turn the key in the lock. She pressed her burning forehead against the cool metal of the door. What the hell had she just done? How could she have been such an idiot as to get into yet more debt, buying expensive junk that her family would take one look at and then discard without a word of thanks? It wasn't as if they would even shower her with expensive presents in return. Or, in fact, any presents at all.

Amber shoved on her overall and hairnet and headed back into the factory, grabbing a pair of rubber gloves from a box left open on the wooden bench seat. There was no sign of Dymphna, who was presumably enjoying her 'production meeting' with Tony, in a hotel near the airport. Only Sarah, who was never late, sat at her place on the line, smugly loading chocolates into a box, eating one occasionally. The rest of the workers drifted in slowly, giggling as the effects of gulping a pint or two took hold.

"Good time?" Mel asked, heaving herself up onto her stool.

"Brilliant, thanks. I got all my Christmas shopping done," Amber said through gritted teeth. How could she have been so stupid? She could have just got small inexpensive presents for everyone. They would never have noticed. Or cared. Instead she had gone completely over the top, buying presents as if she were using toy money. Now it would take forever to pay off the balance on the store card. Shit. Shit.

She jumped again as her phone vibrated in her overalls pocket.

"Hello?" She took out the phone brazenly since Dymphna wasn't around.

"Amber!" Her mother's voice rose to a high-pitched wail. "You have to come over *right now.* Georgina has just told me that I can't make her come home at night. I can't stand any more of this!"

"OK, OK," Amber said soothingly into the mouthpiece. "I'll come now." Wearily she snapped off her phone.

"Problems?" asked Mel. She was slumped across her desk, grabbing chocolates and shovelling them into her mouth.

Amber shook her head in a gesture of despair. "Is there ever anything else in my family?" she sighed. "I've got to go." She climbed off her stool.

"Don't worry. We'll clock you out!" yelled Jules.

"That's it! Let everyone know that she's skiving off. Idiot!" growled Mel.

Amber collected her shopping bags and headed out of the factory, dashing across the carpark with the furtive gait of an escaped convict. It would be just her luck to be caught in the middle of fleeing by Dymphna and Tony returning from their 'meeting'.

Just as she shot through the factory gates a taxi came towards her along the main road. Amber wrenched her hand out of the carrier-bag handles and waved frantically. Her luck was in. The driver gave a cheery salute and pulled to the edge of the kerb. Amber scrambled into the taxi, roughly throwing her bags inside in her haste to leave. There had better be a good reason for this urgent need for an emergency visit, thought Amber, settling herself into her seat. She hardly had the money for the bus fare out to her mother's house, let alone a taxi. But this was supposed to be an emergency. From the phone call it sounded as if her mother was about to slaughter Georgina. Or at least she had better be, or Amber would just have to do it for her, if this was yet another wasted journey.

The taxi driver dropped her off at the house, drumming his fingers impatiently on the steering wheel as Amber counted out the fare.

"Thanks," he snapped sarcastically as she finally dropped the exact amount into his hand.

Her mother had the front door open before Amber had even got out of the taxi. She stood, leaning against the frame, puffing dramatically on a cigarette. "You've been ages! I've had a right row with Georgina," she said tearfully, standing aside to let Amber into the house.

Amber walked into the lounge, coughing in the smoky atmosphere. Ruby must have been in here smoking constantly since she had spoken to her.

"So what's the problem?" She turned to face her mother and felt a jolt of panic as she saw that tears were rolling down her face.

"It's Georgina. She just got up while I was talking to her about not coming in late. She marched up to her bedroom. Came down with a bag and left. She's gone!"

9

"Stella! Come and have something to eat!" Sorcha yelled across the room.

"In a while," Stella mouthed back across the crowded room to her assistant. So far she had managed to avoid having to eat anything at the Christmas party. Fortunately the bar was well away from the buffet table, so she had managed not to have to go anywhere near temptation. If she had gone anywhere near the long table which bulged with grossly fattening sandwiches and pork pies and crisps all oozing fat, she wouldn't have been able to resist the lure of the disgusting food and would have spent the whole night longing to eat, more and more. And then she would have spent the following fortnight loathing herself, seeing the gross bulges of fat that would have settled on her waist and hips. As long as she didn't go near the table and sample anything, then she could resist temptation. Stella took a long swig of her diet tonic water. At least the liquid with its chunks of ice and lemon floating in it looked like a proper drink and no one would start querying why she wasn't drinking. One drink would have been enough to chisel away at her willpower and draw her towards the buffet table. She wasn't going to get fat again. Ever. She had to be aware of every single calorie that passed her lips.

"Glad that you were feeling well enough to come back to work for the Christmas party," Kevin O'Meara, her boss, whispered silkily in her ear.

Stella smiled tightly. She hadn't seen Kevin slinking up beside her. She had spent the whole evening avoiding him, remembering the sarcastic tirade he had subjected her to when she returned to work after Rory had persuaded her to take the day off. Kevin took a long swig of his drink.

Stella suspected that the tumbler full of pale liquid was virtually all whiskey.

"I hope that you'll be well enough after Christmas to work on the special Valentine's edition." Kevin glared at her, his pale green eyes filled with malice. "Your wonderful assistant Sorcha did a brilliant job while you were off." He brushed a lock of long curly hair off his forehead with plump fingers. The unspoken threat was clear in his words. If Stella wasn't going to be at work, then Sorcha was going to take over from her. Simple as that.

Stella nodded, glad that the boardroom was in virtual darkness and so Kevin wouldn't be able to see the blush that she could feel was staining her cheeks. She couldn't blame him for making the threat. She held a responsible position in the magazine and knew that she had let him down badly when she had taken the day off. She knew that she should have been firmer with Rory, but she hadn't been able to stand up to him. The threat from Rory was as clear as it now was from Kevin. She had to be the perfect girlfriend to Rory, pander to his every whim, otherwise she would lose him. Stella loved her job, and she loved Rory. For all his jealous tantrums, she was sure that he loved her. And he was everything that she had ever wanted. Stella was determined not to let him go. She was tired of looking for the right man, one with wealth, looks and power. And now that she had found him, she wasn't going to give him up.

People were starting to drift away from the party. Kevin, having made his point, waltzed away to stand at the door, taking up a position where he could kiss everyone goodnight. Stella collected her coat and headed home. She wished that Rory had agreed to come. She would have enjoyed showing him off to everyone, but he had business to attend to.

* * *

Stella let herself into the darkened flat. In the pale orange light from the gas fire she could see Amber sprawled on the sofa, nursing Teddy across her chest like a baby. Stella snapped on the light.

Amber rummaged in her jeans pocket for a tissue and wiped her eyes surreptitiously. "Had a nice time?" she asked, her voice thick with tears.

Stella ignored her question. "What's the matter?"

Amber hoisted Teddy onto her knees and rubbed his head. "Mum's in a state," she said wearily. "Georgina's packed her stuff and gone. They had some kind of row." Stella took off her coat and went to hang it in her wardrobe. Poor Amber was always stuck in the middle of some family crisis. They seemed to use her as a cushion between them when things went wrong. When things were going all right they couldn't be bothered with her. Stella felt a prickle of annoyance. Amber was stupid to get in such a state over them. Georgina would come back when she had cooled down.

"Yes, I know," Amber whispered miserably. If only her sister clearing off were all that she had to be upset about! She didn't dare tell Stella about her money troubles. Stella had such strong willpower. She seemed to be able to control every aspect of her life, from the tiny morsels that she ate, to the way that she was brilliant with money. Stella would have been furious at Amber for letting herself get into such a mess. Everything was awful and then, to cap it all, she had gone for a drink with the girls from work tonight and had seen Luke and his mates in the pub, sniggering at her – he must have told them all about how he had got her drunk and taken her to bed.

"Will you be OK while I'm at Rory's over Christmas?" shouted Stella through her open bedroom door as she began to take off her make-up. There was another line at the corner of her eyes that hadn't been there before, she was sure of it. She leant forward towards her magnifying mirror. She had to settle down, get married, before it was too late – once her looks had gone no one would want her. "I'll be back just after New Year," she added, wishing that Christmas were over. She felt so *guilty* all the time. Guilty for leaving Amber alone, knowing that she would have a rotten time if she went to her mother's and would come home as soon as she had eaten dinner and given all of her grasping family the expensive presents she had bought for them. Stella had realised, with a jolt of annoyance, why Amber never had any money: she had been saving it all to buy them Christmas presents, while Stella had funded her in the pub and on numerous other occasions. It wasn't that Amber was short of money; it was just that she was squirrelling it away to spend on those leeches! If she had realised that before, she wouldn't have been so generous towards Amber.

Still, she felt guilty at leaving Amber to care for Teddy, although she didn't seem to mind – she had virtually taken over the little dog anyway. But most of all she felt guilty at not going home for Christmas. When Rory had asked her a few days previously what she was going to do for Christmas, she had told him that she usually made the journey home to Mayo until the New Year.

"Oh, you don't want to go all that way surely," he had grumbled. "Stay with me instead."

And so she had readily agreed. It was nice to have the excuse not to make the interminable drive across the country back *there*. Nice to know that she would be spending Christmas in a gorgeous luxury apartment, with a charming, handsome man, instead of in a cramped windswept cottage huddled beneath a grey, grim mountain. It had been hard to explain to her mother, though, that she couldn't come this year. The disappointment was clear in her voice as she told Stella that she hoped that she would come and visit them soon and that she would miss her. Stella had put down the phone with a heavy heart. She hated how relieved she felt, now that she wasn't going back home.

"Sounds like your Lord and Master is here," Amber said, peering out of the window as Rory honked his horn aggressively to announce his arrival.

Stella hastily grabbed the bags that she had lined up by the door and then, seeing Amber's crestfallen face, dropped the bags and crossed the room to enfold her in a bear hug. "I'll see you soon – have a great time."

Amber wrenched her face into a smile. "You too."

* * *

The back seat of Rory's sports car was filled with interesting-looking beautifully wrapped presents. Stella shoved her bags in and settled herself into the passenger seat. She was going to really enjoy this Christmas. It was going to make a wonderful change from the much-hated trip home. Stella had fled from

Mayo as soon as she could and now felt like an alien amongst her family. They were so rough and uncultured. And her sister, Mary, was *so* fat. She really should go on a diet, take a bit of pride in herself.

"Have you got a tree?" Stella breathed excitedly as Rory opened the door to his apartment.

"Nah," Rory shook his head. "They make too much mess." He stood aside to let Stella in, struggling beneath the weight of her bags.

A wave of disappointment washed over Stella, surprising her with its force. Christmas trees were untidy, but Christmas wasn't Christmas without a tree, gently dropping needles all over the floor and crammed with an odd selection of mismatched decorations – like the one that would be no doubt taking up a huge part of the cramped lounge at her parents' house.

"Don't put those bags on the worktop!" Rory frowned as Stella heaved her bags onto the black granite. "I don't want anything to scratch the marble surface," he said peevishly, eyeing her bags suspiciously. "It cost me a fortune."

Later they went out for dinner and then returned to the immaculate, silent apartment. Usually at this time, Stella thought, with a tinge of regret, she would be rolling out of Eagan's Bar with her brothers and sister, holding onto each other for support as they began the long walk home along the road that wound beside the seashore, singing carols as loudly as they could to drown out the noise of the sea hitting the rocks. But this was nicer, she told herself firmly, going to bed with her handsome, wealthy lover, in his beautiful apartment. This was everything that she could possibly wish for.

*   *   *

She woke before dawn, accustomed to early starts, and lay in the vast bed, watching the orange glow of the city slowly change to a murky grey as Christmas Morning began. In Mayo they were probably just having the first power cut of the day as all the children in the West of Ireland turned on their new electrical presents and the antiquated system faltered under the strain.

"How about making me some tea?" Rory opened his eyes and grinned at her, running his hand gently over her stomach and sliding it slowly downwards. "Tea first!" He whipped the bedclothes back off her warm body.

Laughing, Stella grabbed his cashmere sweater and pulled it over her nightdress, then padded barefoot to the kitchen.

She returned a few minutes later with the tea, laid the china mugs on the bedside table and slid back under the covers.

"You're freezing!" Rory groaned, rolling on top of her.

She wasn't quite sure if he was complaining of the fact or was being sympathetic.

"I bet that will be your best Christmas present ever," he grinned after a few moments of frenzied pumping.

He eased himself out of her and fell back onto his pillow, a sheen of sweat on his face, and wiped away the beads of moisture that had collected in the dark haze of stubble above his top lip.

"Definitely," lied Stella. Good grief, she thought, picking up her tea mug – the liquid had barely had time to cool down. Sex was definitely not Rory's strong point. But at least he was nice to her, to make up for his failings in the bed department – most of the time anyway.

"What time shall we go to Mass?" Stella asked, putting down her empty mug.

"Mass?" Rory chortled with amusement. "You don't really want to go *there*, do you?"

Stella's heart sank: no Christmas tree and no Mass. "No, I suppose not."

Rory slid out of bed. "Come on, I want to open my presents!" He pulled on a silk dressing-gown, shoved his feet into leather slippers and padded into the lounge. Stella shoved the cashmere sweater over her head again and followed him. The presents, stacked up on the long dining table, looked oddly out of place in the tidy apartment. There should have been tinsel and lights and Christmas cards lying scattered around. In Mayo the lounge floor would have been covered in discarded wrapping paper, while her mother went around frenziedly gathering up unripped bits large enough to salvage for next year.

"These are yours," Rory said grandly, pulling out one of the dining-room chairs for Stella to sit down and pushing a stack of beautifully wrapped parcels in front of her. "And these must be mine," he grinned, wrapping his arms around the parcels that Stella had wrapped for him and dragging them towards himself.

Feeling very self-conscious, Stella unwrapped her presents as Rory watched her. In Mayo everyone opened their presents at the same time, in a chaos of exclamations of delight and groans of disgust.

"Oh, this is lovely!" Stella unwrapped a red nylon baby doll nightdress with tiny knickers to match. She fingered the fluffy trim around the open crotch of the knickers and cringed inwardly. Surely Rory didn't expect her to wear *them!* A short time later she had accumulated a pile of revolting underwear and a blouse that looked as if it had been made for someone's maiden aunt who was six sizes bigger than she was.

But Amber had got her a gorgeous silk dressing-gown – Stella fingered the luxurious fabric lovingly – this really was gorgeous. She pulled off Rory's sweater and slid into the whisper-thin dressing-gown. This must have cost a fortune. What had Amber been thinking of? Saving so hard to buy such an expensive present! A bottle of bubble bath would have been fine. Stella thought guiltily of the small handbag that she had bought Amber.

Rory began to open his presents, roughly pulling open the expensive gift-wrap that she had chosen so carefully.

"Very nice," he said finally, once he had unwrapped a sizable pile of beautiful cotton shirts and a very expensive leather wallet. "Thank you very much." He lifted one of the shirts. "Did you keep the receipts for these? I might change some of them."

Stella pursed her lips together. "Yes, of course."

Hurt settled like a cloak around her shoulders. Rory had bought her the most awful presents, things that she would never wear, and that he should know that she would never wear, if he had paid any heed to her on the numerous dates that they'd had. She felt as if he had no idea about her at all. And then wanting to change the presents that she had so lovingly chosen for him! That was so hurtful.

Rory scooped up his presents and wandered back to the bedroom with them. Stella followed and shoved hers into one of her bags with a sigh. Men were just so stupid – they never had any concept of what a woman liked. Next year she would have to go with Rory to make sure that they both got something that they liked. For now at least she would make the most of being in this lovely apartment with Rory. Maybe next year she would be married to him, maybe thinking about a family.

That evening they curled up on the leather sofa. Stella, her earlier hurt pushed firmly to the back of her mind, rested her head on Rory's shoulder as they watched age-old films and worked their way steadily down a bottle of red wine.

"I was just thinking," Rory said suddenly, flicking off the television as the adverts came on. "We get on really well, don't we?"

"Yes." Stella began to unbutton Rory's shirt. Perhaps now if they went to bed, he might manage to last a bit longer than this morning.

"Why don't you stay here with me? You could look after me; keep the apartment nice. Give up that bloody silly job of yours."

10

Stella watched Rory walk across the crowded restaurant towards their table. She noticed with a sense of satisfaction how the women cast surreptitious glances in his direction. He looked extremely handsome in his dark grey suit and ice-white shirt. His yellow tie, which would have looked too feminine on a lesser man, only seemed to highlight his dark colouring and blue eyes. Stella gave a sigh of satisfaction. It was wonderful to think that a prize such as Rory was actually hers.

Good-looking, wealthy men were hard to come by. And Stella should know, she had spent long enough trying to find one. Heaven knows, she could have written a book on the subject. Wealthy men came in all shapes and sizes, but not many of them were suitable boyfriend material. There was Mike, with his flashy Lotus and a laugh like a hyena. And the very good-looking Ralph who, when he stood up, barely reached her shoulder – and she had to draw the line at going out with someone who had daintier feet than she did. And Shaun, Mr Lying Bastard. A trail of wealthy mental and physical rejects wound back through the dark recesses of Stella's memory. Some were clearer than others. Some had been so awful she had mentally erased them.

"When are you going to hand in your notice?" Rory sat back down opposite Stella and leant on the table, locking his eyes on hers.

"I – I –" Stella stammered. She loved Rory, he was gorgeous, but giving up her independence, a job that she loved, that she had fought long and hard to get, was too much to contemplate.

"For heaven's sake!" he snapped, folding his arms aggressively across his chest and glaring at her. "What is there to think about? Women shouldn't work – they should stay at home and care for their menfolk. You don't need to work. I'll look after you."

Stella put down her knife and fork. "But I like my job. I love to be with you, but I enjoy working," she said patiently.

Rory grabbed his wineglass and gulped back the dark red liquid, then refilled it so hastily that some of the wine spilled out over the tablecloth. A diminutive waiter shot forward with a damp cloth, dabbing primly at the liquid as it spread slowly across the virginal white of the tablecloth.

"Leave it," growled Rory and the waiter, looking as if he had been lashed with a whip, withdrew rapidly, a hurt look plastered dramatically all over his girlish face.

"Stop denying it, Stella," Rory hissed, narrowing his eyes to glare at her. "There is someone that you're having an affair with at work, isn't there?"

"Oh, Rory!" Stella drew her fingers across her forehead in an effort to straighten out the lines of tension that she knew must be crinkling her skin. "I've already told you – there's no one at work. No one anywhere except you. I love you. You know that. How could I want anyone else? It's just that I don't want to be dependent on you."

"If you say there's no one else then I believe you," he said in a voice that made her think that he really didn't believe her. "But I can't understand why you won't give up your job and be with me. You'd have a great life. More money than you have ever had. All the time in the world to shop."

Stella smiled. His offer really did sound tempting and she wished that she could just agree with him. Just leave her job and go and live with him. It was everything that she wanted. A gorgeous apartment, a handsome, wealthy man. But giving up her independence . . . What if the relationship went wrong?

"I'll give you until New Year's Day to decide," Rory said gently, but Stella was aware of the veiled threat in his voice. Rory took her hand across the table, brought it to his lips and gently kissed each finger. "And if you still want to work, then I think that we'll have to end our relationship."

*   *   *

Stella made her way wearily up the stairs to the apartment that she shared with Amber, Rory's voice ringing in her ears. There was no doubt that he meant every word. She had to leave work or he would end the relationship. She hated the thought of leaving her job. It had taken her years to work her way up to the position of authority she now held. But that wasn't what she minded as much as the buzz that she got from being in the magazine business, the pressure of having to produce the copy ready for a deadline. She loved the stress and the frayed tempers and the glorious feeling of relief and satisfaction when everything went off to press, and then the delight when she saw someone reading the new issue. It was all addictive stuff. But she hated the thought of losing Rory as well. She was twenty-six. Time was running out for her – soon marriage and children would have passed her by. Not immediately, granted, but soon enough. Time slid by very quickly for those who were not aware of it. The last thing she wanted was to be still sharing an apartment with Amber in another few years. It was time that she had a proper home of her own. A husband, children, maybe even a home in the country.

A dark cloud of gloom wafted over her as she shoved open the door to the apartment. Amber huddled waiflike on the sofa with Teddy, a picture of misery, her depression a tangible thing that seemed to permeate the very air. Teddy wriggled out of Amber's grip and hurtled across the floor, short hairy legs a blur of speed, curly tail wagging furiously, yapping with delight to see her again.

"Had a good Christmas?" Stella asked, gently shoving Teddy away from her leg – his sharp needle-like teeth were digging into her skin.

"You don't want to know," Amber said wryly, getting up to help Stella with her bags. Stella felt her jaw clamp tight with tension. She wished that Amber would lighten up – she used to be so bright and full of fun. Things might be bad for her at home, but she should not let it get her down. The last thing Stella wanted, after all the hassle she was having with Rory and the quandary about whether she should leave her job, was to come home and have to put up with a flatmate constantly sunk in virtually suicidal despair. Maybe she should leave her job and move in with Rory – at least she wouldn't have to put up with Amber's constant stream of misery.

* * *

"Do you fancy coming shopping with me?" Stella asked the following morning. She was feeling charitable towards Amber, who was at least making an attempt to be brighter. "Rory has invited me to a party tonight."

"Great. I'm not buying anything though," Amber said firmly, hoping that she would have the willpower to stick to her words. Funny how in the morning her money and family problems never seemed to be so insurmountable. It was only when the dusk fell and the long night settled in that everything crowded in on her and there seemed to be impossible mountains ahead that she couldn't climb.

"Rory wants me to go and live with him!" Stella couldn't contain her excitement any longer. She had been keeping the news to herself, wanting time to think about the consequences and to slowly mull over all of the benefits before she made her decision. But the words had just bubbled out of her mouth, spilling into the air.

Amber shook her head violently. "He wants you to live with him!" she spat scornfully. "Then he can save himself money – he can sack his cleaner, get all his laundry done for free, save on taxis because you'll be driving him about when he's drunk – and what will you have in return? You'll have no security, nothing, and then when he's sick of you he'll just throw you out!"

Stella glared at her friend. Everything that Amber had said was rubbish. Rory wasn't looking at their relationship like that. He didn't see her as just someone to make his life easier. Maybe he wanted to see how well they lived together – maybe he wanted to marry her, but just wasn't sure. Maybe she would make him so happy that he would want to marry her at the first opportunity. Amber was just jealous because she couldn't get anyone nice.

Stella smiled tightly. "I'm sorry that you see things like that, but I don't think that is how our relationship is at all."

The two headed off into the packed streets. Stella was determined not to let Amber's words annoy her. She was entitled to her opinion. Even if it was the wrong one. Already the shops were emblazoned with *'Sale'* signs and filled with determined shoppers, fighting for bargains. Amber trailed after Stella, trying desperately to ignore the clothes and shoes that cried out to her to be taken home. She had made an early New Year's resolution. No more spending until her credit cards and new store-card balances were at manageable levels. Probably in about three years' time!

Ignoring all of the cheaper shops, Stella headed for her favourite exclusive boutique. She shoved her way through the bargain-hunters and battled to a rail of slinky dresses. It would be lovely to spend the day mooching around the shops and picking out bargains, but today there was no time. She needed to buy something and then head home, to get ready for the party that Rory was taking her to later.

"What do you think of this?" Stella pulled a dress off the rail and had the satisfaction of seeing the naked envy in Amber's face as she looked at the sleek caramel-coloured dress. Amber would be better if she stopped buying tons of cheap junk and bought herself a few gorgeous pieces instead, thought Stella, holding the dress up to her front and examining her reflection in the mirror. There was no point in looking any further: this was *the* dress. Rory would adore her in this. Even just held up against her, the dress flattered her pale colouring and its slinky shape would mould itself to her body.

"Go and put it on," Amber said enviously, tentatively pulling out a black dress covered with tiny sequins, before shoving it forcefully back.

Stella headed off into the changing room and put on the dress. Everyone turned to look at her when she headed out into the shop again to show Amber.

"You *have* to buy that!" shrieked Maddie, one of the assistants, abandoning the customer that she was serving and bustling across the shop. "It looks fantastic on you – and you could wear those brown strappy sandals with it!" She was recalling the last purchase that Stella had made in the shop.

Stella looked at herself in the mirror. She had been right: the dress was perfect. It clung to the contours of her body, skimming over her flat belly and the curve of her hips. Thank goodness she had managed to avoid eating very much over Christmas. She had even managed to tip half of her dinner away in the bin when Rory went off to answer the phone.

* * *

"You look lovely," Rory said approvingly, as Stella lowered herself into the passenger seat of his car. He leant over and kissed her gently on the lips. He tasted of minty toothpaste. "Don't forget you promised me an answer on New Year's Day." He glanced at his chunky gold Rolex. "Only four hours to go." He slid the automatic gear-stick into drive and entwined his long fingers in Stella's, driving one-handed. "I hope you're going to say yes – I thought that we could go to Zanzibar to celebrate."

Stella wondered for the zillionth time what she was going to say to him. She watched the frost-dusted city slide by as she relaxed, cushioned in the comfortable, squishy leather seats. Rory had switched on the seat heaters, making her back pleasantly warm – the feeling was one of infinite luxury and comfort, like being cosseted in a warm feather bed.

Leaving work though was such a big step, but she was sure that Kevin would let her work from home, or she could go freelance, or maybe just cut down on her workload, let the pushy Sorcha take over. At first that would be hard, but maybe the benefits would outweigh the downside. She was sure of her decision by the time they reached the party.

On both sides of the street expensive cars jostled for space. Rory pressed the button on the ignition key and the car locks slid into place with an expensive clunk. He led the way towards the house, a tall, imposing building set back from the road, hidden behind a high wall. Tall elaborate wrought-iron gates stood open to let the stream of people into the garden. Stella looked enviously about at the billiard-table-smooth stretch of lawn, surrounded by shrubs all dusted with a glittering of frost that shimmered in the lights from the house. Wide bay windows arched out towards the gardens and inside the house Stella could see that the rooms were full of people, clutching drinks and chatting in small groups. She longed to have a home like this, somewhere gorgeous and elegant, filled with beautiful furniture and ornaments and constantly full of a stream of interesting, wealthy people. And with Rory it was all possible.

"This is Stella." Rory introduced her to their host, a tall, powerfully built man who opened the door to them. "Danny Lyons – he's building the new office blocks near your flat."

Danny took Stella's hand. "Rory, you have all the luck! What did you do to deserve such a beautiful woman?" Then, longingly, to Stella: "Darling, if you ever get fed up of him, I'll be waiting."

"Don't mind him!" A tall, willowy blonde emerged from one of the rooms and glided along the black and white tiled floor towards them. "I'm Norah, his *wife!*" she added, coming to stand beside Danny and poking him playfully in the ribs.

Stella smiled uneasily, unsure of how to react to Danny, or if she had offended his wife. More importantly, would Rory now be simmering with unspoken jealousy?

"Don't worry!" said Norah. "He says that to all the pretty women – I hope he didn't offend you." Norah took Stella's arm and led her along the corridor to a study which was doubling as a cloakroom for the party, Rory following in their wake. "Leave your coat here," she told Stella, then gasped with delight. "What a gorgeous dress! You look wonderful!"

"*Too* wonderful. I'll be spending all night keeping

the other men off her," Rory said sulkily, taking off his black wool overcoat and throwing it onto the pile with very bad grace.

Stella bit her lip. She hated it when Rory got all jealous and possessive – there was no need. It was him that she loved and wanted to be with – there was no need at all for him to feel insecure and threatened. Surely he realised that, now that they had been together for the best part of four months. Stella wished that she had worn a plainer dress – then maybe he wouldn't have to feel as if all the other men were chasing her. She hated the fact that he thought she could be interested in anyone else. She had *him*. He was all that she wanted.

Norah led the way into one of the crowded rooms. "What can I get you to drink?" she asked, peering around the room for one of the black-coated waiters who were circulating with glasses of wine and champagne.

"Champagne would be lovely," Rory told her as she waved in the direction of one of the waiters.

Norah, having found drinks for them, wandered off to circulate amongst her other guests.

Stella sipped the icy cold champagne and stole a furtive look at Rory over the rim of her glass. He was smiling, happily, looking around the room to see if there was anyone there that he recognised. Stella felt herself relax – maybe she had just been imagining that he would be jealous of Danny flirting with her. It was only a bit of fun after all. And he had shamelessly flirted with those dreadful blondes at the restaurant the other evening. What harm was there in it?

Rory wandered around the room, with Stella trailing at his elbow as he mingled with the dozens of people that he knew.

"Come and have a dance with me!" Danny emerged from the heaving throng of people who were cavorting in the centre of the room.

"Come on!" yelled a dark-haired woman, grabbing Rory.

Laughing, Stella allowed herself to be dragged into the centre of the room and began to sway in time with the music as Danny capered beside her. Stella, laughing with delight, looked around for Rory and felt a jolt of dismay.

He wasn't dancing. And he was glaring at her in absolute fury.

11

Stella's heart skipped a beat and the music faded into insignificance. She was aware of Danny, arms and legs swaying like the tentacles of an octopus against the hazy background of the other dancers, and of Rory, his face set in anger. Shooting a tight smile in Danny's direction, she walked off the dance floor to Rory. Anger seemed to almost ooze from his pores. He took a sip of his champagne, looking past Stella as if she were not there. His mouth was clamped into a tight white line when he took the glass from his mouth.

"Lovely party, isn't it?" Stella spluttered incoherently. She had to say *something*, anything to get him to talk to her, so that she could see what kind of a mood he was in.

"*You* look like you're enjoying it anyway," he snapped coldly, glaring in Danny's direction. "Why don't you go back and carry on dancing with Danny?

You were obviously enjoying it."

"I only danced with Danny because he asked me." Stella could feel tears of frustration prickling at the back of her eyes. What was she supposed to do? One dance with Danny, and Rory made her feel as if she was a total slapper, wanting to be with the first man who caught her eye. Refuse to dance and she was being miserable. It was impossible to win. "I'm not doing anything with Danny, just dancing!" She could hear her own voice rising with hysteria. Why was he being like this? She loved him. She didn't want anyone else, so why did he get so jealous the minute she even had anything to do with anyone else? Rory made her feel so dirty.

"So, if you aren't up to anything, why did you shoot off the dance floor when I looked at you? You looked guilty to me. I saw you look at Danny, giving him that look, like 'I've got to go back to Rory now'."

Stella felt a knot of tension twist in her stomach. She shifted uncomfortably, trying to ease the muscles that had cramped uneasily together.

"Rory, please stop being like this," she pleaded, as one large tear rolled down her face. She dashed it angrily away – he wasn't going to make her cry again.

"Don't you start crying!" Rory spat nastily. "You won't get around me like that." He spun around on his heel and marched away, his back taut with tension.

Stella shot after him, weaving frantically through the crowded party, barging people out of the way in her haste to follow him. She had to make him see sense, make him realise that Danny meant nothing, make him realise how much she loved him. Not anyone else. The weight of his anger weighed heavily on her shoulders – he was impenetrable when he was like this. She longed to flounce away, yell at Rory that he could get lost – but that was impossible. She had to make this relationship work. Rory was, or could be, the perfect man for her.

She followed Rory into the cloakroom.

"I'm going home – you stay with Danny," Rory said coldly, grabbing his coat from the pile on the desk and pushing past her to get out through the door.

"I'm coming with you!" Stella cried. She had to make everything all right between them again. She wasn't going to lose him this way, with him thinking that she was some terrible money-grabbing tart who would go off with anyone.

"I don't want you to come!" he shot back, flinging his coat on and marching away. Stella gave a cry of sheer frustration, pulling at the coats, desperately trying to find her own one. Finally she found it and dashed from the room. She hurtled down the corridor and out of the front door, vaguely aware of the curious stares of the people as she barged past them and of Norah's startled cry.

Rory was in the car. Stella ran as fast as she could down the path and flung open the car door.

"You're not leaving me like this!" she said furiously, flinging herself into the car.

For a moment there was silence, then from the direction of the house came the sound of bells ringing and cheering and inside the house Stella could see everyone hugging each other and kissing as the New Year was celebrated.

"Happy New Year," Stella whispered grimly.

"Wouldn't you rather be in there celebrating with your new boyfriend?" Rory hissed maliciously.

"You're my boyfriend. I want to be here, with you," Stella said firmly, reaching across and talking his cold hand. It lay in hers like a dead thing, unmoving. "Rory, please stop this," she said quietly, forcing her fingers into his. "I don't want anyone else. I want to be with you. Surely you can see that."

"I thought that too," Rory said, reaching forwards wearily and pushing the key into the ignition, "but when I saw you smiling at Danny . . ."

"Oh Rory!" Tears of pure frustration rolled down Stella's cheeks. What was she supposed to do? Rory could chat to other girls without her putting him through all of this – this *shit*. She just wanted everything to get back to normal again. Next time she would make sure that she didn't dance with anyone, talk to anyone that might make him angry – she would wear a plainer dress, cling to him. Anything to avoid making him jealous and causing a scene again. It was her fault. It had to be. She had worn a sexy dress. She had enjoyed Danny's flattery. She had never had a boyfriend who had reacted as possessively as Rory, but then she had never had anyone that she wanted as much as Rory. And she was determined that she wasn't going to lose him. Life would never be the same again, without him.

Rory snatched his hand back and shoved the gear-stick into drive.

"Please believe me, there was nothing going on with Danny. Honestly!" Stella could hear the desperation in her voice as she rummaged fruitlessly in her handbag for a tissue. "Please believe me. I am truly sorry if I made you think that I was interested in him."

Rory was silent, gazing intently at the road, as if he was scarcely aware of her presence. Stella could feel panic rising deep within the pit of her stomach. Rory had been angry and jealous before – they had rowed a few times if he thought that someone was paying her too much attention, but he had never been as angry as this, or as immovable. Usually after he had made her feel guilty and cheap he relented and things went back to normal. It was because he loved her so much, he would tell her, that he hated the thought of her going off with someone else.

But this time, he was so cold, so solid in his rejection of her.

Stella found a screwed-up tissue in her handbag and wiped her eyes, but the tears wouldn't stop falling.

"Crying won't make any difference. I told you – you won't get around me like that." Rory hurtled around a corner, narrowly avoiding two drunks who were weaving across the road. "Get out of the fucking way!" he growled through clenched teeth.

Stella was relieved when he finally pulled into the secure garaging beneath his apartment – she had been sure that he was going to crash the car, he had driven so fast and aggressively.

"You can get a taxi home," he said in a voice that was faint and full of menace.

Stella got out of the car and waited until Rory got out and slammed his door aggressively, then stalked towards the lifts that led up to the apartments. She followed close on his heels, feeling his complete and utter rejection of her.

Rory opened the door and they walked silently into the apartment. He snapped on the light and pulled off his coat, ignoring Stella completely. She took off her coat and walked slowly through the rooms. How happy they had been here, such a short time ago! Now she had ruined everything. Why had she ever danced with Danny? How could she have been such a fool?

"I was going to tell you that I would leave work." Stella sank wearily down on the sofa and looked up at Rory.

His face was closed, his eyes blank, mouth clamped into a tight line, white at the edges with tension. He hardly seemed to be aware that she was there.

"I'm going to bed," he announced suddenly, barely glancing in her direction.

"Rory, we have to sort this out," she pleaded, leaping off the sofa, darting across the room and putting her hands on his shoulders. He stood immobile, his face impassive, and unresponsive until finally she dropped her hands. It was useless. She might as well have been trying to get a response from a tree trunk.

"I'm going to bed," he repeated sullenly, turning away. "I don't care what you do." From outside the apartment door came the joyous sound of revellers returning from celebrating the New Year, their laughter penetrating into the stony silence of Rory's apartment. They should have been like that, Stella thought bleakly, laughing together, delighted at the new life that was opening up for them. By now she would have told him that she was going to leave work, they would have been making plans for the future. Instead, their life was frozen, trapped in a misery of misunderstanding and pain.

"No, we have to sort this out! I'm not letting our relationship end like this!" Stella grabbed at his arm, holding tight onto the cool cotton fabric of his shirt. "I love you, for heaven's sake!"

"Get off me!" he growled, shaking his arm violently to dislodge her grip.

Stella clung to his arm. She had to make him stay with her, make him realise how much she cared about him, make everything all right again.

His muscles moved beneath her hand as he wrenched himself out of her grip and grabbed her shoulder. She didn't see the blow coming. She felt the whisper of air close to her face as Rory's fist shot out. She heard a scream but wasn't aware of making any sound, and then there was a feeling of lightness as she seemed to fall through the air. She heard a terrible crunching noise and was aware of an ornamental table splintering into pieces around her. Then there was silence.

She was on the floor, her cheek throbbing terribly,

Rory crouching over her, his face full of concern.

"Stella," he whispered hoarsely, putting his arm around her waist and pulling her gently to her feet.

Stella was dimly aware of the room spinning lazily, dark spots dancing around the corners of her eyes and Rory, guiding her with the utmost tenderness, leading her to the sofa.

"Terrible accident, didn't mean to do that, jerked out my arm, hit you by mistake."

The words drifted lazily into her consciousness. She wanted to close her eyes, sleep. Her cheek throbbed. It was an immense effort to bring her hand to the source of pain, then when she forced her heavy-lidded eyes to look at her fingers, they were sticky and red. Blood, she realised vaguely.

Rory knelt beside her. Stella was aware that he was white and shaking. He was dabbing at her face with a pristine white towel, except that the towel wasn't white any more – huge daubs of red covered the soft pile fabric as if it had been decorated by a modern artist.

"Hospital, this needs stitching," Rory was muttering to himself. Stella forced herself to sit up, fighting desperately to avoid falling into the enticing blackness that she longed to slip into.

"What happened?" she whispered, the earlier row a vague memory that might never have happened.

Gone was the frozen, angry Rory, in his place was a loving, tender man, worrying desperately about her. "I need to get you to hospital – you've cut your face."

Stella could hear the panic in his voice. She let him

lift her from the sofa, supporting her gently with a tender arm around her waist as he reached with his free hand for her coat and arranged it around her shoulders.

"Can you walk?" he said softly, leading her slowly towards the door.

Stella nodded gingerly, wincing as the slightest movement of her head sent pain shooting through her face. She clutched the towel to her face, her whole body racked with shivers as shock began to grip her system.

The walk to the car seemed interminable. Stella was silent as gradually the full impact of what had happened sank into her mind. Rory had hit her. Rory had hit her so hard that he had sent her flying across the room. She remembered the table crunching around her as the force with which she landed on it made it disintegrate around her. Had Rory hit her so hard that he had cut her cheek? Or had she done that when she fell? She couldn't remember.

Neither could she remember, afterwards, the drive to the hospital. She remembered Rory helping her from the car and leading her into Accident and Emergency where the world swam dizzily back into focus. Everywhere beneath the bright lights of the enormous waiting room sat people. They crowded onto the benches around the edge of the room and squashed onto the plastic chairs in the centre of the waiting area. All with a bleak, patient expression of desperation. Drunks, muttering uselessly to themselves, sat amongst small children and old people.

"Sit down." Rory led Stella to a vacant seat. "I'm

going to give in your details."

Stella wondered if she was going to be sick. The violent shivering that had racked her body had stopped – now she just felt numb. She could see every pair of eyes turning with bored disinterest to see who had joined the ranks of the waiting masses.

Rory returned and crouched down beside her. "We have to see the Triage Nurse." His eyes were afraid, burning deep within his pale cheeks.

The nurse, concerned about a head injury, called Stella straight in to be checked. "Come on, that's you." Rory helped Stella to her feet. It looked a dreadfully long way across the crowded waiting room to the open door, inside which Stella could see the plump shape of a nurse watching her progress.

"She fell and cut her face – I don't think it's too bad," Rory said, guiding Stella through the open door.

"I think I'll decide that," snapped the nurse. "You can wait outside."

Rory hovered for a moment, then quailed beneath the nurse's steely glare and backed sullenly out of the room. Stella fought a wave of nausea as she sank thankfully down on a chair.

"Now, what happened?" The nurse pulled Stella's hand, still clutching the bloodstained towel away from her face. Stella saw her wince as she looked at her cheek.

"I fell over," she lied. Rory hadn't meant to hit her – he had said it was an accident. It had been her fault anyway for making him angry.

"I see," sighed the nurse.

Stella glanced at her and could see the disbelief in the plump woman's eyes. Stella slid her eyes away, staring instead at the comfortable roll of flesh above the nurse's belt buckle. Deftly the nurse undid a packet and dabbed at Stella's cheek with a damp wad. Stella winced as the antiseptic soaked into the cut flesh, making it sting.

"Hmmm," the nurse muttered, "this is going to need a few stitches. You're going to need a head X-ray and we'll have to keep you in for observation. Standard for a head injury. And no arguing," she said firmly as Stella opened her mouth to protest. "And I will tell you something else," she said, sitting down suddenly beside Stella, "however much you love this man, any man who can do this to you isn't worth staying with."

12

Amber retrieved the squashy rubber ball from beneath the coffee table for the zillionth time and rolled it gently across the fake leopard-skin rug. Teddy, making ferocious growling noises that ought to have come from a dog twice his size, hurtled across the room and pounced on the ball, seizing it between his tiny needle-sharp teeth. Amber got onto her hands and knees and stretched beneath the table to grab the ball off the puppy. Teddy was the only one of them who didn't seem to be affected by the terrible atmosphere of gloom and despondency.

Ronnie sprawled across the sofa, clutching the remote control, flicking mindlessly backwards and forwards through the channels, while their mother curled into Kenny's armchair, her legs tucked up to her chin, puffing fiercely on a cigarette. "Why won't Georgina talk to me?" she repeated sulkily, sighing miserably.

Amber shrugged. "She will, when she's ready." She wished that Kenny would come back. At least when he was in the house their mother put on some show of normality. Without him she seemed to visibly cave in, as if he was the support that kept her together. Amber gritted her teeth. Maybe if her mother had paid a little more attention to Georgina she wouldn't have gone off like this. Every bit of Ruby's focus was in Kenny's direction – she had made him her life, to the detriment of her children – they could come and go as they pleased as long as their mother had Kenny to fuss over. And now she was upset that Georgina had walked out. It was a wonder that Ruby had even noticed that Georgina was gone, she was so involved with bloody Kenny! And, of course, when Kenny was needed he was out somewhere – no doubt back with his *other* family, his proper wife who was presumably blissfully unaware of her husband's mistress who was bringing up his children at the opposite side of the city.

"Look, I need to get off – I'm supposed to be meeting Stella." Amber got to her feet, tucking Teddy under her arm. Her head throbbed with the strain of offering comfort to her mother who seemed to soak every bit of energy from her, like a needy child.

And now Stella needed her support. Thank goodness she had decided to end her relationship with that Rory jerk. She had supposedly hurt her face in a fall at his flat, but Amber had seen enough of life to recognise a fist mark when she saw it. Stella had told Amber that she'd left because he'd been always chatting up other women while she was there, and Amber had pretended to believe her. At least she had the sense to get out of the relationship. But now, of course, she needed Amber's shoulder to cry on, just as her mother did. Everyone came to her for support. And yet no one ever listened to her problems – they all seemed to think that she just drifted through life happily, without a care in the world. No one wanted to listen to her worries about the mounting pile of credit-card statements and stern letters from the bank that she had stuffed into a drawer. Out of sight, out of mind.

"Why won't Georgina even talk to me on the phone?" Ruby began again, lighting a fresh cigarette from the butt of the first one. Out of the corner of her eye Amber saw Ronnie scowl as he began a fresh bout of frenzied channel flicking. "Her phone just rings and, even when she answers it, as soon as I talk she just switches it off."

Amber rubbed her hand across her forehead – she could feel the muscles of her temples clenching with tension. What on earth did her mother think that she could do about it? She didn't know where Georgina was. Did her mother expect that she would be suddenly able to magic her out of thin air and make everything back to normal again?

"But what *happened*?" Amber asked for the twentieth time. "*Something* must have made her want to leave home."

"She just marched off upstairs and packed her bags and the next thing she had marched out the door,"

Ruby responded as usual. "I only said that she couldn't go out."

"I see." Amber made her voice level. She could imagine the scene, with Ruby shrieking and demanding that Georgina do as she was told. And hot-headed Georgina stomping off like a sulky child. They'd often had rows like this before. Ruby would phone Amber to come and calm the seemingly endless rows that they had. Amber had got used to dropping everything and heading across the city to play the role of diplomat sorting out yet another pointless row.

"You don't know where Georgina is, do you?" Her mother glanced in Ronnie's direction.

"I'm sick of you asking me that," muttered Ronnie, his eyes fixed on the flickering television screen. "I told you – how would I know where she is?"

As Amber rolled the rubber ball across the floor again for Teddy, she glanced at Ronnie. He knew more about Georgina than he was letting on, of that she was sure. As if he could read her thoughts, Ronnie suddenly threw down the remote control and lurched to his feet. "I'm going out."

Their mother, pulling at a loose strand of thread on the arm of her chair, didn't acknowledge his departure, she was so deeply enmeshed in her own emotions.

"I've asked everyone – all of her friends," she said, succeeding in pulling the thread from the arm of the sofa and winding it distractedly around her fingers. "No one knows where she is."

Or wants to say where she is, thought Amber.

"Oh, where is Kenny?" Ruby sighed miserably, looking out of the window as if she expected to see him come marching down the garden path.

Hardly likely, thought Amber, bitterly. Kenny was never there when he was needed. He just wanted to be around for the good bits of life and to sleep with her mother. The cold reality and problems of life were left for Amber to deal with.

Amber sat on the arm of the chair and hugged her mother awkwardly. "Georgina will come home when she's ready, you'll see. She'll soon miss your cooking and washing for her."

Her mother dragged deeply on her cigarette, sending out a plume of smoke from her mouth. "She does that herself anyway."

Amber felt her teeth clench. What sort of a mother did she think she was? Ruby did nothing for her children and then got in a state when they upped and left. Was there any wonder? Georgina had been living with a mother who was obsessed with her boyfriend – nothing mattered except him. Amber hoped that wherever she was she was getting more love than she'd got at home.

"Mind that bloody dog!" snapped Ruby suddenly, lurching from her chair, sending her overflowing ashtray flying. Teddy, bored with chasing the ball, had turned his attention to the sofa and was determinedly gnawing at a corner of it. Amber coughed as a shower of cigarette ash floated gently upwards.

"Kenny got me this!" Ruby crouched beside the

corner of the sofa, examining the damage that Teddy's minute teeth had done. She rubbed frenziedly at the sofa, tutting and muttering to herself.

Amber gathered Teddy into her arms, puffing out her cheeks and letting out a long, miserable sigh. Her mother was supposed to be distraught about her missing daughter, but she seemed to be just as concerned about a sofa that her boyfriend had bought!

"Look, I really must go," Amber said, getting to her feet.

"Bloody dog!" hissed Ruby, rubbing furiously at the sofa.

Amber sighed. Her mother wouldn't even notice that she had gone.

* * *

Amber sent Stella a text message, arranging to meet her near the park. She was a few minutes early and sat on a bench to wait for Stella arriving. Teddy saw her first. Straining at his lead, he jumped up and down in excitement, letting out high-pitched yelps. Amber picked him up, worried that he would strangle himself in his efforts to get to Stella. Hanging determinedly onto the small wriggling bundle, she watched Stella walk down the street towards her. Amber grinned as a car driver, spotting the blonde beauty walking along the pavement, almost drove off the road as he craned his neck to look at her. It wasn't until Stella got closer that Amber could see how much she had changed. A dark bruise that spread across her high cheekbone and a fine rosy-pink line where the stitches had pulled her skin back together still marred her creamy complexion, but it was the lost, hunted expression in her eyes that most worried Amber. Stella looked as if part of her had died.

"Hey, how are you feeling?" Amber stood up and let Teddy go. He bounded towards Stella, pink tongue hanging out as he almost throttled himself straining against the lead in his efforts to get to the other woman he loved.

"Fine." Stella crouched down and stroked the dog, her face hidden from view, but Amber could hear the strain in her voice. "Come on, let's go and get a coffee in that nice café, where we can sit outside." She headed off, without waiting for Amber's reply.

Amber and Teddy followed.

"How are things at your mum's?" Stella asked, glancing quickly at Amber.

"Well, Georgina's still not come back and . . ." Amber's words faded away. Stella wasn't listening, she seemed miles away. Amber felt a surge of concern for her friend. She was obviously terribly unhappy.

They quickly reached the café. Amber went inside to order coffees while Stella went out onto the covered decking to find a table for them, where they could watch the walkers wandering around the park. There was an uncomfortable moment when Amber was worried that she couldn't rake up enough small change to pay for the drinks, but thanking her lucky stars she dredged up enough, handed over the money to a bored-looking waitress and headed outside.

Stella had found a seat at the edge of the decked area and tied Teddy's lead to one of the table legs. The puppy now lay, exhausted by his busy morning, with his head resting on Stella's foot.

"Does your face still hurt?" Amber enquired, gently.

In the pale light beneath the wooden roof of the café Stella's face looked worse, the colours of the bruise more livid somehow.

Stella touched her long fingers to her face in a distracted gesture, feeling the imperfection. She shook her head. "Just a little bit." There was a silence, which lengthened. Stella gazed unseeingly at the cityscape beyond the park, the sheen of orange rooftops beyond the brown, bare branches of the trees, lost in thought.

"Did you hear from Rory again?" Amber asked gently, shattering the pensive silence.

"What?" Stella struggled to focus on Amber's words.

"I said, did you hear from Rory again?"

Stella grabbed her coffee mug and took a long gulp, wincing as the hot liquid stung her tongue. "Yes," she mumbled, the words so faint that Amber wasn't sure if she had actually spoken. "He begged me to forgive him – he wants me to take him back." Amber watched in horror as one single enormous tear welled out of Stella's left eye and slowly trickled down her cheek, the light catching the dark stain of her bruise.

"I thought that he would just accept that I didn't

want to see him again," Stella continued, finally turning and looking straight at Amber. Another tear followed the track of the first one.

Amber felt as if she could almost reach out and take hold of the pain that Stella was feeling, that if she listened hard enough she would be able to hear the sound of her heart breaking.

"He keeps ringing me, begging me to forgive him," Stella repeated, putting down her coffee mug and burying her face in her hands.

"You won't though, will you?" Amber said quietly.

Stella hadn't told her what had happened that night, but she was fairly sure that the bruise and the cut face hadn't come from a drunken fall. That was definitely not Stella's style. Stella had been too involved with him, so hung up on her triumph at having got what she thought she wanted that she hadn't been able to see beyond the glitter of his exterior to the nastiness that lurked beyond. Amber had never trusted him: he was too smooth, too slick.

"Not now . . . but he promised me that he wouldn't do that again . . ." said Stella. Amber's face screwed up in an involuntary wince. Surely Stella wasn't suggesting that . . . ? She reached across the table and put her hand gently over Stella's icy cold one.

"That kind of man never changes," Amber said gently.

"It was my fault. He wouldn't have done it if I hadn't gone off dancing with this guy at a party."

"Oh, Stella, how can you believe that?" Amber said,

slow anger simmering close to the surface. How could Stella believe that she had *made* Rory hit her? The improbability of it made her want to shake her friend. Damn Rory! Damn any kind of violent man! How did they always manage to twist things and make it look as if the violence wasn't their fault. It was always someone else who made them lash out.

"I want to believe it," Stella said slowly. "I want to believe that he wouldn't do it again. It was just a big mistake." She lifted her coffee mug with hands that trembled visibly, the pale brown liquid slopped dangerously, threatening to spill over onto the table. "Finishing with Rory is probably the biggest mistake that I have ever made in my life."

Amber shook her head, looking at Stella in silent disbelief. How could she possibly believe that? Finishing with Rory was the best thing that she had ever done. No one in their right mind should want to stay with someone whose answer to a problem was to use their fists, whether they were a millionaire or a penniless beggar.

"But he was everything I ever wanted." Stella abandoned trying to drink her coffee and put the mug down. "Everything. We made such a great couple. We could have had a great life together. We liked the same kind of things . . ." Her words trailed off miserably.

Big houses, flashy cars, thought Amber. She wanted to shake Stella. She was seriously contemplating going back to Rory because of the lifestyle they would have together. Regardless of the fact that he could have killed her. "Stella," she said sternly. "You – must – be – mad if you think that he wouldn't hit you again. He would. It would only be a matter of time."

Stella glared at Amber. That was the last thing that she wanted to hear.

Silence descended again, Stella staring fixedly at her coffee mug, Amber watching her miserably.

Amber couldn't understand how Stella wanted to believe that Rory would never hit her again. That they could just sail off into the sunset into some happy, golden world of wealth and privilege that she had imagined for herself. And then in time he would hit her again. And again. Until she was broken in body and spirit with no fight left in her to leave him. Amber wanted to shake her by the shoulders, scream in her ear, anything to make her see sense.

The silence lengthened uncomfortably. Teddy woke up and began to scratch himself, his small furry leg thumping on the wooden deck, squeaking with pleasure as his tiny claws reached the itchy spot behind his ears. Amber bent down to rub the soft hair on the top of his head. The sound of laughter floated towards her on the damp afternoon air. Amber looked up to see what had caused such merriment. Her heart gave a painful leap in her chest. Walking past the café was a couple, arm in arm, laughing in amusement at some hidden joke between them. As Amber watched, the woman raised her head to the man and Kenny bent his head to touch her lips with his.

13

Amber had found her sister. She was buried under a mass of credit-card statements and bank letters, and the man at the counter at her bank, who had told her very sternly that they wanted her cheque book back, was sitting on the pile of papers telling Amber that she could have Georgina back once her debts were paid. Then the phone beside him began to ring and Georgina started to plead. "Borrow some money to get me out of here!"

Amber woke with a start, grabbing blindly at her mobile phone which was somewhere on the table beside her bed, sending books and an empty china mug clattering to the floor.

"'Lo?" Her tongue felt as if it were stuck to the roof of her mouth.

"Amber?"

For a long moment Amber couldn't think who the

masculine voice belonged to.

"Uhuhhh." A full bottle of white wine in the fridge and an empty apartment, due to Stella going out with Rory to discuss their relationship, had proved too much temptation. Now Amber was paying the price.

"It's Ronnie," growled the voice impatiently.

"Yeees," she countered, equally impatiently, implying that of course she knew who she was talking to. She struggled upright – her whole body feeling welded to the mattress, every movement was an immense effort. Her head throbbed dreadfully and her tongue felt as if it was two sizes too big for her mouth.

"Let me in. I need to talk to you." Ronnie severed the connection.

"What?" Amber said into the receiver, wincing as it bleeped back at her.

She levered herself out of bed. At least now she was upright she didn't feel quite so ill. She vaguely remembered at some stage during the evening that the puppy had knocked over the bottle of wine. There was a hazy recollection of mopping up liquid with a wad of tissue and Stella being there wondering if the puppy had messed on the floor yet again. Silently Amber thanked Teddy – his clumsiness had probably saved her from the hangover from hell. At least now she would probably merely have the headache without the rest of the life-threatening symptoms. Amber grabbed her dressing-gown, put one arm into the sleeve and then changed her mind – somehow being in a state of undress in front of a nineteen-year-old youth didn't seem right, even if he was your brother. Discarding the dressing-gown, Amber picked up the heap of clothes that she had taken off the night before – there was a damp patch on the knee of the jeans, which she hoped was spilled wine, not puppy wee.

The doorbell began to ring, the shrill noise incessant in the silent apartment. Teddy began to yap.

"Shit, shit," growled Amber, hopping on one foot to shove her other leg inside the damp fabric of her jeans. Then buttoning the jeans as she went, she shot to the door and pressed the buzzer to open the downstairs entrance.

"You took a bloody long time!" Ronnie stomped into the apartment as Amber opened the door.

"Good morning to you too." Amber closed the door behind him.

"I'm bloody starving!" Ronnie stomped in the direction of the kitchen. "I need a fry." Amber ran a hand over her eyes. Was this all part of her dream? What on earth was Ronnie doing in her apartment early on a Sunday morning? She watched as Ronnie flung open the fridge and began to rummage inside, pulling out Stella's lettuce and tomatoes and dumping them unceremoniously on the kitchen worktop.

"Must be some rashers somewhere," Ronnie muttered to himself, tossing a carton of low fat milk onto the counter.

Amber crossed the room and sat down on the sofa. She was bound to wake up in a moment and find that this was all a dream. Teddy lay sprawled on the sofa – he lay tucked against one of Stella's silk cushions, on his back, small legs in the air. He opened one dark button eye and looked guiltily at Amber and then at the small basket in the corner of the room where he should be sleeping. Amber rubbed his plump soft beige belly making one hind leg bicycle with pleasure at her touch.

"Erm, Ronnie, did you want something?" Amber asked, still unable to believe that her gross younger brother had actually come to her flat unannounced on a Sunday morning and was now helping himself to the contents of her fridge.

"I know where Georgina is." Ronnie's mop of dark hair emerged from the fridge.

"Where is she?" Amber was suddenly as alert as a gundog – she could hear her voice rise a pitch.

"I bloody need to eat first." Ronnie began to rummage in the cupboards for a frying pan.

Stella's bedroom door swung open and she came out, looking in disbelief at Ronnie, who, having found a frying pan was tearing open the packet of rashers that he had found. Stella glanced at Amber, who shrugged, and then back to Ronnie, her eyes wide as if she couldn't believe what she was seeing. Amber wondered briefly if she was more surprised at seeing Ronnie in her kitchen or the fact that he had found proper food in their fridge. Heaven knows how old the rashers were!

"You all right, darlin'?" Ronnie lifted his eyes from the bacon rashers as they sizzled in the cooking oil that he had liberally sloshed into the frying pan and grinned at Stella, who wrapped her silky dressing-gown tighter around her and glared at him with distaste. Amber cringed.

"Yes, thank you," Stella said tightly, walking daintily across the room towards Amber. Her eyes blazed into Amber's, silently questioning 'Why the fuck is he here?' Amber shrugged helplessly. Teddy, sensing Stella's approach, gave a deft wriggle and slunk onto the floor, crouching immediately to relieve himself.

"Teddy!" Stella shrieked in frustration as her carpet was drenched in dog wee yet again. *"Outside!"* She hauled the pup by the scruff of his neck and hurried across the room. Ronnie looked up from his cooking, gazing with undisguised interest at Stella as her robe flapped open in her haste to get Teddy outside.

When Stella returned she glared even more angrily at Ronnie, pulling her robe tighter around her body. "I'm going to get dressed," she snapped.

Ronnie grinned at her, oblivious of her dislike of him. Amber cringed inwardly. Were all young men like Ronnie, full of testosterone and bad manners? She wished that he would hurry and finish cooking his breakfast and tell her what he wanted and then she could get rid of him and try to pacify Stella.

Eventually Ronnie upended the contents of the frying pan onto a plate and carried it to the sofa, where he sat down with a sigh of ultimate pleasure and proceeded to shovel the food into his mouth. Amber averted her eyes. The sight of his washing-machine mouth churning the food around made her feel nauseous. Teddy began to scratch at the door to come back in. Amber grinned despite herself at the thought of the effort that it had taken for the pup to climb the stairs from the outside door all the way up to their apartment. She opened the door and stood back as, whimpering with delight at being allowed back in, Teddy bounded into the room, casting sly looks around to see if Stella was still around to chastise him.

"Ronnie, tell me what this is all about?" Amber sat back down, holding Teddy's collar to stop him jumping back onto the sofa for an onslaught on Ronnie's breakfast.

"Hang on – let me eat, will you?" Ronnie said, loading his fork yet again.

Stella stalked back into the room, dressed in a pair of jeans and a long baggy jumper. She was taking no chances of having Ronnie leer at her figure. Immediately she began to bustle around the kitchen, pointedly throwing the frying pan into the sink and spraying the surfaces with disinfectant, her lips clamped firmly into a tight line of distaste.

Ronnie finally finished eating and, giving a loud burp of satisfaction, hauled himself off the sofa and sauntered across to the kitchen. He shoved the plate into the sink. "Can't beat a fry," he grinned at Stella, his eyes roving all over her body.

Stella looked as if she hoped the bacon would give him food poisoning.

"Come on then," he said to Amber. "I've found out where Georgina is. I'll take you to see her."

Suddenly Amber could have forgiven him anything. Now at least she would be able to hear Georgina's side of the story, find out what had really gone wrong with her and their mother.

They hurried downstairs and out into the pale morning sunlight. Abandoned, half on and half off the pavement outside the apartment block, was a small, battered-looking car. The side window on the passenger side was missing, the result of the car having been stolen – either by Ronnie, or one of his revolting cronies.

"That car's stolen!" exclaimed Amber, shaking her head in disbelief. Ronnie never learnt. He seemed to lurch through life from one fuck-up to another. He was bound to get caught for having stolen the car, or for driving it. He had no licence, she was sure of that and, of course, no insurance, that went without saying. Ronnie shot around to the driver's side of the car.

"Ten out of ten!" he growled nastily.

Amber hovered on the pavement. She couldn't go in the car. If they were caught that would make her Ronnie's accomplice. Things were bad enough for her without adding joy-riding in a stolen car to her list of problems.

"Get in the fucking car," snarled Ronnie, throwing open the passenger-side door. "Do you want to go and see Georgina or not?"

"Oh, shit!" groaned Amber, through gritted teeth, caving in and getting into the car. "If we get caught I'll say you bloody kidnapped me!" she hissed, slamming the door so hard that the remnants of broken glass trapped in the metal frame showered to the floor.

Ronnie gunned the car into life, revving the engine aggressively, the high-pitched whine of the engine making the car shudder with the strain. Amber fumbled for the seat belt as Ronnie let out the clutch and the car lurched forwards, its tyres squealing as they sought purchase on the tarmac road. And then they were off, powering down narrow back streets and darting across main roads to hurtle down narrow alleyways. Amber stared fixedly out of the broken passenger window, the passing streets a mere blur of colour as they sped by. The wind from the open window blew Amber's hair around her face, making it impossible to breathe. She couldn't decide if she felt more annoyed, exhilarated or just plain terrified. She stole a glance at Ronnie, dragging back her hair out of her eyes. He was crouched over the steering wheel, looking like something out of a gangster movie, oblivious to the fact that what he was doing was dangerous, stupid and illegal.

After what seemed like several nerve-wracking hours Ronnie slowed the car, the engine note changing to a relieved-sounding hum as they cruised through deserted pristine residential streets. Now that the wind had stopped whipping her hair around her face, Amber was finally able to look at her surroundings. They were driving up a cul-de-sac of neat identical detached houses, each with a small square of close-cropped grass bordered by regimental lines of flowers. With a final flourish in his exhibition of driving skills, Ronnie suddenly shoved his foot down hard on the accelerator and powered the car into the driveway of one of the houses, stopping inches from the pristine paint of a garage door.

"Come on," he said impatiently, swinging open his door before the final notes of the engine had died away.

Amber unclipped her seat belt and stared at the house with a frown. This prim orderly house looked an unlikely spot to find Georgina. Maybe Ronnie had brought her here first on an errand and then they were going on to the dingy bed-sit that Amber presumed Georgina was living in.

Ronnie led the way up a pristine gravel path beside the house and hammered on the glass pane of the front door.

"Ronnie!" Amber yelped, sure that in a second the glass would shatter with the force of his onslaught.

With a dramatic sigh of impatience, Ronnie stepped back from the door and stood on the path, scuffling his dirty trainers against the doorstep. A moment later the front door swung open and there, framed in the light, was Georgina. At least it looked like Georgina, except that this version was neater, cleaner, like someone had taken Georgina and dipped her in glitter.

"Oh," said the Barbie Doll version, her mouth forming a perfect circle, matching her eyes which widened in disbelief to see the pair of them outside. "You'd better come in," she sighed quietly, her unwillingness to let them in obvious in her expression.

She closed the door with deliberate firmness as they shuffled, feeling suddenly embarrassed and uncomfortable in the neat surroundings, into the hall and then led the way down a hallway that smelt of furniture polish and cleanliness.

Georgina led the way into a bright, airy lounge. "You may as well sit down," she growled.

Amber suppressed a grin – whoever owned the house and was letting Georgina stay here certainly hadn't managed to alter her manners. She must be working for a family as a nanny – although there was no sign of any children – perhaps the owners of the house had gone out with their offspring for the day, leaving Georgina on her own. Amber perched herself on the edge of a smart leather sofa. The whole place looked like something out of a furniture showroom. She was half-afraid to move in case she pushed a cushion out of place or jolted an ornament out of line.

Georgina stood by an ornate fireplace, her arms folded aggressively. "What do you want?" she snapped, glaring from Amber to Ronnie, her eyes narrowed with dislike. Ronnie stared at the frayed ends of his baggy jeans.

"We've all been worried about you," Amber shrugged in a helpless gesture.

"Yeah, right!" spat Georgina. "That's a first."

"Mum is *very* worried, she –" Amber began.

Georgina gave a snort of impatience. "Really. Well, that *is* a first. She hardly noticed when I was there – she was too busy running around after fucking Kenny!"

Amber sighed. It was going to be a hard job to get Georgina to go home – everything that she said was right – their mother *was* always too busy with Kenny. But that didn't necessarily mean that she didn't love her children. Ruby just had a funny way of showing it.

Georgina was obviously being well looked after here. Presumably the family she was staying with were kind to her. Maybe eventually she would get fed up with being a nanny or whatever she was doing and want to come home. Maybe then they would be able to patch things up between Georgina and their mother.

"But what are you doing here?" Amber made a sweeping gesture with her hand, taking in the immaculate surroundings.

Then a movement from the doorway caught her eye and she saw a vaguely familiar man walk into the room. Her mind whirred as she tried to place the tall, gangly man, who was standing uncertainly, looking warily at the scene. Then with a flash of clarity she knew who he was. Martin Cavanagh. He had been a newly trained teacher when Amber had been at school – presumably he had then gone on to teach Georgina. She must be working for him, minding his children.

"What am I doing here? I'm living with my boyfriend," said Georgina.

Martin Cavanagh, married, with a child old enough to be Georgina's boyfriend? Amber's befuddled mind made hasty calculations, but just as she reached the inconclusive conclusion that Martin Cavanagh couldn't possibly be old enough to have children her sister's age, Georgina crossed the room, slipped her arms around Martin's neck and kissed him softly on the cheek before turning to look at Amber, a look of triumph burning in her blue eyes.

"Yes. My boyfriend."

14

Stella eased her painful fingers as the handles of her heavy shopping bags bit into the flesh. She dumped the bags onto the lift floor as the doors swished shut. Thank goodness she would soon be home. Well. Home at Rory's. She had spent the afternoon food-shopping, battling against the tide of loved-up couples out celebrating Valentine's weekend. Valentine's *Day* was in the middle of the week, but the world seemed to have overdosed on romance. Everywhere, in town, there were flower-sellers displaying wilted, vastly overpriced cellophane-wrapped bunches of roses. You couldn't possibly be in love, it seemed, unless you had been brought out for an overpriced meal, been given an overpriced bunch of roses and received an overpriced piece of jewellery, preferably a diamond.

Stella was all for romance, but just for now they were taking things slowly. Things were not back on an even keel with Rory – yet. She had pushed the dreadful events of New Year to the back of her mind and told him that they would try again. Today she was going to cook supper to celebrate the resurrection of their relationship. Amber had been furious when Stella had announced quietly that she was going to try again with Rory, but she had been too preoccupied with her sister's relationship with a creepy nerd who used to teach her, to pay too much attention to Stella's life. Stella had felt a bit like a government spin-doctor, slipping some bad news into the newspaper just when there was some dreadful catastrophe, in the hope that it wouldn't get noticed.

Of course, she had to give Rory another chance. What was another another chance between lovers, especially one as almost perfect as *him*? All that Stella had to do was to make sure that she didn't attract the attentions of any other men. Easy. And then everything would be fine. No more rows. No more flying-fist accidents.

This supper would be the perfect start to seal the proper start to their relationship. They had gone out for a few drinks, had dinner together, but this was the first time that they would spend the night together since their relationship had resumed. The leaving work question had never been mentioned again – presumably they would discuss that when their relationship was on a more level footing again.

Stella's indestructible shopping bags had been tested to their limit with all of the provisions that she had packed inside. Two wonderful pieces of fillet steak. Delicious crusty bread, so fresh that the aroma of the cooling French stick filled the lift, making Stella's mouth water. Wine, a delicious red, the best that she could afford. And there was delicious ice cream for dessert, eaten at the table, or maybe in bed . . .

The lift bounced to a halt at Rory's floor, Stella hauled up her bags and, drooping with tiredness, began the walk down the corridor to Rory's apartment. A nice reviving cup of tea was much needed before she would have the energy to make a start preparing the salad and organising the sauce for the steak.

"Did you miss me?" she called, unlocking the door with the key that Rory had given her, and shoving it open with her knee. Rory was standing with his back to her, gazing out of the enormous picture window at the city rooftops. She saw his shoulders shrug. "Sorry I was longer than I thought I would be – I met someone from work."

Rory turned slowly towards her. Stella smiled at him, unable to read his expression, blinking in the bright sunlight from the huge window.

"Really?" He took a stride towards her, moving out of the brightness into the softer light in the middle of the room.

"Yes. Lynda, this girl that I used to work for when I first started at the magazine." Stella felt the air in the room change, prickling with tension. Rory was moving towards her, as if in slow motion, like a slowed-down movie clip. She was aware of her own body, as if she were watching herself taking the salad out of her shopping bag, heaving a bag of potatoes onto the counter, while she was aware of her own voice, loud in her ears. The rhythm of her breathing had changed, becoming jagged, each gasp for oxygen tearing at her throat. Her heart thudded painfully against her ribs, every fibre of her body tightened in panic, sensing the intense barely controlled anger within Rory.

"I was just getting some tomatoes and she tapped me on the shoulder. Amazing that she recognised me. I haven't seen her for ages. She hasn't changed a bit – she could win a gold medal for talking. We went for a coff–"

"Don't lie to me!" Rory's voice thundered. He lunged forwards, grabbing for her arms. Stella scrambled backwards, every movement seeming to take forever, as if her whole being was weighted down, struggling through thick treacle that dragged on her limbs. The bag of potatoes spilt open, cascading to the floor. They seemed to be in their own timeframe, moving at normal speed, hitting the floor, bouncing and rolling, while she and Rory slowly came together. His hands grabbed her arms, his fingers vicelike on her flesh, her feet still scrambling to take her out of his reach. One potato rolled beneath her foot, and overbalancing she toppled to the floor. Rory, still with his inhuman grip on her arms, toppled on top of her.

As she hit the cold, smooth terracotta floor tiles, the slowed-down movie of her life stopped. Rory released his hold on her arms, struggling to his feet, yelling abuse. Scrabbling to get a grip on the floor she half fell, half crawled out of his reach.

"You bloody liar!" he screamed, his face purple with rage, eyes bulging. "Who have you been with?" He plunged forwards again.

Stella knew in that instant, with a dreadful clearness of reason, that he was going to kill her. And in that knowledge, she reached a quiet still place within herself. Death held out its hand to her and, finding a strength deep in her soul, she stood her ground, lurched back at him, screaming with as much force as he had.

"Rory! Stop it! Stop it! Stop it!" She saw him falter, hesitate for a split second and in that moment, she grabbed at her car keys, flung so carelessly on the kitchen counter only moments before. And ran.

Stella thought that she would never get the door lock open – the knob slid between fingers that were slippery with sweat and fumbling with panic. Finally the catch slid back and she wrenched the door open.

"Stella! Don't go!" Rory said so quietly that she half turned in surprise.

Rory was leaning on the kitchen counter, as if his legs wouldn't support him. "Please, I'm sorry. I didn't mean to frighten you. I thought that you were off with someone else." He wiped the sheen of sweat off his forehead with a shaking hand. "I couldn't bear the thought of you being with someone else."

Stella felt her hand freeze on the wooden door, watching him in disbelief. Only a few seconds ago she had been sure that he was about to kill her or do her serious harm. Now he was as placid as a small child that has exhausted himself in a tantrum.

As if by its own volition she felt her hand begin to close the door.

And that familiar voice inside began to sound in her head: Rory hadn't meant to hurt her – he had just been upset because he thought that she was off with someone else. If she hadn't been late he would never have got upset. It was her fault. Yet again.

She looked at the chaos of the kitchen, the spilled potatoes, one still rocking gently to and fro in the middle of the terracotta tiles, surrounded by the debris of lettuce and tomatoes. The dinner that should have been. The meal that would have announced the new beginning of their relationship, after Rory had gone mad before and put her in hospital with her injuries. This time she had been lucky. Whatever wrong Rory thought that she had done, he didn't have the right to take his temper out on her. She valued her life too much. She might want, might really need a wealthy man to be her husband, but not at this price.

Stella shook her head, numbly. "No, Rory," she whispered. Her fingers closed around the door once again and the strength flowed back into them. Wrenching the door open wide, she shot out of the apartment and bolted down the corridor as fast as she could run.

"No!" she heard Rory yell behind her, but then she plunged through the open doors of the lift, pushing the button, her heart pounding painfully in her chest. The doors seemed to take an age to close. Stella felt as if she were living a scene from a horror movie – at any second the villain would pound down the corridor and wrench open the door and then she would be found dead when the lift opened in the carpark two floors below. But the doors swished closed and she was alone. When they swished open a moment later she expected Rory to be standing there, or at least hiding behind the doors waiting to grab her, but as she bolted from the lift no hands reached out to seize her.

Stella ran across the carpark, back to her car, her footsteps echoing loudly around the concrete pillars. Then as she reached her car, she knew that he was there – she could hear his footsteps pounding across the concrete as he ran towards her. She shoved her key into the lock, sobbing in panic, vaguely aware of the concerned, curious glances of some shoppers returning to their apartment. Stella flung herself into the car and pressed the door locks just as Rory reached the car.

"Open the door!" he yelled, hauling on the door handle with all his might. His face was purple, unrecognisable in his anger and panic, his eyes mere dark circles above burning cheeks.

"It's over, Rory!" Stella yelled, not giving a damn who heard her, or what they thought of her. She had to get away, out of this carpark, away from Rory. Far, far away from Rory. She was calm as she pushed her key into the ignition and turned the engine on. It might have been just any ordinary Saturday spent shopping. Her mind, traumatised and terrified, seemed to shut

down, cutting out the dreadful sight of Rory, spittle flying from his mouth, yelling in temper, trying to bash his way into the car. He cannoned off the front wing as she drove forwards, barely aware that he was there, her eyes seeking the exit sign. Then a few moments later, the car surged into the pale afternoon sunlight.

She drove on, trembling, gasping, and some time later juddered to a halt beside the kerb as she burst into tears. She was shaking all over, her knees jerking frenziedly against the curve of the steering wheel. Too upset to notice the curious looks of the passers-by and the angry hoots of car horns from drivers annoyed that she was blocking the road, she sobbed helplessly. Relief to get away from Rory mingled with the dreadful knowledge of what could have happened and entwined with the regret of losing the relationship. It had to end now – she could never trust him again. Stella hunted for a tissue and found one tucked in the side pocket of her door. She wiped her eyes, then stole a glance at herself in the rear-view mirror, her eyes puffy already from crying, her face white with terror. Nothing could be worth putting yourself through this. She had longed for so much from this relationship and it had all disintegrated. Rory had been nothing but a violent bully. She would never marry him, never even see him again. A fresh flood of tears spilled down her cheeks. She must go home. She couldn't sit here, at the side of the road – it was pointless. She had to go on to rebuild her life. Sighing bitterly, she started the car and pulled out into the line of traffic, heading to her apartment.

*   *   *

Stella pounded up the stairs to the sanctuary of her apartment. She shoved the key in the door and burst in. Amber looked up, startled, hastily sweeping a pile of papers together, a guilty look in her eyes.

"You OK?" asked Stella, momentarily forgetting her own plight, Amber looked so miserable.

"Sure," breezed Amber. "Just paying my credit-card bills." She hastily picked up the pile of papers and hurried to her room.

Teddy, hearing Stella's voice, leapt from the sofa where he had been taking an afternoon nap and hurtled across the room, a small ball of brown energy, tail waving furiously, his small teeth nipping at her ankles in a bid for attention. Stella bent down and picked up the dog, burying her face in his soft hair, breathing in the warm doggy smell of him. He squirmed in her arms, small pink tongue working, desperately trying to cover her face in wet licks. He was so delighted to see her – if only Rory could have loved her as much. The memory of her failed relationship clutched at her heart and she sank miserably to the sofa, releasing Teddy and covering her face in her hands.

"Stella . . ." Amber's voice seemed to come from very far away, then Stella was aware of her friend sitting beside her. A warm arm slid gently around he shoulders. "What's happened?" Amber asked gently. "What is it?"

"Rory . . ." Stella whispered his name miserably, feeling the whole weight of the loss of him dragging her down into a deep dark place.

"Oh fuck! I *told* you . . ." Her voice trailed away as she decided not to continue to admonish Stella. She sighed bitterly.

Stella felt the sofa move as Amber got up.

"Put your head down," Amber said gently, shoving a soft cushion onto the arm of the sofa. Stella let her head slide down into the soft fabric and closed her eyes as Amber wrapped a warm duvet around her shaking body. "Stay there for a while. I'll get you some tea and toast and in a while it will all feel OK."

Stella smiled faintly. She wasn't so sure that she would feel OK in a while, but it was nice to be mothered, to let Amber nurse all the feelings of despair away. Teddy clambered onto the sofa and snuggled into the duvet, delighted that someone was going to join him in a snooze on the sofa, his favourite pastime.

*   *   *

In her handbag, dumped onto the floor beside the sofa, Stella's mobile began to ring. Lulled into a dreamy half sleep, by the warmth of the duvet and half a sleeping pill that Amber had slipped into her tea, Stella fumbled for the phone and switched it on. "Lo," she said her voice thick with exhaustion.

"Hi, it's Rory. Are we still on for tonight?"

Stella was instantly awake, listening in disbelief.

How on earth after all that had happened could he possibly think that they could continue with their relationship? The nerve and downright stupidity of him!

"No, Rory," she snapped coldly into the receiver. "It is not on tonight, or any other night. I never, *ever* want to see you again."

"Don't be stupid, Stella," Rory's voice was icy cold, menacing. "You can't leave me. I won't let you."

15

Stella rubbed her sore eyes with her fingertips. She longed to be home, out of this endless line of rush-hour traffic. She blinked again, trying to relax her eyes that ached with the effort of staring through the rain-battered car windscreen at the endless line of tail-lights ahead of her. How was it that, when you really wanted to be home, the traffic was always worse? The cars ahead of her seemed to have been stationary for hours. She began to fantasise about reaching home, slamming the car door and running inside as fast as she could. She wanted to run a deep hot bath and then relax in the water and just let the tension of the dreadful day melt away, while she read the new diet book that she had bought on her lunch break. She had been on a diet for as long as she could remember and had read every book ever written on the subject. This new one was supposed to burn fat quicker than any other way.

As days went this really had to have been one of the worst. Every bone in her body seemed to ache from where she had fallen on the floor a few dreadful evenings ago. Her temples throbbed with tension. The deep purple bruises that marked her arms were stiff and sore. As she had dressed that morning she had seen the bruises in the mirror, each one the imprint of Rory's furious fingerprints as he had exploded into that uncontrollable temper. Misery hung over her, like a black raincloud sitting over the Mayo mountains. Life without Rory seemed dull and featureless, the hope of a wonderful future snuffed out finally.

Now indecision tormented Stella. Maybe it had been her fault *again* – maybe she wasn't treating Rory with the consideration he deserved. Maybe she had driven him to attack her. Finishing with him had seemed so right when she'd discussed it with Amber. She couldn't believe that she had actually thrown down the phone after Rory had rung to see if she was going out. Did she really want the relationship to end? Really and truly? Amber had been delighted – she had no doubts whatsoever that Stella had done the right thing. She had grabbed Teddy and sat with him on her knee waving his front legs like arms in a caricature of a delighted football fan celebrating a big win for his side.

"Thank goodness you've seen sense!" she exclaimed. "He'll always do that again."

Stella had listened to her numbly, wondering vaguely where Amber had got her information from. What the hell did Amber know about violent relationships?

"You would have been always waiting for him to hit you again. You would have become terrified of putting a foot wrong. And in the end you would change so much to keep him happy that you wouldn't even be yourself."

Stella had nodded blankly, hardly able to take her words in. She had just wanted to be with Rory, curled up on his leather sofa listening to music, a glass of wine in her hand, living with the hope that she had finally found the security that she craved. And yet, beneath all of her sorrow and regret, some part of her knew that she had done the right thing. Sometime soon that part would grow, would envelop the part of her that longed for the relationship to work, and then she would be able to go forwards, look for another relationship. But not just yet.

For now she had to endure the feelings of misery and uncertainty, struggle through each day at work until she could return to the sanctuary of her bed. And the blissful release of sleep. Sorcha and Kevin seemed to take great delight in her confusion and misery. Stella felt as if she could do nothing right at work – even the most simple of tasks seemed virtually impossible. She had even submitted a reworked press release for a mascara product with the photographs for a new perfume. Sorcha had spotted her mistake straight away and had made sure that she pointed it out to Stella just when Kevin was walking past. Her boss didn't even alter his stride and for a long while Stella dared to hope that he hadn't heard Sorcha's crowing words. But just when she had almost forgotten the incident Kevin had slid into her office and gently closed the door. Outwardly he hadn't appeared to be angry, but the cold disappointment in his voice, as he told her that the standard of her work was appalling and that it was time that she pulled herself together or else, was worse than any yelling of abuse. In fact, the fear of losing her job was worse than any verbal dressing-down from Kevin, Stella couldn't bear the thought of being insecure once more, not knowing where the next penny was coming from. She had done enough of that when she was younger.

The rain battered against the windscreen in a fresh frenzy, huge hailstones mingled with the raindrops, pounding on the glass and the car bodywork, sounding as if the metal and glass would cave in under the onslaught. Out of the rainstreaked windscreen the car tail-lights inched slowly forwards, the line of red lights stretching as far as the eye could see into the distance of the dual carriageway. Surely this rain couldn't last much longer? Maybe the morning would bring brighter weather – everything would feel better then. She would feel more positive, she would put all of the bad things of the last few weeks behind her and move on with her life. Concentrate on her work. She had to forget Rory. Show Kevin just how good she was at her job. Put Sorcha, with her simpering little side-snipes into her place, show her once and for all who was boss. Tomorrow. It would all seem better tomorrow.

But first she needed to get home and soak in a hot bath.

The car gave a lurch – momentarily the radio and windscreen wipers stopped and then started again, so quickly that Stella thought that she had imagined it. The line of traffic ground to a halt again. Stella braked and then the car was suddenly silent, the windscreen wipers stopped midway up the glass, the rain pouring unchecked down the sloping screen, quickly obliterating the view of endless red tail-lights. Stella turned the ignition key. The engine spluttered and then was silent.

"No, no, no, not now!" pleaded Stella, turning the key again, pumping her foot on the accelerator, hoping for some sign of life from the car. The little car had never let her down before – it was like a friend, faithful and honest. How could it fail now, on what had to be the filthiest night ever, and just when she really needed to go home?

Without the heater blasting out hot air, the car was suddenly freezing cold. Stella turned the key again – she had to get the car started.

"Come on, you bloody thing!" she raged, thumping her fist on the centre of the steering wheel in sheer frustration.

The line of cars ahead began to move, the tail-lights of the car in front moving away, their red glow flickering through Stella's rain-covered windscreen as if they were mocking her plight. The car behind flashed his headlights, the brightness reflecting in her rear-view mirror and making her wince. Then from behind her came the noise of car horns, from frustrated drivers annoyed at being delayed further. Stella jumped as a man thumped on her driver's window. Gingerly she wound it down, blinking as the rain poured in.

"Move out of the fucking way!" a middle-aged man snapped, rain dripping off the end of the newspaper that he had spread over his head.

"I'd love to," snapped Stella, sarcastically, "but the bloody car won't start."

The man wrenched open the car door. The icy rain poured in on top of her.

"Get out of the way!" he growled.

Stella scrambled out of the car, feeling the rain immediately soaking her head and through the shoulders of her coat and her best leather kitten-heeled shoes.

"Fucking women drivers!" complained the man, sliding into the driver's seat, while Stella wondered at how easily she had relinquished her car to him. He could have wanted to steal it or mug her, or anything. A thousand thoughts flickered distractedly around her befuddled mind, barely taking in the fact that the car was immobile and would have been impossible to steal.

The man turned the car key aggressively, his bulk seeming to fill the small area in between the steering wheel and the seat. "Bastard thing won't start!" he growled between clenched teeth, glaring at Stella as if she had deliberately broken down.

"Yes," Stella whispered, close to tears. There were a thousand smart answers that she could have given him, but just at the moment she couldn't think of anything to say – she just wanted to get home and into some dry clothes.

Two men ran towards the stricken car, heads bowed against the rain that was soaking through their business suits.

"Quick!" one of them yelled, his voice almost lost in the traffic noise. The two of them shoved their shoulders into the back of the car and the big man leapt nimbly from the driver's seat and steered the car with one hand while he helped to push the car to the side of the road. The three of them bounced the car off the road onto the grass verge, and then as quickly as they had appeared vanished into the rainswept darkness. The line of cars began to move again, tyres sloshing through the puddles, leaving Stella standing on the grass verge.

Miserably she got back into her car. The seat was damp where the water from the man's wet clothes had soaked into the fabric. Hopefully there would be reception for her mobile phone to call someone. Who on earth did she know well enough to ask them to come out and help her? She reached over to the passenger seat and rummaged for her phone in her handbag. She looked up as a pair of bright headlights bumped up onto the grass verge and stopped behind her car. She watched through the rear-view mirror as the lights were switched off and a man came towards her car. Hastily she jammed the door-lock down and inched open her window.

"I thought that it was you." Henry Murphy grinned at her from beneath the brim of a very battered-looking cowboy hat.

Stella's heart sank. Of all the predicaments to find herself in, this had to take the biscuit. Stranded on the dual carriageway in the rain and *he* was the best Sir Galahad that life could provide her with!

Stella unlocked the door and opened it slightly. Henry crouched down beside her, shielding her from the worst of the rain. Water dripped slowly off the brim of his hat onto his corduroy trousers, and Stella could smell the distinctive odour of horses above the tang of traffic fumes.

"I was driving along the opposite carriageway and I thought that it was you. I saw you standing in the road while the men pushed your car off the road. It took me a while to turn around and get back to you."

Stella twisted her lips into a polite smile, wishing that he hadn't bothered. She didn't like him. She didn't like anyone so obviously penniless and scruffy. And she *really* didn't like the way her heart seemed to beat at double-quick time whenever he was around.

"Please don't let me delay you." Stella chanced a look at him. His face was dreadfully close to hers. She could see the raindrops glittering on the untidy strands of his hair where it curled unchecked beneath his hat.

"You aren't delaying me."

His mouth was wide, his lips full. She watched them move over a row of perfectly even teeth. She didn't dare look at his eyes, in case she discovered what was making her heart flutter so uncontrollably.

"Come on. I'll take you home. We'll have to get a

garage to come and tow your car in – we can't do anything about it now."

He reached in and took her hand – his skin was icy cold against hers. His hand was very big, gently clutching hers as if she were a tiny delicate bird that he was afraid to hurt. Stella let him pull her to her feet. Then he abruptly let go of her.

"Jump into my Jeep," he said, reaching inside her car and grabbing her handbag and keys. "Quick, get out of the rain!"

Stella dashed for the Jeep. The heavy door gave a crunch of protest as she wrenched it open. She glanced back, watching as Henry shoved down the lock on her car and slammed the door shut.

"You must be frozen!" Henry exclaimed, bursting into the driver's seat a second later. "Here, you can wear this jumper of mine." He stretched his arm into the back seat, rummaging around in the darkness. "Take off your wet coat." Stella did as she was told, pulling the heavy jumper he gave her over her head and grimacing with distaste at the smell of horses and dogs that wafted from the fabric. "Throw your coat into the back," Henry told her, firing the engine into life. "Now you had better give me directions."

The Jeep jolted off the grass verge and surged out into the line of traffic. Stella threw her coat into the back, narrowly missing the collie dog that was curled up on a pile of horse rugs. The dog lifted his head and regarded her balefully for a moment before lowering his head onto his paws again with a sigh.

"It's not far – turn off the dual carriageway at the next junction," Stella told him. Thank God it wasn't far. There were limits to her endurance and sitting in this dirty, rattling Jeep was almost too much. Heaven knows what was under her feet, she thought, tentatively pushing away a cardboard box full of thoroughbred sales catalogues.

"Are you going to Fairyhouse? One of Rory's horses is running there." Henry virtually had to shout over the rattling noise that the Jeep was making.

"Not sure," Stella shouted back. She should tell Henry that her relationship with Rory was over, but part of her held back. She didn't want Henry to know. Something that she could see dancing behind his eyes, when she dared look at him, made her feel that Henry would be rather pleased to hear that she was single again.

"Just here," Stella said a few minutes later, pointing at a gap between the parked cars where Henry could pull over close to her flat. "That was very kind of you." She smiled at him gratefully. She scrambled from the Jeep as Henry turned off the engine.

"I'll walk you in," he said hastily, leaping out of the vehicle before she could protest. He shot around to the pavement with a coat which he held over her head as they ran towards the apartment block. Stella could feel the warmth from his body against hers as he hunched over her, protecting her from the rain.

Suddenly Henry was jerked away and the coat fluttered to the ground as a fresh onslaught of rain thundered down on Stella's head. Stella felt her mouth drop open.

Rory had hold of Henry's sweater and was shaking him like a terrier with a rat.

"You bitch! You must have been carrying on with him while I was there!" shrieked Rory. *"I fucking knew you were seeing someone else, but not him!"*

16

Stella felt disbelief mingle with an uncontrollable anger. In the harsh glow of the street-lights, with the torrential rain pouring down on them all, the scene had a surreal quality, as if she were watching a scene from a movie.

Rory stood in the middle of the pavement, his hair slicked to his head with the rain, fists clenched as he roared again and again: *"I knew you were seeing someone else! You two-timing bitch!"*

"Leave her alone!" Henry snarled. "There's nothing going on between us. Never has been." He shook his head vehemently.

Stella wondered if she could hear a note of regret in his voice.

"Her car had broken down and I stopped to give her a lift."

Rory lowered his head, shaking it slowly, like a raging bull about to charge. His eyes blazed in his pale face. "Stop lying," he growled between clenched teeth. "You may as well admit it now." He swung a clenched fist in Henry's direction. Blind with temper, the punch missed by a mile.

"I wasn't seeing Henry!" Stella yelled, astonished to find herself standing in front of Henry as if to protect him. "You and I finished days ago because of you acting like this all of the time, Rory! So who I get a lift from is none of your business!"

"Get out of my way!" Rory snarled, seizing Stella by the shoulders and shoving her out of the way.

"Get off her!" screamed a voice and Amber launched herself at Rory, her diminutive frame full of anger, tiny fists flailing in his direction.

Rory, shocked by the sudden onslaught, stumbled backwards.

"I was just walking Teddy," Amber said, putting her arm around Stella, "when I heard that idiot screaming and carrying on." She glared at Rory who stood sullenly in the rain. "Go on, you. Piss off! Leave Stella alone!"

Rory shuffled his feet, all of his anger suddenly depleted.

Then at the same moment all of them seemed to notice Teddy, who, released by Amber as she launched her attack on Rory, was now wandering around the pavement, weaving in and out of their feet.

As if she had a sudden premonition of what was to come, Amber suddenly dropped to her haunches. "Teddy, come here!"

Stella could hear the sudden panic in her voice. She saw Rory turn, look at the puppy who was snuffling around close to his feet, and then in one movement he scooped the pup into his arms and, shooting them a look that was pure malice, turned and ran with it in his arms.

"Rory! No!" screamed Stella, shooting across the road after him.

"Fuck off! It's your turn to get hurt now, Stella!" Rory heaved open his car door, threw Teddy inside like a rugby player passing the ball and before she could reach him, he had jumped into the car and slammed the door shut.

Stella stood in the street watching the car disappear into the distance with Teddy's small brown face looking at her out of the back window.

Fighting a dreadful feeling of nausea that was threatening to envelop her, Stella slowly made her way back across the street, narrowly avoiding being run over by a car that hooted angrily as she almost walked into its path. Amber crouched beside the wall outside the apartment block sobbing noisily, while Henry stood uncomfortably beside her looking shell-shocked.

"Why didn't you stop him?" snapped Stella at Henry. None of them could have prevented Rory from taking Teddy, none of them were close enough, but somehow she wanted to lash out at Henry, hurt him for being the cause of her precious dog being taken by Rory.

"I . . ." Henry shrugged helplessly, as if he knew that

to argue with Stella would be useless – she was too distraught.

"He'll kill the dog. I know he will!" wailed Amber, covering her face with her hands. "He just wants to hurt you. He's a maniac."

Stella felt hot tears of shock and hurt begin to trickle down her cheeks. She crouched down beside Amber. "Come on. Let's go inside out of the rain – we can't do anything out here," she said gently, putting her arms around Amber and trying to haul her to her feet.

Amber got up. She stood beside Stella as limp as a rag-doll, all of the life gone out of her. "Rory, please don't hurt him," Amber whispered miserably, burying her face against Stella's shoulder. Stella felt a warm pair of arms encircle the two of them. The damp cotton of Henry's shirt brushed against her face. She could feel the warmth of his arm against the icy cold of her cheeks and feel the hard muscle beneath the fabric.

"Come on. Let me take you inside," he said gently.

Stella launched herself backwards out of his grip. "Why don't you bloody well clear off? Haven't you caused enough trouble?" she snapped, furiously. If Henry hadn't been around, none of this would have happened.

Henry stepped back as abruptly as if she had punched him. "Fine," he said coldly. Stella glared at him as he stood there, his face pale and set beneath the unearthly glow of the streetlamp.

"I'll go then." He paused, standing in the middle of the pavement uncertainly, as if he were struggling to find something to say, some words that would make everything all right.

"Go on then!" raged Stella.

"Right!" Henry turned on his heel and walked away, the sound of his drenched clothes and the water sloshing in his shoes loud in the stunned silence.

Stella stared after him as he stalked across the road, got into his Jeep and drove away. Beside her she heard Amber sigh miserably. "We should have got him to drive after Rory," she said bitterly, turning away and walking towards the apartments.

Stella stood in the rain for a long time, watching the tail-lights of Henry's Jeep disappear down the street. She wished that she had never, ever, ever met Henry Murphy.

"Oh God, Amber!" Stella groaned, shaking her head in disbelief. Turning around, she found the pavement was deserted. Amber had gone inside. Fighting back tears, Stella made her way inside.

Amber was in the lounge, pacing up and down frenziedly. "What's he done with the dog?" She looked at Stella, her eyes wide and frightened, her hair hanging in wild disarray around her face. "You don't think that he'll hurt him, do you?"

Stella winced. That scenario was too awful to contemplate.

"No." She shook her head firmly. "He might be a maniac, but he's not cruel to animals." Stella hoped that she was right. Rory was angry enough to do anything to get back at her.

Amber sank down onto the sofa and buried her head in her hands. Stella watched as the water from her clothes slowly dripped onto the fabric, making dark stains.

"Make him bring him back!" Amber pleaded, her voice almost lost in the sound of her sobs.

Stella stood in the middle of the room, uncertain as to what she should do. Then suddenly she picked up the phone and punched in Rory's number. After a few rings he answered.

"Stella!" He sounded delighted to see her number come up on his phone. "Are we on for tomorrow night?"

Stella gasped in disbelief. Had he somehow managed to erase the memory of what had just happened? Had he forgotten that he had attacked her – twice – and had just threatened someone who had helped her when her car had broken down? Had he forgotten that he had just stolen her precious dog?

"No, Rory, we are not." She tried to keep her voice as calm and neutral as she could. "Rory – could you bring the dog back, please?"

"That bloody thing!" He snorted in amusement. "Peed on the floor of my car. I threw it out by the new Sycamore Park Estate. Some kids went away with it."

Stella's mouth dropped open. She stared at Amber, who was looking at her expectantly, her eyes full of hope that he would bring Teddy back.

"I see," she whispered, struggling to speak for the enormous lump that had suddenly welled in the back of her throat.

"Come out with me again," Rory was saying. "I'll buy you another dog, a nice pedigree one, not a scruffy mutt like that one."

Stella clicked the receiver down. There was nothing more to say to Rory. How could he have just thrown the pup out? Her precious little dog. Teddy. He might be just a scruffy mutt in Rory's eyes, but to Stella and Amber he was an adorable part of their lives. How could Rory have been so cruel? Just to hurt her?

Stella opened her mouth again, but no words came out. She looked at Amber and saw the hope die in her eyes.

She walked around to the sofa and sank down. Suddenly she didn't feel as if her legs would support her.

"He let Teddy out of the car at the Sycamore Park Estate."

Amber leapt to her feet. "Come on! We'll go and find him!"

Stella pulled her back down onto the sofa. "We can't. It's almost midnight and I have no car. We'll have to wait until morning."

Amber glared back at her. "First thing then. We'll ring in sick and go and look for him."

*　　*　　*

Kevin was speaking. Stella could see his mouth opening and closing, but couldn't take in what he was

172

saying. Teddy had been missing for three days now and the belief that he would be found safe and well was beginning to fade. The harsh reality was hard to face. They were never going to see him again. He was out there somewhere, alone and frightened. Maybe he had been chased away by the children and was lying injured somewhere. Maybe dying.

Stella and Amber had spent every spare moment walking around the drab streets of the housing estate, looking for Teddy. They had knocked on countless doors, asking if anyone had seen the dog, but every reply had been negative. They had walked around the wasteland that bordered the estate, sinking ankle deep into mud and clambering over abandoned mattresses and old fridges, calling the dog's name and listening to the mocking replies of the grubby estate children who trailed curiously after them.

"So how do you think we should present this article?" Kevin asked, looking quizzically at Stella over the top of his half moon glasses.

"Oh, I . . ." Stella began.

"About the health spas!" said Sorcha, tapping a long fingernail against the pile of papers that she had laid in front of Stella before the meeting began.

"Yes." Stella fought to get her thoughts in order, trying to banish the picture of Teddy lying whimpering pitifully beneath a bush. "Perhaps we could do a top ten of the best spas?" she said lamely.

Kevin clasped his pudgy, sausage-like fingers together. "Excellent," he preened, pursing his fat lips.

"Now," he said, flapping his hands in front of him, "I think that Sorcha would do a great job of sampling them all and coming up with the top ten." He beamed across the table at Sorcha, who fought to control her cry of delight and just managed to turn it into a strangled cough.

Stella shuffled her papers, trying to hide her disappointment. Normally that job would have been given to her, but she seemed to have lost all of the drive that had made her so good at her job. Sorcha had been snapping at her heels for long enough. Now she was clearly overtaking her. Soon Stella would be the assistant and Sorcha would be given the editorial job.

The day dragged on. Stella stole yet another glance at her watch: time seemed to be standing still. There were hours yet before she could head out of the office into her car and head back to the Sycamore Park Estate, for yet another heartbreaking search for Teddy.

"You've made a mistake on this article," Sorcha crowed, unable to keep the glee out of her voice.

Stella almost choked on Sorcha's overpowering perfume as the girl leant over her desk to throw the article in front of her. Out of the corner of her eye Stella saw Kevin mincing past. Sorcha had timed returning the article to Stella until Kevin was around. Stella had lost count of the times that she had altered things that Sorcha had made mistakes on, without even mentioning it to her. This was pure spite – Sorcha just wanted to show Stella at her worst so that she could wheedle her way into Kevin's good books.

Finally the time came to leave the office. Stella tried desperately to string out the time that it took her to pack away her things so that she wouldn't appear to be too eager to leave. Sorcha looked up from her desk as Stella walked past.

"Oh, is it time to go *already*?" she asked loudly. "I'll just stay here and finish these. You get off, Stella."

Stella clenched her teeth. Yet again Sorcha had managed to make her look like a bad employee in front of Kevin. But she had to leave. She was due to pick up Amber from outside the factory and then the two of them were going to spend the remaining hour of so of daylight walking around the housing estate hunting for Teddy.

But yet again the search was fruitless and as the darkness began to fall they had to admit defeat. They went back to Stella's car and sat shivering, aching with tiredness and misery as they drove home silently.

*   *   *

The doorbell rang. Amber leapt to her feet expectantly and ran to open it. Stella listened hopefully to the sound of voices coming from the front door. Maybe someone had found Teddy and brought him back. She looked up a few moments later, longing to see Teddy wriggling with delight in Amber's arms, but instead Henry stood in the doorway. Amber slid past him, disappeared into her bedroom and closed the door quietly. Stella stood up, wondering why he had come.

"Hello," she smiled tightly.

"I came to say thank you," Henry said stiffly, not returning her greeting. "Rory just came to see me. He wouldn't believe that we were not having an affair."

Stella made a spluttering sound. The very idea was ridiculous.

"And so," Henry continued, glaring coldly at her, "he's taken his horses away from my yard."

"He took my dog and threw him out of his car and now he's lost!" Henry wasn't the only one who had lost something because of Rory's stupidity.

"I've just lost half of my business." Henry glared at her coldly, the muscles at the side of his jaw clenched with tension, before he added sarcastically: "Thank you very much."

17

Amber reached across the production line, scooped up another handful of chocolates and shoved one into her mouth. "Uh uhhh," she said into the mouthpiece of her phone, biting through the icing-sugar coating into the chocolate truffle. She propped her head in the crook of her arm and slumped across the conveyor belt amongst the chocolates. Mel, taking advantage of her position, reached across the stationary conveyor belt and flicked one of the chocolates at Amber's head. The voice on the other end of the phone reached shrieking pitch. Amber sat up with a sigh.

"Yes, Mum," she said as her mother launched into another tirade of misery about how awful Georgina was for not contacting her. Across the table Mel caught her eye and grinned sympathetically. Amber raised her eyes in a gesture of frustration. She was sick of hearing about how awful her mother thought Georgina was. If she had paid her any attention in the first place then they probably wouldn't be having these problems now. She had been too busy with her married boyfriend and now she was concerned when her daughter found affection elsewhere. Bored with talking to her mother, Amber grabbed another chocolate and threw it high in the air before catching it in her mouth. Mel gave a short laugh of delight, which died suddenly on her lips. Amber saw the look of amusement in her eyes change to sheer horror as she glanced at the door.

"You're going to have to get her to phone me!" her mother shrieked down the phone.

"Yes, Mum, I'll . . ." Amber followed Mel's horrified gaze.

Dymphna stood at the end of the table, her arms folded aggressively across her scrawny chest. Amber hastily snapped off the phone and shoved it into the pocket of her overalls. A tense silence had descended on the factory floor. All of the girls hastily stopped gossiping and scuttled back to their places on the conveyor belt. Someone started the belt and the chocolates began to slide along the length of the room as the girls hastily shoved them into boxes, casting tentative glances around the room to see who had skived off for the afternoon, taking advantage of the fact that Dymphna was usually absent.

"Good to see that you've been working hard," Dymphna said in a voice that dripped with sarcasm. She stalked around the factory floor, glaring at the empty seats, making a mental note of who was missing.

Finally she disappeared into her glass-fronted office, where Amber could see her talking on the phone and making notes in a black book.

The remainder of the afternoon was spent in a hushed silence, while the girls worked frenziedly.

"Where's Tony?" mouthed Jules to Amber.

She shrugged in reply.

"Why aren't they having their usual meeting, rolling around a hotel bedroom?" whispered someone else.

Amber miserably shoved another handful of chocolates into the tissue-paper lining of the gold-coloured box. Somewhere, someone would receive this box as a gift – it would bring happiness, touch a heart. Would whoever opened it and ate the contents have any concept of the misery that was around the box when it was packed? As if there wasn't enough to worry about, now Dymphna had come back to spoil the one easy afternoon that they had in the factory. Life really couldn't get much worse. Her mother was raging on the phone all the time about Georgina and there was no peace even at the apartment. Teddy was still missing – there had been no sightings of him after a small snotty-nosed little boy with a grubby jumper and a cut knee had told Stella that he had seen the dog heading off across the wasteland with what were probably tinker children. Stella had been in the depths of despair ever since. They had finally stopped going to the estate – it was pointless. They had knocked on every door and asked if anyone had seen the dog, hunted through every inch of the waste ground, looked under every rotting mattress and into every rusting, smelly fridge to see if the puppy was inside. But there had been no sign of him. Stella had even phoned the police and the radio stations had put out Teddy's description. She had even visited the dog pound and come back heartbroken at all the beautiful, homeless dogs that she had seen. And if the missing dog was not enough, every time the postman arrived he brought fresh doom to Amber. The letters from the bank and finance companies were slowly getting nastier and nastier.

The tense atmosphere lasted until the bell rang to announce that the day was over. Someone turned off the conveyor belt and the ceaseless line of nut-encrusted chocolates that they had been packing groaned to a halt. Everyone slid off their seats and headed into the changing rooms, gladly casting their protective hats and overalls and rubber gloves into the bins.

Once outside the tense atmosphere vanished.

"Fuck!" exclaimed Mel. "I couldn't believe that Dymphna came back. She *never* comes back on a Friday afternoon. She's always too busy shagging Tony."

"Wait till she gets hold of Ann on Monday morning," giggled someone else. "Her and Bernie were in the pub for the afternoon." Laughing and chattering, the girls headed out of the factory gates.

Amber made her way wearily home. There had to be a better way of living than this relentless grind of work and bills. This weekend she was determined that she was going to stay in, save some money, sort out those awful bills. At least if she stayed at home she would be able to resist the temptation to spend more money.

She pushed open the front door to the apartment, looking furtively at the hall table and the doormat. Relief flowed over her – at least there were no more horrible letters demanding money. She headed up the stairs, wrinkling her nose at the strange smell that seemed to pervade the whole house. The smell got stronger as she went towards the apartment – then, as she turned her key in the lock and went inside she gasped with the overpowering stench.

"Fuck!" Amber stopped dead in the doorway, eyes wide with disbelief. The apartment was full of flowers.

Stella sat miserably at the dining-room table, her eyes red and swollen from crying.

"What the hell is all this?" Amber asked, shaking her head in disbelief.

"Rory," Stella sighed, wiping her eyes with a tattered tissue. "He keeps sending me flowers – every few minutes they've been arriving since I got home. All day at work . . . he keeps telephoning, asking me to go out with him . . . begging me to forgive him."

Amber leant silently against the door, numbly surveying the room. Flowers filled every vase that they had and lay abandoned in cellophane packets on every surface, their smell overpowering in the confines of the apartment. Slowly she walked across the room. Huge lilies mingled with roses and the white blossoms of flowers that she couldn't even name.

"We could open a stand and sell all of these," Amber

joked, feebly, trying to make light of the situation, afraid of the fear that she could see in Stella. She sat down beside her and took hold of her hand. It was icy cold.

"I can't stand much more of this," Stella wept bitterly, her voice full of desperation. "First the dog, and now this. He really is mad."

Amber patted Stella's hand, distractedly, not knowing what to say, or how she could make her feel better.

"He's been telephoning me all day – he's made me look a right fool. Kevin was going mad – we're not supposed to get personal calls. Sorcha, of course, loved every second of it all, especially when Kevin blew his top when the tenth lot of flowers arrived." She groaned miserably. "I don't even know if I've got a job any more. Kevin told me to go home and sort things out." She jumped as the doorbell rang. "Oh God, please no more!" she begged, looking at the door as if she expected Rory to dash through wielding an axe.

Amber got up slowly and went to the intercom. Her finger was trembling as she pressed the buzzer to speak.

"Hello?" she whispered tightly.

"Amber?" The fearful feeling turned to relief which quickly faded to annoyance. Her mother. What the hell did *she* want? This had to be the first time that she had ever come to the apartment. She had phoned plenty of times, when she wanted something, but she had never paid a social call. This must be a real emergency.

"Come up," Amber said into the intercom.

She cast a furtive glance in Stella's direction. This was a terrible thing to inflict on her, just at this moment. Ruby was bad enough when you were in a good mood, but when things were as traumatic as they had just been for Stella . . . Amber wasn't sure that she'd be able to stand even a few minutes in Ruby's company, especially without a strong drink to fortify herself for the ordeal.

"It's my mum," Amber said, already apologising for her arrival.

Stella made a small sound of acknowledgement. A moment later the sound of footsteps pounded up the stairs towards the apartment. Sighing, Amber opened the door. If her mother had come to borrow money then she was wasting her time.

Ruby shot through the open doorway with Ronnie hot on her heels.

"Hello," Amber said wryly as they marched past without acknowledging her.

"Who died?" Ronnie said gruffly, looking quizzically at the rows of flowers. Amber glared at him as he looked Stella slowly up and down as if he were appraising a piece of meat.

Ruby walked straight past Stella, with a short "Hello, darlin'", plonked herself down on the sofa and began to rummage in her handbag.

Oh no! Amber opened her mouth to protest, but all that came out was a strangled noise of horror as her mother dragged a battered packet of cigarettes out of her handbag and, flipping the pack open, pulled a cigarette out and rummaged in her jacket pocket for a lighter. With a sigh of pure pleasure she lit the cigarette and blew a huge plume of smoke out through her nostrils. Amber cringed. Stella hated anyone smoking around her – she had never allowed anyone to smoke in the apartment.

"I'm bloody sick of this," Ruby snapped, dragging deeply on the cigarette.

Stella slid from her seat and casting a wry smile of sympathy in Amber's direction headed for her bedroom.

"Sick of what?" Amber asked, gritting her teeth to keep her temper. Another dragon's plume of smoke headed towards the ceiling.

"Georgina living with this bloke," her mother snapped, petulantly. "It's time that she came home and stopped all of this messing around."

"Well, she seems happy enough with him," Amber said and then instantly regretted it as her mother screeched in reply.

"She's living with a man old enough to be her father! Her bloody teacher, for fuck's sake!"

"*Ex*-teacher," Amber said, knowing that there was no point in arguing with her mother – she could never win. Ruby always had to have the last word. When she had made up her mind no one could change it.

"I don't bloody care who he is! Everyone will be gossiping when they find out – she's making a fool of me."

Amber opened her mouth to speak and then changed her mind. What was the point of protesting that everyone in the district was probably gossiping about *her* affair with a married man? They would hardly bat an eyelid because her daughter had gone off and found herself someone decent to live with.

"Bloody hell!" exclaimed Ruby, gazing around the room in amazement, finally noticing that the apartment looked like an upmarket florist shop. "Who's got an admirer?"

"They're from an ex-boyfriend of Stella's."

"Bloody hell! Must have some money – flowers cost a fortune. Stella must be daft if she's dumped him."

Amber cringed, wishing that her mother would just shut up. The last thing that Stella needed was to be reminded just how wealthy Rory was. She was well shut of him.

"I'm going to go round to *his* house and get her back." Ruby forgot about the flowers, her attention focusing once more on her own problems. She threw the butt of her cigarette into one of the vases of flowers. There was a hiss as the red-hot end hit the water. Gathering up her handbag, she stood up. "And *you'll* have to come with me. You're the only one that Georgina will listen to. You'll have to make her see sense and come home."

"Right," Amber said through gritted teeth. She knew from long experience that while her mother was in this mood the best thing to do was to just go along with her.

*   *   *

They reached their destination at breakneck speed, Ronnie jerking to a halt outside the silent, tidy house.

"Georgina!" yelled her mother, hammering on the glass door pane so hard that Amber thought she would surely break it.

After a moment Georgina opened the door and stood back silently to let them in. Amber shot her a look of sympathy, but Georgina ignored her.

"You're coming home with me," her mother snapped, her voice strident in the quiet house.

Georgina gave a snort of sarcastic laughter and led the way into the lounge, shaking her head silently. Martin sat on the sofa, bent over a pile of schoolbooks that he was marking. He looked up, his grey eyes cold behind his round glasses.

"*You bastard!*" shrieked her mother, pointing a long, nicotine-stained finger at him. "I'm taking Georgina home. Get your things. *Now!*" she snapped in Georgina's direction.

Martin got slowly to his feet. "I think that decision is up to Georgina," he said politely, padding softly across the room and putting his arm around Georgina.

Ronnie, his head lowered like a bull, thundered across the room. "She's coming home with us!" he yelled, pounding into Martin with all his weight. With a movement that looked oddly out of place from the passive, shy-looking nerdy man, Martin seized Ronnie by the shoulders and propelled him across the room, banging him against the wall and holding him there by the neck as he wriggled furiously like a fish on a line.

"Go away, all of you, and leave us alone," Martin said. "Georgina is staying with me." He abruptly released Ronnie, who skulked from the room hunched over, clutching his throat.

Ruby stared at Martin as if she wanted to explode. Amber saw her mouth open and close like a fish gasping for air, as if she couldn't find the right words of abuse to yell at him. Then, realising that she was outfaced, she spun on her heel and stalked from the room without a backwards glance.

Amber shrugged helplessly and smiled weakly. "Bye then," she said, glancing back at Martin holding Georgina in his arms, comforting her, kissing her hair.

He raised his head and growled "Just leave us alone!"

18

Amber was glad when it was Monday morning. When her alarm clock went off she reached out to turn it off with what was almost a sigh of relief, rather than the usual groan of horror. For once she was glad that the weekend was over. It would actually be nice to be back in the relative peace of the factory, amongst the factory girls, listening to their stories about lost boyfriends and awful mothers-in-law. Anything had to be better than being at home.

The weekend had been awful. Stella had sat amongst the wilting flowers, jumping every time that the phone rang, mourning the lost puppy. Rory had sat outside in his car for most of the weekend, looking up at the flat with a stricken face. Ruby had been on the phone every few minutes, upset about Georgina. Amber found it hard to have sympathy for her. Who cared if Martin was way older than Georgina, and if he

188

once had been her teacher? That was years ago. She was over eighteen. At least she had a nice house to live in and he obviously cared an awful lot about her.

Amber rolled over in bed, grinning at the memory of the way that Martin had launched himself at Ronnie. He might have looked like a nerdy weed, but he certainly knew how to look after himself. They should all just leave them alone to get on with their lives. Her mother was going to lose Georgina for good if she kept behaving like that.

Amber got up and went out into the kitchen to get some tea. The apartment was back to normal – every flower had gone and all of the vases had been cleared away. Stella sat at the kitchen table, dressed in her best, knock-em-dead business suit. She looked coldly efficient.

She smiled tightly at Amber. "I've thrown out all of those flowers." There was a forced, brittle note to her voice, as if she was trying very hard to keep her composure. "It's time to put the whole Rory saga behind me. And Teddy . . ." her voice faltered a little at the mention of the dog's name and then she thrust her jaw forwards and continued firmly. "I have a life to regain. And a job to wrestle back from that bitch Sorcha." She crunched into a piece of toast and chewed determinedly.

"Right. Good for you," answered Amber, raising her fist in a power salute. And I am going to have to get my life under control too, she mused, switching on the kettle and shoving bread into the toaster. She really had to do *something* about those credit-card bills.

Work wasn't the blissful relief that Amber had thought it was going to be. A hushed, tense atmosphere hung over the factory floor. All of the girls who had been absent the previous Friday afternoon were marshalled into Dymphna's office first thing in the morning and had all come back looking red-faced and thoroughly chastised.

"The bitch has docked our wages!" hissed Maggie.

"Well, what did you expect?" said another woman smugly. "We were all here working while you lot were skiving off in the pub."

Maggie stood up, her face like thunder, but catching sight of Dymphna out of the corner of her eye she sat back down again, and sat glaring sullenly at the woman. Dymphna stalked around the factory floor, her footsteps slow and rhythmic, pausing occasionally to stand behind one of the workers, watching each one delicately placing the chocolates in the fancy boxes as if they were made of glass, rather than just dumping them in as they usually did. The atmosphere was oppressive and Amber found it hard to breathe in the silence, as everyone's eyes followed Dymphna's progress around the room, waiting for the moment when she would pounce and give one of them an almighty dressing-down for some imaginary wrongdoing. Tony appeared and strode arrogantly across the factory floor, importantly clutching a clipboard to his chest. Amber tilted her head slightly and watched him head into the glass-fronted office that he shared with Dymphna. A moment later Dymphna followed him.

"What is it with those two?" wondered Mel at break-time, as she leant against the iron railing that bordered the flight of concrete steps where the women sat for a cup of tea and a cigarette in the open air.

Amber shrugged. "Lover's tiff, has to be. Otherwise why all the tense atmosphere and meetings in his office?"

"Maybe she's pregnant and he doesn't want it," grinned Jules maliciously.

"Nah, maybe she's pregnant and it's someone else's!" Amber joked.

"Shit!" yelled Mel, frenziedly stubbing out her cigarette on a concrete step. "We're late back *again!*"

* * *

The day dragged on. Amber was sure that Dymphna had altered the clock so that the hands moved more slowly than they should. Surely time should not go so more slowly? Finally there was only half an hour to go. Amber breathed a sigh of relief. She couldn't wait to get out of the factory and go home. At least the atmosphere should be lighter there – if Stella had continued with her positive thinking policy.

"Amber, Maggie, Ann and Bernie – can you all come into my office?" Dymphna stood in the doorway to her office, her thin lips twisted into a smug smile.

"Aghhh," groaned Amber. "She's going to give out

at us again for being late back after break." She slid off her seat and made her way wearily into Dymphna's office. "Shut the door!" Dymphna snapped, when they were all crammed into the confines of the glass-fronted room.

Amber shot a look out of the window and grinned across at her friends, raising her eyebrows comically. They all lined up in front of Dymphna's desk, watching while she sat down slowly and then began to flick through the sheets of paper on her clipboard. She reminded Amber of a large cat, spinning out the torture of a small mouse, taking the maximum time to move in for the kill. Finally she put down the clipboard and sat back in her chair, looking at each one of them in turn. Amber began to feel as if she were back at school, standing in front of the headmistress, something that she had endured on a fairly regular basis, to be reprimanded for some feeble misdemeanour. She let her mind drift away as she had done in the headmistress's office, wondering what she should make for her dinner and what was going to be on telly that evening.

"I've given you every chance, so this should come as no surprise to any of you." Amber came back to reality with a jolt. "What?"

Dymphna turned her mean gaze on Amber, looking her up and down as if there were a bad smell under her long, thin nose. "I said," she repeated, in a pained tone, "your work has been terrible, your attendance appalling, your attitude disgusting and so I'm letting you go."

Amber's mind drifted off again, unable to take in what Dymphna was saying – from far away she could hear the sound of her voice, strident and ear-grating, and see her thin lips moving over an uneven row of yellowing teeth. It was as if she were listening to her speaking from under water. The occasional phrase came clearly . . . "wages to the end of the week . . . P45 . . . accompany you to clear out your lockers . . ."

And then the four of them were walking across the factory floor with Dymphna stalking alongside them like a jailer escorting a bunch of criminals to prison.

The factory floor was deserted. Everyone had gone home. They hadn't even been given the chance to say goodbye to their workmates. Dymphna leant against the wall, watching as they emptied out their lockers, a faint smile of pleasure twitching the corners of her lips and dancing in the depths of her eyes. Maggie was sobbing as she cleared out her locker, miserably shoving packets of biscuits and her make-up bag into her handbag.

"You fucking bitch!" snarled Bernie, glaring at Dymphna who began to finger her two-way radio nervously, ready to call security if any of them made a move to punch her. "You haven't seen the last of us! We'll fight this! This is unfair dismissal!"

Amber collected a bottle of deodorant and a tattered pair of runners from her locker, abandoned there when she was on a health kick and was running to work, or maybe it was when she couldn't afford to get the bus and *had* to run to work – she couldn't remember. She hastily shoved her overall over the three boxes of chocolates that she had hidden in her locker for consumption at Easter. Maybe now wasn't a good time to try to take them home. And then they were going out through the foyer, punching their time cards into the machine for the last time. Then they were out into the fresh air and walking across the carpark. Dymphna accompanied them right to the factory gates, making sure that they had passed through into the world beyond before she turned away silently, satisfaction at her dirty work etched in every line of her posture.

"I'll get that bitch!" spat Bernie glaring back across the carpark at Dymphna as she walked away.

"I can't believe what she just did," complained Ann, her voice high with disbelief. "We'll fight this!"

But despite their brave words, they all knew none of them would do anything at all. Too much trouble, too much grief and they hadn't a leg to stand on anyway thanks to Dymphna's detective work.

Amber shook her head numbly, said a quiet goodbye and walked away. What was the point in saying anything? There was no point in hanging around the factory, discussing what had happened. That would change nothing.

She caught the bus and sat at the back watching the world pass by. Life was going on for everyone else. The shops were beginning to fill with spring fashions – beautiful flimsy dresses in pinks and lilacs, gorgeous shoes, things that Amber would have loved to buy. The first stirrings of panic began to set in. Pictures of the piled-up credit-card bills danced before her eyes. How was she supposed to pay off her debts now? How would she pay the rent on the apartment? The bus glided past a young homeless boy sitting on a hotel step rattling a paper cup at passers-by. Soon she would be like that. Homeless, penniless, and hopeless. She sighed bitterly. This was ridiculous. She would get another job; there was no need to panic; money would come from somewhere; she just had to be positive.

Stella was already home when Amber got back to the flat.

"Hi," Amber tried to sound cheerful.

"Hi," said Stella, smiling brightly. "Nice day?"

"Great," Amber replied, trying desperately not to cry.

Stella would fly into a major panic if she knew that Amber was out of work. She worried about money anyway and the thought that she was sharing an apartment with someone who was jobless would freak her out completely. Amber decided that she couldn't tell her until she had another job and the threat of poverty had been lifted from Stella's horizon.

"I'm off out later," Stella grinned. "Time to pick myself up. No more moping about Rory and Ted–" She swallowed hard, trying to compose herself. "An art gallery opening. Lots of nice men, with plenty of money."

Amber shook her head and smiled. Stella didn't take long to bounce back.

"And Rory is bound to get fed up of sitting outside

in his car soon," Stella added, heading off to her bedroom to get ready for the evening.

Amber bit back tears. She wished that Stella wasn't going out – she didn't want to be alone for the evening with just her thoughts for company. She would only start to panic about finding another job and start looking at those credit-card bills – again.

Stella emerged like a whirlwind from her bedroom, wafting expensive-smelling perfume in her wake. "OK, I'll see you later," she breezed, casting a furtive look out of the window to see if Rory was parked on the street. Then, with a visible sigh of relief that meant the coast was clear, she hurried out, banging the door briskly behind her.

Silence descended on the apartment. Amber took one look around the room. The walls seemed to be closing in on her. Grabbing her handbag she dashed from the room in Stella's wake. She had to get out of the apartment – she couldn't stay there alone. She would think too much. Once outside on the pavement she slowed her panic-driven pace. Now what would she do? She couldn't go to a bar. She had to save every penny.

A seed of thought sparked: Kenny might know of where there might be jobs. He would be able to put in a good word for her. And a moment later she was heading on another bus to her mother's house.

*   *   *

Amber walked up the street towards her mother's house. Kenny's car was parked half on and half off the pavement.

Kenny opened the door after what seemed like an age. "She's not in."

Amber forced her lips to twist into a smile. He really had to be the most unpleasant man that she had ever met.

"Well, I'll come in for a while," she said, meeting his eyes.

"Uhhhhhhh." Kenny shrugged, raising his eyebrows and turning his full lips downwards. He moved out of the doorway slightly so that she had to brush past him to get into the house.

Amber almost gagged at the overpowering smell of his aftershave. She wished that she hadn't come. Now that she was here she couldn't imagine asking him for help. She would wait until her mother came back, then make her excuses and leave.

Kenny followed her into the lounge and inclined his head, indicating that she should sit. The room smelt of stale smoke and cheap perfume.

"Where has she gone?" Amber asked, as Kenny plonked himself down in the armchair opposite her.

"Just up to the off-licence to get me some cans." He picked up the newspaper and began to read it. Outside a car sped up the street, the noise of its engine loud in the silent house.

"So," Kenny said finally, looking at Amber over the top of the newspaper, "how are things with you?"

His voice was coldly polite, but Amber could feel the unpleasantness that oozed from his every pore. He didn't want her here. He hated every bit of her. She could feel it.

"Fine," she said, hearing the note of sarcasm loud in her voice. She didn't want to talk to him, lay her life bare for him to pick over.

Kenny lowered his newspaper and looked at her quizzically. "Doesn't sound very fine to me!" he responded, equally sarcastically.

"Actually, I just lost my job," Amber blurted out. Why had she said it? It was a stupid idea to think that she would get any sympathy or advice here. Well, she might as well ask him now. "Do you know of anything going?" she said timidly.

"Girl like you should have no problem getting work. Plenty of jobs for someone as intelligent as you." Kenny picked up his newspaper again. "Your problem is that you always take the easy way out." Then he added nastily, "Maybe you could get work as a bed-tester."

19

Stella lowered herself slowly into achingly hot water, which slopped dangerously close to the edge of the bath as she moved. This really had to be the very best way to spend an evening in. Forget curling up with a good book, or a video. A hot bath with beauty treatments an inch thick on her face and over her hair was the ultimate way to relax. Slowly, so that she didn't slop the water over the edge of the bath, she reached over to the low table, grabbed the headphones of her Walkman and pressed the play button. She slid the ear-pieces in and closed her eyes, letting the beautiful voice of Lucie Silvas wash over her. At least now she was in her own world, away from Amber's misery and the ever-constant threat of the phone ringing with Rory on the other end begging her to forgive him. Amber was virtually suicidal, since she had lost her job. For three days after she had been sacked, she had pretended to go out to work and come home after Stella, until finally she had broken down in tears and confessed. Stella had told her that she would soon find another job and not to worry about it, that she could cover the rent for a month or so. When she had suggested that Amber try to talk to her mother's boyfriend, who was some big shot businessman, Amber had collapsed in fresh floods of tears and told Stella that he had already suggested that she could find work as an escort. Since then, Amber had seemed a little better, the air of doom and gloom that had followed her for the few days when she'd kept her terrible secret lifting a little. She had gone out daily job-hunting, spending hours poring over the newspapers and filling in application forms.

Stella began to sing along to her favourite track on the CD, extending her long, slender limbs as she exfoliated each one with the expensive Christian Dior that a wealthy boyfriend had once bought her on a shopping excursion. She stopped singing, suddenly aware that she could hear banging on the bathroom door. Scowling, she pulled off the headset and sat up, slopping water out over the rim of the bath.

"Stella!" yelled Amber, hammering on the bathroom door once more.

"Yes!" Stella yelled in reply. What did Amber want *now*? She had taken to pestering Stella for help in filling in the application forms that now littered the flat.

"Stella!" Amber yelled again, her voice filled with urgency.

Stella heaved herself out of the bath, grabbed a

towel and held it around herself while she opened the door.

"Stella!" Amber almost fell in through the door as it opened. "Come out quickly! Guess who's here!" She was squeaking excitedly, hopping from one foot to the other. She stopped as she took in the state of Stella, her eyes narrow with annoyance glaring from behind the thick green face-mask, yellow fruit-smelling slime sliding slowly off her hair. "Maybe you'd better finish your bath first! But be quick!"

Amber darted off again. Stella let the towel slide from her shoulders and clambered back into the bath. She pulled out the plug, watching regretfully as the hot water gurgled away down the plughole. Whatever was exciting Amber so much? Stella couldn't imagine that there was anyone she would like to see just at this moment, unless it was George Clooney, but he was very unlikely to come calling. She gasped as she turned on the shower and a blast of icy cold water hit her in the face.

Drying herself quickly, she shoved on her dressing-gown and, sighing with annoyance, marched out of the bathroom.

"Nice singing," said Henry Murphy, his eyes widening with amusement as she emerged into the living room, still tying the belt of her dressing-gown around her waist.

Stella gave an involuntary gasp of dismay. How could Amber have let *him* into the apartment? And not *warned* her? She must be mad!

"Hello," she said coldly, shooting a furious glance at Amber who was making a peculiar scrabbling gesture at her cheeks.

Henry leant against the back of the sofa, looking gorgeous in a dishevelled way. Torn, faded jeans clung to the long muscles of his thighs and the collar of his shirt was frayed where it touched the long sweep of his neck. His eyes were dancing with amusement.

Stella cringed inwardly. He had heard her dreadful tuneless singing. Pure anger sent prickles of heat all over her body. This really was dreadful. Of all the people that could have come while she was in the bath Henry had to be the worst. And now he was sitting in *her* lounge looking at her as if she were some really amusing comic turn.

"Henry's got something for you," Amber said, scratching at her cheek furiously and rolling her eyes at Stella.

"Oh yes?" Stella said coldly, glaring first in Amber's direction – why *was* scratching her cheek like that? – and then at Henry. She wished that she were safely dressed in her business suit, feeling in command of the situation instead of feeling foolish and vulnerable, standing barefoot and damp in her oldest dressing-gown with her hair all awry and without even a scrape of lipstick or mascara to cover the nakedness of her face.

Henry grinned, levering himself upright. "Something that you might like," he said, getting a large cardboard box from the side of the sofa.

Stella frowned at Amber as Henry bent over the box and began to open it. Is he *mad?* she mouthed.

But Amber was now animatedly pointing to her face.

Then Stella realised with a jolt what Amber's scratching was all about. She still had some of the face-mask smeared on her cheeks.

But then something brown and hairy exploded from the box.

"Teddy!" the girls yelled in unison, as the dog bounded across the room, ears flapping, mouth wide open in a grin as he leapt from one of them to the other, unable to conceal his delight at seeing them again.

"You're wonderful, Henry!" grinned Stella, scooping Teddy up into her arms where he wriggled furiously, trying to lick her face with his small pink tongue while his whimpers of delight rang loudly around the room. Henry, she noticed above the wriggling dog, had gone quite pink and was grinning from ear to ear. "Where did you find him?" She didn't want to ever let Teddy go again. She stroked his wiry coat, revelling in the feel of it beneath her fingers. He smelt of dog shampoo, woody and clean.

"Some lads who do a bit of shooting found him on the wasteland behind the Sycamore Estate. I heard who had found him through one of the lads who works at my stables and went around to see if it was the same dog." Henry watched Stella bury her face in Teddy's furry coat, long strands of brown hair sticking to the green face-mask that was smeared on one of her cheeks and knew that the bottle of whiskey and crisp one-hundred euro note that it had cost him to get the dog back had been worth every penny. Even if it did mean he would have to live on toast and marmalade for the rest of the week.

"Let me cuddle him!" pleaded Amber, taking the dog from Stella and gesturing with her head towards the bathroom.

"Yes, OK." Stella unwillingly released her hold on the dog and quietly slipped away back to the bathroom.

She closed the door and let hot tears of relief fall slowly down her cheeks. She had thought that they would never see Teddy again, imagined that he had died somewhere, all alone and afraid. And now he was back, safe and sound. Thanks to Henry. A sudden picture of his amused expression flashed into her mind and she launched herself across the bathroom to the sink and peered into the mirror, barely stifling a cry of anguish. She had come out of the bathroom in such a temper that she hadn't washed her hair or face properly. A clump of yellow goo still clung above her right ear and a large smear of green face-mask was still on her face, now with numerous curly dog hairs stuck in it. And as if that wasn't bad enough, the green mask still remained in the creases at the sides of her nose, which was red from the bath and her excitement, and in her hairline at the temples. What an idiot Henry must think she was! And hearing her awful singing as well!

Stella scrubbed at her face with a flannel, then rinsed her hair again with the shower-head, washing every trace of the hair and face-masks away. Then she slapped some moisturiser on with a hand that trembled with agitation, applied some make-up with special attention to her red nose, added a touch of mascara and a sheen of lipstick. Then she combed her hair, slipped into the jeans she had been wearing earlier and a fresh T-shirt and went back into the lounge.

Henry was sitting at one end of the sofa while Teddy sat at his feet looking up at him adoringly. Amber sat at the other end, her face mirroring Teddy's expression of admiration.

"Ah," Henry looked at Stella appraisingly as she came back into the room, "you looked just as nice before."

Bastard! Stella felt herself prickle with annoyance. What an idiot he must have thought she looked, in her tattered dressing-gown with her face all smeared! Now he was laughing at her. Somehow, whenever she was around this man, she seemed to make a fool of herself.

Amber leapt from the sofa as if it was suddenly burning hot. "Excuse me," she simpered. "Early night, I've got an important interview in the morning. You sit here, Stella." Amber indicated the vacant end of the sofa, like a sycophantic waiter guiding a tetchy client to the best seat.

Stella sat down unwillingly as if she were at the dentist for a filling without an aesthetic.

Amber sidled towards her bedroom door, ignoring her friend's alarmed expression.

Stella didn't want to be left alone with Henry. He

made her feel uncomfortable, gawky, as if her arms and legs were too big for her body and she had little control of them. And she didn't like the way that her eyes strayed, as if by their own volition, to gaze at the contours of his body or the planes of his face.

"It was very kind of you to find Teddy for us and bring him back."

"Glad to be able to help," grinned Henry. "Um . . . you and I seem to have got off on the wrong foot . . ." He looked around the room as if he were afraid to meet Stella's eyes. "Maybe we could be friends now."

"Sure," Stella shrugged.

"Would you like to come for a drink then?"

"Errrm . . . well . . . OK," Stella replied, caught completely off guard.

"Now," Henry said. It was a statement, rather than a question.

Stella opened her mouth to protest and then closed it. What if Rory was sitting outside again in his car? She hated the thought of another scene out in the street. But Henry had been very kind to bring the dog back – at the very least she owed it to him to be friendly. Just because he was scruffy and smelt of horses didn't mean that he wasn't a nice person. They *had* got off on the wrong foot. And maybe she was too sensitive about being laughed at.

And just because she was looking for a millionaire and would never, not in a million years, *ever* entertain a relationship with someone like him – that didn't mean that she couldn't go out for a friendly drink with him.

"I'll get my coat." She got up, went into her bedroom and pulled her coat out of the wardrobe. One quick drink couldn't hurt.

"Are you going out with him?" hissed Amber, her face alight, slipping into the room a moment later.

"Yes," Stella said slowly, annoyed with herself to find that she was standing in front of her mirror, reapplying her lipstick and for some reason adding a squirt of perfume behind her ears.

Amber did a war dance around the room. "Wonderful! He's really lovely!" she hissed.

"No, he's not!" Stella snapped.

Amber gave a snort of amusement. "Oh yes, he is. And from the way he was looking at you I'd say that he's crazy about you."

"Well, he's wasting his time!"

Amber pulled a face and sniggered knowingly but to Stella it was not a laughing matter. She had to protect herself, make sure that she never ended up scratching a living, struggling to make ends meet like her mother had. She simply had to marry someone who had some money, to protect her own future.

At least when Stella emerged from the apartment a few minutes later with Henry, there was no sign of Rory. Hopefully, he had got bored with the endless waiting in the car, then the fruitless running alongside her begging forgiveness.

Henry opened the door of his rusting Jeep to let Stella in. She noticed that this time the floor was clean of the mass of newspapers that had littered it last time.

"There's a pub just down here, isn't there?" he asked, gesturing down the road as he turned on the engine.

"Yes!" Stella yelled above the rattling that was coming from the bodywork of the Jeep. She grinned in spite of herself. Henry was such gentle easy company. It was a pleasure to be with him after her tense relationship with Rory where she had to watch everything that she said for fear he would get jealous again.

* * *

Henry pushed his way to the bar while Stella found a seat and tried to regain some of her hearing which she was sure had been damaged by the noisy vehicle. Henry returned with two drinks and sat down beside her, grinning as he clinked his glass against hers. "Here's to friendship!"

Stella took a sip of her drink, then started as her phone shrilled in her pocket. Her stomach tightened itself into a knot of tension as she fumbled for the phone, its ringing loud in the half-empty bar.

"Stella?" Rory was crying, his voice coming out in pitiful gulps.

Stella swallowed hard, feeling Henry's eyes on her.

"Please come out with me, just once more. I miss y–"

Stella snapped off the phone. The less she spoke to Rory, the sooner he'd understand that she wouldn't have anything more to do with him.

A second later the phone rang again. Angrily she snatched it up. She'd have to turn it off altogether if he didn't stop ringing, but somehow she was afraid to. Just in case Amber needed to phone her. With Rory sitting outside the apartment so often, the two girls were afraid of what he might do if he lost his temper again, and they had taken to having their phones with them at all times in case one of them needed help.

"Yes!" Stella snapped into the mouthpiece, and then almost dropped the phone in shock as a voice came through that she really didn't expect.

Her mother, Irene.

"Stella," she said in her soft Mayo accent, "is that you?"

20

Stella pulled a wry face at Henry by way of apology for taking the phone call when they were chatting. She moved to the doorway, where it was quieter, so that she could hear her mother above the hum of noise from the pub.

"Stella, can you hear me?" her mother shouted. She was extremely nervous of using the phone, still regarding it as some newfangled piece of equipment, even in these days when there were computers and microwaves and satellite TV even in the darkest recesses of the Mayo countryside.

"Yes, I'm here," Stella answered shortly. Chatting to her mother came second only to speaking to Rory in terms of undesirable phone calls. She kicked the toe of her shoe against a discarded cigarette packet, in annoyance.

"We really need you to come home!" Her mother's

voice was so loud that Stella could have heard it if she had lifted the phone right away from her ear at arm's length. Listening to her bellowed speech, Stella was instantly transported back to the small, cramped kitchen, with the ancient range that belched out smoke and covered all of the surfaces in a white powdery dust and the sink so old that the enamel was worn away in places. She could imagine her mother, in one of the awful, old-fashioned, shapeless dresses that she always wore, sitting beside the range, holding the phone as if she thought that it would bite her, while the rest of the family crammed along the sagging sofa playing games on their mobile phones and Game Boys.

"Yes, I will. Soon." Stella was irritated by the request. She would rather walk through fire than willingly go back to Mayo.

"Your dad is sick," Irene continued.

Stella closed her eyes, trying to blot out the words. Her father was always sick.

"It is serious," Irene persisted, ignoring the resentment implicit in Stella's silence. "When will you come home?" Her voice was so loud that a couple of men who had come out into the fresh air for a cigarette grinned in amusement.

Stella felt as if she were sixteen again, telling her parents that she was getting a job and leaving home. "I'm not sure – I'll have to see how things are at work." Stella glared at the men. "Bye," she whispered, terminating the call. She had no intention of going home if she could help it. She had escaped from her childhood, made a new life for herself in the city. An annual trip was enough.

Shoving her phone back into her pocket, Stella walked back into the warmth of the pub.

"Problems?" Henry asked as she sat back down at the table.

Stella shrugged in reply. "Just my mum asking me to go home – my dad is sick."

"Oh dear," Henry said sympathetically, gulping his drink down in one. "I guess you'll need to get straight back to the apartment then."

Stella shook her head. "No," she told him firmly, "I'm not going home."

"But if your dad is sick …" Henry drew his eyebrows together.

Stella sighed, shaking her head. "He's always sick – this is nothing new. *She* probably just wanted some excuse to get me to go there because I didn't go at Christmas."

"Don't you think that you should go?" Henry reached across the table and took Stella's hand gently.

His fingers were warm, strong and comforting. She let her hand remain in his.

"Where do they live?" he asked softly.

"*Mayo!*" Stella spat out the word. The very name made her shudder. The very mention of it brought back horrific memories of her childhood: the grinding poverty, the brooding mountains that seemed to hold her captive beneath their greying slopes, her mother always slaving away in the kitchen and around the yard, hauling in huge bags of turf – while her father stayed in bed, or shuffled grey-faced from the bedroom to the kitchen. "I'm not going," she asserted firmly.

Henry looked at her, his gentle eyes roving over her face. Stella looked away, gazing at the row of bottles above the bar. Henry couldn't understand how she felt, how she hated everything about home.

"You should go," he said gently. "Maybe there is something seriously wrong with your dad. You shouldn't cut yourself off from your family completely."

Stella bit her lip, anger bubbling deep within her. What made him think that he had the right to tell her what she should do?

"Just go for the weekend," he said. "Two days and then you can come back. It won't hurt you and it will keep them happy."

Stella took a sip of her drink. Maybe he had a point – at least, if she did make the trip to Mayo it would satisfy her mother, keep her off her back for another six months or so.

"You're probably right," Stella nodded her head. "I'll go this weekend, just for Saturday night."

"I could drive you over there. If you like ..." He smiled disarmingly. "You shouldn't risk taking your car – not since it broke down on you. I'd be quite happy to stay in a B&B somewhere. I'm not very busy with the horses at the moment since . . ." Rory's removal of his horses from Henry's yard went unspoken, but the memory of Rory's terrible tantrums hung heavily in the air.

"Fine." She felt as if she was being railroaded but at

least if he was going to drive then she could sleep for the journey, instead of having to look at the dreary mountains and miserable bogs.

* * *

As Stella closed the door to the apartment, Amber's head appeared around her bedroom door. "Just thought that I'd come in here in case you brought Henry back in for a coffee," she grinned, emerging from her bedroom and heading for the sofa where she snapped on the television.

"Glad that you didn't – I was just watching a really good film." She stretched herself along the length of the sofa, sighing with pleasure. Teddy scrambled up beside her and lay on his back with his head cradled in the crook of her arm, watching Stella warily through half closed eyes, in case she should shout at him to lie on the floor. When he realised that she was too distracted by her own thoughts to notice what he was doing, he closed his eyes, drifting immediately off into a twitching, whimpering sleep.

"Isn't Henry lovely? Fancy him going to all that trouble to bring Teddy back!" Amber grinned wickedly at Stella. "He's gorgeous, isn't he?"

"If you like that kind of thing," Stella said huffily. She wasn't going to admit to Amber how gorgeous she actually did find him. Amber would get all excited, thinking that there was a new relationship on the cards. And that wasn't possible.

"So, how did it go?" Amber asked, scratching Teddy's soft, hairless tummy.

"Great," muttered Stella sarcastically, throwing herself into the armchair. "I'm going to Mayo this weekend with him."

"What!" Amber exclaimed, sitting up so quickly that Teddy fell onto the floor. "You're a fast worker!"

"No, I'm not," snapped Stella, petulantly. "I don't even like Henry. He just offered to drive me, that's all. I have to go home. My dad is sick – as if that's anything new – but my mother is insisting."

"Don't like Henry!" Amber gave a cry of amusement. "Well, he's obviously mad about you. And you *do* fancy him! You go all pink every time you see him."

"Haven't you got a job interview in the morning?" snapped Stella, tight-lipped with annoyance. Henry *was* cute, but she seriously didn't fancy him. And as for going pink, it must have been a trick of the light.

*   *   *

True to his word, Henry arrived at the apartment on Saturday morning. Darting warning glances at Amber, willing her not to make any smart comments about them going away together for the weekend, Stella followed Henry outside to the Jeep. She glanced furtively up and down the road to see if Rory's car was parked on the street again. He had stayed away for days now and, if it hadn't been for the daily arrival of an enormous bouquet of flowers and the twice-daily phone calls pleading for forgiveness, she might have thought that he had got over her.

Amber watched from the window, grinning broadly. Stella studiously ignored her – she had heard enough of her silly comments about the lovely couple that they made and how they should watch out and not go strolling in the hay fields together.

Henry heaved her holdall into the back of the Jeep, beside his own ancient leather bag. The Jeep seemed to have acquired another layer of dirt since the last time she had seen it – and she was sure that the rust had spread.

"Let's go," Henry said above the groan of protest from the vehicle as he slammed the rear door.

Stella got gingerly into the passenger seat, relieved that she had worn her dark-coloured jeans and sweater. The inside was almost as dirty as the exterior. The engine fired reluctantly into life, accompanied by a worrying rattle that reverberated through the Jeep. Stella looked longingly at her own car, tucked neatly off the road in one of the parking spots reserved for the apartment residents. She must have been crazy to let Henry persuade her that *his* rusty heap of junk was more likely to make the journey to Mayo.

They began the journey, the Jeep heading resolutely west. There was little traffic. Everyone with any sense, mused Stella, was heading *into* the city to spend quality time wandering around the shops looking for lovely things to buy, instead of heading off into the back of beyond. As the dual carriageways ended and the narrow, winding potholed roads began Stella began to feel a dreadful sense of foreboding. She hated the countryside. She had grown up with undiluted countryside, in the middle of nowhere, miles from anywhere, and she hadn't liked it – one bit. Now she lived in the city, the centre of all things, close to everything – and that was how she liked it. Green fields stretched for miles at either side of the road, broken only by hedges and walls and endless herds of cattle and sheep. Not a shop in sight. The Jeep sped through tiny villages where grim clumps of houses seemed to huddle together for warmth against the incessant Atlantic gales. Henry peered over the stone walls and hedges.

"Isn't this beautiful?" he mused, jerking the steering as they headed towards the ditch after he'd spent too long gazing at the scenery instead of concentrating on the road.

Eventually they stopped for lunch in a small village café. Stella had been delighted at his offer to buy her lunch – she was starving – but eating in a hick town café, with plastic tablecloths and sauce in little packets wasn't quite what she had in mind.

She stalked haughtily into the café behind Henry.

He didn't seem to mind the café. He happily tucked into a vast plate of chips with a greasy sausage plonked unceremoniously on top by the fat woman who seemed to act as both chef and waitress. Of course, thought Stella, scanning the menu for Caesar salad, this was probably the type of place that he was used to. Someone like him had probably never dined anywhere even remotely nice. Eventually she settled for a cup of tea and a scone, telling Henry that she had eaten a huge breakfast.

They set off again. The sun, now beginning to drop into the west, hung above them like a beacon to mark the direction.

"I have to stop," Henry said, swinging the Jeep off the road into a lay-by. "This is all so beautiful." He turned off the engine, heaved open the Jeep door, got out and leant against the long square bonnet, gazing at the mountains.

Stella got out. She wasn't going to even look at the scenery – she hated the mountains, but she might as well stretch her legs.

"Look at that!" Henry breathed in an awestruck tone.

Stella looked. Below them in a green valley a long lake shimmered, mirroring the green and greys of the mountains that surrounded it and the cloudless blue sky above. And across the lake the mountains soared, timeless and majestic, clothed in a mantle of a thousand shades of green broken by glittering outcrops of granite. Stella looked at the brooding, forbidding slopes that had held her captive as a child.

"Beautiful," she admitted grudgingly.

*   *   *

It was the middle of the afternoon before they finally reached the village where Stella had grown up. Nothing much had changed in Abbeymoy. The wide streets were still empty, the inhabitants of the village sheltering inside behind twitching net curtains, gossiping about one another. The shops were still the same: the butcher's with its pathetic selection of meat displayed unimaginatively on silver platters and the general store with its age-old window dressing of faded boxes of breakfast cereal thrown together with plastic buckets and boxes of nails. Stella shivered in spite of the warmth of the Jeep. How she hated returning to Abbeymoy! The bitter memories of her childhood were too strong, too painful. The Jeep sped past the institution-cream walls of the small school that Stella had first attended, and then out onto the coast road.

"Not far now," Stella told Henry quietly as the familiar feeling of gloom and oppression seeped even deeper into her psyche.

"Fancy growing up around here!" Henry exclaimed as they reached the coast and the road turned westwards again, following the line of golden sand broken into small coves by the rocky headlands and the blue of the sea, the horizon mingling with the blue of the sky. "Lucky you!" He wound down the window, letting the salt tang of the air blow into the vehicle, masking the all-pervading odour of horse and dog.

"Here!" Stella pointed to a small laneway that wound between tumbledown stone walls. She had never brought anyone who knew her here. It would have been too embarrassing for them to see the hovel in which she grew up and the people who she belonged to. But Henry didn't matter – she couldn't have cared less what he thought about her. He lived in a hovel himself and probably had come from a similar background to hers. He wouldn't look down on her for her simple roots. The Jeep bumped along the potholed lane and then turned into the driveway of a small house. "This is it," Stella said quietly, hardly able to bring herself to look at the stark lines of the whitewashed cottage.

"OK, I'll come back for you tomorrow afternoon," Henry told her as she got out of the Jeep. He followed her out and handed her the holdall. "I'll head off and find somewhere to stay and explore." He seized her shoulders and planted a warm kiss on her cheek.

"Thanks." Stella took the bag from him. "See you then." She turned away. She didn't want him to come inside, at least not until she had seen just how tattered everything looked. Maybe if things didn't look too bad she would invite him in tomorrow. But not now.

She waited until the Jeep had driven away before she put her fingertips to her face. She could still feel the touch of his lips on her cheek. Slowly she made her way into the cottage. The door as always was open. She shoved it hard – the frame had warped, making it hard to open without a lot of force.

"Hello!" she called, wrinkling her nose as the smell of the turf fire hit her. Her footsteps echoed on the lino floor.

"Stella!" Irene dashed from the kitchen, where she had doubtless been hastily tidying up.

"Hello!" Stella kissed her mother on the cheek as Irene enfolded her in a joyous bear hug. She could smell the turf smoke in her mother's hair.

"You look lovely," Irene said, looking at Stella, holding up her hands in a gesture of admiration, before shyly smoothing the collar of Stella's suede jacket as if she were afraid that she had damaged it while she was hugging her daughter. "Will you have a cup of tea?" She laughed. "I don't have any of that cap-o-cheeno stuff that they're all drinking now! But I do have some fresh-baked scones – your favourites."

"Tea is fine." Stella wished that her mother would stop fussing over her.

Irene bustled around the kitchen as if this was a State Visit, stealing glances at her daughter as if she could not believe that she was really there. She kept up a stream of chatter, reporting local news that was of no interest to Stella and asking her questions she really didn't want to answer.

As soon as Stella had drained the last dregs of her too-milky tea and forced the last morsel of scone into her nervous stomach, Irene said "Come in to your dad – he's been looking forward to seeing you."

Stella followed her unwillingly down the corridor into the main bedroom.

Her father lay in the bed, dozing.

"Paddy!" Irene said softly.

His eyes opened briefly, closed and then opened

with a start, as if he couldn't believe what he was seeing. "Stella!" he exclaimed, his voice weak but still full of delight.

"Hello, Dad." Stella went slowly across the room and bent to kiss her father.

He had always been ill, for as long as she could remember, one sickness after another, but now he really did look terrible. His skin looked as if it was too big for his frame, hanging in yellow folds around his jawline and beneath the blankets his legs and arms looked stick-thin. This time there really was something seriously wrong with him.

21

Stella walked into the kitchen and sat down heavily beside the kitchen range. A fire burnt in the grate as it did every day, winter and summer. The fire was essential in the old cottage to warm the water. On the rare occasions that the weather was hot, every window and door had to be opened to let out the stifling heat. Today, despite the warmth of the air, Stella shivered, huddling beside the fire. She gasped for air, as if she had been suffocated in the bedroom where her father lay. She could only vaguely ever remember a time when her father had been healthy. She could vaguely picture him in a huge pair of fisherman's bright yellow over-trousers that covered his legs and ended somewhere up close to his chest, returning home in the first light of morning, from fishing trips up and down the Mayo coast.

Those memories were hazy. The predominant ones

were of him lying in bed, or sitting in a battered armchair beside the fire, yelling at them for making too much noise or to get him something.

His face had lit up when he had seen her sitting on the bed beside him. But she had recoiled from his touch, wanting to shake off his hand when he reached out and covered hers with his bony, icy cold one. It wasn't possible to forget all of the loathing she had felt for him for all of the years of her ruined childhood.

"What's wrong with Dad?" she asked, shaking her head as her mother offered her another cup of tea. Her stomach had twisted itself into a knot and there was a huge lump in her throat.

"Cancer," her mother whispered the word as if it were the most dreadful blasphemy. "Prostate . . ."

Stella watched her mother picking up the teapot and then putting it down again as if she was not sure what she should do with it. Suddenly Irene slumped down onto one of the low stools that the family used to sit around the table and buried her head in her hands, weeping silently. Cancer . . . the very word made Stella shiver. But surely nowadays it could be cured? Thousands of people got cancer – they had treatment and then they were all right again.

Stella got up and moved away from the warmth of the hearth. She pulled out a stool and sat beside her mother. "How bad is it?" she whispered, touching her mother gently on the arm. She could not say the dreadful word . . . cancer. That would only make it more real.

Irene lifted her head, gave a determined sniff and wiped her eyes with a tissue that she fished out of her apron pocket. "It's a stage four cancer . . . it's spread into the bones of his pelvis."

"Spread?" Stella whispered. "Why didn't it get noticed before?" She was filled with an indignant rage against her father – surely he must have noticed that something was wrong!

"He is always in so much pain anyway," Irene shrugged wearily, "so I suppose that masked any other signs."

"Is he . . ." Stella struggled to find the words, "is he going to live?" she blurted out finally. There was no easy way to deal with this. No polite language to ask the dreadful questions.

Her mother shrugged her narrow shoulders, playing distractedly with a fork that she had picked up off the table, turning it over and over in her rough, work-worn hands. "How can they know?" Irene stopped trying to dab away the tears and let them fall down her cheeks. "He starts radiotherapy next week and they say they'll get the pain under control, but who knows?"

The words hung heavily in the air.

Irene got up from the table, the fork clattering down as it fell from her fingers. Stella watched her walk from the room – her shoes were tattered, looking as if they were years old.

"I've put your bag into your old room," said Irene, returning a few moments later.

"Thanks." Stella felt a jolt of annoyance twist in her stomach. Why did her mother feel that she had to do everything? Could she not have left the bag in the hallway for Stella to move herself? "I'll just go down to the room. I want to change my shoes." She got up and went down to the bedroom she had once shared with her sister. Mary still slept in the room. Stella's old bed lay in the corner, untouched, the familiar faded quilt still covering it.

She changed her shoes, then sat down heavily on the bed and stared at her surroundings: the lino floor, so dreadfully cold on winter mornings, and the bare, soulless walls. Now, though, a modern DVD player and computer sat on a table beside the window. Everything was so familiar, and yet so dreadfully alien. It was as if she had never been away, the familiar sense of being trapped in a world that she didn't belong in was so strong. She wished that she could just go away again. And never come back. She had tried so hard to escape from her family, turn her back on the grinding poverty she had grown up with.

The door slammed and the sound of voices filled the silence of the house. Her brothers had returned. Dragging herself unwillingly off the bed, Stella went towards the sound of their voices.

Her two brothers were sprawled on the sagging sofa. Patrick, the oldest, sat with a cigarette tucked between his lips, smoking it without removing it from his mouth. Seamus, his unruly hair covered in dust from some plastering he had been doing for someone, had his head buried in the newspaper.

"Hi." Stella stood in the doorway, looking at them both. She loathed the pair of them. Big and uncouth, they were a world away from the kind of men that she now mixed with. Once they had all been friends, when they were very young, but then she had changed, seen that there was more to life than living in a hovel in the wilderness, more to life than scraping a living from fishing, waiting all the time for the brutal, merciless sea to claim their lives.

"How ya doing?" asked Seamus, bending down to unfasten his boots, which their mother removed and put beside the hearth.

"Fine," Stella said tightly, sitting down beside the fire, struggling for something else to say. She hadn't a thing in common with any of them any more – their lives were so far apart.

It was easier when she came home at Christmas. Then they were able to return to the easy rapport they had enjoyed as children when it had seemed that it was the four of them against the rest of the world. The cottage was usually busy, filled with a constant stream of visitors piling into the house to eat chunks of brown bread and drink the poteen that one of the neighbours brought regularly for their father.

At those times the cottage would be filled with the sound of laughter and merriment. It was almost easy to forget the usual tense silence that hung in the air, as their father, short-tempered with pain, chastised them for making too much noise.

Mary came back later. She was fatter than ever, her enormous thighs squeezed into a tight pair of bright red leggings.

"How's life in the big city?" she asked Stella amiably.

Mary always reminded Stella of a cow – she had that peaceful bovine quality, as if she were happy to let life drift by her, needing nothing more than regular food and company. She pulled out a stool from beneath the table and sat down, her wide bottom spilling over the edge of the seat. She seized a slice of brown bread, spread butter thickly on it and began to chomp happily, looking at Stella as if she were some alien creature she had just discovered in the kitchen.

"Great," Stella replied.

That exhausted all of their conversation.

After dinner the lads melted away from the room to go to the pub. Stella heard the sound of their car engine dying away in the silent night air. Mary disappeared to her bedroom to mess around on the computer.

"Your dad would love you to sit with him," her mother said gently, handing Stella yet another cup of tea.

Stella stood up hesitantly, and went unwillingly down to the bedroom.

Her father was asleep, his breathing faint and shallow, for a moment his pain erased. Stella sat down in the armchair beside him. She watched his still form in the pale glow of the bedside light. His face was relaxed, the harsh lines that normally scored his cheeks smoothed away, and Stella could picture him as the handsome man she had so loved when she was a child, before he had become bent and angry with pain. After a while, when he did not wake, she slid quietly from the room, guilt at leaving him alone mingling with the relief at not having to talk to him.

*   *   *

Henry came back the following afternoon. Stella fought the urge to stand outside with her bag packed, waiting for him to come and rescue her and take her back to Dublin. Every hour seemed to drag. Mary's soft bovine snoring had kept her awake half the night and then she had woken with a jolt when Patrick and Seamus had roared back up the lane in their noisy car, returning from the pub. She had gone to Mass the next morning, sitting in the pew with the rest of the family, trying to ignore the curious stares of the locals who would no doubt be speculating about the kind of life she led in the wild city. And then she had sat with her mother beside the sleeping form of her father, making polite, stilted conversation about the weather and her job, anything other than mentioning cancer and death. If it hadn't been so sad she would have laughed at the improbability of the situation. Chatting about how little it rained in the city compared with on the coastline, sitting beside a man who was dying, who she might never have the chance to talk to again.

Stella never thought that she would ever be

delighted to see Henry Murphy, but when the sound of his Jeep could be heard rattling up the lane, she breathed an audible sigh of relief. Soon she would be out of here, heading back home. Back to the city where she belonged. She invited Henry inside, because it would have been rude to do otherwise. He fussed over her mother, telling her how nice the house was and what a lovely spot it was built in. He might have been royalty for all of the fuss her mother made of him. She embarrassed Stella dreadfully by telling him how pleased she was that Stella had found such a nice man. Stella cringed yet again, especially when Henry put his arm around her shoulder and told her mother that he had every intention of looking after her.

Even her brothers and Mary came out of their shells in his presence. Patrick and Seamus chatted happily about their souped-up car and Mary told him about the latest game that she could play on her computer.

"I'd love to see the beach," Henry said later, after they had drunk numerous cups of tea and listened to her mother, who had bloomed under the beam of sunlight from Henry, rambling about the flowers that she intended to grow in her bare patch of garden.

Unwillingly Stella got up. She didn't want to stay a moment longer than she had to, but it would be rude to refuse Henry.

*   *   *

Henry walked alongside Stella up the beach, their

shoes crunching on the golden sand. It was nice to be out of the gloomy atmosphere of the house, away from her mother flapping around everyone like a nervous, flustered hen, and away from her rough, uncouth, siblings with their country ways. The tide was out and the beach stretched for miles ahead of them. High above on the grassy headland was a patchwork of small fields bordered by grey stone walls, each presided over by an identical small whitewashed cottage and the newer, sprawling bungalows built as second homes by wealthy foreigners and city dwellers. The bungalows looked incongruous beside the ancient cottages – too new and tidy, with neat gardens of low shrubs especially selected by garden designers to withstand the Atlantic storms of harsh winds and salty air. The gardens contrasted sharply with those of the old cottages, where every inch of grass was used to feed cattle or the inhabitants, neat rows of earth heaped up into potato rows alongside enormous cabbage heads and the lacy leaves of carrot plants.

"Let's sit here," Henry said, guiding Stella towards a long, low flat stone that nestled in a sheltered curve in the rocks.

Years ago the rock had been used as a picnic table when they had been young. Stella remembered summer holidays spent on the beach, spreading out their simple lunch of home-made brown bread and strong cheese made by one of the local farmers. Long days where she had played with her brothers and sisters on the sand, bored, longing to be able to visit the city, to head off to the zoo, or to a holiday camp like the others at school did. They spent their days teasing the city children who came to holiday at the nearby town and who headed out to 'their' beach in expensive cars with proper picnic sets and beach chairs. And then when they got older, the long rock had been a famous spot for bringing a boyfriend or girlfriend to, perfect for romantic liaisons, hidden from the prying eyes of the village.

Henry stared out to sea. Today it was cooler. Instead of the tropical blue of the hot days, the sea was a myriad shades of green which mingled with the white heads of the waves. Far into the distance the sea blurred to become part of the horizon, blending in with the grey of the gathering clouds. Stella recognised the signs in the sea, a skill learnt through a childhood spent listening to the men who made their living trying to harvest lobsters from the ocean. They sat in silence, Stella wishing that Henry would hurry up and have enough of looking at the scenery, drinking in the beauty of the sea ringed by the tall mountains. She wanted to get back to the city, back to pavements and traffic, back to reality.

"You should try to make things up between you and your dad," said Henry, picking up a small stone and lobbing it down the beach.

Stella shook her head. "I can't," she whispered, bowing her head so that Henry wouldn't see her tears as she mourned her lost childhhod.

A dreadful guilt gripped her like a clinging briar. She wished she had been able to say what she felt to her father, rather than the ridiculous stunted small talk that had passed for communication between them. But somehow she hadn't been able to find the words. It was hard to frame the words when she did not know what they were herself. He had made her childhood a misery, with his short temper and seeming lack of interest in anything other than sitting beside the fire. And yet somewhere at the back of her mind she remembered a different man, a gentler, good-humoured man who had laughed and played with them all. She had loved that man.

22

Amber slammed a plateful of brown bread down on the tray. She hadn't got the time to be playing nursemaid to her mother. Kenny had phoned her the night before asking if she could come over and look after her mother. She was sick in bed, supposedly too ill to get up, and Ronnie had to go to work and since Kenny knew that Amber wasn't working, then there was nothing to stop her coming over to help. She slammed down a mug of tea next to the brown bread, not caring that the hot liquid slopped out over the edge. This was totally unfair. She hardly had a penny to her name. She was desperately trying to get a job and Kenny had now got her playing nursemaid to her mother.

She sighed bitterly. She hated Kenny, loathed him, totally and utterly. He could have helped her to get a new job if he had wanted to – he had tons of friends who ran businesses around the city. Instead all he could come up with was some dreadful, sordid suggestion about 'bed-testing'. He was cruel and nasty. And then when there was a problem, it was Amber who had to go and pick up the pieces. It was always Amber they turned to, she thought bitterly, picking up the tray and carrying it upstairs. It hadn't seemed important to them that she had barely enough money to cover her bus fare to make the journey to her mother's house. They didn't care about that. They didn't care that for the second month running Stella had let her off paying the rent on the apartment. They didn't care that Stella was becoming increasingly tetchy about Amber eating her food. Her sarcastic comments about Amber having no money and how difficult it must be to find work were becoming less and less of a joke. And they certainly didn't care about the nasty letters that Amber was getting from the credit-card companies about non-payment of her bills and the extra interest they were charging her. No – all they cared about was using her, for their own interests.

Amber walked slowly up the stairs to her mother's room and pushed open the bedroom door with her toe.

Ruby lay curled beneath the pretty flowered duvet, her hair spread out on the pillow, her face relaxed in sleep. She looked like a teenager, and certainly didn't look ill.

"I've brought you some breakfast," Amber said, slamming the tray down on the dressing-table with as much force as she dared. Ruby stirred slowly, unfolding and stretching upwards, finally opening her eyes to stare at Amber.

"Oh," she said in a voice thick with disappointment, "I thought for a minute that you were Georgina come back." She sank back against the pillows, looking for all the world like a heroine in a period drama on the television. "I've left messages on her phone to say that I'm sick – she can't be so heartless and unfeeling as to stay away!"

Amber twisted her lips into a bitter smile. "Sorry to disappoint you, but I was the best that Kenny could get." She gestured towards the tray. "I've brought you some breakfast," she repeated. Then, trying, but failing to keep the sarcasm out of her voice, she asked: "Do you think you can manage to eat anything?"

"I'll try," her mother said in a pitiful little-girl whine. "I've had no appetite since Georgina upset me so much. My stomach is in knots."

Amber pushed the pillows up behind her back and straightened the duvet around her legs.

"I have no strength to do anything," Ruby moaned weakly, as Amber laid the tray on her knees. "My nerves are terrible." She picked up one of the slices of brown bread, as if she struggled to lift its huge weight, and then wolfed down the whole slice in a few hungry bites.

Amber clenched her teeth and stared out of the window through the lace curtains at the identical row of houses over the road. She would scream in temper if she looked at her mother.

There was absolutely nothing wrong with Ruby. Just

a severe case of play-acting for sympathy, hoping that this charade would make Georgina come back. No doubt Ronnie had been despatched to the house to tell Georgina how sick their mother was, since leaving a message on her mobile phone hadn't worked. Amber hoped that she would take no notice.

"Will you manage to get up later, do you think?" Amber asked, pretending to be concerned about her mother's alleged illness.

"Oh," Ruby sighed, swallowing another mouthful of brown bread, "I don't know. Maybe. I might try to come downstairs and lie on the sofa under a blanket."

And I could fan you and feed you grapes, thought Amber, watching the mug of tea disappear as quickly as the bread.

"Could you manage to eat anything else?" she then asked sweetly as she lifted the tray.

"No, I've no appetite." Ruby slumped back onto the pillows and drew the quilt around her shoulders with a dramatic shudder.

Amber shook her head – she would hate to see what her mother could eat when she *did* have an appetite. "Maybe you'll feel well enough to get up when *Fair City* is on?" Amber curled her foot around the door to pull it open.

"I'll try," came the weak reply.

Amber stamped back downstairs. Her bloody mother ought to get a part in the soap for the performance she was putting on. Amber glanced at herself in the mirror that hung in the hallway, shaking her head in annoyance at her reflection. How could she let herself be used by her mother and Kenny? Why had she not said 'Sorry, but I cannot come over. I have important things to do. Like finding a job.' Instead, they only had to snap their fingers and she jumped to attention.

She went back into the kitchen, filled with self-loathing. How could she let herself be used? Why was she not stronger? Kenny hated her – he had always made that obvious. She wasn't part of the little family that he had created with Ruby and his children. Amber had never been part of that little unit. Kenny didn't care if she was starving out on the street as long as he could use her when he wanted to make his life easier. And that of her mother.

Everything was Kenny's fault, Amber thought, snapping on the kettle to make herself a cup of coffee. If he wasn't around then her mother would have to stand on her own feet. He had strung her mother along for years, *and* his own wife, living a double life, with two families. Amber despised her mother for letting Kenny treat her like a convenience. She knew that Kenny had another wife and another life somewhere else and yet she accepted it. But you could bet your life that the other family knew nothing about *their* existence. Amber wondered what his wife would think if she knew that he was playing house with another family. You could bet that *she* wouldn't accept it. They had seemed so happy when Amber had seen them walking together in the park. It wasn't fair that he was using her mother, wasting her time, wasting her life with no future to offer her. If only he would go and leave them alone.

And that was the moment when Amber decided. Kenny really would have to go. If his wife knew about her mother's existence . . .

He arrived later on during the afternoon. Amber was running the iron aggressively over one of Ronnie's shirts when she heard the sound of Kenny's big car purring down the street.

"Hey, how's it going?" he said a few moments later, opening the front door with his own key.

"Fine, thanks," Amber replied tightly, and then watched resentfully as he took off his coat, threw it over the banister and ran lightly up the stairs to her mother's room. Amber turned off the iron and folded up the ironing board, listening to the sound of laughter and voices that drifted down from the bedroom. Her mother couldn't be very sick if she was well enough to make jokes with her boyfriend.

A thought struck her. She turned back and looked into the hallway, to where Kenny had thrown his coat. There was an envelope sticking out of his pocket. An electricity bill – she recognised the logo on the corner that jutted out. That would have Kenny's address on it. Amber could find out where he lived when he wasn't here, messing up her life. Amber took a stride towards the coat, her heart pounding. Then she stopped. She couldn't bring herself to look at the envelope.

She turned away.

"Amber, bring us up some tea, will you?" Kenny

roared jovially downstairs. Something exploded deep within Amber. She was sick of Kenny! Sick of the way that he treated her as if she were of no importance whatsoever. She shot out into the hall and slid her hand into the pocket. Her fingers closed around the cool paper of an envelope. She pulled it out. He lived in the best part of the city – of course, she thought angrily, shoving the envelope back into his pocket.

Later her mother came downstairs and stretched out weakly on the sofa, while Kenny tucked a tartan rug around her legs.

"Maybe I could manage a cup of tea and a slice of toast." She smiled faintly in Amber's direction. "With plenty of butter and some of that nice jam!" she called as her daughter headed into the kitchen.

"Do you think that you'll be well enough to come to the cinema at the weekend?" Amber heard Kenny ask Ruby.

She shoved the kitchen door shut viciously, certain that she would thump her mother if she had to listen to any more of her playing at being ill.

"I expect you'll stay here the night to make sure your mum is OK," Kenny said a little later, watching lovingly as Ruby tucked into her third slice of toast and jam.

Amber nodded resentfully in agreement. She didn't want to be here at all; she wanted to be back in her own life at the apartment with Stella and Teddy, trying to find a job and get things back on track, not playing unpaid skivvy to her mother and her lover.

Stella would be upset that Amber wasn't around. She was nervous enough with Rory hanging around the apartment, making his awful pleading phone calls. And now there was trouble in Mayo – her father was really sick. Amber should be with *her* – that was where her priorities lay, not with Kenny and her mother who were just taking advantage of her.

* * *

Amber slept fitfully in the strange bed, listening for her mother waking periodically and demanding attention like a spoilt child. She woke just as the first streaks of dawn light crept into the room through a gap in the bedroom curtains and knew that she had to do something to get rid of Kenny. He was the cause of all of the problems. Without him her mother would have time for her family again, rather than running around after someone who was using her as a convenience.

Unable to bear staying in bed any longer, now that her mind was made up, Amber got up. She made tea for Ronnie and took it in to him to wake him up. He grunted ungratefully as she snapped on the bedroom light and put the tea mug down on the bedside table.

Then she made breakfast for her mother, while Ronnie stamped around upstairs, getting ready for work.

Finally, grunting a farewell, he went out, slamming the door behind him.

Amber made her own breakfast. She was surprised

at how hungry she felt. But with a job like the one she had to do today she would need all the strength that she could muster. Then she made toast and tea for her mother and took it upstairs to her.

"Oh, it's still a bit early," Ruby complained, blinking like a mole as she emerged from under the quilt.

"Sorry but I have to go and do the shopping, otherwise there'll be nothing for you to eat," Amber said dumping the tray down on her mother's legs. "I'll take some money out of your purse." And then, before her mother could protest, she fled back down the stairs, grabbed her mother's purse from the sideboard and dashed out the front door before she lost her nerve.

It was an easy journey – plenty of buses ran out from the city to the exclusive residential area where Kenny lived his other life. Amber supposed this was to make sure that the exclusive residents of the exclusive residential area didn't have to be bothered standing for ages waiting for buses to take them into the city to their exclusive jobs, or to spend their packets of money. Even the buses seemed nicer than the ones that ran out from the city to her mother's home. They were cleaner and more modern and the drivers were far more polite, waiting patiently while she fumbled in her mother's purse for the correct change, instead of slamming the doors and leaving you to struggle to stand upright as the bus lurched along while you counted out the money.

The bus driver, as she had asked him to, told her the right place to get off and even gave her directions to

Larch Avenue, bidding her a cheery goodbye as she climbed down onto the immaculate pavement. Watching the bus disappear along the tree-lined road, Amber felt her courage desert her. Perhaps this wasn't such a good idea. But then, as she had come this far, she forced herself to set off in the direction of Kenny's house. The streets were deserted. Enormous, tall detached houses stood at either side of the road, all bordered by tall walls and iron railings behind which she caught glimpses of immaculate gardens, overflowing with flowers and smooth acres of lawn.

Finally she turned a corner into Larch Avenue. She licked her lips – her mouth felt as dry as if she had been walking for days across a desert, and her heart pounded uncomfortably in her chest. She could just walk past the house, just look at where he lived with his other family. She didn't have to *do* anything. The houses here were larger than the others, real mansions of red brick, with wide expanses of glass conservatories beside them – one even had a swimming pool, covered by a huge glass dome. Amber stopped to stare at the sheer opulence of the place from behind the tall, ornate iron gates, designed to keep out unwanted visitors. Above her head was a number, emblazoned on a sign, decorated with flowers entwined with hearts. Amber's heart stopped. *This* was Kenny's house. She stared at the house, filled with a mixture of rage and jealousy. How could he mess around with her mother when he had a home here? She started as the huge iron gates suddenly gave an expensive-sounding clunk and then slid back silently. A large, brand-new and very shiny silver estate car passed by and slid through the gates. The woman driver cast a look down her nose at Amber, as if she was a beggar envying her position in life. Fear and uncertainty were replaced by a jealous rage in Amber. How dare the woman look down her long nose at her, as if she was a piece of dirt! She slipped through the open gates and marched up the sleek tarmac drive in the wake of the car.

The car stopped and Amber drew level with it.

The woman let down the car window a fraction. "This is a private house," she snapped, a tinge of fear in her voice,

Amber glared at her, taking in the beautifully highlighted blonde hair, her youthful complexion, her long elegant white fingers topped with neatly done nails fearfully clutching the steering wheel, her expensive clothes – and wanted above anything else to hurt her, to see the façade of wealth crumble as she saw her life disintegrate into the sham it was.

"I think there is something that you should know about your husband," Amber said softly.

23

Amber saw countless emotions flash across the woman's face, like on one of the hologram toys in a cereal box that looks one way and then, when you move it, the light catches it and the picture is different. Her mouth opened and then closed again and the fingers relaxed and then clutched at the steering wheel again.

"What?" she exclaimed. Her eyes were very blue, fear and confusion dancing within their depths.

"He's deceiving you," said Amber, watching confusion clear to terrible realisation in the other woman's eyes.

Kenny's wife was staring wordlessly at her, waiting for her to go on.

Then Amber's courage deserted her. The terrible anger evaporated and she just gaped at the woman, groping for words, suddenly aware of the appalling thing she had done.

Then she turned and fled back down the drive, running as fast as she could, feeling the hard surface of the pavement jarring her ankles, and listening to her own breath coming in short, jagged gasps.

She glanced back over her shoulder, as if she expected to see Kenny's wife pounding along the pavement after her, but there was no one. She unbolted a small side gate and rushed through it.

A bus was coming down the road.

She tore across the road to the bus stop and shoved out her hand. A moment later she sank into a seat at the back of the bus and watched the beautiful residential houses slide by the window as the bus drove out of the exclusive area and headed towards the city once more.

The whole day seemed to have taken on an unreal quality, as if she had dreamed the whole thing. Surely she couldn't have really gone to Kenny's house and told his wife that he was having an affair? Kenny would kill her if he knew what she had done. What was it she had said? "There is something that you should know about your husband." And something about him deceiving her. Then she had fled. The woman would probably think that she was some lunatic and take no notice of what she had said. Hopefully.

She was so wound up that she missed her stop and had to walk miles back to the shop to get something for them to eat for dinner.

*   *   *

Kenny was at the house when Amber returned. His big car sprawled in its usual place, half on the pavement and half on the road. Amber faltered halfway down the street to the house. What if Kenny's wife had already told him about her visit from a madwoman? There was no choice, though – she had to go in and face the music. Amber pushed open the front door and went inside, half expecting a bellowed roar of temper from Kenny, but there was only the low hum of noise from the television. Amber took off her coat, hung it up and went into the lounge. Kenny and her mother were on the sofa. Her mother, tucked into her blanket, looking every inch the wilting heroine in a Victorian novel, lay with her head on Kenny's lap.

"There you are," complained Kenny. "I thought that we'd have to send out a search party for you."

"I had to do some shopping." Amber heaved the bags through into the kitchen. "Good," Kenny's voice carried down the hall. "Make your mum something to eat then, will you? I've got to get off – I'll be back later."

In the kitchen Amber sat down heavily on one of the chairs, her legs suddenly feeling as if they couldn't support her any longer.

She could imagine Kenny's big car cruising up the sleek drive, him easing his bulk out of the car and going towards the house, then the blonde woman rushing to meet him, demanding to know what it was that she should know about her husband, describing the girl who had come to see her that day . . .

What on earth had possessed her to go to Kenny's

house? She let out an involuntary whimper of fear. Why had she been so stupid? Why could she not have just let things alone? She ran her hands through her hair in a distracted gesture. How on earth was she going to get out of this pickle? Finally she decided that there was no way out. She had to stay and face the music, wait until Kenny returned and see if he demanded to know why she had been at his house that afternoon. She boiled some eggs for her mother and made more toast, then carried them into the living room.

"Here's something to eat." Amber laid the eggcups down on the small coffee table and pulled it closer to her mother.

Ruby sat up and eagerly began to knock at the shells of the eggs.

"How do you feel now?" Amber asked, hoping it sounded as if she meant it.

"Terrible," answered her mother, taking a mouthful of boiled egg. "I'm as weak as a kitten – I have no strength, no energy . . ." Her voice, filled with self-pity, trailed off.

"Will I take you to the doctor's tomorrow?" asked Amber, watching her mother over the rim of her teacup.

"No!" Ruby shuddered. "No. I don't need a doctor, I just need Georgina to come back and stop messing around. It's she's making me ill. Moving in with that man. He's old enough to be her father."

Amber gave a snort of exasperation and quickly turned it into a cough when her mother looked at her sharply.

"I'm going to ring Stella," she told her mother, going back into the kitchen, grabbing her mobile phone out of her handbag and punching in Stella's number.

"When are you coming back?" Stella asked peevishly. "Rory's been hanging around the apartment again and I hate being on my own."

Amber sighed. Now Stella was pulling at her heartstrings. Everyone wanted Amber to be with them, to nurse them and protect them, but there was no one looking after Amber. She listened miserably to Stella recounting the story of Rory waiting for her when she returned from work, hanging onto her coat sleeve while she was yelling at him to let her go, all of the time pleading with her to give him another chance. One of the neighbours had come out eventually and told him to clear off. Now she was scared of being alone.

"I can't come back tonight," Amber told her. "My mum's still not well. Maybe tomorrow."

"Fine!" snapped Stella, resentfully. "Teddy misses you terribly." Then she added maliciously, "How is the job-hunting going?" The fact that Stella had paid the whole rent on the apartment for two months now and also had given Amber money to help her out lay before them, like a huge block in their friendship.

Unspoken resentment festered between them.

The front door opened. "I've got to go," Amber yelped, snapping off her phone and dropping it on the floor as Kenny came in.

"You're a bundle of nerves!" Kenny grinned as he threw a large carton-filled paper bag down on the table.

"Chinese, to tempt your mum. Do you want some?"

Amber nodded bleakly. Her throat felt so tight that she was sure that she wouldn't be able to swallow anything.

"Don't worry. I'm sure she'll be fine," he said gently, interpreting her nerves as worry about her mother, not sheer panic about the terrible trouble she was certain she had unleashed.

On autopilot Amber got knives and forks out of the drawer and plates out of the cupboard. Why had she tried to hurt them? How could she have been so stupid? She had longed for Ruby and Kenny to split up. Anything to stop her mother giving all of her love and affection to him and maybe turn a little of it in her children's direction. But now she wasn't so sure that she wanted to be responsible for splitting them up.

The front door banged again and Ronnie bounded into the kitchen, kicking off his enormous runners and dumping his lunch box down on the worktop.

"I bet that you don't want any of this Chinese?" Kenny said, waving the bag in Ronnie's direction.

"Nah," Ronnie joked, lunging for the bag and attempting to wrestle it from Kenny. "Come on," Kenny said, cuffing Ronnie affectionately around the head, "your mother is about to starve to death." He dumped the bag back onto the table and began to unpack the cartons, tipping the various dishes onto plates. He looked so totally at home, it was hard to imagine that he had another life with a wife in his big fancy house, thought Amber, wiping grease from the kitchen table.

They carried the plates into the living room and sat in front of the television to eat. Ruby tucked into hers with a voracious appetite. Not bad for someone who is supposed to be at death's door, thought Amber. Tomorrow she really did have to go back to her own apartment, pick up the threads of her life and make a real attempt to find another job.

Amber started as someone banged on the front door.

"You lot are bloody popular tonight," growled Kenny jovially, glaring in the direction of the door.

"I'll go," sighed Ronnie, levering his bulk out of the armchair.

Amber stared blindly at the television screen. The picture swam out of focus. She knew instinctively, without even seeing who was at the door, that the time had come. Above the background hum of noise from the television, all of Amber's senses focused on the sound of the voices from out in the hall, loud as if they were magnified, though Kenny and her mother were oblivious to them.

Amber could hear every creak of the door as it swung open, even hear the rush of the night air as it blew into the hall, Ronnie's exclamation of surprise and a woman's voice, hissing with anger, Ronnie's bellowed "Oyyy? Where the fuck do you think you're going?". And then, just as she had imagined, the blonde woman burst into the living room.

She stopped in the doorway, as if she had been jerked to a halt by a rope that she had reached the end of. Her pretty face was frozen in shock, as if she was surprised to actually see what she had hoped she wouldn't see. There, sitting on a sofa, in front of a television was her husband, with another woman's head resting in his lap.

The world seemed to stop. Outside Amber could hear the voices of a gang of youths, laughing as they walked past the house, but inside the scene was frozen, like a television screen when the film breaks down. Ronnie, his face like thunder, standing in the doorway, stunned as he realised who the woman was. Kenny, his expression like that of a guilty child who has been caught pinching chocolate bars, looking slowly from his wife to his mistress, caught like a rat in a trap. And her mother, who for the first time, in all of the days of her supposed sickness, for once looked genuinely ill, her face grey with fright.

The woman took a stride forwards, standing uncertainly as if, now that she had proof of what she had suspected, she didn't quite know what to do with the dreadful knowledge she had just gained.

"Someone told me that there was something that I didn't know about my husband," the blonde said. Her voice was quiet, composed, although Amber could see that she was trembling like a leaf. "I thought that I knew everything." She shook her head in disbelief. "All about how hard he worked. All about how much he loved me." She looked at Kenny, her face closed and impenetrable, lost in her own world of private pain. Then she looked at Ruby, taking in a woman years older than she was, half as attractive, her hair lank around her face from days of being in bed. "He's supposed to be meeting an architect now to discuss putting a gym room next to the swimming pool at our home. I felt stupid following him. I thought I was making a fool of myself. I didn't really believe . . . this." Her eyes locked onto Ruby's, who then looked away guiltily. Then she stood uncertainly in the room, as if she had just realised where she was. Her eyes roved around, no doubt taking in the awful, cheap décor, the simple house that had become her husband's bolthole.

Then in an awful moment of clarity, she looked straight at Amber. The light of recognition shone in her eyes.

"Hello again," she said, smiling tightly. "Thank you for enlightening me about my husband." She was speaking in a tight, polite voice – she might as well have been thanking her for giving up a seat on a bus.

Amber was silent, unable to speak, her mouth dry with shock and fear. She saw her mother's eyes turn towards her, and beyond her Kenny's eyes, filled with shock and loathing.

"I'll show myself out," the blonde said as politely as if she had just come on a visit, and then she walked gracefully, head held high, out of the room.

Kenny stood up, shaking off her mother in his haste. Amber could smell the raw fear emitting from him.

"Adèle!" he cried desperately, plunging from the room in the wake of his wife. A second later through the open door came the sound of a car, screeching off at top speed and then the dull roar of Kenny's vehicle as it roared off in pursuit.

There was a silence, so thick and heavy that it seemed to fill the room, making it impossible to breathe. Ronnie moved slowly into the hall, closed the front door and then came back and sat down heavily, leaning his arms on the table and shaking his head as if he couldn't believe what he had just witnessed.

Their mother struggled to her feet, fighting to free herself from the blanket which seemed to have entangled itself around her, trapping her in its soft folds. She leapt across the room to stand face to face with Amber, her skin ghostly white, her eyes blazing with a terrifying fury.

"You stupid bitch!" she spat, as her legs crumpled beneath her and she slowly slid to the floor. "Get away from here and never come back!"

24

Stella handed Amber another tissue.

Amber blew her nose loudly and wiped her swollen, red eyes miserably. "Oh, how could I have been so stupid?" she wailed fretfully. "Why did I have to go to Kenny's house and stir things up?"

Stella sighed. She wished that Amber would stop wallowing in self-pity and give her time to think. There were so many thoughts whirling around in her mind, so many memories, half-forgotten feelings that she wanted to put into perspective. She needed time to be alone, to gather her thoughts, to think about her relationship with her father.

Even Teddy looked fed up with hearing Amber wailing. He lay in his basket, his small head resting on his paws, his round, black button eyes peering miserably out from behind their curtain of shaggy hair, his ears clamped sadly to his head.

"Kenny and Mum have split up now," Amber looked imploringly at Stella, as if she could forgive her for her actions, "and it was all my fault!"

Stella gritted her teeth – she had heard this twice already.

"He won't see Mum again and she's in bits!"

Stella picked up the shredded, damp tissue that Amber had discarded and threw it into the bin. There was nothing that Amber could do to turn back the clock – she should just start to get on with her own life again. She had to leave Kenny and his wife and her mother to sort out their own mess. Sooner or later, his wife was bound to have found out about them, no matter how long they'd been together. Maybe Amber had done her mother a favour. Now at least she wouldn't have to waste any more time on a married man. And it was time that Amber sorted herself out and got herself a job instead of expecting Stella to always be there to pick up the pieces.

The phone rang. Stella snatched it up eagerly – even listening to Rory sobbing on the phone about how sorry he was for all that he had done to ruin their relationship had to be an improvement on listening to Amber's story over and over again.

"Hello," Stella said in the cold, impatient voice she reserved for calls she assumed were Rory.

"Stella, it's Henry."

Stella felt a warm glow spreading slowly upwards from her belly, radiating heat. "Oh! Hello!" Stella heard the pitch of her voice change. Her voice seemed to think that she was delighted to hear from him, while her brain certainly wasn't. Now what did he want?

Amber had stopped crying and was looking at her, amusement dancing at the corners of her puffy, red eyes.

"I've been thinking about you. I know that you must be worried about your dad," he was burbling, the words spilling out as if his mouth couldn't get them out quickly enough. "I thought that maybe you would like to go out tonight. Maybe for dinner. Take your mind off things."

Stella's brain cringed at the thought of spending another evening with him. Her brain shrieked *"No!"* but before she could frame the word her mouth had said, "Yes, thanks."

"Great! I'll see you about eight."

Stella put down the phone with a sigh. What had she let herself in for? Why had she not said no? It was stupid to give him any encouragement.

"Was that Henry?" grinned Amber, her misery forgotten.

"Yes," Stella mumbled. "I've just told him that I'll go out for dinner."

"Great stuff."

"It isn't great stuff at all," sighed Stella. "It's terrible. Why the hell did I say yes?"

At just before eight o'clock the buzzer sounded to announce that Henry was downstairs.

Amber dashed to the intercom before Stella had the chance to get to it. "Come up!" she said.

Stella sat on the sofa, rubbing Teddy's soft ears, listening to the sound of Henry's footsteps coming towards the door.

"You look lovely," mouthed Amber, standing ready to open the door.

Stella sighed. The last thing that she had wanted to do was to look lovely – she had wanted to look ordinary as if going out with Henry was of no importance whatsoever. She had put on her oldest jeans and a top that she hated, with only a minimal slick of make-up and yet when she'd looked in the mirror she seemed to glow with life.

The footsteps stopped outside the front door, but before he could knock, Amber opened it. "Come in," she breathed, simpering shamelessly at him.

"Hello, Amber," said Henry but his eyes were already on Stella. "Stella!"

Teddy abandoned Stella and hurtled across the room, bounding up and down to get attention from Henry.

"He loves you too," Amber smirked.

Henry bent to pet the little dog. "Are you ready then, Stella?" he asked, as tongue-tied as a youth on a first date.

Stella gazed at the dog who was winding himself around Henry's legs, giving small cries of delight. She stole a furtive look at Henry and was horrified to find that he looked as gorgeous as usual. However could she fancy him so much? She was only ever attracted to sharply dressed men in dark suits and crispy cotton shirts with elegant silk ties and brightly polished shoes.

It just wasn't *possible* that her heart could be fluttering so much at a man dressed in a baggy pair of cords and a shapeless hacking jacket, from which she could smell the unmistakeable odour of horse. And his hair needed cutting.

He was too attractive and too unsuitable and she just couldn't go out with him . . . on her own . . .

She stood up and reached for her handbag.

"It's OK if we bring Amber with us, isn't it?" she said. It was a statement, not a question.

Henry looked completely taken aback.

"No . . ." Amber began to protest.

"Nonsense," Stella told her. "Get your coat!"

"But I don't −"

"Amber − you need a night out, take your mind off things."

Amber went uncertainly to get the coat.

"She's had a terrible time recently," Stella told Henry firmly.

"Fine," Henry said, looking bemused and disappointed.

They left the apartment and walked out to Henry's Jeep. Rory's car was parked behind it. He got out of his car as they approached.

"Stella," Rory said softly.

"Go away, Rory!" said Stella, her voice quavering slightly.

"Leave her alone!" snapped Henry.

"It's OK," Stella said softly, putting her arm on Henry's.

"Come back to me, Stella!" Rory's voice rose to a plaintive whine.

"No," Stella said firmly.

Henry unlocked the Jeep and they got in.

"Stella!" Rory cried, the note of desperation loud in his voice.

"Oh God!" breathed Amber as the Jeep pulled away, leaving Rory standing in the road watching them. "Why don't you get the Guards to sort him out?"

Stella shook her head sadly. "He's just very sorry about what he did. I don't want to make things worse for him by getting them involved. He'll get fed up sooner or later."

Henry shook his head angrily. "He's a raving nutcase. I think he's bloody dangerous. You should do something about him. I'm worried that he'll hurt you." He seized Stella's hand and grasped her fingers for a few moments until she shook his hand away without replying.

"Are you OK back there?" he called over his shoulder to Amber, who was perched on a pile of horse rugs. Fortunately they were new, still wrapped in their plastic covers and so didn't smell of horse, but the plastic was slippery and every time Henry went around a corner Amber found herself sliding further and further off her makeshift seat. She began to wish that she hadn't come. It was awful to have to play gooseberry. But Stella had really wanted her to come, as if she were afraid of what might happen if she was alone with Henry. Amber sat in the back of the Jeep and watched the two of them together, making stilted conversation, as if they were afraid of each other.

Henry led the way into the restaurant. He had a table booked. A third place setting was quickly laid out for Amber, who sat down, feeling more like a gooseberry than ever in the intimate surroundings of the dimly lit restaurant.

"Menu, madam."

Amber glanced up to take the menu and felt her mouth drop open. The waiter was absolutely gorgeous.

"And for you, sir." He almost knocked over Henry's wineglass as he returned Amber's fixed gaze.

"Paul?" Henry exclaimed, looking quizzically at the waiter. "Paul Kennedy?"

The waiter tore his eyes away from Amber. "Henry Murphy!" He gave an exclamation of recognition and shook Henry's hand.

"Well, Paul, this is amazing" Henry grinned. "How are things? I knew you weren't racing much any more, but didn't know what you were doing . . ." his voice trailed off.

Paul sighed. "I wasn't getting the rides any more, so I've had to find something to do to earn a living." He gave a wry wave of his hand to indicate the restaurant. "Got too cocky, missed rides, didn't respect the trainers, usual stuff." He sighed again. "Got too successful too quickly and couldn't handle it."

"Ah," Henry said sympathetically.

"That's how it goes," Paul said chirpily, handing a menu to Stella. "I'll be back to take your order in a while," he assumed his waiter role, "but would you like a drink now?"

"We'll decide in a while," Stella told Paul – she was the only one of them not dumbstruck by his surprise appearance.

"Well, fancy that," Henry mused, watching Paul walk away.

I do, very much, thought Amber, also watching Paul walk away. He had the smallest, neatest butt that she had ever seen.

"He used to be one of the best young jockeys," Henry said, dragging his eyes towards the menu. "I'd wondered what had happened to him."

Racing *again*, thought Stella, glaring at her menu, wishing that she hadn't come out. She should have stayed at home and rung her mother to see how things were with her father.

They ordered their food and then sat, waiting, making stilted conversation, lost in their own separate worlds.

When the food arrived Amber could barely eat. Her stomach seemed to have been filled with butterflies. She toyed helplessly with a beautifully cooked steak, while Stella pushed a heap of Caesar salad around her plate.

"Could you pass the pepper, please?" said Stella.

Henry handed Stella the tall wooden pepper pot, his fingers brushing hers. She jerked her hand away as if his fingers were red hot and had burnt hers.

Paul returned to the table. "Is everything all right for

you?" he asked, his dark eyes meeting Amber's.

"Fine thanks," Stella told him.

Amber seemed beyond speech.

Eventually, when their plates were cleared away and they sat sipping hot, strong coffee Paul came, coffee mug in hand, and pulled up a chair. "Mind if I join you?"

"Not at all," grinned Henry, shifting his chair around slightly to make room.

"I can take a break, now that the restaurant is almost empty," Paul explained.

"Great."

Amber was gazing at Paul, her face flushed.

"You seem to be doing well with the horses," Paul said to Henry.

Stella raised her eyes to the ceiling. Horses – that was all they could talk about.

"I've a great chaser at the moment," Henry told Paul. "She's called Hollyberry. I think that she could be a Grand National horse – she's just getting better from a nasty virus that laid her low for a good while. But when she's on form . . ."

Stella looked at Amber, intending to shake her head in annoyance at the boring conversation, but Amber was lost, gazing misty-eyed at Paul.

"I haven't really been able to find the right jockey for her – she takes some riding. "Maybe you'd come and have a look at her?"

"I'd love to."

The conversation droned on. Eventually the other

waiters began to cast annoyed glances at Paul for taking so much time out.

"I'd better go," Paul grinned, standing up and draining his coffee cup in one gulp, his eyes locking onto Amber's.

"So had we," Henry glanced at his watch. "It's getting late."

He paid the bill and the three of them walked out into the cold night air, Amber dragging herself away from the restaurant on feet that seemed to be made of lead. If only she had been brave enough to ask Paul for his phone number, or slipped hers into his hand! He had clearly fancied her as much as she had fancied him. How could she have missed out on such an opportunity? It wasn't as if gorgeous men came along every moment.

As they reached the Jeep, Henry suddenly gave an exclamation of annoyance. "Blast!" he said reaching in his pocket and pulling out a business card. "I forgot to give this to Paul." His eyes twinkled as he turned to Amber. "Amber, would you mind running back with it for me?"

Amber gave a cry of delight and flung herself at Henry. She seized the business card out of his hand and ran hell for leather back towards the restaurant.

25

Amber glared at her reflection in the mirror. "Bloody hell," she grumbled. The yellow dress she had picked out was completely wrong. It was gorgeous. That was the problem. The pale yellow fabric clung to the contours of her body, flaring gently out from her hips, skimming gently over her flat belly, the tiny, spaghetti-thin straps showed off the creamy skin of her shoulders. She looked gorgeous in it. But . . . there was no way she could wear it for a first date with Paul. It was too nice. Damn. She wriggled her arm around her back to tug down the zip and let the dress slide down over her hips. If only Stella were here, she would know exactly what Amber should wear. She might even suggest some casually elegant outfit from her own wardrobe. But she had headed off to Mayo, alone. Her father had taken a turn for the worse. She had been tearful but composed when she had driven away. Amber knew that she longed to make up with her father, to heal the rifts between them before he died, but she hadn't been able to bring herself to say the words to him.

Amber gazed longingly at Stella's bedroom door – she would have loved to have gone in and found something to wear, but after the fiasco with the lovely red dress she didn't dare. She had got away with it the last time, but she might not be so lucky again. Throwing the yellow dress on her bed, Amber opened her wardrobe door again and peered hopefully inside.

"What am I bothering for?" Amber asked Teddy, who sat on the bed watching her. Teddy cocked his head to one side, as if he were considering her words.

"He's probably just like all the other bloody men anyway. Use 'em and lose 'em. That's the motto men go by!" She shifted clothes from side to side as she looked.

Teddy sighed and lay down on the bed, resting his head in his paws as he watched her.

"He probably won't even turn up." Amber pulled a pair of jeans from the bottom of the wardrobe. "These will do." She threw them onto the bed and pulled out a top to go with them. "I'm not going to go to any effort," she grumbled, pulling the jeans on. "Don't want to make a show of myself while I'm being stood up."

She stood in front of the mirror again and gave a groan of frustration. Even if he did stand her up or even if he *did* turn up but turned out to be a complete bastard, there was no way she could go out dressed like a tramp.

"You choose," she said to Teddy, pulling off the jeans

and slumping down onto the bed beside him. The little dog gave a whimper of pleasure and wriggled onto his back, waving his legs in the air, hoping to get his belly scratched. Amber tickled the soft, hairless skin of his belly. "OK," she sighed, a moment later, "third time lucky." She pulled a pair of black trousers out of the wardrobe and a simple turquoise shirt. "This really will have to do." She changed into the new outfit, applied a touch of mascara and lipstick and then smiled at her reflection. "Perfect," she grinned.

* * *

Of course there was no sign of Paul outside the pub. And Amber was, as usual, deliberately nearly ten minutes late. A crowd hovered around the doorway, smoking furiously in the cool evening air. Amber searched the faces. No, no Paul.

Well, what had she expected? Had she really thought he would be there waiting for her? Still though, her heart sank with disappointment.

But maybe he was inside. She went into the pub.

The pub was crowded, the hum of noise unbearably loud after the relative silence of the pavement. Amber moved through the drinkers, glancing around to see if Paul was at the bar or sitting down at a table. No sign. He hadn't come. He had stood her up, just like all of the others that she had got involved with. Men were such cruel bastards. They built you up, made you think that they liked you and then they dumped you. Often before they even had a chance to get to know you. Amber turned around and began to walk back out of the pub. She might as well go home – there was no point in hanging around here. A man was coming in through the door as she reached it – she could see his outline in the frosted glass. She stood back to let him pass as the door swung open, her eyes downcast, feeling battered with misery. She watched a pair of smart shoes stop in front of her, topped by a trendy pair of jeans covering long legs.

"Amber?" a voice asked.

Amber looked up "Paul!" She couldn't believe it. He had come. To meet *her.*

"You weren't leaving, were you?" he asked, smiling.

"Yes, I was. I was going home," Amber replied, feeling as if she were living in a dream. In her mind she had made him into the ultimate male bastard and now he was here. He had turned up. "I thought you weren't coming," she muttered.

"I said that I would come, didn't I?" he said huffily, leading her towards the bar. "What sort of bastard did you think I was?"

Amber looked at him, tongue-tied.

"What do you want to drink?" he said shortly.

"Coke." The whole evening was ruined now. She'd got into a temper because she thought he wasn't coming. And now he'd got into a temper because she'd thought he wasn't coming. It was impossible to win.

Paul bought them both drinks and carried them to

an empty table. They sat in stony silence.

"How could you think that I wasn't coming?" he asked at last, crossly, playing distractedly with a beer mat. "I was a little late and I apologise for that – but surely you should have realised something might have delayed me."

"You weren't here. I just thought that you wouldn't bother coming."

Paul shook his head in disbelief. "That I wouldn't bother! But I *told* you I would be here. I wouldn't just not turn up without a serious reason." He took a long swig of his lager. "Could you not see how much I fancied you the other evening?"

Amber sipped her drink and looked miserably around the pub. She had ruined the evening. "I really did think that you wouldn't come. Used to being stood up, I guess," she shrugged.

Paul grinned suddenly, his face softening. "You can't be serious! Anyone that stands you up must be stupid or something!"

"I've met a lot of stupid men," Amber said softly and then smiled and the dreadful atmosphere that had existed between them vanished like a morning mist as the sunshine breaks through.

The evening flew by, with Amber barely noticing the ebb and flow of people around the pub. She and Paul were lost in a world of their own, talking about their lives, their hopes for the future, their likes and dislikes. Paul had grown up in Kildare, surrounded by racing yards and horses. He was terrible at school, he told her with a hollow laugh of regret, always sneaking off to go to the races with one or another of the trainers. And then when he'd left school the racing yards were the only option, especially when he had no ambition to do anything else. He told her about starting to ride, learning to race, the success that came too early, before he could handle it. Told her with candour about how he had earned too much money, driven a fast car, thought that he was the best, thought that he was indispensable. He had shaken his head wryly at the memory. And then, when he became far too cocky, no one wanted him. There were other jockeys just as good who were reliable and nicer to the trainers and owners. And then no one would give him rides and he had fallen quickly from grace – the world that had put him on a pedestal had kicked it out from under his feet.

Amber told him with equal candour about her gross stupidity in going around to Kenny's home. How she had wanted to hurt them all. And how she had succeeded and how now she had lost everyone.

"We'd better go," Paul said suddenly, as the barman whipped their empty glasses from the table.

Amber stood up. She felt as if she had unburdened her soul talking to him. He seemed to understand how she felt, without condemning her for her actions.

The pavement was deserted, all of the smokers having long since headed off home or to the chippy.

"I'll walk you home," Paul said, taking her hand.

Happily Amber entwined her fingers around his. They walked silently through the empty streets – there didn't seem to be any need to fill the silence with mindless chatter. Amber resented every footstep that took them closer to home, closer to the moment when he would say goodbye and vanish into the night.

"This is where I live," she said, halting outside the apartment block.

"I don't want to leave you," Paul said huskily. Gently he entwined his fingers in her hair and drew her face towards his. For a long moment they stood, face to face, breathing in the same air, feeling the warmth from each other's skin and then, with infinite slowness and tenderness Paul gently lowered his lips onto Amber's. He slid his arm around her back, drawing her closer to him, so that every inch of their bodies touched.

"Now I really don't want to leave you," he whispered, when they finally came up for air.

"Don't then." Amber touched his face softly as if she couldn't believe that he was real.

"OK then, you've twisted my arm," he grinned, taking her hand again and leading her in the direction of the apartment.

"Night," one of the residents said as they passed on the stairs.

"Night," Amber said shortly. Now everyone would know that she had brought a man back for the night.

Amber put her key into the apartment door, a bolt of regret shooting through her. She had vowed never to be used by a man again. Never to sleep with someone just because she fancied them. And now here she was again, putting herself straight back into that position.

Paul seemed to sense her hesitancy for he pushed open the door and led her inside, shoved the door shut and very tenderly began to kiss her once more.

Amber felt all of her hesitancy vanish. She knew that she would probably regret this in the morning. Paul would vanish. How could any man respect a woman who slept with him on the first date? But then maybe he would have vanished anyway and she would never have seen him again. She might as well enjoy herself. Amber leant back against the living room wall, letting Paul kiss her, feeling his hands roving all over her body, while she kissed him back with equal passion.

Then suddenly Teddy exploded towards them, barking furiously at the strange shapes that were moving around in the dark.

"Bloody hell, what's *that?*" Paul laughed as Amber switched on the light to pacify the small dog.

"It's OK, Teddy!" She picked up the terrier, cradling him in her arms, while his tail wagged furiously, his face filled with embarrassment at having barked at one of his own family.

"I'm getting jealous of all the attention you're giving that dog," Paul said huskily, taking Teddy out of Amber's arms and placing him gently onto the floor. "Show me where the bedroom is."

Taking his hand, Amber led him into her room.

Much later, when all was silent, Teddy pushed open the bedroom door with his nose and padded quietly towards the bed. Amber and Paul lay entwined in each other's arms, their bodies covered only by the sheet that

Paul had pulled over them before they had finally collapsed with exhaustion. Teddy jumped up onto the bed, looking disdainfully at Paul. Then, with a sigh of pleasure, he curled up in the small of Amber's back and went to sleep.

*   *   *

"Paul," Amber moaned, as she woke to feel him covering the back of her neck in warm, wet kisses. She turned and then gave a cry of disgust. Teddy lay beside her on his side, licking her neck.

Paul lay beside her, sleeping. Her cry woke him and he stirred, reaching for her and pulling her into his arms. Teddy slunk guiltily away, landing with a thud as he jumped off the bed. Amber saw him glance back regretfully as he slid out of the doorway. Amber stared at the ceiling as Paul began to doze again. She had done it *again*. She had vowed that she would never sleep with a man on a first date again and she had. How easy he must think her! He would wake in a while and make some excuse to leave and then she would never see him again.

As if he could sense her thoughts Paul stirred again, sighing with pleasure as he slowly began the ascent into wakefulness.

"Hey," he said softly, propping himself up on one elbow, "you look gorgeous in the morning."

Amber wriggled out of his grip. What was the point of prolonging this? She might as well let him get up and head off – that was probably what he wanted to do anyway – he would just be looking for an excuse to leave.

"I'll make some tea," she said.

"Come back here!" He pulled Amber back towards him and pinned her to the bed, covering her face in kisses until she giggled helplessly. Then he began to kiss her more slowly, his lips covering hers hungrily.

"I'd better go," he moaned, a long time later. "I'm supposed to be working at lunch-time."

"Right," said Amber, her heart sinking. She prepared herself for the usual see-you-around-then brush-off. In a moment he would swing himself out of bed, pull on his clothes and then say those immortal words. She lay on the bed and watched as he dressed, trying to memorise the strong lines of his back, the muscles on his thighs and the way that the hairs on his forearms were standing up in the cool air.

Finally dressed, he sat down on the bed, pulled her towards him and whispered, "I can't wait to see you again. Would you come out with me again tonight?"

26

Amber did a war dance of victory around the apartment after she had dressed that evening. This time things were going to turn out all right! Paul was a genuine nice guy. He wanted to see her again – tonight! He had kissed her goodbye that morning as if he didn't want to ever let her go. Amber stopped jumping around and checked her reflection in the mirror. Tonight she was wearing the yellow dress that she had discarded the previous evening as being too dressy. It was perfect for the evening. The pale yellow looked gorgeous against her skin. She seemed to glow with happiness, her eyes dancing with delight, and her curly dark hair looking like a sexy cloud around her face, rather than its usual wiry frizz.

Stella had rung from Mayo. Her father's condition hadn't changed – she was going to stay a bit longer. She had sounded tired and miserable, her voice distant as if she were a million miles away, not just over a hundred.

And so, taking advantage of her absence, Amber had decided to cook dinner for Paul. Not that it was going to be much of a dinner. She had found some pasta in the cupboard and some mince in the freezer and had plundered a bottle of red wine from the store that Stella thought she had hidden. Hopefully she would be able to replace it before Stella came back. But the apartment was empty and what was the point of sitting talking in a pub, when they could be alone together?

The whole day had gone brilliantly. Filled with happiness, Amber had set off into town once Paul had left for work. Life suddenly seemed very good, full of hope for the future. Even the mountain of debt that she was buried under didn't seem quite so big. She had wandered into one of the shopping centres and gone into the supermarket – maybe there would be work there that would be OK until something better came along. As on those perfect days when nothing can go wrong, she had seen a notice that they were looking for staff, the supervisor was available to interview her and a few minutes later she was walking out with a bright blue nylon overall under her arm and instructions to start in a few days' time. It wasn't the career of the century, but it would certainly do for a while – and there was the added bonus that when she had been there for a while she would get discount on the clothes that the supermarket sold. Amber had wandered around the clothes section with her overall tucked under her arm, picking out a new lilac skirt and top that she would buy with her first week's wages. It would be wonderful to be able to shop again. And, of course, to pay off the credit cards.

Amber glanced at the clock. Paul had said that he would be here at eight – it was almost that now. Filled with nervous energy, she flitted around the room, brushing an imaginary crease out of the tablecloth, straightening a fork that had gone out of line.

Teddy padded around the room, getting under Amber's feet, wondering why she wasn't paying him any attention.

"Teddy, get in your basket," she ordered finally, so filled with nervous energy that she felt as if she were about to burst. The spaghetti was almost cooked and the mince, into which she had tipped a bottle of pasta sauce, simmered fragrantly on the stove. Everything was perfect.

The doorbell rang and Amber danced to the intercom and turned it on.

"Hello," she whispered huskily into the mouthpiece.

"Amber?" Ronnie's thick accent reverberated through the room. "What's the matter with you? Have you got a cold or something?"

"Ronnie?" Amber yelped in surprise. "What do you want?" The last time she had seen her brother he had been standing in the living room of their mother's house, glaring at her as if he wanted to kill her.

"It's Mum."

Amber could hear the raw anxiety in his voice.

"She really is ill this time. You've got to come. I don't

know what to do with her."

Amber leant her head against the cool wall, "Oh fuck," she breathed, banging her fist against the door in frustration. Everything had been so perfect for this evening. Slowly she straightened up, glaring decisively at the intercom. This time she would let them sort themselves out. It was time her family stood on their own feet. Her mother had made it clear the last time that she wasn't welcome ever again. And now that there was a problem, it was her that they came running to again. She would tell Ronnie that she wasn't going to come.

"Ronnie," she said firmly into the mouthpiece.

He grunted in reply.

"Ronnie . . ." she said again. "Hang on. I'll be down in a minute."

Cursing her own stupidity, she turned off the cooker. What was she doing? How could she be such a walkover? Then, filled with regret, she went to the phone, found the number of the restaurant and dialled it.

"I'm trying to get in touch with one of your waiters, Paul –" She couldn't remember his surname.

"He's not here. Off for the night," came back the curt reply and then the phone went dead.

"I know that," Amber growled. "I wanted a mobile number for him."

She picked up her handbag. Maybe Paul would be outside when she went downstairs. She could tell him then that she had to go to her mother's. He would understand. She went out, slamming the door behind her and ran down the stairs.

Ronnie was leaning against the outside door. "Come on," he growled, "hurry up!" Amber looked hopefully up and down the pavement, but there was no sign of Paul.

"I'm expecting someone," Amber snapped. Paul had to be here any moment, and then she could explain to him.

"For fuck's sake come on, will you?" Ronnie shoved his hand under Amber's elbow and propelled her towards the car. He virtually manhandled her in and slammed the door.

Shit, shit, thought Amber, why had she not thought to leave a note on the door for Paul? Now he would come and find no one in. What on earth would he think? Obviously that she wasn't interested in him. Ronnie gunned the car into life and headed off with screaming car tyres.

Halfway down the road, Amber saw Paul. He was walking towards the apartment, a big bunch of flowers in his hand and a bottle of wine under his arm.

"Stop, Ronnie!" she yelled, clutching his arm. "I need to talk to this man!"

"No time," hissed Ronnie, jerking the car into a higher gear and accelerating.

Paul looked at the car as it sped past, attracted by the screaming engine. For one long, terrible moment his eyes locked onto Amber's and then the car had passed him and sped onwards.

Amber let out a whimper of despair. "Oh, no!" she wailed. Paul had just seen her in Ronnie's car – now, not only would he think she was a pushover who would sleep with someone on a first date, but he'd think she was a two-timing slut as well!

Ronnie sped down the back roads, cutting through narrow alleyways and rutted lanes to their mother's house.

"What's wrong with her *this* time?" Amber snapped.

Ronnie slowed the car fractionally so that he could talk to her. "Kenny's gone and she can't cope – she's in bits – I can't get any sense out of her at all."

"But she can never cope!" Amber moaned. She was sick of her family. The whole lot of them, they were ruining her life.

"She really can't cope this time." Ronnie shot across a main road and onto another back road. "She's done nothing but cry for days. Now she's just sitting there, whimpering. I just don't bloody know what to do with her."

Amber swallowed hard, suddenly overcome with guilt. After all, she was the cause of all the upset – it was she who had caused the break-up. It had been what she wanted, but now she wasn't so sure.

"But, Ronnie," she protested, "I caused the break-up. I told Kenny's wife. Mum won't want me within a million miles of her. She told me that."

Ronnie shrugged, glancing in his rear-view mirror at a Garda patrol car that was heading in the opposite direction. "Well, I can't do anything with her. You caused it all. You'll have to sort it out."

The house was in darkness when they drew up outside.

"Mum!" called Ronnie, turning his key in the front door lock and pushing the door open. He dashed inside, punching the light switches, flooding the house with light as he darted from room to room.

Amber stood in the hallway, uncertain of what to do, now scared of the devastation that she had caused.

"Mum!" Ronnie called again, pushing past Amber and thundering upstairs. "Mum, where are – "

Amber heard him stop abruptly.

"Oh, there you are!"

He had found her.

She found that her knees were trembling and that she had stopped breathing in panic. For a moment she had thought that maybe their mother had killed herself, or hurt herself somehow.

"She's here!" Ronnie appeared at the top of the stairs, his face greyish-white in the harsh glow of the hall light.

Amber walked up the stairs, like someone going to the gallows, dreading the reception she was going to get from her mother. Ruby had been so violently furious the last time she had seen her.

Amber walked into Ruby's bedroom. It seemed like a lifetime since she had been here before, nursing her mother through her imaginary illness, the nervous tantrum because Georgina had left. Had that only been a few days ago?

Her mother lay in bed, a shrunken shape beneath the duvet, her eyes staring blankly at the wall.

"Mum?" Amber was suddenly afraid of her mother's condition. It was as if she wasn't really there at all. Slowly her eyes turned to Amber who could see the pain behind them as her mother tried to focus and then realised who was there.

"Amber," she whispered wearily. All the life and hatred had gone from her.

"I'm here," Amber whispered, crouching beside the bed and stroking her mother's hair. "I'm sorry. I didn't mean to hurt you. I just wanted to get back at Kenny for not helping me find a job."

Her mother struggled to sit up. She gave a small hollow laugh. "She would have found out one day anyway, I suppose." Tears began to flow unchecked down her sunken cheeks. "It was just that I'd got so used to having him around. He meant the world to me. I can't believe that he's gone. That I'll never see him again."

Amber put her hand across her mouth to stop herself from crying out. It was hard to witness the devastation that she had caused.

"I'm so sorry," she whispered, sitting on the bed. Her mother looked such a tiny, frail figure, her fingers twisting a corner of the sheets in desperation. "Did you speak to Kenny?"

Ruby shook her head. "He must want it to be over. He'll stay with his *wife!*" She spat the word 'wife' as if it were an awful taste on her tongue.

"How can you know that?" Amber asked, watching her mother struggling to keep her composure.

Ruby shrugged. "I just do," she sighed, lying back against the pillows as if she had given up on life.

Amber went back downstairs. Ronnie sat in front of the television, oblivious to her. Amber looked at him angrily. He could have looked after their mother himself, but he just hadn't wanted to bother.

The phone rang. Ronnie ignored it completely. Amber snatched it up.

"Hello?"

There was a stunned silence from the end of the phone, and then a voice said, "Amber? You stupid cow!"

It was Kenny.

"How could you have been so dumb as to go round to my house? Didn't you think about the trouble that it would cause?"

Amber was silent, horrified at her own stupidity.

"Let me speak to your mum." He sounded furious with her, his voice full of hatred. Amber turned to shout for her mother, but she was already beside her. She snatched the phone from Amber's hand.

"Kenny," she breathed, "Kenny!"

Amber shook her head wryly. The affair was about to start up again.

*   *   *

"Drop me here," Amber told Ronnie as they reached

the end of the road that led to the apartment. "I want to walk, get a bit of fresh air."

Ronnie swerved the car in to the pavement and revved the engine impatiently while Amber scrambled out.

"See ya," he nodded as she slammed the door, then shoving the car into gear he sped off, the engine roaring in protest as he pushed it to full revs before changing gear.

Amber stood on the pavement, listening to the sound of the car growing fainter and fainter. Slowly she turned and began to walk towards the apartment, her legs feeling as if they were too heavy to move, each stride an enormous effort. She felt as if all of her energy had been sucked out of her and replaced by a strength-sapping numbness.

After a few strides she could go no further and she sank miserably down on a low wall in front of a house and began to weep bitterly. Tonight should have been so different. It was meant to have been the start of her new life with a new boyfriend and a new job. Except that the new relationship had never been given a chance to blossom. Now she was alone *again*.

Amber stood up. She'd better go home. She could cry in bed – at least there she would be warm! She rounded the corner of the road and turned towards the apartment. And then her stride faltered.

A vagrant was sitting in the doorway of the apartment. That was all she needed. It was too dark to make out the man clearly. It certainly wasn't Rory – he always sat in the comfort of his car while he did his stalking. Lounging on the front doorstep wasn't his style. Fear crept slowly over Amber, making her heart pound. How was she going to get into the apartment past the man? The road was deserted. What if he attacked her? She stopped walking, waiting hesitantly, unsure of what she should do.

The dark shape unfolded itself and stood up. Her heart pounded.

"Amber?" said a familiar voice.

"Paul!" Amber yelled, and ran headlong into his outstretched arms.

27

Stella wondered if it would be rude to shove cotton wool in her ears to block out the sound of Amber's awful singing. Ever since Stella had arrived home from Mayo, it had been like living with a banshee. Amber couldn't sit still – she leapt around the apartment, singing tunelessly, bursting with excitement at having finally found what she told Stella was the love of her life. As Amber launched into a fresh burst of 'You're the Love of my Life', Teddy looked balefully at Stella.

Stella was finding it hard to tolerate Amber's noisy cheerfulness. She needed rest and quiet to recover from the trip and the grim experience of her father's illness. Despite his pain, Paddy was clinging to life with a grim determination.

"I think he may make it," the doctor had told them. "He doesn't seem quite ready to go."

'*Go.*'

Stella had glared at the doctor. Why could he not say 'die'? Why were they all so afraid to mention the word?

She had come home. There didn't seem to be any point in sitting around the house wishing she could pluck up the courage to go and tell her father that she loved him and that she wanted to put all of the bad feelings behind them . . . in case . . . *it* happened.

Now Amber's exuberance grated on her nerves. She was so full of life and happiness. She was even delighted about the new job that she'd got. In a supermarket checkout for heaven's sake! She had no ambition whatsoever.

The phone rang. Amber stopped in mid-shriek and bounded across the room.

No doubt it would be the waiter on the other end and then the two of them would spend hours talking gooey rubbish to each other.

"Hello!" Amber snatched up the phone, her voice full of excitement. "Oh," the note of excitement died, abruptly, "Henry. Do you want to talk to Stella?"

Stella shook her head, waving her arms at the door and pointing to indicate that Amber should tell Henry she was out.

"Here she is," grinned Amber, holding the receiver in Stella's direction.

"No," mouthed Stella, glaring furiously at Amber.

"She's just coming," Amber said again into the receiver.

With a face like thunder, Stella snatched the receiver out of Amber's hand.

"Hello," she said, trying to sound icily polite and failing miserably. She glimpsed Amber grinning at her and dropped her hand quickly – she had automatically been smoothing her hair as she spoke to Henry.

"Stella!" She could hear the naked delight in his voice. "How are things out in Mayo?"

"He's doing OK," she answered briefly.

Henry was always kind and thoughtful. Rory never even gave her past life a thought and he certainly wouldn't have cared about her parents. Stella could just picture what Rory would have thought of the humble little house and her simple parents if he had ever met them.

"I just wondered," he continued, "if you would like to come out for dinner with me?" Stella groaned inwardly – she really didn't think that was a good idea.

Amber, eavesdropping unashamedly, nodded her head furiously, mouthing, "Go on! Go on!"

Stella shook her head, glaring at Amber. She couldn't go out with Henry. She didn't dare. What would happen if they were alone together and she let herself look into his eyes?

Amber poked her viciously in the ribs. "Say yes!" she hissed in Stella's ear.

"OK – that would be lovely!" Stella heard the words spilling out of her mouth as if they had a life of her own.

She heard Henry ask her over to his place, tomorrow. He would love to cook dinner for her himself. He was a dab hand with roast lamb, he told her.

She replaced the receiver and turned angrily to Amber. "What did you make me do that for?"

"*You* said yes – I didn't make you say anything except talk to him!" Amber laughed merrily.

"Oh, God," moaned Stella, "I've just agreed to have dinner at his place. What *have* I done?"

"The right thing," Amber said and danced around the room, launching into an awful, tuneless rendition of 'Love is in the Air'.

* * *

"For someone who didn't want to go out you're making a big effort," Amber said wryly, raising her eyebrows and looking quizzically at Stella, who was beautifully dressed in a dark pair of trousers and a cream-coloured top.

"Well," snapped Stella, tetchily, "you never know who you're going to meet when you're out."

"I thought that it was just dinner at his place," giggled Amber, her eyes dancing with amusement.

"Well, I like to look nice." Stella glared at Amber. "For *me*."

Amber nodded her head solemnly. "Of course," she said seriously, trying to suppress a smile.

* * *

Stella marched out of the apartment, filled with self-righteous anger. How dare Amber suggest that she'd got dressed up to impress Henry! That certainly wasn't the reason. Somehow she had just wanted to look nice for the evening. Nothing to do with Henry. There was no sign of Rory in the street. Breathing a sigh of relief, Stella got into her car and headed out of the city.

She had soon left the bright lights of the city behind and sped along the narrow country lanes of Kildare. It was funny how different everything looked when you were driving yourself, rather than being a passenger. With Rory she had looked at the scenery, rather than the road signs. However, soon she recognised the road where she'd found Teddy the day she'd visited Henry's yard with Rory.

She drove on but before long was in unfamiliar territory.

"Damn!" she cursed.

Meeting a huge tractor on a tight bend in the road, she hastily steered the car into the hedge, hearing the thorn bushes scraping along the bodywork. The road seemed to get narrower and narrower – she had definitely taken a wrong turn.

"Shit, shit!" Now she was going to be late.

A short way further on she found a wide gateway and reversed into it to turn the car around. For one awful moment the wheels spun around, not able to grip on the slick turf and then suddenly with a lurch the car shot free and bounced out onto the road. Stella shoved her foot hard on the accelerator and drove back to the point where she had probably taken the wrong fork in the road. Taking the alternative route, she drove on, scanning the landscape for familiar landmarks.

Soon, to her immense relief, she saw the beautiful grey stone of Thornhill House, just visible through the green canopy of leaves, and shortly after spotted the entrance to Thornhill Stables, almost hidden in the bushy growth of the hawthorn hedge.

She slammed on the brakes.

The van behind her screeched to a halt, skidding and almost sliding into the bumper of her car. She felt a red-hot blush flush over her face as the driver of the van honked loudly on his horn. In her rear-view mirror she could see him waving two fingers in her direction in a rude gesture.

Slowly Stella drove down Henry's bumpy driveway towards his cottage, wishing that she hadn't accepted his invitation. What on earth had possessed her to say yes? She enjoyed being taken out for dinner in slick city restaurants, not having it cooked for her by some country horse trainer. This was only prolonging the agony of having to give him up.

She would turn around, go home, and make sure that she didn't talk to him again. The driveway was too narrow to turn around on and she didn't want to risk turning in any of the gateways that led off the lane – they all looked far too muddy and she could just imagine how amused Henry would be if she got stuck on his driveway, especially if she had to tell him that she was trying to bolt for home.

So on she went.

However, when she finally reached the stable yard

in front of the cottage Henry's home stood in darkness. The stable yard was deserted. A black pall of disappointment settled on her shoulders, surprising her with its intensity. Not paying attention to what she was doing, she drove into the middle of the yard, braked hard to avoid hitting a scrawny black and white cat, and stalled the car. She looked around at the deserted cottage and yard. There was no sight of the Jeep. Henry had obviously forgotten that she was coming. He had gone out without her. Stella scowled, suddenly wanting to see him very much.

The cottage windows stared blankly out into the yard. From the stables a few horses gazed out at her car, their ears sharply pricked, eyes bright and intelligent, curious about who had driven into the yard. The black and white cat stalked back across the yard, jumped up onto her car bonnet, eyed her disdainfully through the windscreen and then settled down to wash itself, enjoying the warmth from her car engine.

Surely Henry wouldn't have gone out and forgotten her? Stella's pride wouldn't allow her to believe that this was possible. He must be somewhere around. Maybe there had been a power cut and he was in the kitchen, waiting for her to arrive. Stella got out of the car and walked across to the cottage, shivering in the brisk wind that cut across the pastureland and swirled around the yard, sending stray strands of straw skittering across the uneven cobbles.

She hammered on the back door, hearing the noise echoing around the silent cottage. Henry wasn't there.

She walked around the back and spotted the Jeep parked by one of the barns away from the stable yard. And there was a light in the barn He must be there. Picking her way across the yard, Stella made her way towards the light, grumbling under her breath about her own stupidity. Henry hadn't had the courtesy to even remember she was coming, so why was she chasing after him? She should just get back into the car and drive away. Sod Henry! But still her feet brought her relentlessly towards the light, picking her way over the muddy patches and the patches of more awful substances that seemed to virtually fill the near-derelict yard.

Lights from the mansion blazed through the woodland at the edge of Henry's gallops, shining across the sandy track and closely cropped turf. Stella paused to look at it, mesmerised as always by its beauty, before the chill evening wind made her shiver and carry on towards the light in the barn.

She paused in the entrance to the barn. "Henry!" she called uncertainly.

"Fuck! Stella!" came the horrified reply. Henry's head appeared from one of the stables at the far end of the barn. "Shit! Is it that time already?"

Stella smiled tightly. "Yes." This was some reception. She had never been so insulted in her life! Well, this was it! In fact, she had just been provided with the perfect excuse not to see him again.

A cold anger building, she walked down the length of the barn towards him. The barn contrasted sharply with the unkempt cottage and stable yard outside. It was immaculate. Large stables stood at either side of a wide corridor, each divided by smartly painted wood and tall iron railings. The stables were mostly empty, save for a few at the far end, in which two pretty brown horses watched her approach.

"Sorry," confessed Henry, grimacing at his own stupidity. "I completely forgot about the time." He kissed her softly on the cheek.

Stella could feel the coolness of his lips on her skin after he had released her from his gentle grip.

"This foal won't suckle," Henry told her, stepping back into the stable. Inside the stable, knee-deep in straw, stood an enormous chestnut horse, beside which was a little foal.

"What's wrong with it?" Stella grimaced at the odd-looking animal. "Is it . . . deformed?" The foal looked as if its legs were too large for its tiny body, and as if the head was too big for its short neck to support.

Henry gave a laugh of delight. "They always look like this! You'll see, he'll soon look like his head and legs belong to him."

The foal took a step forward, wobbled on his long legs and fell, sprawling heavily into the straw. Stella gave a gasp of sympathy and moved forward as if to help him. The big chestnut horse laid back its long ears and rolled a wild-looking eye in Stella's direction.

"Don't come in," Henry warned quickly.

Stella stopped. There was no way she was going near that great orange brute.

"Woah, girl!" Henry ran a gentle hand over the chestnut mare's long neck, calming her with his voice and hands.

Stella watched silently, enthralled at the graceful way in which he stroked the mare and the way that she was changed from a fearful mass of muscle to a gentle creature by his touch.

"I need to get the foal to suckle." Henry held the foal, supporting him while the gangly creature fought to control his enormous legs, his whiskery muzzle sweeping up and down the mare's hind legs and beneath her belly, while she stood patiently. "He has to learn to put his head beneath her belly and then upwards for her teats," Henry explained, gently trying to guide the foal while holding him up with his own legs. "And he just can't get the knack."

Stella watched as Henry tried, tried and tried again, wondering at his patience. Then she jumped back from the doorway as the orange horse let out an almighty squeal. "There," Henry said, grinning delightedly, "he's found the milk bar at last!"

Once the foal had suckled, Henry moved away. The foal tried to walk again, catching his long legs in the straw and tumbling down.

"Come and stroke him," Henry said, opening the stable door.

Stella walked in uncertainly, keeping one eye on his cross-looking orange mother. "She's calmed down now – she won't mind," Henry said, seeing Stella looking nervously at the mare.

Stella crouched by the foal as he lay in the straw, all legs and enormous head. Gingerly she stoked the warm fluffy fur of his belly and then touched his velvet-soft muzzle, enthralled at how such a gangly little creature could possibly grow up into something as huge as his mother.

"Oh bloody hell!" exclaimed Henry suddenly, leaping to his feet. "I was so busy with the mare that I forgot to put the dinner on for you!"

Stella gave a short laugh – suddenly it didn't matter any more.

Henry washed his hands and arms to the elbow at a nearby tap. Then they walked slowly along the wide corridor. He turned off the lights and they walked together across the dark yard and into the house.

Henry closed the door behind them and then stood in the semi-darkness, looking at Stella. She could sense the incredible tension that buzzed between them. Then with infinite slowness he gently touched her cheek.

"Stella," Henry whispered softly, "you look absolutely beautiful tonight."

27

Stella steered her car slowly along the rutted lane away from Henry's cottage, trying to avoid the deep potholes highlighted in her car headlights. At the end of the drive she turned out onto the tarmac road, drove a short distance and then pulled over into the lay-by on the opposite side of the road where Rory had stopped the first time they had come to visit Henry. She turned off the engine and threw open the door, breathing in huge gasps of the cold night air as if she had just come to the surface after being underwater for a long time. With movements jerky with panic she swung her legs out of the car and sat, with her head in her hands, letting the cold air seep into her consciousness, bringing her back to reality. Slowly she raised her head.

Far below, through the trees, highlighted in the pale glow of the full moon, was the gorgeous mansion. It stood, a proud, dark solid shape surrounded by the pale silvery sheen of the surrounding fields and gardens. The round face of the moon reflected in the lake close to the house. And beyond the house, off to the right, was the sagging rooftop of Henry's cottage and the bulk of the barn behind it.

Stella levered herself to her feet and leant against her car bonnet, gazing longingly at the mansion. *That* was the sort of place that she wanted to live in. Not some tumbledown cottage like Henry's. She ran a trembling hand over her forehead, feeling the tension in her skin. Her temples throbbed. She had to get a grip on herself – she couldn't let herself fall for Henry. She pictured a nightmare scenario, living in the battered cottage, becoming a bitter drudge, shabby and careworn like her mother. She shook her head to clear the scene from her thoughts. That couldn't happen.

She shivered, got back into her car and pulled out onto the road again, with a final look back at the mansion as it slid away out of her line of vision. She brought her hand to her cheek. She could still feel the touch of his fingers against her skin from when he had gently pulled her towards him, and brought his lips tenderly down onto hers. The world had spun dizzily on its axis, as if she would fall, but his arms had encircled her, holding her as if he had the strength to support the two of them. He had kissed her so gently, his lips moving against hers as if she were the most precious thing that he had ever touched, while one hand gently cupped the back of her head. She had felt the warmth from his body, felt the strength that lay within him as his body gently brushed against hers.

And when they had drawn apart they had stood for a long moment, as if surprised and afraid of what was happening between them.

Henry had moved away first. "I don't know what we'll have to eat," he had said huskily.

Stella had followed him into the kitchen, hardly aware of the chipped cupboards and grotty furniture. She had smiled as he opened the fridge. On the bottom shelf was a leg of lamb, resting in a baking tray, ready to be put into the oven.

"Too late to cook that," Henry shrugged wryly, crouching beside the open door and peering hopefully inside. "Looks like this is the best I can offer you –" Puffing out his cheeks and letting out a huge sigh. he pulled rashers of bacon and some eggs out of the fridge.

He had fried the rashers and eggs while Stella sat on one of the rickety chairs watching him. And then she had surprised herself by polishing off everything that he had put on her plate, plus a slice of toast. Normally she would have made herself eat half of what was given her, nibbling at the bacon rashers and telling him that she didn't like the yellow bit of the egg. But something happened to her when she got near to Henry.

Something that she didn't like.

She had to cut him out of her life.

After they had eaten, they spent a long time side by side on the sofa, enjoying coffee, then a glass of wine and then coffee again, chatting about everything under the sun. But the moment when Henry slid an arm gently around her shoulders acted like an alarm signal to Stella. She had risen abruptly and announced she must go.

That had been a sensible thing to do.

Why then had she accepted an invitation to go to the races with him the following weekend? He had a horse running, he had told her – it should do well. It would make up for not getting any dinner. And she had accepted, eagerly. But now she was cursing her own stupidity. She should have made some excuse. And now she had just got further into the mess by accepting his invitation.

*　　*　　*

"What are you doing?" Amber asked as Stella headed into an expensive-looking boutique.

"Just having a look," Stella said brightly, holding the door open for Amber to follow her.

They were in town having lunch together to celebrate Amber's new job. Stella had rather wished that Amber had removed her electric blue nylon overall though before they sat down to eat, but Amber seemed oblivious – she never seemed to care what people thought about her.

"What about this?" Stella pulled a tweed suit off the rail. She held the jacket up against her, looking in the mirror to see. The creamy tweed fabric highlighted her pale colouring, and the darker suede trim looked lovely against the colour of her hair.

"For the races, you mean? I thought you didn't want to encourage Henry?" Amber looked quizzically at Stella.

"I don't!" Stella snapped. "But I still want to look nice. I'll get a lot of use out of this suit." She headed towards the checkout to pay.

*   *   *

Stella arrived at Henry's cottage at the appointed time a few days later. She parked her car close to one of the stables and got out.

"You can't park there," snapped the short dark-haired man that she recognised as Henry's groom, Jimmy. "Go near the cottage."

Stella got back into her car, prickling with irritation. What a rude bunch these racing people were! The car bumped across the yard to the cottage.

"Happy now?" Stella growled under her breath.

The yard was a hive of frantic activity. Jimmy and a scrawny middle-aged woman with a leathery face were shooting backwards and forwards across the yard from the barn to the ancient lorry that stood in the middle of the yard with its ramp down. Henry appeared out of the cottage, clutching a pile of brightly coloured satin jackets.

"Hi!" He came across the yard towards Stella, greeting her with a kiss on the cheek. "We'll be off in a minute," he said, glancing in the direction of the stables. "Everything ready, Kathy?"

The leather-faced woman gave him a thumbs-up

signal as she jogged back towards the barn. A few moments later Jimmy and Kathy emerged from the stables, both leading horses. Kathy led a pretty bay who walked politely beside her into the lorry. Jimmy hung onto the lead-rope of a prancing grey horse whose ears were flat back against his elegant neck and whose eyes were rolling. The horse glared at Stella who shrank back against the wall in fright.

"Come on then," Henry said as they heaved up the heavy ramp.

Nodding briefly, Kathy skulked back in the direction of the barn and Jimmy clambered into the lorry and settled himself down on the small ledge behind the driver's seat.

"After you." Henry held open the passenger door of the lorry for Stella to climb in. Stella swallowed hard – she wasn't sure that her skirt and new high-heeled boots were made for clambering up into lorries.

Amusement danced in Henry's eyes. "You'll have to hitch that skirt up," he grinned.

Pursing her lips angrily, Stella wriggled the skirt upwards and began the climb up into the lorry cab. Then much to her annoyance, Henry put his hand onto her bottom and shoved her into the cab.

Jimmy gave a snort of amusement. "Nice legs," he grinned.

Glaring at him angrily Stella settled herself into the seat. She had expected to be driven to the races in the Jeep – that would have been bad enough – but to go in a lorry!

Despite all that, Stella would have enjoyed the journey – it was amazing how far you could see while high up in a lorry cab – but the whole way she was worried about how she was going to get down onto level ground again. However, when the time came, Henry had the solution.

"Jump down into my arms," he grinned, pulling open the passenger door when they pulled into the carpark at the race meeting. Taking a deep breath Stella slid, very ungracefully, down out of the passenger seat into his arms. Henry took Stella into the racecourse, past the security guard, and then went back to organise the horses for their races, telling Stella that he would see her in the parade ring, pointing in the direction of a grassy oval bordered by a white fence.

Stella began to relax, wandering happily around the racecourse admiring the outfits of the smartly dressed men and women. At one edge of the course there were stalls selling everything from beautiful handmade leather handbags to gorgeous silky scarves. Stella wandered around the stalls, losing herself in the pleasure of shopping until it was time to go and meet Henry at the parade ring.

Without her noticing, the racecourse had filled up. There were people everywhere, wandering aimlessly, chatting on mobile phones, gazing intently at the names of the horses written on tall boards beside the bookmakers. She made her way to the parade ring. A crowd of people clustered around its edge. Stella shoved her way through and then hesitantly ducked under the rail.

The horses, all bounding with energy and power, were being led around a tarmac track that circled the grassy oval. Stella took a deep breath and dived across the tarmac onto the grass, her eyes raking the groups of people, looking for Henry. At last she saw him and walked across the grass, hampered by her high heels which kept sinking into the soft turf.

"Hey, Stella!" Henry grinned with delight when he spotted her. "This is Eileen and Tom Joyce, the owners of Moody Man."

Stella shook hands with the tall, elegantly dressed man and his tiny, fragile-looking wife.

"Hasn't Henry done a good job on him?" Eileen asked Stella.

Stella nodded, hoping that she looked knowledgeable – she didn't even know which was their horse! A red-faced man in a tight-fitting tweed suit rang a bell, bellowing something unintelligible, and from the low wooden building beside the parade ring came a line of jockeys, all dressed in brightly coloured silks, slapping short whips against their stick-thin legs.

"Here's Jamie, our jockey!" Tommy Joyce stuck out a finely boned hand in the direction of a pale-faced young man, who looked as if a strong breeze would blow him away.

The red-faced steward rang his bell again and the horses were led into the centre of the ring. Sheila spotted Henry's prancing, angry-looking grey horse. Henry legged Jamie up onto his back.

Stella leapt out of the way as the horse began to caper, throwing his head up and down. She backed away quickly – she didn't want to get in the way of those flying hooves.

The horses went out onto the course. Stella craned her neck to watch as they circled at the start of the race and then set off, a long caterpillar of colour against the green background of the surrounding farmland. After what seemed only a few moments the horses were thundering past the winning post, with Moody Man in third place. Henry glowed with pleasure as Eileen kissed him and Tommy shook his hand at the same time.

"Now time to see what my horse can do," Henry said, once all the excitement had died down.

Jimmy, the groom, reappeared with the elegant bay horse.

"This is Princess Pushy," Henry told Stella as the horse walked around the parade ring. She was very different from Moody Man, calmly taking in her surroundings, gazing at everything through kind brown eyes, her ears sharply pricked, noticing everything that was going on around her, yet accepting it all fearlessly.

"I bred her myself," Henry said proudly.

The jockeys trooped out once more, as Henry legged Jamie up onto Princess Pushy's back.

Stella turned as someone tugged at the sleeve of her jacket.

"Stella," Rory said, "how good to see you again!"

Stella felt her heart give an uncomfortable lurch of fear as Rory towered over her, gazing maliciously in Henry's direction.

"How are you getting on with the prodigal son?" he asked nastily, jerking his head towards Henry.

"Fine thanks," snapped Stella, wondering fleetingly what on earth he meant.

But before she had time to ask, Rory continued, "I don't know what you see in someone like him when you could have been with me."

Out of the corner of her eye Stella could see Henry glance in their direction, his expression full of concern.

"He's just a loser," Rory spat, and then seeing Henry approaching dropped his grip on Stella's jacket sleeve and with a final, defiant glare in Henry's direction, turned abruptly on his heel and stalked across the parade ring.

Stella heaved a sigh of relief. What a nasty shock he had given her! She hadn't expected to see him today, though indeed she should have done.

"You OK?" Henry put his arm gently around her shoulder.

Stella nodded, fighting the urge to lean against his chest and weep with fright.

"Come on," Henry said. "Let's go and see what Princess Pushy can do."

They went out to the Trainers' Stand and found a place to watch the race. Stella was horribly aware of Rory's presence, only a few seats away from them.

The horses made their way down to the start line.

"This is her first proper race," Henry told Stella, gripping her hand in his. "She's done a few point, to, point races, but this is her first real race."

Far away on the other side of the course the race began, the horses surging away towards the first fence.

"Cod and Chips is Rory's horse," Henry told her, as the commentator began to reel out the names of the horses as they ran. Princess Pushy was right at the front of the pack, her elegant cream muzzle shoved resolutely forwards. Cod and Chips, Stella heard the commentator say, was in fourth place. The horses surged past the stands, a blur of colour and movement, against the cacophony of noise from the crowd. The horses took off as one to jump the solid-looking fence nearest the stands.

Then Henry's grip tightened on Stella's hand. Princess Pushy had fallen, the elegant bay mare skidding incongruously along the ground before she scrambled to her feet, looking bemused.

"I'd better go and see if she's all right," Henry said distractedly, letting go of Stella's hand and shoving his way out of the stands. There was a roar of delight from the crowd as Cod and Chips surged over the finishing line ahead of all the other horses. "See," Rory, growled, coming to stand beside Stella, smirking smugly at her, "I told you that Henry was a loser."

29

"Why won't you come?" Amber asked.

Stella shook her head firmly. "Henry's just not my cup of tea. He's very nice, but I don't want to be with him."

"I'm not asking you to have anything to do with Henry," Amber said, a petulant note appearing in her voice. "I just wanted you to come and see Paul ride the horse for him. This could be the start of Paul race-riding again."

Stella shook her head again, shaking Teddy off her lap as she got off the sofa.

"I don't want to give Henry the wrong idea," she muttered, switching on the kettle. "I don't want him to think that we could have a relationship."

Amber watched her as she lifted the tea caddy, and then put it down again, before lifting the coffee jar, beginning to open it and then changing her mind once more. She had been really affected by going out with Henry. More than she was admitting, maybe even to herself.

"He thinks the world of you," Amber told her. "You should just get on with things. Just go out with him and enjoy yourself."

"No," snapped Stella, slamming down the coffee jar, hauling the top off the tea caddy and shoving a tea bag into a mug. "I can't."

Teddy weaved himself around Amber's legs and plonked down, his small head resting on her feet, looking up at her in the hope that she would throw the ball for him.

"What else are you going to do?" Amber tried again. "Coming out for the day with Paul and me has got to be better than staying here." Amber knew that she had won then. She saw a fleeting look of fear flash over Stella's face.

Since she had seen Rory at the races he had redoubled his efforts to get her back, sitting outside the flat most nights, telephoning her constantly at all hours of the day and night and sending gifts of flowers and jewellery. A small heap of gold necklaces and pretty silver bracelets lay on the kitchen worktop, tangled incongruously into the cards declaring undying love. Amber knew that Stella was afraid. Whenever she was home she wandered aimlessly around the apartment, unable to settle, listening for the phone to ring that would either herald another bout of pleading from Rory, or another grim update on her father's health from Mayo. Stella had thrown herself into her work to escape from the horrors beyond the stark walls of her office.

Things were going well for Stella at work. Sorcha, Stella had told Amber, had been very firmly put in her place. Stella had turned the tables on her by working twice as hard and being twice as good at her job. Stella had even been offered a promotion, which would make her Kevin's equal rather than working beneath him.

Amber had no such ambition. She loved her new job, sitting merrily on the supermarket checkout with a constant stream of interesting people to talk to as she scanned their groceries and speculated on what kind of lives they had. Paul would often come into the supermarket and stand patiently in the queue for Amber's checkout. Somehow he would have slipped a note into one of the things that he was buying, asking her to meet him for coffee, or making naughty suggestions that made her blush and giggle.

Stella brought a cup of tea back to the sofa and sat down wearily.

"OK," she said wearily. "You win. I'll come."

* * *

Paul picked the two of them up the following morning. Amber had dressed casually in a pair of jeans and a baggy sweatshirt. Her hair was being particularly uncooperative and stuck out at all sorts of angles, in spite of her dampening it down with water, and applying tons of stuff supposed to control frizz. Even so, her hair was as unruly as ever, and so she had stuck a baseball cap on top of the whole mass, so at least she could see without it blowing all over the place.

"You look nice," Amber said to Stella, grinning at Paul and nudging him to look. Stella too was dressed in jeans, but still managed to look elegant and stylish. For someone who supposedly wasn't interested in Henry, she seemed to make an awful lot of effort when she was going to be around him.

Paul still drove the flashy sports car that he had bought himself when he was earning a fortune as a jockey. He loved the car, but now, with his wages from working as a waiter, could barely afford to run it, with the result that the petrol gauge constantly read empty, or dangerously near to it. Today, however, after a good night at the restaurant when he had earned a small fortune in tips, the petrol tank was full.

Paul levered the front seat up so that Stella could climb into the small back seat, with her legs stretched sideways. Amber threw Teddy into the back with her.

"He's a good back-seat driver," she joked.

Stella gave directions while Paul drove.

"This is lovely," said Amber, as they headed out into the countryside.

Soon they were bumping down the potholed drive to Henry's cottage. Paul grimaced as the bottom of the car scraped along the ground when it hit a particularly deep pothole.

"Oh my!" breathed Amber, as the car came to a halt

in the yard. "Isn't it absolutely gorgeous?" She got out of the car, breathing deeply through her nose to savour the warm country smell of horse manure and of the freshly churned earth that blew down from the gallops. "Just imagine living somewhere like this!" She turned slowly around, oblivious of Paul and Stella who were leaning on the car, watching her with bemused expressions.

Paul had grown up on a farm in the country, so he took all of the fresh air and open space for granted, enjoying the convenience of the city and yet feeling totally at home when he came back to the countryside. To Stella the countryside reminded her of her childhood, poverty and loneliness.

Amber moved into the centre of the yard and then slowly spun around.

"Look at that beautiful old building!" She stopped revolving and stood still, awestruck, gazing at the faded old stone of the barn. "Look at the colours of the stone – and the roof!" She gazed up at the stone barn, loving every inch of the battered old building, seeing incredible beauty in the stone, weathered to a thousand different shades of cream and grey, standing proudly beneath a slate roof, whose tiles were chipped and cracked with age. "Just imagine the work that went into creating something like that," she mused, looking at the way the vast stone lintels had been placed in the windows high above the stable yard, in what would once have been grooms' accommodation. "I would love to have somewhere like this, to make it live again," she breathed, ignoring Stella's scathing looks.

"Old places are hard work, always needing repairing," Stella grumbled, remembering the draughty cottage where she grew up.

"So do new ones," scoffed Paul. "My flat is in a new block, only built last year, and there are things going wrong with that already."

"Imagine living in that gorgeous cottage," Amber said enviously, looking across the yard to Henry's home. "It just needs some roses around the door and a few hanging baskets to make it look like a chocolate-box picture. Oh, look, Henry's here!" She darted a look at Stella who was staring determinedly at a blackbird trying to pull a worm out of the soil close to where Paul had parked his car.

"Hi, you're all very welcome!" Henry came across the yard to join them.

Amber stifled a giggle as Henry, looking so hard at Stella, almost fell over Teddy who was trying to pull up a tuft of grass from between the cobblestones.

"Hi, Stella," he said, kissing her softly on the cheek.

"Hi, Henry," Stella replied.

Amber could hear how her voice softened when Henry was around.

"It's lovely out here," Amber told him, indicating the yard and cottage with an expansive wave of her arms.

"Where is the horse that you wanted me to look at?" Paul asked, looking around the yard at the horses' heads that were gazing out at them. "Henry?"

"Er," Henry said, tearing his eyes away from Stella, "sorry . . . er . . . what did you say?"

Amber nudged Paul and muttered between her teeth: "Talk about lovelorn, look at the two of them!"

"Horse? Which horse did you want me to look at?" Paul asked again, nudging Amber in the ribs to make her behave.

"Yes," Henry said distantly, "horse . . . yes . . . this way."

Henry led the way across the yard to one of the stables, yelling for Jimmy to get a saddle and bridle.

"This is Princess Pushy." Henry pulled open one of the stable doors.

Paul and the girls followed him inside. The elegant bay mare pushed at Henry with her cream muzzle, hoping that he would give her a treat.

"Is this the horse that fell when we went racing?" Stella asked, stretching out her hand gingerly to touch the mare's silky, soft neck.

"Just bad luck," Henry said firmly, deftly undoing the fastenings on Princess Pushy's dark-blue rug and sliding it off over her muscular quarters. "She ran in a few point-to-point races – I think that she's got a great future ahead of her. And I think that your style of riding would suit her, Paul." Henry smiled as Paul ran an admiring hand down the mare's neck and rubbed her face gently.

Jimmy shoved his way into the stable, using the saddle that he carried like a battering ram to shove them all out of the way. The mare was quickly saddled and bridled and then Jimmy led her outside into the yard.

"You can try her, see what you think," Henry told Paul, legging him easily up into the saddle.

Amber grinned at Paul. He looked so at home on the mare's back as he rode off across the yard, his legs dangling by her sides as he fumbled to put his feet into tiny stirrups. Stella walked beside Henry as they toiled up the hill from the yard to the gallops. Princess Pushy and Paul jogged in front of them. Amber had her heart in her mouth watching the two of them. The horse pranced, tossing its elegant head up and down, champing at the bit as if it wanted to rid itself of the burden it carried.

Then there was a blur of brown streaking from the undergrowth as Teddy hurtled from beneath a bramble bush, straight between the horse's legs, and ran at full speed towards them. Amber didn't have time to be afraid before the mare gave a huge leap into the air with fright at the sudden appearance of the little dog. Somehow though, when Paul and Princess Pushy came down to earth the two of them were still together.

"I think maybe Teddy had better go on a lead," laughed Henry, totally unconcerned.

"Oh, we left it in the car!" said Amber.

Henry fished a long piece of baler twine out of his pocket and tossed it to Amber.

Teddy wriggled furiously as Amber tied the twine to his collar. At least he was enjoying himself. She was hating every minute. She was sure that Paul was going to be thrown off and killed or at the very least injured at any second. It was even worse when they started to go faster. Princess Pushy pounded around the gallops, her long legs a virtual blur with the speed that she was travelling at. When Henry suggested that Paul try her over one of the jumps it was all that Amber could do to stop herself from falling onto her knees and clutching at his hand, begging him to take Paul off the horse immediately.

Paul turned the mare towards the solid-looking jumps, speeding along the gallops standing in his stirrups, crouching low over her neck. Amber felt her breath catch in her throat as they took off, soaring through the air, so high and so fast, in perfect harmony. And then as they landed Amber felt the most almighty jolt of adrenaline course through her body – this had to be the most incredible thing that she had ever seen. The most terrifying, but the most thrilling.

"That was amazing," Amber said as she jogged back down to the yard beside Princess Pushy.

"She's a wonderful mare," Paul called back over his shoulder and then rolled his eyes at Amber.

Paul had leant down to kiss her when he rode up beside them after he had jumped the mare. Amber could taste the sweat on his upper lip; his face was icy cold, his cheeks red from the wind. He was back where he belonged.

Stella and Henry were walking behind them, their heads close together, seemingly oblivious to anything but each other.

Then, as they neared the yard Amber heard Henry swear: "Fuck, I had forgotten about *him!*" An elegant Range Rover was parked in the yard, its owner lolling casually against the bonnet.

"Hope I'm not interrupting you." The owner of the Range Rover strolled over to the gate to let them back into the yard.

"Not at all," Henry said with a cool edge to his voice. He held out his hand for the man to shake. Amber could hear a note of tension in his voice. "These are friends of mine – Stella, Amber and Paul – just come to have a look at my mare. This is Derry Blake, one of Ireland's top trainers."

Derry turned towards the girls, his lips twisted in a smile that Amber saw didn't reach his eyes. His eyes flickered briefly over Paul and then back to the girls as if he had already decided that Paul was of no consequence.

Derry was one of the most handsome men that Amber had ever seen. He was elegantly dressed in smart tweeds and casual cord trousers, and he smelt deliciously of expensive aftershave. Yet Amber instinctively recoiled from him – he looked far too much of a charmer for her liking.

Paul slid off Princess Pushy and nodded curtly in Derry's direction before leading the mare towards her stable.

"I can come back some other time," Derry said, then added, "although I thought you were in a hurry to sell The Entertainer?"

"Don't go," Henry snapped. "Stay. Let's get this over with."

Amber turned to Stella – they should get out of the way, let Henry and Derry sort out whatever business they had to do. To her horror she saw that Stella was absolutely mesmerised by Derry Blake.

30

Stella's alarm clock was going off, its noise loud and insistent. She fumbled for the bedside table, made a grab for the clock and then realised that it was her phone that was ringing. She was instantly awake. It was the middle of the night – that had to mean bad news.

"Stella!" Rory's hysterical voice screeched in her ear.

Stella felt her mouth drop open with surprise. She had been expecting to hear her mother's hushed voice telling her some awful news about her father, which would mean she would have to scramble straight out of bed and begin the long, dark drive back to Mayo. She caught sight of the clock, its red numbers glowing in the semi-darkness: 2:15 a.m.

"Stella!" Rory shrieked again, when she didn't reply immediately, his shrill voice thick with alcohol. He was very drunk. "You have to come back to me," he ranted. "Have to . . ." she could hear the sound of him sobbing.

"I can't live without you!" Stella propped herself up on one elbow, furious at having had her night's sleep so brutally disturbed.

"Rory," she said, trying to inject patience in her voice, "listen to me. I can't go back to you. The relationship is over. You have to understand that."

"I'm going to kill myself!" he roared, sounding as petulant as a small child denied sweets.

"OK, Rory!" Stella severed the connection. She couldn't bear to listen to him any longer. He had threatened to kill himself dozens of times as if he thought that this would make Stella change her mind.

She huddled beneath the bedclothes once more, shivering with nerves. Why could he not leave her alone? She really couldn't cope with this any longer. Maybe she should go to the Garda and complain about him, as Amber and Paul had been telling her to. She had really hoped that before long he would get fed up when he realised that his threats were not going to make any difference.

She felt hot tears of frustration roll down her cheeks and onto the pillow. She hated the thought of what Rory was going through, hated the thought that she was causing him pain, but she couldn't resume their relationship. He was never going to make her happy. And besides which, he would never actually carry out his threats of killing himself – that was all for attention, like a girl telling an ex-boyfriend that she's pregnant in the hope that he'll go back to her. There was no hope. The relationship was over. Forever.

Stella lay in the blissful place between wakefulness and sleep, cocooned in the warmth of the quilt.

Then the phone rang again, dragging her once more into wakefulness.

"Hello," she said impatiently.

"I'm going to crash my car off the motorway." Rory's voice was cold, filled with anger.

Stella dashed away the tears. How could he be so cruel as to keep torturing her like this? Why could he not just leave her alone and get on with his life? "Rory," she could hear the hysteria rising in her own voice, "stop it! Stop being like this! Just go home and go to bed. We can talk in the morning." She couldn't bear his unrelenting cruelty, twisting his life around so that she was responsible for his happiness.

"No, Stella," Rory said, his voice suddenly calm, almost jovial. "I'm going to crash my car now. And it will be all your fault."

In the background Stella could hear the sound of Rory revving up the car engine. This was ridiculous, tomorrow she was going to have to go to the Garda about him, make them stop him from harassing her – and maybe they would be able to make him get some help.

"I'm going to drive off the motorway now," she could hear Rory saying, the car engine loud in the background, screaming in protest as he drove it faster and faster.

"Rory! Stop it! Stop it!" Stella was panicking now. What if he really carried out his threat?

"It's all your fault!" His voice had a singsong lilt to it, rising at the end. "All your fault." He was silent then. Stella could hear the roar of the car engine, even the sound of the road beneath the wheels, then suddenly he spoke again. "Bye, Stella." His voice was icy cold and cruel.

Stella felt her heart pound in her chest as through the earpiece she heard a dull thud. Then a thousand different noises all joined together into one dreadful cacophony of scraping, banging, metal tearing. Suddenly the connection was severed and she lay in bed, shivering violently, listening to the mundane noise of the phone bleeping.

Slowly she replaced the phone on the bedside table. She was trembling all over. Surely Rory hadn't really carried out his threat to crash his car? Was he really prepared to kill himself in the hope that she would feel guilt about his death for the rest of her life? Surely he wouldn't be that stupid? So was it just a cunning act? Could he be that cruel?

Stella turned on the bedside light and caught sight of herself in the mirror, wide-eyed with shock, her face grey and pinched with fear.

"Amber!" she shrieked. "Amber!"

"Whaaaa?"

Stella heard Amber stirring in the adjoining room. In response to her cries Teddy shoved his nose around the bedroom door, hurtled across the floor and bounded up onto the bed to see what the matter was with his mistress. He shoved his small, cold nose into her neck, wriggling furiously, trying to cheer her up. Stella was so shocked that all she could do was to feebly try to push Teddy away, but there seemed to be no strength in her arms at all.

"Teddy, get down!" Amber came into the room, sweeping Teddy off the bed and sitting quickly down beside Stella, her face full of concern. "What is it? What's happened? Is it your dad?"

Stella shook her head numbly, her mouth opening and closing as she fought to frame the words. "Rory – it's Rory. I think – he's – he's just killed himself."

"Good!" snapped Amber, but then seeing the stunned, fearful look in Stella's face, she said quietly, "You don't actually believe that?"

"He just phoned me. Said he was driving off the motorway."

"Yes, but that doesn't mean that he was going to actually do it. He's just trying to get your attention."

"He did crash though," Stella gasped. "I heard him do it. His phone went dead."

Amber shook her head. "Let me ring him." She picked up the phone beside Stella's bed. "What's his number?"

Stella desperately plucked the phone number out of her mind. She could barely remember what it was, she was in such a state. Amber shoved the phone up to her ear, watching Stella as it tried to connect. The unobtainable sound of the phone bleeping was loud in the silent room.

"Now what do we do?" Stella asked a few moments

later. They had been sitting silently on the bed. Teddy had snuck back onto the bed and lay sprawled between them, enjoying the unexpected attention, as they both stroked his fur distractedly. Amber puffed out her cheeks and shrugged. "I dunno."

Stella was always the one who knew what to do about problems. It was impossible to sleep now with all that trauma.

Amber made tea and they curled up at opposite ends of the sofa to sip the scalding liquid. "We'll be worn out in the morning now," grumbled Amber, watching the hands of the clock slide slowly around.

"Maybe we should ring the Garda?" Stella whispered bleakly. "Or the hospital?" Before they had time to ponder further Stella's phone rang again.

"I bet that's him," Amber growled, filled with uncontrollable anger. How could Rory be such a prick as to put them through this trauma?

"Hello," Stella said fearfully.

Amber concentrated hard on rubbing Teddy's ears, watching Stella's reaction to the phone conversation. She could hear the sound of a voice, muted, talking rapidly.

"Yes . . . yes . . . yes . . . OK . . . thank you." Stella put the phone down, shaking her head numbly while she brushed away the tears from her eyes. "He did crash the car," she said wearily. "I can't believe that he would be so stupid. He's on his way to hospital, in a serious condition. He gave them my name and number as his fiancée, his next of kin."

*　　*　　*

Even in the middle of the night the hospital was busy, like a small city living separately from the rest of the world, its inhabitants wandering aimlessly around dim corridors and sitting in small, bleak huddles. Stella and Amber made their way to the Accident and Emergency unit. There was a long queue of people waiting to talk to the bleary-eyed receptionist, who sat behind a glass panel, speaking only through a small chink in the glass. Stella and Amber joined the end of the queue, shuffling forwards at a snail's pace. Finally it was their turn.

"You have a friend of mine here, Rory McFadden – he was in an accident," Stella told the receptionist, then lip-read her reply above the angry buzz of noise from the seating area. "We have to go through into the waiting room," she told Amber.

The casualty department waiting room was crowded, row upon row of chairs filled with slumped, bewildered-looking youths, dripping blood from various parts of their anatomies. Feeling as if she were living some bizarre nightmare, Stella found them seats at the edge of the waiting room. It was ironic that the hope and dreams of her relationship with Rory were to end in this drab nightmare of a place. At one end of the waiting room were double swing doors, through which a constant stream of people went in and out, nurses rushing in looking stressed and exhausted, patients walking in and then emerging bandaged and cleaned up. Beyond those doors somewhere was Rory. He could be dead now for all she knew. The receptionist hadn't been able to give them any information. Stella found a crumpled tissue in the corner of her coat pocket and dabbed at her eyes uselessly. Nothing seemed to check the tears that persisted in falling at an alarming rate down her cheeks. If only she had been nicer to Rory, maybe he wouldn't have been driven to try to kill himself. If only she had been the kind of person that didn't make him jealous and upset all of the time, they could have had a great relationship. If only . . . the words churned around and around in her mind, while she wondered desperately what was happening. Pictures, memories and visions from a lifetime of television films and documentaries flashed through her head: she saw Rory bloodied and battered, being resuscitated, the doctors giving him up for dead. If only . . . she began to weep again, silently, her shoulders shaking.

Amber took Stella's hand. "This is not your fault," she said firmly. "You didn't make him crash his car. Whatever blame he tries to put on you, remember that."

Stella nodded her head, silently. It was true, of course, but somehow it was hard to believe.

An old lady came in. She was dressed in a huge baggy coat that reached almost to the floor and was clutching a battered carrier bag to her chest, her enormous, bulbous red nose almost touching the grubby plastic. Her eyes darted constantly from side to side, her mouth worked, talking to herself as she shuffled around the casualty department, ever watchful for the Security men who would haul her outside into the darkness when things quietened down and they had nothing else to occupy themselves.

One of the lads got up and began to shout, bellowing loudly that he had been waiting for hours. Two burly Security men shot from their office beside the triage ward. Outfaced by their bulk, the bellowing youth sat down again, glaring at them sullenly. Hearing Stella's name announced over the Tannoy, Amber seized Stella's hand, "Come on, let's go in." She steered her through a set of double doors into the emergency department.

"You have to wait your turn," a skinny, exhausted nurse snapped, waving her arm at them as if to shoo them back into the waiting room.

"We're here to see someone who was in an accident. Rory McFadden."

"In there." The nurse waved her arm in the direction of a row of curtained cubicles. "The third one."

"I'll wait outside," Amber said, her courage deserting her as they walked towards the cubicle.

Stella walked on as if she hadn't heard her, shoving back the brightly patterned curtain and disappearing inside.

Rory lay on a high bed, with the metal sides pulled up as if he were an ancient old man in danger of rolling out. A long cut ran diagonally across his forehead and a pretty young nurse was putting the final stitch into it to pull it all together.

"Stella," Rory grinned weakly. His face looked grey, in the patches that were not covered in purple bruises and bright red scratches.

"Is this your wife?" asked the nurse, gently clipping the end of the thread.

"Just a friend." Stella hurried to answer, emphasising the word 'friend'.

"He's very lucky, just a few nasty cuts and concussion. We'll have to keep him in for the night. What a lovely man he is! Imagine driving off the road just to avoid running a cat over!" The young nurse looked delighted that she was going to be looking after this hero. Rory obviously hadn't confessed to the fact that he had just tried to kill himself.

Stella had lived through absolute hell the last few hours expecting that he would be dead, or at least would die of his injuries, and now she had found out that he had merely got a few cuts and a bang on the head.

Stella stood by the foot of Rory's bed, numbly looking at him. She despised him for what he had put her through.

"I'll leave you to it for a little while," the pretty nurse said, smiling sweetly at Rory, before she swished back the curtain and disappeared.

Stella sat down heavily on the bed, watching Rory silently, so filled with anger that she couldn't trust herself to speak. How often was he going to pull this stunt? Was he going to torture her, every time that he felt miserable, with threats of killing himself?

"I thought that you were dead," she muttered bleakly, not able to bring herself to look at him. Instead she concentrated on the bleeping of machinery and the moans that came from the other cubicles.

"I wanted to be," Rory said gently. "I wanted to hurt you for leaving me. Punish you . . ." His voice faded away as he struggled to find the words to explain.

Stella shook her head miserably, numb with tiredness and frustration.

"I drove the car off the embankment." He gave a short laugh at his own stupidity, which ended in a yelp of pain as bruised muscles protested. "Someone saw me and pulled me out. There was a concrete bollard a few feet away, if I had hit that I would have been killed. Trust me to mess it up."

Tears began to trickle down Stella's cheeks. She searched for a tissue and, failing to find one, pulled a handful of paper towels from the dispenser and wiped her face on the coarse scratchy fabric.

Rory slipped his hand into hers and she jerked her hand away violently.

"Don't you touch me!" she snapped.

"Stella," Rory said his voice thick with tears, "I'm so sorry. I was so stupid."

Stella nodded her head, unable to speak.

"I realised the instant I drove off the motorway that I'd made a terrible mistake." He gave a hollow laugh. "The car was rolling over and over, smashing to bits around me, and all I could think was that I wanted to live."

Stella made a faint snort of amusement. "Bit late then," she whispered, stealing a glance at Rory.

"I'm sorry for everything that I've put you through. I've been an idiot about everything," Rory's hand found Stella's and this time she didn't snatch hers away.

"I miss you," he began and then feeling her hand withdrawing hastily added, "But I am going to get over you. I promise I won't bother you again."

Stella nodded. She felt utterly exhausted, too numb to speak.

"Get off home now," Rory said gently. "I'll be OK."

She stood up to leave as the pretty young nurse came back into the cubicle and began to fuss around Rory, plumping up his pillow and straightening the blanket that covered his legs.

Stella grinned suddenly, turning to face Rory. "Yes, it looks as if you will be OK now."

31

Amber *knew* that it was a hopeless idea. But maybe, just maybe she might be lucky. Paul had said that he thought Princess Pushy had a good chance of winning or being placed in the race. Paul had been riding the elegant mare for a few months and was really getting on well with her. She seemed to really try her hardest when he was riding her.

Amber walked slowly up the line of bookmakers, looking at the blackboards on their stands that listed the names of the horses running in the race. Beside each horse, the bookmakers had chalked in the odds. Because she had fallen in her first race the bookmakers hadn't given Princess much chance of success and so the odds on her were very long. Paul had told Amber, when they arrived at the races, that she ought to put a bet on the mare. Now he had gone off with Henry to change into the brightly coloured purple and white silks that he was to wear. Stella had drifted off in the direction of a stall that was selling handcrafted handbags – as if she didn't already have enough, Amber thought. And Amber had been drawn relentlessly towards the double row of brightly coloured umbrellas that sheltered the bookmakers as they took fistfuls of money off eager gamblers. At first she had only meant to put on a small bet – one of the bookmakers.had a notice above his board saying he was accepting a minimum bet of two euros. That was plenty of money to gamble, Amber had decided, fishing in her bag for her purse. If the mare won she would get . . . she worked out the amount quickly in her head. A nice little amount. She could probably afford to buy a new top or two. Her eye fell on her purse, the wallet section of which was crammed with the money she had transferred from her wage packet earlier. The bulk of it was to go to Stella for the rent on the apartment and for her to buy food and pay the bills. While the rest, a pitifully small amount, was to pay for her bus fares and to try to make some impact on the frighteningly large balances on her credit-card statements. It hardly seemed worth paying anything into any of them as the amount that she did pay off every month barely covered the interest that was being accrued. The credit-card people must have a great laugh when her payments went through to them: 'Take off ten euros and then add twenty!'

Amber pulled out the money, a slender bunch of crisp notes. She closed her fist around the notes as if they were alive – her skin seemed to tingle with the touch of them.

Paul had said that the mare stood a good chance of winning. It would be a shame to lose out on the chance to gain so much money if she did win. Amber quickly worked out that if she bet her wages and the mare won, she would have enough money to pay off all of her debts and still have some left over. In her mind she already had the leftover sum spent on the pretty cream dress dotted with tiny pink flowers that adorned the mannequin she could see from her place on the checkout at the supermarket.

Amber walked in a daze along the line of bookmakers, being jostled from side to side by the frenzied throng of gamblers desperately looking for the best odds. It would be sheer stupidity to gamble all of her wages. The mare could lose the race. There were so many other good horses. Nothing was certain. She should just bet a few euros and then, if she lost, it wouldn't matter.

"Jockeys up," came the announcement over the Tannoy, blaring loudly close to Amber. The race was about to start. In the parade ring the jockeys were being thrown up onto their horses, ready to go down to the start of the race. Amber cringed guiltily. She should have been back in the parade ring to wish Paul good luck – instead she was still with the bookmakers deciding what to do. The announcement spurred the gamblers into a fresh panic. They swarmed everywhere, shoving money in the direction of the bookmakers, who snatched it eagerly from outstretched hands, shoving it into cavernous black leather bags and muttering the details to their assistants who jotted down the amounts on a huge ledger.

Amber joined one of the queues, being shoved forwards by the swell of people thrusting towards the red-faced bookmaker, sweating with the effort of having to take the money so quickly. Suddenly Amber was at the front of the queue, her purse in her hand. The bookmaker looked at her expectantly. If a cartoonist had drawn him he would have given him the face of a pig – he had a huge, round, red face, with large ears and a wide long nose like a snout.

"Yes, darlin'?" he bellowed, twitching with the urgency of getting her money before the race began.

"I want to put . . ." Amber's fingers closed on the bunch of notes. She would just bet ten euros, that was enough, ". . . this on Princess Pushy!" She thrust all of her money into his hand.

"Count that," the bookmaker ordered, casually tossing all of her money to his assistant, who counted the notes equally casually and then threw them into the depths of the leather bag. The bookmaker handed her a ticket.

"Two hundred on Holbrook," yelled the man behind her, shoving forwards to push Amber out of the way.

Amber looked yearningly at the bag, wishing that she was still clutching her money. It had seemed to jump out of her hand into the bookmaker's as if it had a life of her own.

It was too late now though – she couldn't get it back. She tore back to the parade ring, dodging around people in her haste to get to Paul before the start of the race. The horses were just beginning to go out of the parade ring onto the course. Amber ducked under the guardrail and hurtled across the turf. Jimmy was leading Princess Pushy around the parade ring, Paul astride her on the impossibly small saddle. He looked decidedly ill. His face was a curious shade of grey-green and his lips were clamped tightly shut as if he thought that he would vomit if he opened them. Amber skidded to a halt.

"Paul!" she shrieked, waving to attract his attention. Paul looked, and managed a small, nervous smile. "Good luck!" she cried. He had been so full of himself in the lorry on the way to the races, sitting in the passenger seat beside Henry, his feet propped up on the dashboard, reading the newspaper, laughing and joking with Amber and Stella who were squashed onto the narrow ledge behind the seats. Now he looked terrified.

"Don't worry," Henry said, coming to stand beside Amber. "He'll be OK once he starts racing."

Amber nodded slowly – she hoped so.

"I'm going to find Stella and head up to the stands to watch the race," Henry told her, his eyes already scanning the spectators looking for Stella.

The parade ring began to empty. Amber bleakly followed the line of people out onto the stands. There, circling below them, close to the stands, were the horses and riders. Amber craned her neck to see Paul, standing on tiptoe to look above the heads of the other spectators who all seemed to be either very tall, or wore ridiculously large hats, making it impossible for her to see anything. Finally she managed to get a glimpse of the horses and their riders. They were walking in a large circle, the riders chatting to one another, their demeanour relaxed as they lolled casually in their saddles. Then she spotted Paul, riding apart from the other jockeys, every line of his body oozing tension. And then the horses began to walk forwards for the start of the race.

The starter dropped his flag and the race began.

Amber could hardly bear to watch. Her hand ached with the loss of her money. How she wished that it were still in her hand, ready to give to Stella, rather than being gambled on the outcome of a race. How could she have been so bloody stupid? Before the race began she knew that the money was lost, but still at the back of her mind was the hope, the dim possibility that maybe, just maybe, Princess Pushy could win and then she would go home with her pockets crammed with money.

It was sheer anguish watching the race. Her emotions veered wildly from wild hope – her heart thumping so hard that it was hard to breathe as Princess Pushy shoved her way to the front of the runners, her long legs raking over the ground, shooting over the fences like an equine missile – to the agony of despair as the other runners swept past her at the final fence and surged on towards the finish line, leaving her to toil up the hill alone, trailing in last.

"Brilliant! She did great!" gasped Henry. "She needed that run to give her the experience! She'll probably get placed the next time."

Amber hadn't even been aware that he was nearby.

"They didn't fall," Stella grinned, shaking Amber's jacket sleeve with excitement. "He's safe, thank goodness!"

"Come on, we'd better go and find Paul!" Henry darted off across the stand, hand in hand with Stella.

Amber watched them go, feeling sick. What had she done?

A whole week's wages gone in a few moments. And she didn't even have anything to show for it. What on earth was she going to say to Stella? Maybe she should say that she'd been mugged and the money stolen? How could she have been so stupid? If only things had been different, she would now have been celebrating and congratulating herself on how clever she was, instead of cursing her own stupidity! Amber trailed after the others, letting herself get jostled by the spectators who were dashing back to the bookmakers to collect their winnings, clutching betting tickets aloft, their faces split with broad grins of delight.

Princess Pushy was being led around by Jimmy. Paul had gone to weigh in after the race and get changed. Henry patted the mare.

"She has it in her to be a champion!" he beamed, hugging Stella to him.

Amber glared resentfully at the mare who stood

with her head down, sides heaving, her enormous body a network of veins that stood out beneath her sweat-darkened coat.

Soon Paul was jogging across the grass towards them, his hair – still wet from the shower – slicked to his head.

"She was brilliant," he grinned, slowing to a walk. His face, red from exertion, glowed with delight. He grabbed Amber and swung her around. "Next time you'll be able to win a fortune on her, you'll see!"

Amber swallowed hard to stop herself from crying. How could she explain to him that she had just *lost* what to her was a fortune?

"You have a good mare there, Henry!" Derry Blake sauntered up to them. He shook hands with Henry and nodded curtly at Paul. "You rode her well." Derry sounded surprised as if he hadn't thought that Paul would have been capable of riding her at all. "Henry, I'll pick up the horse I bought off you in a day or two."

Amber could see the regret in Henry's eyes – he obviously hadn't wanted to sell The Entertainer.

As if he picked up on this, Derry added maliciously, "I'm sure that he'll improve no end when he comes to my yard."

Amber could see Henry struggling to find a reply. He was no match for Derry's razor-sharp disdain.

Derry's eyes roved casually over Amber, dismissing her as of no consequence, and then lighted on Stella.

"Stella," he said silkily, brushing past Amber to seize Stella's hand and bring it to his lips, "how lovely to see you again!"

He reminded Amber of a snake, slithering gracefully, hypnotising its victim, ready to pounce.

"We had better take Princess Pushy to the lorry – we should be getting home," Henry said. There was a note of desperation in his voice as if he had been outfaced by a stronger rival and knew that he stood no chance.

"Perhaps I'll see you at the Murtaghs' party." Derry slowly released Stella's hand as if he were unwilling to let her go.

Stella was speechless, as bemused by Derry's megawatt charm as a gauche child.

*   *   *

It was almost midnight when the girls finally got home after first driving back to Henry's to put the mare in her stable. Stella went out to take Teddy for a walk when they got back to the apartment.

"See you in a little while," she said to Amber, pulling an unwilling Teddy out of the door – he had been cosy and warm curled up in his basket and didn't want to go out into the cold night air.

The door closed and Amber collapsed onto the sofa in panic. How was she ever going to get out of this scrape? Why was she so stupid with money? Stella had laid a line of newspaper around the kitchen in case Teddy had an accident. One section was stained dark where the dog had wet it. Bleakly Amber went to clean it up. She couldn't sit still, thinking of what a fool she had been. Scooping up the newspaper she shoved it into the bin and then paused. There, on the floor in front of her, was her salvation.

Amber eagerly crouched down as if she had found gold inlaid into the floor. On her hands and knees she began to read the advert that she had spotted on the newspaper. An enormous feeling of relief seeped slowly through her body, like sinking into a hot bath after being out in the cold.

'Consolidate all of your loans into one simple repayment. Borrow enough to pay off all those annoying loans and have cash back to treat yourself!'

Tomorrow she would go to the offices of the loan company and fill in the simple paperwork, just like the advert said. After tomorrow she would have no more awful credit-card bills, just a small repayment. She would have money again. It was the answer to all her prayers.

32

Amber picked one of the chocolates out of the crisp paper and put it gently between Paul's lips. How glad she was that she hadn't been the person who had toiled over a conveyor belt filling this box! The job at the supermarket was far nicer. No one complained when she chatted to the customers and there were always the new lines of clothes being brought into the ladies' section, just across the store from her checkout. And finally it was lovely to be able to afford to buy the chocolates so that she could spend an evening in with Paul, eating and drinking the lovely bottle of wine that she had found in the off-licence. It had been expensive, but now that she had got rid of all of her credit-card debts things were a lot easier. The girl in the loan agency had told Amber what her monthly repayments would be – for the next five years. They did seem rather expensive, but the end of the month was a long way away. And it had seemed worth spending the money on chocolates and wine. After all, it wasn't every night that she got to spend time alone with Paul. He had the night off from work – now that he was racing again, he had cut his hours down at the restaurant. He was only working a few nights a week rather than every night. And it wasn't every night that Stella went out, leaving them with the place to themselves.

Stella emerged from her bedroom looking like a film star in a slinky gold dress that fell to her ankles, the soft fabric draping itself around her body like a second skin, clinging to her curves.

"Wow!" breathed Paul, then gasped as Amber elbowed him mock-jealously in the ribs.

"Behave!" she hissed.

"The Murtaghs' party is supposed to be a really good do," Paul said, his voice tinged with envy. "I've never been asked, never been good enough for that kind of crowd. But of course now that you're mixing with *the* Henry Murphy . . ."

Stella laughed at Paul's sarcasm and gave a snort of derision. "Yes, turning up for parties in a battered old Jeep really gives a good impression," she mocked, grabbing her bag from the table. "I bet Derry Blake won't come in a battered old car," she added wistfully.

"Henry's worth two of *him!*" snapped Paul irritably, heaving himself upright to glare at Stella.

"I'll walk you out, Stella," Amber said, getting to her feet and popping another enormous chocolate between Paul's teeth to shut him up before he could annoy Stella further. She followed Stella out the door and down the stairs into the cold night air.

"You look lovely," Amber said, pausing in the doorway as Stella buttoned her coat over her dress.

Stella smiled wryly. "Henry probably won't even notice."

Amber shook her head with a smile. "Of course, he'll notice – he never takes his eyes off you."

"Really?"

"You know he doesn't," Amber grinned. "Surely you can see that he's crazy about you."

Stella winced. "I don't want him to be crazy about me though," she sighed. "I think he's lovely, but I don't want to get involved with someone like him."

"But you *are* involved," Amber said gently. "Can't you see that?"

Stella kissed Amber softly on the cheek. "'Night,"

Amber leant against the door frame and watched Stella get into her car. "Don't hurt him," she whispered as the car pulled slowly out of its parking spot.

* * *

Paul stretched luxuriously as Amber sat gently down on the sofa and leant over him, kissing his mouth softly. He had been drifting off to sleep, lulled by the heady wine and the warm flat. He ran a leisurely hand around the back of her neck, drawing her closer to him.

"I hope that Stella is very, very late back," he muttered huskily, sliding his tongue in between

Amber's lips.

"Very, very, late," agreed Amber, wriggling so that she was lying on the sofa, stretched out beside Paul, every inch of their bodies touching. He slowly undid the buttons on her shirt and she gasped as he slid his hand inside, caressing her skin.

"Do you think that we might be more comfortable in my room?" Amber whispered, nibbling gently on the soft skin beneath his ear.

"Definitely," he agreed, whimpering as Amber's fingers travelled slowly down his chest and came to rest tantalisingly at the waistband of his jeans. "Come on then!" he shouted suddenly, tipping Amber onto the floor with one deft movement and darting towards the bedroom. Teddy, thinking that this was a great game that he would love to join in, leapt from his basket and ran yapping across the floor. Paul shot into the bedroom with Amber hot on his heels, dragging Teddy, who was clinging to her jeans with his tiny needle-sharp teeth, after her.

"Sorry, mate," Paul said a moment later, depositing Teddy outside the bedroom door and closing it firmly in his crestfallen face. "But you're not welcome in here."

"We should send Stella out more often," Paul said, throwing himself onto the bed and watching Amber with his hands behind his head. "You're *some* floozy," he grinned, as she began to take off her shirt and jeans.

"I wonder if she's enjoying herself?" mused Amber, taking off her socks and getting into bed.

"I bet she is," he replied as he pulled off his jeans.

"The Murtaghs' parties are pretty legendary – all the posh, rich crowd go. Stella will feel right at home."

"Hmmmm," Amber mused, gently stroking Paul's face, "I prefer a bit of rough."

A few moments later the silence of the apartment was broken by the door buzzer sounding.

Teddy exploded into a frenzy of barking.

"Who the fuck is that?" groaned Paul, rolling irritably away from Amber.

"I'll get rid of them, whoever it is. Wait there." Amber wrenched back the bedclothes and hastily dressed again. "Hang on!" she yelled, as the buzzer sounded again.

She went outside and pressed the intercom. "Yes?"

"Amber, it's Georgina," came back her sister's tinny-sounding voice.

Paul appeared naked in the bedroom doorway. "Whoever it is – get rid of them!" he growled.

"I can't," said Amber miserably, screwing up her face in anguish. "It's my sister, the one that ran off with her teacher."

Paul ran one hand through his hair in a gesture of frustration. "This had better be important," he growled, snatching his jeans off the bed and beginning to pull them on, whimpering softly all of the time, so that Amber giggled.

Teddy sat watching him, his head on one side, wondering why he was making such a strange noise.

"You're too young to understand," Paul said, bending over to scratch Teddy's whiskery face.

Amber pulled open the door and stood watching for her sister to appear. A few moments later, two heads emerged from the stairs: Georgina's and that of the nerdy-looking Martin.

"You'd better come in," Amber said, hoping that she didn't sound too resentful. She hoped that this wasn't just a social call – it would be awful to have missed out on a luxurious night of pleasure with Paul for that. But somehow she knew that it couldn't be. She and Georgina had never been close, even when Amber lived at home.

Georgina had changed since she had left home. She had grown into a woman. Gone was the plump teenager, and in her place was a confident, self-assured young woman. She was still not slender, but the chunky teenager buried in puppy fat had long since disappeared. Moving away from home had obviously done her good. The only sign that she was nervous was the way that her hand clutched at Martin's long pale fingers, as if she were afraid that he would make a bolt for the door and leave her alone with Amber. Martin, taken away from his usual position beside the school blackboard, looked more like a nervous teenager than she did. He was smartly dressed in a blue cotton shirt, which brought out the colour of his eyes, and a tweed jacket and cream chino trousers. He kept running a nervous finger around the edge of his collar as if it were too tight for him. There was a faint sheen of sweat on his brow, beneath his trendy haircut, which tonight was slicked into spikes with gel, in a very different style to the nerdy way that he styled it while he was teaching.

"Sit down," Amber said graciously, catching Paul's eye as he came back into the room, dressed once again. He pulled a sad clown's face at Amber behind her sister's back, turning his lips down, hunching his shoulders and then rubbing his eyes as if he were crying. Amber shot him a warning look.

"This is Paul, my boyfriend," she told them as Paul sat down with a barely audible sigh.

"How are things?" Amber asked, thinking how bizarre it was that she was now making polite conversation with her pain-in-the-ass sister, when she wanted to be back where she had been a few minutes previously – in bed with Paul.

"Things are great – aren't they, Martin?" said Georgina, looking at him for reassurance.

"Yes, great," he agreed, nodding in a way that reminded Amber of one of the toy dogs that sit in the rear windows of cars. He looked petrified, as if he thought that Amber was going to yell and scream at him for stealing Georgina.

"Great," nodded Amber, not daring to look at Paul in case she giggled. This was the most bizarre exchange, sitting and repeating the most stilted conversation ever. "So," she asked suddenly – it was time to get to the point, "what can I do for you?"

Martin looked as if Amber had just jumped up and bitten him. "We . . . er . . . that is . . ." he stammered.

If the whole scene hadn't been so tense, Amber would have found it really funny. When she had been at school he had been someone to fear, always with a lightning-fast put-you-down to subdue any pupil that stepped out of line – his acid tongue had been legendary. Now he was sitting in her living room tongue-tied and terrified.

Georgina entwined her fingers, compulsively twisting them together. Something glittered, catching Amber's eye, and a jolt of realisation shot through her just as her sister jumped to her feet and blurted out: "We're getting married!"

It was a diamond engagement ring that she was twisting around her finger.

"Fuck!" breathed Paul in astonishment.

Martin shot him a look, suddenly reverting to being a schoolteacher faced by a naughty schoolboy, and then suddenly subdued when he remembered that he wasn't at work.

"Ahh!" was all that Amber could manage to say.

Martin grasped Georgina's hand and pulled her back to sit beside him. She glared at Amber defiantly, as if daring her to criticise them.

"That's lovely," Amber finally managed to say. "Great news," she added, as if to convince herself that it was anything but earth-shattering. She understood instantly why they had come here first. Georgina wanted *her* to break the news to their mother, see what the reaction would be before the two of them risked their lives going around to tell her themselves. Cowards, thought Amber – they want me to do their dirty work for them. As usual.

"Have you set a date yet?" Paul asked, amusement dancing in his expression. He looked as if he were torn between wanting to slap Martin on the back and congratulate him, or ask him if he should do a hundred lines saying '*I will not swear in front of my teacher*'.

"Not yet." Martin seemed to have regained his composure, now that the traumatic news had been broken and they hadn't received a terrible reception. "Hopefully sometime next summer."

Amber nodded slowly. "Lovely."

"Great, isn't it?" Georgina continued. They were back to square-one, monosyllabic conversation.

"And I suppose that you want me to come with you to break the news to Mum?"

"Yes!" breathed Georgina as if Amber had suddenly come up with a brilliant idea.

"Well," Amber said slowly, "I don't know if I'll be much help to you." Georgina's face fell. "Mum kind of fell out with me. I split her and Kenny up."

Georgina listened wide-eyed.

"But I'll come with you anyway," Amber said solemnly – there was no way that she was going to miss *this* scene.

Martin had a neat little car that they all piled into. Paul dived into the back seat beside Amber who was grinning helplessly at the bizarre nature of the occasion. Paul, feeling desperately horny now that his planned evening of unadulterated sex had been thwarted, ran his hand up and down the inside of Amber's thigh, whispering suggestively in her ear. Martin drove quickly and skilfully, with none of the flashy showing off that Ronnie loved to demonstrate, but they were left in no doubt that they were in the hands of someone who loved to drive – fast. Georgina navigated through the residential areas, until they drew to a halt outside Ruby's house. Martin turned off the engine and they all sat in a pensive silence, no one wanting to go in and face the wrath of Ruby.

"In we go then," Paul mocked lightly, as the schoolteacher pushed open his door with all the enthusiasm of someone going to the guillotine.

Ronnie answered the door.

"What do you want?" he growled, seeing Martin standing on the doorstep.

"We want to see Mum," Georgina replied bravely, squaring up to Ronnie, who took a step backwards to allow them to pass.

"What is it?" Ruby came out of the kitchen as she heard the voices. "Oh!" She stopped in her tracks as she saw Georgina and Martin.

This really is a night for stimulating conversation, thought Amber, slapping Paul's hand behind her back as it caressed the swell of her bottom. Georgina sat down on the sofa, glaring defiantly at her mother. She stared around the room as if she had never been in it before. Her mother sat heavily down on the chair opposite them and sat looking as if she couldn't believe her eyes.

"It's great of you to come," Ruby burbled as if she were making polite parlour conversation – and failing miserably.

Martin cleared his throat suddenly. Amber could see the sheen of sweat glowing once again on his pale brow. He ran his finger around his collar again and then clutched at Georgina's hand. "We've come to tell you – out of courtesy – we aren't asking your permission, or your blessing, or you to be pleased, or for you to come . . ."

Ruby's eyes widened as she tried to follow his words.

"We're getting married," he finished suddenly as if he had run out of breath. Ruby was silent, as if his words were still sinking in, a quizzical expression on her face. Slowly she nodded her head, looking towards the kitchen.

Kenny came out of the door and stood, arms folded, a faint smile playing on his lips. "Am I invited?"

33

Stella stole a look at Henry. He looked gorgeous in his tuxedo. Tall, elegant and impossibly handsome.

As if he sensed her eyes upon him, he glanced at her and she looked away shyly.

"I'm really glad that you agreed to come with me," Henry said. He almost had to shout above the rattling and squeaking that the Jeep was making. "This should be a great party." He turned the Jeep in between a tall set of gates.

Stella caught a glimpse of the outline of rearing lions and tall proud stags set into the ornate ironwork.

"I hope there will be plenty of people here that I can talk to about bringing their horses to me to train," Henry mused, joining the tail-end of a long queue of cars and Jeeps that were jammed along the wide, straight, tree-lined avenue that led up to a magnificent four-square house set on a rise above them. "I could do with a bit of extra business since . . ." His voice trailed off, the unspoken truth that it was because of Stella that he had lost the best part of his business hanging momentarily in the air between them.

Stella suppressed a sigh. Losing Rory's horses had made things very difficult for Henry. A huge part of his income had vanished. Losing a few horses wouldn't have mattered to a big trainer. Someone like Derry Blake.

Stella found her thoughts straying to Derry. He fascinated her. If only Henry could be like him. Wealthy and powerful, just the kind of man she wanted. Henry was lovely, kind, very handsome, but so, so terribly poor. That was obvious in every part of his life: his tatty Jeep, his tumbledown cottage, his shabby clothes. But Stella knew that she was falling in love with him. Had fallen in love with him, hopelessly, but every fibre of her intellect rebelled against that love. She had to have someone wealthy. Had to. There was no way that she was ever going to end up like her mother, scratching a living, always having to worry about where the next penny was coming from, making do with second-best.

She wasn't going to end up with Henry. No way. Not under any circumstances. But she could go out with him – without things having to get serious. That was all right. But she must never let Henry know how she felt about him. The relationship had to be light, friendly. Just loving friends.

The long line of vehicles finally crawled closer to the mansion. A man, wearing a fluorescent jacket and waving a powerful torch aggressively in the air, was directing the cars into a field, through a muddy gateway in the post and rail fencing.

"We'll go a bit closer, I think," Henry mused, winding down his window as they neared the fluorescent-jacketed man.

"Everyone has to go into the field," he snapped, jerking his torch in the direction of the gateway. "Oh, sorry, didn't realise it was you, Henry – you go on up to the house – park in the courtyard."

Henry grinned. "Cheers, Fintan!" He gave the man a thumbs-up signal. "How's Geraldine?" he added, ignoring the angry hoot of a car horn behind the Jeep.

"She's a lot better now, thank you for remembering," the man grinned, moving quickly away to direct the car behind them into the field.

Winding up his window Henry drove on towards the house. "We'll go around the back of the house, into the old courtyard," he said as they reached a fork in the driveway. "That way goes up to the house." He pointed to a gracefully curving drive, lit by flickering flares, that wound around a velvety smooth expanse of grass, broken only by tall, ornate yew trees, each trimmed into a precise rectangular shape. "This drive was once used for carriages," he explained, steering the Jeep along a driveway that curved away from the house, through parkland dotted with ancient trees before it led beneath a huge archway into a vast cobbled courtyard. "Those were staff houses at one time." Henry jerked his head in the direction of the cottages that lined the edge of the courtyard. "Times have changed now," he added with a wry laugh. "Now the rich folk have to take every penny that they can out of these big old money pits they call houses. The Murtaghs rent these out as holiday cottages."

He parked the Jeep beside an ornate fountain that trickled water over a woodland nymph carved in stone and into a huge circular pond.

"Very upmarket holiday cottages, though," Henry mocked lightly, glancing at the large chandelier that they could see hanging in a room of one of the cottages.

"Come on. We'll go in the back way." Henry shot around to open the door of the Jeep for Stella to get out. The door gave its now-familiar screech of metal against metal, as he wrenched it open and then banged it shut forcefully.

Henry led the way to a door, half hidden in the dark shadow cast by the towering, square house. He shoved his shoulder against the door, barging it open. It gave way unwillingly – obviously it hadn't been used very recently.

"Hang on," he mumbled.

Stella stepped into the darkness of a cold, damp room. She could hear Henry fumbling around the walls.

"Light has to be here somewhere," he muttered. Stella blinked as Henry found the switch, flooding the room with light. "These were once kitchens and laundries," he told her, seeing her look of wonderment at the shabby, damp rooms. "I don't think the Murtaghs ever come down here." He shook his head, sighing at the abandoned rooms, with their peeling paint and piles of unidentifiable cardboard boxes and rubbish. "I used to spend hours down here when I was a child," he sighed at the memory. "I used to come and play with the cook's children."

"Nice," Stella said politely.

Henry grinned, taking Stella's arm. They walked along echoing corridors towards the sound of the party that filtered down from above them. Stella was musing over everything that Henry had told her. So his family had lived in this area when he was young – or perhaps his parents had worked here at the house and that was why he knew the place so well?

She was just about to ask him when they came to a narrow wooden flight of steps leading upwards. He led her up the stairs. At the top, he shoved open a door and helped Stella out into the midst of a crowded party in the most luxurious house that she had ever seen. Stella fought to close her mouth which had gaped open in amazement.

"Hello, Henry!" someone yelled, as Henry shoved the door closed behind them. Stella felt as if she were Alice in Wonderland as a uniformed man carrying a silver tray laden with tall, slender cutglass champagne flutes, bore down on them.

"Thanks!" Henry seized two of the glasses and handed one to Stella. "Cheers," he grinned, clinking his glass against hers.

Stella took a long swig of the champagne, gasping as

the ice-cold bubbles hit the back of her throat, tingling as they hit the roof of her mouth.

"This is gorgeous," she breathed, overawed by the sheer opulence of the house. They were standing in a huge domed hall. Acres of creamy marble floor seemed to stretch forever at either side of them. A dozen double doors led off the hall, all standing open to reveal luxurious rooms filled with heavy wooden furniture and glittering crystal chandeliers.

The whole downstairs of the mansion was filled with what seemed to be the tallest, most elegant, beautiful people that Stella had ever seen. They moved with a self-assurance and confidence born of wealth and power, as if they had been gilded at birth with an aura that set them apart from everyone else.

"Here are the Murtaghs." Henry seized Stella's hand and led her across the marble floor towards a middle-aged couple. "Cecilia and Gerald Murtagh . . . Stella O'Rourke.

"Oh Lord, Henry," giggled Cecilia, "Cess and Gerry, please." She had a rich voice that sounded as if she had a dozen plums in her mouth. Stella tore her eyes away from Cess, aware suddenly that she was staring. Cess was magnificent. She was tall and plump, but the gorgeous red silk dress that she wore only seemed to highlight her voluptuous figure, skimming over her waist and plunging to reveal the creamy skin of her glorious breasts. Dressed in a baggy pair of jogging bottoms wandering around a supermarket she would have looked common and vulgar but, dressed in a way that brought out the best points of her body, she was an imposing sight. Beside her Gerry cut a dashing figure. He was so tall that he seemed to hunch over as if to bring himself down to the level of his companions. He was as thin as Cess was fat. Again, dressed in ordinary clothes sitting on a bus, he would have cut a nondescript figure. It was amazing, thought Stella, taking a long swig of her champagne as Cess and Gerry glided away to meet more of their guests, how wealth transformed someone's image, from the commonplace to the extraordinary.

Together Henry and Stella wandered around the beautiful rooms, filled with beautiful people. In one room an enormous mahogany dining table creaked with the weight of food that it carried: huge turkeys, dressed salmon, the biggest side of beef that Stella had ever seen, with vast bowls of lush salads and a steaming dish of tiny potatoes, swimming in butter. Another table was laden with the most amazing and colourful desserts. This was one room that Stella knew she should avoid, especially after she had drunk a couple of glasses of champagne.

Music boomed from a darkened room from which sweating couples emerged to grab glasses of champagne from the waiters and gulp them down like lemonade.

"Maybe you'll have a dance with me later?" Henry suggested shyly, looking warily towards the flashing lights that could be seen inside the dark room.

Stella's favourite room was an enormous lounge.

Three huge squashy sofas were arranged in a rectangle around a cavernous fireplace and all around the edge of the room were dark wooden bookshelves, crammed with books of every description.

"Shall we go and get something to eat?" suggested Henry. "I don't think I've eaten since this morning." He frowned, trying to remember when he had last eaten.

"No, you go. I've already eaten," Stella said hastily. She didn't want to go near the buffet table. If she had anything at all to eat she wouldn't know where to stop and then she would feel the dreadfully familiar guilt of having overeaten. As long as she didn't go near to the food she would be fine. "I'll just wander around on my own until you come back," she smiled at Henry, who lingered uncertainly for a moment, torn between his hunger and his desire to stay with Stella.

"OK, then," he said, the hunger winning. "Are you sure that you'll be OK?"

"Yes, fine. You go on." She virtually had to push Henry in the direction of the food.

It felt strange, suddenly, not to have Henry beside her. She felt curiously naked, as if she had forgotten her handbag, or to put on her shoes. She wandered off down the long hall, exploring the house, squeezing past groups of people who all seemed to be chatting animatedly about horses or racing. The hall was lined with enormous portraits, originals in oil, in gorgeous ornate frames. One, a picture of a blond man astride a huge grey hunter, looked oddly familiar. Stella paused to look at the picture, fascinated by how familiar the man looked – maybe he was the ancestor of someone famous, or something.

"You're with Henry Murphy, aren't you?" A willowy blonde came to stand beside Stella, gazing up at the picture.

"That's right," Stella nodded, warily, not sure of who the blonde woman was.

"Lucky you!" she breathed, looking Stella unashamedly up and down. "He has never even given me a second glance," she sighed, turning once again to gaze up at the picture. "Do you think that could be one of Henry's relatives?" the blonde asked, wiping an imaginary bit of dust from the frame and examining the tip of her finger.

"Maybe," Stella said lightly. But she didn't know how to take the remark. Was the woman implying that Henry's ancestors had been the illegitimate results of liaisons between the servant girls and their aristocratic masters? Or was it just a snide reference to Henry's poverty?

"Stella," a familiar smooth voice said beside her.

She turned and smiled up into the handsome face of Derry Blake.

"How careless of Henry to leave you alone," he said silkily, resting one arm on the wall above her, effectively trapping her.

"He's just gone to get something to eat," Stella replied, seeing out of the corner of her eye the blonde woman slipping away.

"Come on, I'll get you a drink. Someone as gorgeous

as you should not be left alone." Derry placed his hand on the small of her back and guided her across the room. "Bottoms up!" He handed her a glass of champagne.

Stella sipped and watched Derry over the top of her glass. There was something dangerous about him, dangerous and intriguing.

Derry leant forward and whispered, huskily, "I would love to fuck you."

Stella felt her mouth drop open with the sheer effrontery of the man. Then as she opened her mouth to frame a reply she felt Henry slipping his arm gently around her waist and drawing her possessively to him.

"Thanks for looking after Stella," he said, smiling tightly at Derry.

"My pleasure," Derry smiled back, his eyes narrow with dislike. "Any time." But his final words were directed straight at Stella.

*   *   *

The night wore on. Henry finally claimed his dance with Stella as the music slowed from a booming disco beat to gentle romantic songs. They swayed slowly around the dance floor. He was lovely to dance with, holding her tenderly, his cheek resting gently against her hair. She leant against his body, letting the music take them around the floor. She felt so safe, so protected by him. So comfortable.

And then all too soon they were outside, clattering

down stone steps onto a gravel forecourt. Dawn was just breaking. Bright purple and pink streaks spanned the horizon, mingling with the remnants of the darkness and the pale grey sky of morning.

"Henry, your tie," laughed Cess, hurrying out of the front door with Henry's bow tie draped in her hand.

Henry gave a sigh of disgust at himself for being forgetful. "Excuse me!" He released his grip on Stella's hand and ran lightly back up the steps. Stella stood and watched him, smiling faintly, luxuriating in the warm feeling of being with him.

"May I give you this?" Derry was at her elbow. He slipped a heavy expensive-feeling business card, embossed with black and gold lettering into her hand. "I meant what I said. Call me."

34

Stella watched Henry coming back down the steps towards her, his reclaimed bow tie clutched in his hand. He looked gentle and kind, and very happy, shaking his head in mock annoyance at himself. Behind him, standing at the top of the steps, stood Derry, staring intensely at Stella, his face impassive, amusement glittering in his eyes.

"Good job Cess found my tie," Henry laughed, seizing Stella by the hand. "I'd have been looking for it all over the house. This way!" He led the way along a path that ran around the edge of the house, towards the courtyard where they had left the Jeep. "I need a good woman to look after me!"

Stella glanced quickly at him. Had she heard him right?

"And I know just the one for the job." He put his arm around her shoulder and drew her towards him.

Stella leant against him, soaking up the strength from his body while her heart sank. If he meant her, he was in for a big shock. She enjoyed his company, he was wonderful, gorgeous, but she had no intention of making him her life partner.

The field where everyone had parked their cars was empty now, save for a lone Range Rover, which was left beside the gateway.

"I really enjoyed the night," Henry said, pulling out of the driveway onto the main road.

"So did I," Stella agreed truthfully. She had indeed had a wonderful time. She laid her head against Henry's shoulder and let herself be lulled into a doze by the jolting and rattling of the Jeep. This whole situation was crazy: she was falling in love with someone that she could never be secure with. Tomorrow she would have to pull herself together. Be firm with herself and never see Henry again. It wasn't fair, on him or her. She woke as the Jeep jolted down the drive to Henry's cottage.

"Hungry?" Henry asked, as Stella sat up, rubbing her eyes, sleepily.

"No," she lied. She had eventually succumbed to eating a small plate of delicious salads at the party, figuring she needed it to soak up the alcohol. "I would like coffee though."

The driveway down to Thornhill Cottage was lovely, the early morning light shining on the branches of the trees and the grass as if it were all freshly painted especially for them. At either side of the drive cowslips and honeysuckle danced in the faint breeze, their delicate heads almost hidden by the lush growth of grass. From a distance even the cottage and yard looked pretty, the dawn light shimmering on the silvery grey of the rooftops and setting the ancient stonework alight in a thousand different colours.

The yard was silent as Henry drove in and turned off the engine. His old black Labrador, George, padded stiffly out of one of the hay-sheds, awoken by the noise of the Jeep. He stood in the centre of the yard, and gave a single bark of welcome, his whole body moving as he wagged his tail in delight at having his master home. "Morning, George!" Henry crouched down to rub the old dog's head and pat his portly body. For a long moment Henry looked longingly towards the stables, where the horses looked eagerly over their stable doors, expecting their breakfasts. One banged hopefully on the door with his elegant hoof, demanding his food.

Stella could see him itching to go and check the horses, to make sure that everything was OK with them all after he had been away for *so* long.

But then he turned abruptly away. "I'll get you that coffee," he said giving a final, lingering look around the stable yard before walking decisively towards the house. "The grooms will be here in a little while," he said, as if to reassure himself that his precious charges wouldn't be deserted for much longer.

Stella's car was parked beside the cottage, where she had left it the night before. "I'll get my bag and get changed," she told Henry, reaching inside her tiny evening bag for her car keys.

"Oww . . . I like you in that dress," Henry said, stroking her waist regretfully. "Mind you," he smiled suddenly, "I like you in anything."

"Thanks," Stella said faintly, embarrassed by his words. This was all moving too fast for her, in a direction that she didn't want it to. She grabbed her bag off the back seat of her car. She should leave as soon as she could. He was obviously falling in love with her, and she was letting him – and she was enjoying the feeling.

She shook her head to clear the sudden vision of the cottage with hanging baskets swinging from beside the battered wooden door, except that now it was brightly painted and she was humming to herself as she hung out a line of gleaming white washing. Then, as in the movies, when the happy music screeches to a halt, she stopped the vision. Good heavens, what was she thinking? She was going to have a smart, new townhouse, with a brand new car sitting on the drive, a good-looking husband in a suit, tons of money in the bank, swanky holidays every year. *That* was what she wanted.

Stella headed upstairs to put on her jeans.

"Need any help?" Henry called up the stairs.

"No, thanks!" Stella yelled back hastily, wrinkling her nose at the delicious smell of frying bacon rashers that was drifting up the stairs towards her. A minute later she hurried back downstairs, before Henry decided to come up to give her a hand to change.

"Yes," Henry nodded, as Stella walked into the kitchen. "You do look just as gorgeous in jeans." He darted quickly back to the toaster, where the toast he had been making had got stuck. Thick black smoke poured out of it, making Stella cough. She darted forwards, pulling the toast out, giggling at his hopelessness.

"Come here," she said mock-bossily, taking the frying pan out of his hand and pushing him gently in the direction of the table. "You set the table, I'll do the girly stuff."

"Suits me."

"How on earth do you manage, really?" She smiled happily, poking at the bacon rashers with the metal spatula.

"I *like* burnt food," Henry mocked, pretending to be hurt. He was very close to her suddenly. "Well, actually, George does," he said softly.

Stella was intensely aware of his closeness. It was as if the heat from his body were radiating towards her. Her eyes were level with his mouth and she concentrated hard on watching his lips moving over his even, very white teeth. His breath smelt of mint – had he cleaned his teeth in anticipation of kissing her?

As if he read her thoughts, Henry gently lowered his head. For a long moment their lips were inches apart, the anticipation tingling in the very air between them. And then, infinitely slowly and tenderly, Henry lowered his lips onto Stella's.

"I should . . . erm . . . the bacon," Stella said some

moments later, turning slowly away. Her body felt as if it were limp, all the tension gone from it.

"Yes," Henry answered dreamily, his arm still lingering on her waist. "Right." he seemed to be forcing himself to concentrate, surfacing back to reality as if he had been underwater.

"Here!" Stella forked bacon and eggs and the freshly made toast onto two plates. She had almost finished her breakfast, savouring each mouthful, before she realised what she was doing. She *never* ate breakfast. She glanced up suddenly. Henry was watching her from across the table.

"It's great to see you eating," he grinned. "I thought that you never ate. I was afraid you were one of those weird anorexics or bulimics."

Stella smiled weakly. "Really?"

After they had eaten Stella cleared away the plates and Henry said he must go out to the yard, unable to keep himself away from checking out the horses any longer.

"I'm sure that Jimmy and Kathy will be able to manage without you for a while longer," Stella smiled.

Henry shrugged self-effacingly. "I know." He shook his head wryly at his own inability to trust anyone but himself. "It's just that the horses are all I have."

Stella watched him go, shaking her head at her own insanity – falling in love with someone whose life was as precarious as Henry's. This had to stop.

By the time Henry returned, Stella had washed up and tidied the kitchen.

"Right then," Henry said sternly. "I have delegated. Jimmy and Kathy are in charge for the morning."

Stella smiled, raising her eyebrows and looking at Henry quizzically.

"Let's go wild, head off for a walk, just enjoy the sunshine." He seemed amazed that he had managed to tear himself away from his responsibilities, even for a few hours.

"Come on then!" Stella helped herself to a jacket from the pile that hung in the hall. "Right." Henry grabbed another jacket and followed her outside.

Even George looked surprised to see Henry heading out of the yard without the horses. After a moment, he bounded after them, delighted to be going for a walk. It was lovely to be outside in the fresh air. The coolness of the early morning still lingered, but with the promise of a warm day later, when the sun rose fully. Dew still dampened the grass, clinging to their shoes and leaving a trail of footprints across the fields. They walked silently, savouring the silence, while George padded stiffly behind them, his thick black tail waving in delight. Behind them some of the horses were coming out onto the gallops. Henry paused, turning to look, unable to resist watching his prized horses working, and then after a moment he tore himself away.

"Madly Deeply looks like he's going well – should be ready for Clonmel," he muttered, ducking under the post-and-rail fence that bordered his land and holding out his hand to steady Stella as she followed him.

They followed a path that led through the

woodland, winding steadily uphill, through the ancient oak and sycamore trees. It was warm inside the woodland, no breeze stirring the leaves. Henry stripped off his jacket and flung it over his shoulder. "This is wonderful!" Stella took in a deep breath of the earthy woodland scent as they padded along, their footfalls muted by the peaty earth.

"There's a fairy fort up here," Henry said, leading the way as the path forked, turning sharply up the hill. He grabbed Stella's hand, pulling her up the steep incline, winding through the ancient, thick trunks of the trees, into the shadowy dim light of the canopy made by the leaves.

At the top of the hill the trees thinned out into a grassy field and there on a small incline was a circle of trees around a circular mound of rocky earth. They reached the fairy fort and leant against one of the silvery trunks of the sycamore trees, taking deep breaths of air into lungs that protested with the effort of the climb.

"Oh, there's my house!" Stella said, looking at the scenery once she had got her breath.

"Your house?" smiled Henry, gazing in the direction of the mansion that Stella so often admired when she was travelling to Henry's cottage.

"I would love to live somewhere like that," Stella mused.

Henry shook his head, snorting faintly with amusement. "I think that maybe you will. One day."

Stella turned to face him. "If I win the lottery

maybe?" She smiled wryly.

"You should have a house like that," Henry said, putting his hand gently around the back of her neck and drawing her towards him.

Stella let herself step into his arms.

"I want you so much," he breathed softly, cupping her chin in his hand and tilting her face up to meet his.

The soft green canopy of the leaves of the tree made an almost mystical shelter from the outside world. Gently Henry unbuttoned Stella's shirt, sliding his cool hands around her waist, stroking her smooth skin, as if he couldn't quite believe that she was real.

"Take off your jeans," he murmured, his long fingers already fumbling with the button.

Stella felt intoxicated by the heat and pure unadulterated lust for him. She slid quickly out of her jeans, wanting to be entwined against his skin, revelling in the feel of his lips against hers, in the pure pleasure of longing for another body. Henry cupped her buttocks, naked in her tiny lace thong and drew her to him once again. She could feel his cock, pressing urgently against her belly. Then reluctantly pulling away from her, he slipped out of his jeans, grinning and unabashed by his nakedness.

"Sit down," he whispered hoarsely, pulling apart from Stella and helping her to sit beside him, handling her as gently as if she were made of fine cut glass. Slowly they unfolded their limbs until they lay side by side, cushioned by the warm grass that made a deep comfortable bed for them.

"Stella, Stella," Henry whispered, gently, pulling her towards him so that they lay, every inch of their bodies touching. "Jesus – you're so lovely," he murmured.

Stella ran her hands over his skin, feeling the firm swell of his muscles beneath his skin, letting her hands play across the smooth plane of his back and then onto the firm athletic muscles of his belly, sliding relentlessly downwards.

The sunlight played on her face as Henry slowly rolled her onto her back, the grass prickling momentarily, and then all external sensation was lost as their bodies entwined, hungry for each other. Their hands grasped each other, lips locked onto one another until they were breathing the same air, the sweat from their bodies mingling. And then the phone rang.

For a long moment the shrill noise of the phone didn't penetrate their consciousness as they lay, lost in each other. It was Stella who heard it first, recognising its shrill note. She lifted her head, listening.

"Oh, sorry," she said, "I have to answer that – it might be my mum."

Henry rolled away, lying with his hands behind his head, gazing up at the sunlight filtering through the leafy canopy.

"Yes," Stella snapped, lying on her belly to speak into the phone.

"Stella, it's Mum. Please, can you come home? They've taken your dad into hospital."

"OK, I'm on my way." Stella snapped off the phone. The earth felt suddenly very hard beneath her body, the grass prickly. "Henry," Stella said quickly, rolling to face Henry.

"I know," he said before she spoke. "You have to go home."

Stella nodded, already reaching for her knickers. She felt suddenly embarrassed about her nakedness, wanting to get back into her jeans and shirt as quickly as she could. Henry watched as she dressed, as if he wanted to savour every moment of seeing her body.

"Come on, please!" He didn't seem to appreciate the urgency she felt. She had to get away, get to her car, drive to Mayo. Now.

Half an hour later she was hurtling away from Henry's cottage, belting her little car up his drive as fast as it could go. The dread of the hours yet to come mingled uncomfortably with the sense of relief that she now felt. Her mother's phone call had just saved her from making *the* biggest mistake of her life.

35

Stella found that she was trembling all over. She drove like the wind, wanting to put as much distance as she could between herself and Henry. How could she have been so stupid as to let herself get carried away like that? She had wanted him so desperately. She shook her head, wiping a sweat-dampened hand across her forehead, reliving every gorgeous, terrible moment of her encounter with Henry. What would they have been doing now, if it were not for that fateful phone call from her mother. They would probably have been lying in each other's arms, like a pair of lovebirds, billing and cooing at each other. What path would her life have travelled along then? She would have doubtless become Henry's official girlfriend. And then what? The lovemaking with him had the promise of being delicious, something that would have been hard to walk away from once she had been with him. Thank goodness that hadn't happened. She had been given a second chance to get a grip on her emotions. She couldn't let herself get carried away. Must not. Falling in love with Henry was just not an option.

She pictured her mother, a shapeless, careworn figure, dressed in shapeless awful clothes, a skirt so old that the hem drooped, and an ancient jumper threadbare at the elbows. Heaving bags of turf in from the shed, carting water up from the well, her face haggard with the exhaustion of caring for her husband and running the house with no money, no prospect of a better future. That was where being in love with a poor man got you. And that wasn't for Stella. Ever.

She pulled to the side of the road. There was no point in going back to the apartment – she had everything that she needed – her toilet bag, make-up, she could borrow spare clothes from her sister. Heavens above, what was she thinking of? It was doubtful that anything of her sister's would fit her, even if she could bring herself to wear the dreadful junk that her sister clothed herself in. The best option was to buy something in Westport – that at least would save her the time of having to go back into the city. Stella pulled out her map and plotted out her route west. Then she phoned the apartment to make sure that Amber would look after Teddy for a few days.

Amber was obviously making the most of having the apartment to herself. She sounded drowsy as she answered the phone. "Heylo?"

Stella could hear Paul in the background, saying

something about the ice cream melting and bedclothes.

"It's Stella."

There was a scuffling noise as if Amber was thumping Paul to make him behave. Stella could imagine the two of them lying in bed doing just what she had been about to do. Except that she had been about to do it under a tree, out in the open. She prickled with an unexplainable anger. Amber just drifted through her life without a care in the world. Messing around with a no-hope job in a supermarket, with a waiter for a boyfriend. Amber was going to end up nowhere in life if she didn't buck up her ideas, have a bit of ambition, ditch the waiter and get herself a man with a future ahead of him.

"Listen," Stella said huffily, "my mum rang. Dad's . . ." She couldn't bring herself to even say the words that would make the fact that he was dying a reality. "I have to head straight to Mayo. Will you look after Teddy for a few days?"

"No problem!"

Stella could hear the delight in Amber's voice at having the apartment to herself for a few more days.

The phone call made, Stella started the car again and headed west. A few more miles further down the road the phone rang again. She pulled over to the side to answer it.

"Stella?" It was Henry – she could hear the sound of horses' hooves clattering along tarmac in the background. "I just phoned to see how you are."

Stella felt a jolt of pleasure at hearing his voice. He

was so kind and thoughtful, so concerned for her wellbeing.

"I'm OK," she replied, knowing that she was anything but. If only he knew what just the very sound of his voice did to her and how hard it was going to be to tell him that she couldn't see him again.

"I enjoyed last night," Henry continued, "and this morning!"

"Henry, I have to go." She ignored his quip about their morning stroll and what had happened between them. She wanted to be alone with her thoughts – just talking to him distracted her.

"Listen, best of luck with things at home."

"OK. Look, I need to go." Stella severed the connection.

It was the middle of the afternoon before she headed into the village. It was only a few weeks since she had been here, but already everything looked different, the village looking brighter in its summer mantle. The village shop was festooned with the buckets and spades and rubber balls that would be bought by the holidaymakers who descended on the village in the summer months. Even the dull-looking houses seemed more cheerful, the bright sunlight glittering on their paintwork. The village café, which only opened during the summer months as every winter its owner headed off to a villa in Spain an aunt had left her, had gleaming plastic tables and chairs on the pavement outside for holidaymakers to enjoy burgers and Cokes out in the sunshine.

Even the whitewashed cottage looked bright and cheerful in spite of the tragedy that had taken over the lives of those who lived there. Stella parked her car on the grass outside and dragged her small overnight bag out of the back seat. Patrick came out to greet her.

"Mum is at the hospital with Dad," he said quietly, his face pinched with tiredness.

Stella was silent, unsure of how to frame the questions that swirled around in her mind. Was their father dying? The doctors had all sounded so positive about him getting better. They had seemed so optimistic that they would be able to control the cancer.

"He got really sick," Patrick told her, sensing her feelings. "It was the bone cancer, the secondary cancer – calcium from the bones was getting into his bloodstream and it made him sick. He couldn't keep down his painkillers." Patrick's voice trailed away as he remembered the dreadful night that the family had just gone through, watching their father. "Hypercalcaemia," he said finally, his lips twisting around the unfamiliar word that the doctors had said was wrong with his father.

"What does that mean?" Stella asked, afraid of Patrick's reply.

"They will put Dad on a drip, get his pain back under control and use some drugs, bisphosphonates, to sort out the calcium problems." Patrick took Stella's bag from her and led the way inside.

Seamus and Mary were slumped on the sofa, hands cupped around mugs of tea, looking for all the world as if they had been up at an all-night party. Except that they had been up all night and it had been no party.

An hour later they were all walking through the dim echoing corridors of the hospital. "*Primrose Ward,*" Mary read aloud, scanning the long list of wards on a map of the hospital.

"This way," Seamus headed off down a long corridor.

Then, as they saw the sign '*Primrose Ward*' above the door Patrick's steps came to a faltering halt. "I think I'll go and get some coffee first," he said, gazing through the glass doors into the ward, where patients lay surrounded by the winking lights and bleeps of machinery.

"Me too," Seamus and Mary spoke together.

"You go in. Dad will love to see you," Mary went on, opening the door into the ward, leaving Stella no choice but to go in.

Stella walked slowly down the ward, gazing at the beds that lined either side of the room, afraid of intruding on the patients that lay there.

Her father lay in a bed halfway down the ward, his eyes closed. He looked relaxed in sleep, all of the pain smoothed away from his face. Her mother sat in an armchair facing him, her hand entwined in her husband's.

"Hello, Mum," Stella said softly.

"Oh love, you're here!" Irene smiled, getting stiffly to her feet and hugging Stella.

"How is he?" Stella perched on the edge of her

father's bed. He had lost weight again and his skin had a grey tinge to it.

Irene opened her mouth to speak, but all that emerged was a half-strangled sob. She sat again and clasped Paddy's hand.

"The others are down in the café." Stella gently touched her mother's arm. "Why don't you go and get a cup of tea with them. I'll sit with Dad."

Irene nodded, her lips twisted together as if she were afraid to speak in case she began to sob. Unwillingly she released her grip on Paddy's fingers and walked away down the ward. Stella eased herself into the chair that her mother had vacated.

There were a lot of people in the ward, visitors coming and going, crowding around the beds, chatting to the patients, nurses hurrying up and down the ward, their rubber-soled shoes creaking on the lino floor. Stella looked everywhere except at her father. She felt a fraud being beside him, as if she were playing the role of a caring relative, when in reality she had no feelings. She was frozen inside where he was concerned.

"Stella . . ." His familiar voice startled her.

"Yes, Dad?"

"I felt rough last night," Paddy said weakly, his hand moving across the bedclothes in Stella's direction.

Stella smiled tightly, unable to bring herself to meet his eyes. He always felt rough; even before the cancer there had always been something wrong with him.

"Have you come all the way from the big city just to see me?" Paddy smiled, teasing gently, as he struggled to sit up.

Stella nodded, watching him for a moment and then jumping to her feet to rearrange his pillows so that he would be more comfortable.

"I love you, Stella," she heard her father whisper as she leant over him.

"I love you too . . ." The words had escaped from her mouth before she had the time to stop them.

It was evening when a doctor came to Paddy's bedside. "We have the calcium under control," he said, looking intently at Paddy, as if he were some unusual specimen, "and the pain. We will monitor things for a day or so, and if all goes well we can hope he will be able to go home soon."

*   *   *

Stella went into the kitchen and lifted the blind up from the window. It clattered up noisily. Behind it the window was misted with condensation, a long crack stretching from one side to the other. Outside it was already bright, the early morning sunshine glittering on the sea. Stella stood at the window, gazing out at the small, windswept garden behind the cottage, the stunted plants that her mother tried so hard to cultivate withered by the constant battering from the Atlantic. Beyond the garden, small fields bordered by stone walls formed an untidy patchwork down to the golden gleam of the seashore where the white breakers charged up onto the sand marking the passing of time.

The cottage was silent, everyone else still slumbering. Stella made tea in two mugs and padded softly down the corridor to her mother's bedroom. The dawn light had begun to slowly filter through a gap in the curtains, casting a dim light over the room. Her mother looked up, smiling faintly. She looked exhausted, huge purple smudges marking her cheeks beneath her sunken eyes.

She handed her mother one of the mugs of tea and sat down beside her.

"Your father was . . . is a wonderful man," her mother said quietly.

"Oh . . . yes," said Stella. She sipped her tea, wondering if they were referring to the same man. He had never seemed very wonderful to her. He had always been bad-tempered, shouting at them to be quiet, always ill, spending days in bed, or propped on the sofa while her mother ran errands, bringing tea to him, coaxing him to eat with little titbits. They had always been poor, wearing hand-me-down clothes. Stella had always blamed him for not working, not being able to give them the things that they so obviously needed. Her mother was always too busy running around after her husband to look after the children, to give them the attention that they all so desperately craved.

"You probably don't remember him before he became ill," Irene continued softly. "He was such a good father, always playing with you, helping with the nappies and feeds."

Stella felt a tinge of regret for the man she wished she could remember.

"But then the accident changed him."

"Oh, yes," said Stella vaguely, taking another sip of her tea. She had heard her mother refer to 'the accident' a few times in the past but, as a child, she had learnt not to ask questions about it.

"He never made much of a fuss about it," her mother said. "The ironic thing was that he saved the lad's life and ruined his own life in the process."

The lad's life? What *was* she talking about? Confused memories rushed into Stella's mind. "You know," she said slowly, "I never was clear about what happened . . ."

"Oh, you wouldn't be – you were too young at the time and I never talked about it much after – I didn't want to bring back memories that were painful for your father. In any case, he wouldn't allow me to talk about it. He was a very proud man. He was never going to say: I was injured and now I need pity."

"So, what did happen exactly?"

"Well, some lads had come down from Dublin for the weekend," her mother said, cupping her hands around her mug. "They went out on a boat, got into difficulties. Paddy was out in his boat, checking the lobster pots. He went to rescue one of the lads who had fallen in the sea. He was drowning, panicking. Your father dived in and saved his life." She smiled at the memory, shaking her head, bleakly remembering the proud man that her husband had once been. "But after he managed to rescue the lad, he got trapped between the two boats. Damaged his back, harmed his insides. He was never the same again."

Guilt rushed through Stella. If only she had known! But she had been so young and they had chosen not to tell her.

"Of course, after that he was never really able to work much," her mother continued. "There was never enough money. He was so proud. He hated not being able to provide properly for you all." She shook her head at the memory. "I never minded. I loved him so much. We were happy with our simple life. We had each other. Even if he was sick, he was a wonderful man. We were very happy together."

"I never knew any of that," Stella whispered humbly.

"He must have seemed angry to you, but it was because he was so often in pain and angry at himself for not being able to give you the things he wanted to."

A strand of sunlight shone through the curtains. Stella watched the dust dance in the chink of light, coming to rest on the simple furniture.

"He loves you so much," her mother said.

36

Amber looked into her purse. Under the circumstances it was the most ridiculous thing that she could possibly have done. She *knew* there was only a twenty-euro note and a handful of dingy coins in it. But still she looked.

"Well?" The huge man towered over Amber, his bulk seeming to fill the doorway.

Even Teddy was terrified of him. When he had come up to the door of the apartment Teddy had yapped furiously, guarding Amber from the stranger. Then as the man glared at him, the small dog had thought better of it and had slunk away, bushy tail between his legs, to hide in his basket, embarrassed at his failure, leaving Amber to deal with the 'intruder' alone.

"I don't seem to have enough money," Amber said, hearing her own voice, high and afraid.

"Not good enough, darlin'." The man rested one

arm on the door frame and stood there, large and very intimidating.

Amber wished she had pretended she wasn't in when he had rung the doorbell. He had sounded pleasant enough when he had spoken into the speaker. "Nigel," he had introduced himself, "from the loan agency. Your repayment seems to be overdue – I wondered if there is a problem? Can we have a quick chat about it?" Nigel had a high, squeaky voice – he sounded as if he were about twelve years old.

"Sure, come on up," Amber had said, grinning cockily into the speaker. There was a *bit* of a problem with the repayment. Basically the repayment had gone on a *rather* nice handbag and a matching pair of shoes. They were just what she had needed for the race next week when Paul was due to ride one of Henry's horses. Actually, buying the shoes and handbag was saving money. The dark brown leather bag and the shoes with the fancy stitching and inlaid snakeskin would go perfectly with a cream coat that she had bought years ago. So she wouldn't need to buy a new outfit, just update an old one. Thereby saving a fortune. Even if it had meant spending the repayment money.

Nigel had sounded like the kind of lad who would understand all about people having problems with repayments. She would soon smile and flirt her way out of this little problem. Tell him that she would give him the money next week.

But Nigel, when he appeared at the door to the apartment, didn't somehow look quite like a Nigel.

More like a Fang, or a Basher. He was enormous. At least six feet tall and almost as wide, with a huge head that seemed to rise straight out of his shoulders.

"So," he leered, as Amber gulped at the sight of him, "what's the problem with this repayment then?" He had a wide mouth with a dazzlingly white row of teeth, one of which glittered with a tiny gold star embedded in its centre. His eyes were hidden behind huge dark glasses, making it impossible to read his expression. Except that Amber didn't need to read Nigel's expression. He oozed anger and menace.

"Well, I, er ..." Amber felt her face alter from a petrified white to a terrified red.

"You should have deposited the repayment in our office at the end of last month," Nigel growled. He lowered his chin, so that he could look at Amber over the top of his dark glasses. His eyes had the cold, merciless look of a shark.

"I forgot," Amber said lamely.

"Uh uh," Nigel grunted, thick dark eyebrows raised over the top of his dark glasses. "Well, I'll take it with me now."

"Right." Amber glanced desperately beyond Nigel to the top of the stairs. Would she be able to dodge past him and escape? Nigel looked as if he were well used to stopping people from escaping, so she ditched that as an option. Maybe Teddy could seize him by the throat and maul him into submission? Teddy was watching the proceedings from his basket, one eye open, wearing a guilty expression. That didn't seem like a viable option either. "I'll get my purse."

As she opened her purse Nigel seemed to grow, expanding until he filled the doorway, rather like a volcano about to erupt. Amber swallowed hard.

"I'll take that." He reached forwards with a huge paw-like hand and with incredible delicacy seized the single crisp note from her purse. "Thank you." Nigel stuffed the twenty-euro note into a brown envelope and wrote her name on the front of it. "So," he sniffed, menacingly, "what are you going to do about the rest of the money?" Amber opened and closed her mouth. What *was* she going to do about the money? The twenty was all that she had in the world – heaven knew how she was even going to get to work in the morning without her bus fare!

Nigel answered for her. "I'll call in two days' time. You be here with the money. Or I will have to pay you a little visit at work." With that he turned and stomped off down the stairs. Amber leant against the door frame, feeling as if Nigel had punched every inch of her.

Now what was she supposed to do? She had never dreamt that the loan company would be so heavy-handed about wanting their money back.

Paul came later, clutching a carrier bag of Chinese food and a bottle of wine. Amber swallowed her pride and asked him if she could borrow some money.

"I've left my bank card at work by mistake," she shrugged wryly. "I just need to borrow enough to get to work."

Paul grabbed a thick wad of money out of his

pocket. "I've just got paid for riding a horse that belonged to a friend of Henry's," he grinned delightedly.

Amber couldn't take her eyes off the money. There was enough there to pay off her monthly repayment, but she couldn't bring herself to ask Paul. It would be too embarrassing to confess to him what an idiot she had been.

They ate the Chinese and then Paul headed off. He needed an early night – he had to be at the gallops early in the morning.

Amber lay awake all night, turning over and over in bed fitfully, wondering hopelessly where on earth she was going to get the money from. She wished that Paul had stayed the night – that would have taken her mind off her impending sense of doom. But then, she decided, it was probably a good job that he hadn't – she would have ended up asking him for the money.

By morning the only person that she could think of to ask for a loan was Ronnie. He was working and she had done enough for him over the years. He owed her a favour, but being owed a favour and asking to have it repaid were very different things. She couldn't concentrate at work. All day the only thing she could think of was that at the end of the day she'd have to go around to her mother's house and see Ronnie. It was an awful prospect – she dreaded to think what kind of reception she'd get. It had been difficult enough the last time that she'd gone to her mother's with Georgina to announce her engagement. Kenny had been back on the scene, smug at having got *his* life back in order. No doubt he had promised his pretty blonde wife that he would give Ruby up, begged forgiveness and promised to never stray again. And then as soon as her back was turned he was back with his mistress. Messing up two sets of families. Her mother had been offhand, no doubt still furious at Amber for having upset their cosy nest in the first place and then feeling embarrassed at the affair restarting.

Amber couldn't settle at work. She made mistake after mistake, handing out the wrong change, scanning groceries twice and throwing tinned stuff on top of delicate boxes of eggs when she was helping to pack the shopping. All day she kept casting furtive glances to the end of the line of people queuing for her checkout, expecting at any second to look up and see Nigel standing beside her, his hand open, ready to take the money out of her till.

Even that seemed a terrible temptation, all that money, just sitting there in front of her. Surely no one would miss the little bit that she needed? But she couldn't bring herself to do that. Eventually the clock slid around to the end of her shift and she slid thankfully off her seat and headed out of the supermarket.

She caught the bus to her mother's house with the last of the money that she had borrowed from Paul. Her heart sank as she rounded the corner at the bottom of the road. Kenny's car stood in its familiar spot, half on and half off the pavement. As she walked towards it a disgruntled woman, pushing a toddler in a pushchair, had to go out onto the road to get around the huge vehicle. Amber walked on, trying to frame the words that she would have to say to Ronnie – trying to figure out how she could beg for money without seeming desperate. What a joke! Nigel would tear her limb from limb if she didn't come up with the money. She knocked on the door, feeling sick.

"Oh, it's you!" Her mother answered the door, and then stood, glaring at Amber.

"I want to see Ronnie," Amber said glaring back at her mother. How could she be so stupid as to take Kenny back? Once they had broken up she should have tried to move forwards without him, instead of just caving in and collapsing into a heap. One day he would leave her again and the next time maybe his wife wouldn't be so forgiving.

"He's not here," Ruby said, resting one hip against the door frame. "He's working away." Then she added unwillingly, "You'd better come in." She stood upright and walked into the lounge.

Kenny sat in his usual place, reading the newspaper, a mug of tea resting on the arm of his armchair.

"Amber!" he exclaimed, feigning delight.

"Where's Ronnie? I need to talk to him." Amber couldn't keep the desperation out of her voice. Without begging some money from Ronnie she was as good as dead. Nigel would make sure of that.

Kenny laid down his newspaper. "Are you going to tell her, or shall I?" he grinned. Ruby sat down. Now

Amber noticed she looked very pink, as if she were bubbling with excitement that she could barely contain.

"Ronnie's moved out," Kenny said. "He's got a place of his own."

Amber looked from one of them to the other. It was hard to imagine Ronnie summoning the energy to move out – something momentous must have happened to make him.

"He didn't want to come with us," grinned her mother.

"Why, where are you going to?" snapped Amber, unable to bear the way her mother was squirming with excitement.

Ruby went and sat on the arm of Kenny's chair, resting her arm around his shoulders possessively. "*You* tell Amber," she beamed.

Kenny rested his hand on her leg. "My marriage is over," he said quietly. "When you told my wife about us, it brought everything to a head. I thought that I had the best of everything. But then when I had to do without your mother I realised that it was her I truly wanted to be with."

Amber could feel her eyes widen with amazement. They were really going to be together, properly.

"I've bought my wife out – she's moved out of the house on Sycamore Avenue," Kenny grinned. "So we're moving in there."

Amber glanced at her mother and saw a broad smile of triumph flash across her face. She looked as if she had lost ten years in the few weeks since Amber had seen her last. Happiness oozed from every pore.

"Bloody hell," was all that Amber could manage to say. After all the years of being used by Kenny, things had actually come right for them.

"It's all down to you," beamed Kenny, jerking his head as if in acknowledgement of the enormous service that Amber had done them. "If you hadn't stirred things up with my wife I would have never done anything to change the situation. I thought that I was doing the right thing for everyone, but then I realised the opposite was true and everyone was unhappy."

Amber thought she was actually going to be sick, listening to all the sugar-coated drivel he was spouting.

"Ronnie didn't want to move to the new house," Ruby told Amber. "He said that he wouldn't feel comfortable there."

Amber nodded. That was easy to understand – it was hard to picture her rough-diamond brother living in the refined atmosphere of Sycamore Avenue. "Where has he gone to?"

"He's got a job in Galway – he moved down there last weekend. We were going to tell you." There was a tinge of guilt in her voice.

"Tell me when, exactly?" whispered Amber bleakly. Now what was she supposed to do? Kenny and her mother's news had distracted her from the urgent task in hand. She didn't even have the money to get home.

"What do you want Ronnie so urgently for anyway?" Kenny quizzed.

Amber put her face into her cupped hands, to stop

the tears that were suddenly spilling down her cheeks. "Ooh," she groaned. She might as well tell them. Maybe Kenny would help her out, now that she was practically going to be his stepdaughter. "I've made such a mess of things."

"Oh, bloody hell!" laughed her mother, when Amber had finished telling them about the financial mess that she had got herself into. "Just money problems! I thought that you were going to tell me that you were pregnant!"

Amber glared at her mother. She might be stupid, but she wasn't *that* stupid.

Kenny however wasn't amused. At all. "You bloody idiot!"

Amber glanced at him, shocked. He really was angry.

"Why didn't you stop spending money before you got into this mess?"

Amber winced. She had known that she should stop, but it had been impossible – any money burned a hole in her pocket; she had to spend it. Kenny was shaking his head. Amber felt as if she were a small child again, in front of the headmaster.

"You have to put a stop to this mess now. Once and for all," Kenny growled.

"I will," Amber nodded her head, seriously. Of course, she would, once she'd got out of this current situation. "But I have to pay this guy tomorrow."

Kenny looked as if he were about to explode. He was muttering in exasperation under his breath as if he couldn't believe her stupidity. Finally he looked up and said: "I'll come with you tomorrow and sort out this debt."

Amber breathed a sigh of relief that quickly turned to horror as Kenny continued, "I'll take over your debt. You'll owe me the money – I'm going to give you a job at my car hire company – it's time you had a decent job – and I'm going to take the money you owe me out of your wages and give you pocket money until you have paid your debt and hopefully learnt how to manage your money properly."

37

Amber shrugged helplessly. "I don't know where he is."

Henry glanced at his watch yet again. He had been growing more and more agitated as the morning wore on.

"Try ringing him again," he said, trying to make his voice sound bright as if he were not concerned.

But Amber could tell by the anxious glances that he kept darting to the end of the driveway that he was hoping to see Paul's car appear at any moment.

"I knew that he would let Henry down," Stella said huffily, coming across the yard with yet more mugs of tea. They seemed to have been drinking tea constantly for the last few hours. "He said that he would be here first thing." Stella handed a mug to Henry, who slopped a good part of his tea onto the cobbles, a sure indication of the agitated state he was in.

Amber turned away, gazing up at the woodland behind Henry's stable yard. How peaceful it looked up there, the woolly green heads of the towering oak trees standing proudly as they had for generations. Stella was really starting to annoy her. Actually *had* been annoying her for the last few days.

* * *

She had been really happy and relieved when she returned from seeing her father in Mayo. But then she had lapsed into an extremely emotional state, no doubt in reaction to all the stress. Amber had been kind to her, nursing her, wrapping her in a duvet on the sofa, where she had sat hugging Teddy to her, his hair wet with her tears. Amber had sat with her, listening for hours as she spoke of her father, how miserable she had been as a child and how now she was so happy they had the chance to put all of the ill feeling behind them. She wished she had told him that she loved him years ago. He could have died thinking that she hated him. It could have been too late. She wouldn't have been able to turn the clock back.

After a few days Stella had pulled herself together. She had got out of bed one morning and come into the kitchen to find Amber. She looked calm, composed again. More like the Stella that Amber knew. Stella had crumbled a slice of toast between her fingers as they sat to eat breakfast. Amber wondered how she even existed, she seemed to eat so little.

"I'm going to end it with Henry," Stella had said finally. "There's no point in carrying on with this."

"Why?" Amber had asked, shaking her head in bewilderment. They seemed so involved with each other. They were meant to be, anyone could see that.

"I'm getting too fond of him," Stella said and there was more than a touch of bleakness in her voice.

"What?" Amber asked incredulously. Surely you were *meant* to get fond of someone when you were in a relationship?

"He's not for me," Stella said flatly.

"Of course, he is!"

Stella shook her head, "No." For a long while she was silent, sipping her tea, resting her elbows on the table. Her expression looked desperately sad. "My mother loved my dad," she then said quietly. "After he was injured they had nothing. Mum says that she never regretted that. She loved him and was happy with him. And that it didn't matter to her that they had nothing."

Amber smiled faintly. "Well, surely if you love someone nothing really matters – whether you're rich or poor, sick or healthy. The love is there whatever."

Stella glanced up at Amber, her eyes narrowed with annoyance. "No. I don't believe her. How can she have been happy living like *that?* Struggling all the time?"

Amber was silent, afraid to answer. Afraid that if she did, she would say something that Stella didn't want to hear.

"So," Stella drained the last of her tea and put down her mug decisively, "I'm going to end it with Henry."

"Please don't do anything until after this weekend though," Amber pleaded. "Henry is so wound up about this big race. Paul was with him a few days ago – he said Henry is like a cat on a hot tin roof. Can't settle. If they win this race he's hoping that more clients will come to him. Make life a lot easier for him." Amber saw a frown flicker across Stella's forehead. "You owe it to him," she told her. "It *is* because of Rory that he lost so much business in the first place."

Stella's jaw clenched.

"If you're going to end it with him, *please* wait."

Stella sighed. "Right!" she snapped. "But once this race is over . . ."

* * *

Now Amber began to wish that she hadn't persuaded Stella to stay with Henry until after the race. She was as taut and tetchy as could be, her face pale and drawn.

"What has happened to Paul?" she began again, resting her hand on Henry's arm, touching the fabric of his jacket as if she wanted to imprint the feel of him into her memory.

Amber shook her head, shrugging miserably. "He was just going out with some mates last night." Amber saw a wry look flash over Stella's face. "He's not the kind to get blind drunk and end up sleeping in a gutter somewhere!" But still, at the back of her own mind, prickled a seed of doubt.

Where *was* he? He had told her it was a lads' night out. He hadn't been out on his own since they had started to see each other. He had seemed to prefer spending time sitting quietly in a corner of the pub with Amber, sipping a Coke, or curled up at the apartment watching television with her – or if Stella were out, curled up beneath the duvet, their arms and legs entwined. She had almost had to force him to go out with his friends. In fact when one of them had phoned to ask him to come he had initially refused. Amber had made him ring back and say that he would go. Now she regretted her rashness. What if he had gone off with another girl? Maybe at this moment he lay beneath someone else's duvet, licking ice cream off her belly.

"We'll have to go," Henry said, getting jerkily to his feet. "We can't wait any longer."

Amber pressed the redial number on her phone, listening bleakly as it rang momentarily and then switched straight to a recorded message – Paul's voice brightly saying in her ear that he was sorry that he couldn't come to the phone. "Where are you?" Amber hissed, before saying into the mouthpiece, "Paul? Henry is going to have to leave. He can't wait any longer for you. Please phone me, or him." Maybe Paul was with someone else and didn't want to talk to her. If that was the case maybe he would phone Henry.

Kathy led Princess Pushy across the yard and into the battered horse lorry, her face like thunder. "Will you be able to get someone else to ride her?" she snapped at Henry, shooting a glance of dislike in Amber's direction as if it were her fault that Paul wasn't here.

Henry nodded, following the woman and the horse into the lorry and shutting the partition as Kathy ducked underneath it. "It's just that she goes so well for Paul. She really likes him," he said, running lightly down the ramp and heaving it closed. The undertone was that it was as well that Princess Pushy liked Paul, because just at this moment in time, no one else did.

Stella walked across the yard, carrying the empty tea mugs. Amber climbed into the passenger seat of the lorry, looking back to see Stella gazing around the yard as if this were the last time that she would ever see it. Amber began to feel sick, a sharp pain dug into her side, like a stitch, as if she had been running a long distance. She shifted uncomfortably, digging her fist into her side to try to ease the pain. What a nightmare of a day this was turning out to be! Paul had gone missing and Amber didn't know if she was ever going to see him again. And it looked as if Stella had no intention of ever seeing Henry again after today either. She had been true to her word, standing by him for the race that meant so much for him, helping to ease the stress that he was under. But after the race she was going to end it all, so she had told Amber.

Stella climbed into the lorry, flashing a sympathetic smile at Henry. "It will be OK, you'll see," she smiled, talking gently to him.

Amber could see Henry visibly relax when she was around. She soothed him, just like Paul had seemed to soothe Princess Pushy. It was as if she lifted all of the clouds that surrounded Henry. Amber wanted to shout at her, to shake her, anything to make her not leave Henry. They were so right together. Any fool could see that.

Henry started the lorry. "Maybe he'll meet us at the races." He seemed to speak more to reassure himself than anything else.

"Don't worry," Stella reached across and put a gentle hand on his knee, "you'll find someone else, if Paul doesn't turn up."

Henry smiled bleakly at her. "I know – it's just that I had such hopes for the two of them."

Amber stared fixedly out of the window, cursing Paul – and Stella. She was going to break Henry's heart when she dumped him. And why? Because of some silly idea that she had of finding a rich man. She thought that she wouldn't be happy if she were with someone who had nothing. Love didn't work like that. It was so obvious how much they cared about each other. Stella was going to be lost without Henry. She was being ridiculous. Why break your own heart, because your head is leading you in a different direction?

*　　*　　*

The races were already crowded when they arrived.

Kathy went to get the horse ready, grumbling sourly that they had left things very late and that Princess Pushy wouldn't be relaxed and warmed up enough.

"She'll be OK," Stella snapped at her.

Amber grinned. In spite of her own misery, Stella protected Henry like a mother hen, shielding him from any anxiety Kathy was trying to stir up.

"Go and declare Princess Pushy," said Stella. "We'll meet you in the parade ring. There will someone around who will ride her. Go and look in the Weigh Room." She had learned a lot about racing since she had started going out with Henry. She gave Henry a gentle shove in the direction of the Stewards' offices.

People were pouring into the races as Amber and Stella walked into the concourse. This was one of the biggest races of the year. And Henry had been convinced that Princess Pushy stood a good chance in the race. She had been working so well with Paul riding her. But now . . .

Amber trailed miserably after Stella across the racecourse. She wore the new boots and carried her matching handbag. The whole outfit did look beautiful – it should do after all of the trouble it had got her into, she thought, catching sight of herself in the reflection from the glass in the Owners' and Trainers' Bar. Paul would have loved her in this. Now she was beginning to get frightened. What if he had been in an accident? Stella had been so convinced that he had gone out and got drunk and was just sleeping it off somewhere. But that would be so unlike him.

Amber glanced at her watch. They would be home in a few hours' time and then she would have to phone the hospitals to see if he was lying there, injured.

Injured. The very thought made the pain in her side grip again.

Stella and Amber leant on the guardrail around the parade ring, watching the horses walk around, delicate hooves barely seeming to touch the tarmac as they danced with excitement. Amber could feel the anger that emanated from Stella, as she stood silently watching the horses go around.

"I've found someone!" Henry dashed up to them, alight with excitement. "Toby McEvoy's horse has been pulled out – he was lame this morning, so Toby has agreed to take the ride on Princess Pushy."

Stella grabbed his hand, kissing him with delight, "Brilliant!" she exclaimed, the relief loud in her voice.

"Great," agreed Amber, feeling very much as if she shouldn't be with them. After all, it was her boyfriend that had caused all the trouble.

Henry put a kind arm around Amber's shoulder and squeezed her gently. "Don't worry – I'm sure that there is a really good reason why Paul isn't here. He wouldn't just let us down. He's not that kind of man."

Amber smiled gratefully, ignoring the look of scorn on Stella's face. She obviously thought that Paul was *exactly* the sort of man who would let anyone down.

Kathy brought Princess Pushy into the parade ring. The elegant mare looked fabulous. She walked calmly around the ring, her delicate ears sharply pricked, taking in all that was going on around her.

"I hope that she goes well for Toby," Henry fretted, twisting a lead rope between his fingers. Stella took his hand, squeezing his fingers gently.

The jockeys trooped out of the Weigh Room, their brightly coloured silks billowing in the fretful wind that had blown up.

"Good afternoon," Toby shook hands with Henry and nodded politely at the two girls.

"She's a good mare," Henry began, taking Toby to one side to tell him how to ride the race.

Amber glared at the jockey's bowed legs. She didn't like him at all, and neither did Princess Pushy from the way she laid back her ears and kicked out with a hind leg when Henry legged Toby up onto her back.

"Steady, my lady," Kathy tried to soothe the mare as she jogged, tense beneath Toby's weight.

The horses began to go out onto the course, Kathy struggling to keep control of Princess Pushy, who was prancing sideways, tossing her head up and down, thoroughly upset by the stranger that was on her back.

"She doesn't like Toby!" wailed Henry.

"Paul!" screamed Amber, not sure whether to be delighted or furious. Paul was running across the grass towards them, a huge black eye on one side of his face.

"Where the fuck have you been?" snapped Henry as Paul slithered to a halt, panting for breath.

"In a Garda cell!" he gasped.

38

Stella wanted to hit Paul, to give him a black eye to match the one that he already had. How dare he let Henry down! And in a Garda cell! That was just what she would have expected. Amber looked as if she were about to burst with pleasure and relief, she was so delighted to see Paul back. Even Henry looked relieved to see him, although it was too late for him to ride the horse.

"A Garda cell!" exclaimed Henry. "What the hell were you doing in a cell?"

Paul brought his hand up to his face as if his black eye were really hurting him. "I went out with some lads last night. We were in a bar and I heard some lad, a jockey he was, bragging about . . . stuff. So I hit him. And he hit me back."

"What?" Henry said incredulously. "Bragging about what stuff?"

"Come on," Paul said. "They're going down to the start." He looked regretfully at Princess Pushy who was cantering away from the parade ring, looking very unhappy, swishing her tail and bucking as if she wanted to rid herself of Toby.

"Bragging about what stuff?" Henry persevered as they walked towards the Owners' and Trainers' Stand. Paul stopped, ignoring the angry glares of those who had to squeeze past them on the way to the stands.

"You remember when Morgan Flynn's horse fell and killed a jockey and then afterwards some of his horses got poisoned and died?"

Henry nodded. "Go on."

Amber and Stella looked at each other – this was stuff that they had never heard.

"Well, this lad who was bragging was someone who had once worked for Morgan. He had got the sack for stealing and decided to get his own back. The accident was the perfect cover – everyone thought that the poisoning was something to do with that."

"And so you hit him and ended up in a cell for the night?" Stella could hardly keep her temper. "But I tried to phone you – it wasn't answering."

"My phone had got broken in the scuffle – though in any case the Gardai would have taken it from me." Paul pulled his phone out of his pocket to show them. "And this morning I just wanted to get here as quickly as I could. I knew there wasn't time to stop and use a phone box. I hoped that I would make it before you had to give the ride to someone else."

"Well, you didn't!" Stella snapped. How could he be so stupid as to let Henry down? Why could he not have just walked away, not got involved in a fight?

"I would have made it," Paul grinned disarmingly, "but the Gardai stopped me for speeding!"

"Oh God!" Henry started to laugh.

"I thought that you were dead!" Amber threw her arms around Paul, who locked his lips against hers as if it were months since they had seen each other rather than just an evening.

They hurried up onto the stands, to a place where they would all be able to see the race. Stella pushed her way in so that she was standing beside him. At the far side of the course they could see the horses circling as they waited to start. It was easy to spot Princess Pushy. Toby was riding her apart from the others, trying to get her to settle, but the mare jogged, tossing her head up and down. Even from across the racecourse they could see the white patches of foaming sweat beneath her saddle patch and on her graceful neck.

Stella glared at Paul. He should have been riding the mare. She knew him and went well for him. He owed it to Henry not to let him down. Henry had stuck his neck out to give Paul a second chance when no one else would, when all of the other trainers wouldn't let him ride for them. And this was how Paul had repaid him.

Paul was looking across the racecourse miserably, his face full of guilt, his eyes never leaving the frenzied shape of Princess Pushy. The steward who started the race climbed up the starter's stand. The horses began to form a ragged line across the track. Princess Pushy lashed out at another horse, her powerful back legs raking into the air, sending Toby sprawling up her neck. The starting flag fluttered downwards and the horses plunged forwards towards the first jump.

"Oh shit!" gasped Paul, as Princess Pushy refused to start, turning sideways as the horses shot away from her. One of the stewards cracked a long hunting whip at her bottom and she jumped forwards in surprise, scooting after the other horses.

"She's racing," breathed Henry, relief sounding in his voice as he gazed with narrowed eyes at the brown caterpillar of horses' legs that was surging around the track towards them. Princess Pushy caught up with the horses – they could see the familiar colours of the silks that Toby wore merging with the other jockeys as they soared over the first jump. Around the track they went.

"She's there," Amber pointed unnecessarily at the heaving mass of horseflesh and grim-faced jockeys.

The horses thundered past the stands and then surged on around the course, soaring over fence after fence as they raced.

"Two fences to jump!" the commentator's voice bellowed out of the loudspeaker, *"They're rounding the home turn."*

"She's in second place," Henry said incredulously, gripping Stella's hand so hard that she winced.

"Princess Pushy coming up on the outside!" screamed the voice of the commentator, *"Only the final fence to jump. It's Late Again closely followed by Princess Pushy."*

The commentator was hoarse with excitement, his voice rising higher and higher. Stella stood on tiptoe to watch the horses rushing towards the final fence. Late Again's chestnut face appeared over the jump, with Toby flying through the air alongside him.

"Princess Pushy has refused. Toby McEvoy's gone over her head!" shrieked the commentator. *"Late Again wins the race!"* he bellowed as the chestnut horse surged past the winning post alone.

They watched, hearts in their mouths, as Toby rolled himself into a ball close to the jump, sheltering from the lethal hooves of the horses as they came flying over in Late Again's wake.

"McEvoy is on his feet! He's not hurt!" yelled the commentator as Toby picked himself up.

"Thank God for that!" breathed Henry.

"Oh fuck!" Paul gasped, sinking down into his seat. "She would have won if I had been riding her."

"If you hadn't been so stupid!" Stella snapped.

Henry sank down beside Paul, speechless with misery. The stands began to empty as people dashed down to get drinks and place their bets before the next race.

"Hadn't we better go down to Princess Pushy?" Stella couldn't bear the utter misery that emanated from Henry.

Henry shook his head, bleakly. "Kathy will deal with her." He sounded totally defeated.

"Come on. I'll get you a drink." Paul gave Henry his hand and hauled him to his feet. Henry sighed and shrugged. "Ah well, maybe next time we'll have better luck," he said quietly and headed off down towards the Owners' and Trainers' Bar, his shoulders hunched in misery.

The bar was crowded, everyone congratulating the owners of Late Again, a syndicate from a pub in Galway who were all already very drunk. The bar heaved with the happy throng.

They found a quiet corner, away from all the merriment, where they could drown their sorrows. Paul pushed his way to the bar, while Henry sat on a bar stool at one of the high tables and watched the celebration enviously. Stella prickled with anger at Paul and Henry. It was all Paul's fault, but yet Henry seemed to accept the terrible thing that had happened and was putting it behind him and moving on. Stella could barely bear to be near Paul, or Amber who was so delighted to be with him. In Stella's eyes he had lost Henry the race.

A few moments later Paul came back, with the glasses clutched in his hands.

"Henry," Paul grinned, "there's a guy at the bar who wants to talk to you about putting a horse with you – and in having you train it – and me ride it – if I can turn up on time!" he joked, delighted to be imparting such good news.

Henry's face lit up. "Excuse us," he said, smiling at Stella. "I'll just see what this man wants – I'll be back in a few minutes."

Stella glared at Paul's back as he weaved his way

through the crowds beside Henry.

"There should be scorch marks in his coat from the way you're looking at him," Amber said quietly, sipping her drink.

"He deserves it," Stella said coldly. "He lost that race for Henry. He ruined the day." Amber gave a short laugh. "For someone who doesn't care about Henry, you seem to be caring an awful lot about how he feels." She raised her glass mockingly at Stella.

"Paul obviously doesn't care very much about anyone," Stella retorted, turning to Amber, her eyes narrowed. Paul was no good. Amber would be able to see that if she had any sense whatsoever. "I don't know why you bother with him. You've just been given a great new job. A clean slate. You should get yourself a better boyfriend."

"Better than being a *waiter* and part-time jockey, I suppose," Amber retorted, spitting out the word 'waiter' vehemently.

Stella was silent, staring across the bar at Henry and Paul, who were talking animatedly to a short, balding man with very large teeth. "He's going nowhere, Amber," she said the words forced out through her clenched teeth. "He'll let you down and break your heart."

"Just like you're going to break Henry's when you finish with him!" Amber hissed, watching the sudden look of guilt that flashed across Stella's face.

"That's my business," Stella growled sullenly.

"Well, Paul is my business," Amber snapped back,

full of hostility.

"You didn't mind me looking out for you when you had no money," Stella said acidly.

"You didn't mind me looking after you when Rory was stalking you. Or mind me looking after *your* dog when you went away," retorted Amber, fighting the childish urge to bawl and pull Stella's hair.

"Well, thanks for that!" Stella said tartly.

Stunned by the ferocity of the hostility that darted between them, Stella and Amber sat in sullen silence waiting Henry and Paul to return.

"You aren't really going to finish with Henry, are you?" Amber asked suddenly, breaking the silence.

"I have to," Stella answered, looking at Amber, her eyes filling with sudden tears. "I can't carry on with this."

"Because you've fallen in love with him?"

Stella nodded, bleakly. "I can't stay with him. I just can't. Being poor . . ." Her voice trailed off. It was too hard to describe how she felt. Why she felt that she had to finish with Henry before it was too late.

Amber shook her head, silenced by the intensity of her sadness. Stella was being such a fool. How could she give up a man who clearly worshipped her and who she so obviously felt so much for? The whole thing was crazy. She certainly had some deep-seated problems. In fact, she needed to see a shrink.

"Well, it looks as if I've got myself a new client," Henry grinned, returning a few moments later. He pushed himself up onto the bar stool and took a long swig of his drink.

"I hope that some good has come out of today then," said Stella tightly.

"Maybe we should head off," Amber said, putting her hand on Paul's arm urgently.

"Oh, right." Paul sensed the tension in Amber. "See you soon, Henry," he nodded in Stella's direction, "Stella."

Amber slid off her chair. "Bye, Henry." She pecked Henry gently on the cheek. "You're a real nice guy." Then without saying a word to Stella she grabbed Paul's arm and strode away without a backward glance.

"What was all that about?" Henry frowned, gazing at Amber as she barged her way through the Galway syndicate group, sending one man's glass flying.

"I told her that Paul was no good," Stella said tartly.

Henry frowned quizzically, "What on earth for?" He stared at Stella as if he couldn't believe what he was hearing.

"Because he let you down, because he'll let her down," Stella replied sullenly.

Henry smiled, touching Stella's face with his fingers, tracing a line from her high elegant cheekbones to her chin. "Leave them to sort their own relationship out. It's none of your business. No matter what you think. And as for me –" he gave a snort of laughter, "well, today turned out OK anyway!" He drained his drink. "Come on, we'd better head off – Kathy will be ready to leave now."

Stella slid off her stool and followed Henry out of

the bar, the sound of merriment following them out of the door.

They drove home in silence. Kathy sat in the back, snoring softly as she dozed, her jean-clad legs stretched over the back of the seat Stella sat in. She didn't wake up until the lorry air brakes hissed when Henry stopped in the yard at his cottage.

"I'll finish off," Kathy said.

"Come on. We'll go inside." Henry helped Stella down from the lorry. It seemed a lifetime since they had been in the yard during the morning, waiting for Paul. Stella felt as if she had aged a thousand years, the journey from the lorry to the house seemed as if it were a hundred miles long, every stride an immense effort. She couldn't go inside with him. She couldn't trust herself to be alone with him again. If he were to kiss her once, she would be lost again and this time there might be no going back. She had to end the relationship. Now. While she still could.

Henry shoved open the cottage door and stood back to let Stella pass.

"Henry," Stella said suddenly, her voice sounded very tired, almost mechanical. Henry leant down and kissed the soft skin on her neck.

"I think we should go up to bed," he muttered, moving forwards to gently enfold her in his arms.

Stella felt herself waver. Her whole being cried to be with him, to go to bed with him, to become part of him, to stay beside him forever, where she belonged. But she couldn't.

"Henry," she spluttered, "I have to end this. I can't see you again." She wriggled out of his grasp, glimpsing his hurt bewildered face, highlighted in the soft light from the hall and then she was charging across the yard, hurtling towards her car as if she thought that he was going to grab her and make her stay. Make her listen to sense. Make her love him. But he didn't. She reached her car, fighting to shove the key in the lock, slamming the key into the ignition while Henry stood in the doorway, his face closed with shock.

She drove away from Henry's yard, wondering if this time she really had made the biggest mistake of her life.

39

Stella threw the remains of her sandwich into the bin at the side of her desk. Actually there was rather a lot of sandwich uneaten, but she just didn't seem to have any appetite at all. She had spent what seemed like a lifetime trying to control what she ate. Now she didn't want to eat at all. She sat up quickly as Sorcha came into her office. She must not let Sorcha see how upset she was, otherwise she would start to undermine her position again by criticising her work. And Stella didn't want to go down that particular road again – it been hard enough the last time when she was upset about Rory. Now she was upset again, about Henry and Amber, but this time she had to keep things under control, not to betray how terribly disturbed she was.

Sorcha picked up a typewritten feature from Stella's desk.

"Do you want me to check this?" she asked, her lips

twisting into a snide smile.

"No, thank you," Stella smiled back brightly, feeling her teeth grate together with the effort. "It's fine. I've checked it myself." And she had, very carefully – anything to keep her mind off the horrible thoughts that churned around. The memory of Henry's hurt face when she'd told him that she didn't want to see him again. And Amber, her very, very best friend – who now hated her, with a vengeance. If only she could unsay the things that she had said, she thought miserably, trying to force her unwilling mind to focus on checking the article she had just written. But it was too late for going back. She had found a new apartment and was moving out.

*   *   *

Amber had been shocked into silence when Stella had told her that she was moving out. They had been keeping a frosty near-silence ever since they had rowed at the races. There had been days when they had scarcely said a word to each other, apart from "Here is your mail," and "I'm out tonight". They had shared the apartment, acting like polite strangers.

The night that Stella had come in from the races, Amber had said, "You didn't really finish with Henry, did you?"

"Yes, I did," Stella had replied, unable to believe herself that she had actually done the terrible deed, how her mouth had said those words while her heart had screamed out for her to stay with him.

"You bloody stupid idiot!" Amber had said, her hand full of toast halfway between her plate and her mouth. She had frozen, glaring in disbelief at Stella, then she had laid the toast down and silently got up and left the room. After that they had hardly spoken. And after a week Stella knew that things would never be the same between them again.

They had been friends for two years, since Amber had come to share Stella's apartment. They had liked each other immediately and living together had been easy, but now there could be no going back. Stella couldn't change her mind and Amber couldn't forgive her. Too much had been said and too much ill feeling had passed between them to ever be forgotten. And so, after a week, Stella phoned an agent and asked if there were any other apartments or house shares available. And, as if it had been fated, there was a house, in Ballsbridge, where the girls who rented it were looking for another to share it with. They were, the agent had told her, all lovely girls, all working, all around the same age as Stella. They would get on brilliantly, so the agent said. And none of them had any objection to Teddy being there, as long as he didn't chase the cat that belonged to one of the girls. Stella had gone straight around to the address the agent had given her. The house was lovely, an old Edwardian house, set in a tiny garden.

One of the girls, October, had answered the door when Stella arrived. "Hello!" She had a clipped English accent, very polite and correct, that matched perfectly with her neat oval face and precisely trimmed bob. She was very pretty in an elfin kind of way, with enormous brown eyes that scrutinised Amber from beneath her fringe. "The others are all out. Julia is helping out in one of her uncle's shops, just for today. She thinks that she might like to have a shop of her own." October sounded as if she thought this was the most bizarre thing anyone could do with their time. "But they're all very nice girls. I'm sure you'll get on with them." She showed Stella around the house. It was gorgeous – spacious and airy, with a shared kitchen and lounge downstairs. Each of the girls had their own bedroom. Stella's one was at the back of the house, looking out onto a lovely garden with a paved patio and an inviting swing-seat beneath a cherry tree. Her room was far larger than the one at the apartment and had a small en-suite. Stella couldn't think why she had stayed in the apartment with Amber for so long. Here at least she would be mixing with a nice set of girls. They would be able to introduce her to a new set of men. Maybe now she was on the right track to finding a thoroughly nice millionaire.

Stella had told Amber that evening. Amber had been in the shower when Stella had come in from work. Stella stood in the living room waiting, unable to settle, slowly pacing the room, listening to the sound of the water running, as she had tried to frame the words. She had arranged for the lease on the apartment to be put into Amber's name. Now that she was working for Kenny she should have no problem paying the rent.

Maybe Paul would move in with her to help pay the rent – if not, she would just have to find someone else to share with.

The water stopped running and Stella knew that the time had come. A moment later the bathroom door opened and Amber came out wearing a dressing-gown, a towel swathed around her head.

"Hi!" Amber always forgot that they had fallen out when she saw Stella, launching into a bright conversation until, halfway through getting her words out, she would remember and the sentence would falter and die on her lips.

"Amber, I've found another place to live. I'm moving out at the weekend." Stella heard the words escaping from her mouth as if she were watching a video of herself. She could have stopped if she had wanted to, but still she said the words, wishing that instead she was asking for forgiveness, telling Amber that it was all a terrible mistake, that they should repair their friendship, put everything behind them.

A tendril of Amber's hair had escaped from the towel. Stella watched a drop of water slide down it until it spilled onto the shoulder of her dressing-gown.

"I see," Amber said coldly, her eyes narrowing with dislike. "Thanks for telling me." She turned away, her mouth clamped into a tight straight line, her jaw thrust resolutely forwards.

There was no sign of Amber in the morning when Stella got up. She had gone out with Teddy.

Stella was in the kitchen when they returned.

"Hang on, let me take your lead off," Amber's voice came from the front door.

A moment later Teddy bounded into the kitchen.

"Teddy!" Stella bent down as the little dog hurled himself at her, leaping at her legs, his sharp front paws clawing at her calf muscles.

"Hi," Amber said shortly, coming into the kitchen. She leant against the door frame, a half-smile playing on her lips, unable not to be amused by Teddy's antics. "So when are you going?" she asked, staring fixedly at Teddy.

"I'll pack up this week and be out on Friday." Stella stood up. If only she could bring herself to put her arms around Amber and tell her how sorry she was. Then everything would be back to normal.

"What about Teddy?" Amber said sullenly.

"He's my dog," Stella said quietly.

Amber gave a snort of derision. "You might have found him, but I've spent more time with him than you," she said coldly.

"Yes, well . . ." Stella couldn't think of a reply. They had shared the dog, he was a family pet, when she and Amber had been each other's family. "He's still my dog," she finished lamely.

"Suit yourself," snapped Amber, adding "Bitch!" quietly under her breath.

* * *

By Friday Stella couldn't wait to move out of the

apartment and make a fresh start. The atmosphere had deteriorated into one of open hostility. She woke on Friday morning with a sense of relief. At last she was going to be away from Amber and making a fresh start. She would at last put the nastiness of the last few weeks behind her. There was very little to move, just her clothes and personal possessions. They were already packed away in the new luggage bags that she had bought especially. She might as well make a good impression when she arrived at the house.

There was no sign of Amber when she left her bedroom. Presumably she was out walking Teddy. Amber has spent the last week cradling the dog as if she couldn't bear to let him out of her sight, looking at Stella coldly as if she was about to take her child away from her.

As soon as Amber returned with Teddy she would leave. She carried her bags downstairs and packed them into her car. Then there was nothing more to do but wait for Amber to come back. She sat on the sofa and looked around the room. She had been happy here – there were such good memories tied up in these walls.

Amber pushed open the door. "So you're going then?" She held Teddy in her arms, the small dog wriggling furiously, trying to get to Stella.

"Yes." Had Amber thought that all of this was a joke? She sounded so surprised.

"I'm ready to go – I was just waiting for you to come back." Stella heaved herself to her feet, not daring to look at Amber. She was aware of her own bleak expression and that there were tears pouring down Amber's face.

"I'll bring Teddy out," sobbed Amber.

Stella groped her way to the door, blinded by the tears that suddenly sprang to her eyes. Her car was parked outside against the pavement, filled with her boxes and bags.

Amber let out a strangled sob, burying her face in Teddy's hair. "Here," she spluttered, pushing the dog towards Stella. Teddy squirmed delightedly in Stella's arms, enjoying the attention, trying to shove his wet nose into her neck to lick her. Stella longed to throw her arms around Amber, tell her that everything was all right. To bring her bags back inside the apartment and spend the rest of the day laughing about how stupid they had been. But it was too late.

Amber folded her arms. "See you then," she mumbled thickly and then before Stella had a chance to reply, turned on her heel and shot back into the apartment.

Numbly Stella put Teddy into the car. He put his front paws on the dashboard, peering through the windscreen excitedly, dying to know where they were going. His curly tail waved furiously as he glanced at Stella, his mouth open, panting eagerly.

"Right then," Stella said feigning a decisiveness that she didn't feel as she slid into the driver's seat and shoved her key into the ignition.

A short time later she was pulling up outside the new house in Ballsbridge. The drive outside the house was jammed with expensive cars, a small Mercedes sports car, a flashy looking Mini Cooper and the one she knew belonged to October, an exotic-looking Lotus sports car. Stella left her own car outside on the road – it would have looked very nondescript beside the expensive cars that belonged to her new housemates. Hauling one of the bags, with Teddy beneath her arm, Stella made her way up the drive, skirting carefully around the sports cars. She rang the bell, balancing Teddy on her hip as she did so. A moment later the door swung open.

"Yes?" A tall, willowy blonde girl stood aggressively in the doorway. In her arms was an enormous fluffy grey cat, which took one look at Teddy and seemed to grow to twice its size in the girl's arms, emitting loud hissing and yowling noises, before it exploded from her arms and vanished into the house.

"I'm Stella," Stella gulped, quailing beneath the girl's furious gaze. "I'm moving in today. And this is Teddy."

"Julia." The girl eyed Stella coldly and held out a cold, limp hand for Stella to shake, dropping the contact as soon as she could.

Her hand reminded Stella of one of the dead fish that she had hauled from the boats on the beach in Mayo years ago, when she was a child. She pronounced Julia as if it were 'Juli-yah'.

"You had better come in." She made it sound as if she were doing Stella the most enormous favour letting her cross the threshold of the house. "That was Gucci that your . . ." she looked Teddy up and down as if she had never seen anything like him before, "dog" she finally decided, "upset. I thought when October said you had a dog that you would have something like a Labrador, something nice. I didn't realise that it was a mongrel." She made it sound as if Teddy was the most revolting mutt ever created, rather than the most adorable sweet little dog.

"October and Xanthe are in the lounge," Julia waved her hand in the direction of the lounge, before wordlessly heading off in search of her cat.

Stella sighed, holding tight onto Teddy who was wriggling with impatience. Hopefully Xanthe would be nicer than Julia.

She wasn't. Xanthe took one look at Teddy and shrieked, "That dog has to live outside! There's a kennel in the garden. It will have to be chained to the kennel!"

Xanthe got to her feet, fluttering her long hands in agitation, her long dark waterfall of hair swinging from side to side as she gestured agitatedly.

October smiled languidly at Stella. "Whatever," she sighed passively. "I think there's a chain out there." She gestured in the direction of the garden. "The last people in the house had a dog."

Stella nodded. This was terrible – but what could she do? Things had to get better. They had got off to a bad start.

She took Teddy outside into the garden, attached the chain to his collar and left him yelping furiously.

"I'll give you a hand to bring your things in," October said as Stella came back into the lounge.

"Where do you come from?" Xanthe asked, still fluttering around the room, looking agitatedly out at the garden and wincing dramatically every time Teddy yapped. "Mayo, but I've lived here for –"

"Mayo!" exclaimed Xanthe, turning her green eyes on Stella. "Mayo? I didn't think that anyone actually *came* from Mayo!"

40

Amber turned the pages of her diary, counting slowly. There had to be some mistake. She couldn't possibly be *that* late with her period. But, conscious of an ever-sinking feeling deep in her belly, she knew that she was late. Very.

"Bloody hell," she mouthed miserably. That really was all she needed. She couldn't be pregnant. It just wasn't possible. Fate wouldn't be that cruel, surely. And yet the dates were there, in black and white. She was very late.

Amber sniffed hard – she wasn't going to cry again. She had done too much of that recently. Things should have been going so well. Were going so well. Amber loved her new job. She was good at it. Working with people was wonderful – every day brought a fresh challenge. There was always some problem to be solved, someone who wanted to hire a car without a driving licence, or the car that they had hired wasn't going to be suitable. Like the man who had hired a small car because it was cheap and when he and his very large – as in 'fat' – family arrived to collect the car they couldn't all fit in. Amber had to organise a different car to be brought from a different depot. Quickly.

She smiled at the thought of the family trying over and over again to get into the car, the three children squashed into the back seat, while the parents heaved themselves into the front, their faces all pressed close together. Amber had missed telling Stella about it. How they would have laughed! She had told Paul and he had roared with laughter, but somehow it just wasn't the same. It was wonderful to have a kind, loving boyfriend, for once in her life, but she missed Stella like hell. Missed curling up with her on the sofa, Teddy sprawled between them while they watched some girly programme on the television. And girly gossip, bitching about the people that they knew and the people that they worked with. Somehow when she said the same things to Paul they sounded nasty and snide – another girl understood. Well, other girls that was, except Della her new flatmate.

Della was … well, Della was like a lady wrestler. With lots of make-up on. She was enormous. Not in the pudgy fat kind of enormous, just solid, hefty, with thighs like tree trunks and strapping forearms that a navvy would have been proud of. And she had no sense of humour whatsoever. She merely went to work or sat in front of the television, her solid face impassive behind a thick layer of orange make-up. At least, Amber had thought when she first met Della, she would never have to worry about having her boyfriend pinched. Della didn't look as if she were interested in anything, except watching television and eating chocolate. She could consume bar after bar, her jaws moving with the rhythmic slowness of a bovine while her eyes never moved from the flickering images on the television screen.

Della was the complete opposite of Stella. How odd that their names were so similar, as if they were opposite sides of a coin! And just at this moment Amber missed Stella terribly. Stella would have made Amber feel as if she could cope with this awful pregnancy scare. Amber could imagine her snatching the diary and counting the dates, her long fingers tapping the pages as she turned them. And then she would have dismissed the scare as irrelevant – "You're only a few days late, don't worry," – and sent Amber off to the shops to rent a girly video and buy a bottle of wine, or she would have helped to do something about it. "I'll be godmother. I'll baby-sit. I'll help you find a crèche. I'll help you tell the father." Telling the father . . . that was an awesome task.

Paul was gorgeous. He was the best thing that had ever happened to her. Even if Stella hadn't thought so. He was kind, considerate, infinitely good-looking. Very sexy. But telling him that she was pregnant . . . if she was . . . that was something else altogether. And telling her mother and Kenny. Just after she had got her life back on track. Kenny had been true to his word, docking money out of her wages to pay her rent and to pay back everything that she owed. The debt was going down, slowly. And at least there would be no more visits from Nigel. No more visits to the shops for some time either, if she wanted to eat. Kenny was very strict with the amount that he gave her, allowing only enough for her bus fares and for food.

How would they react? To Amber the thought that she might be pregnant was scary, but not terrifying. She wanted children. Someday. To have a baby as an unmarried mother and hold down a job and rear a child wasn't a dreadful prospect. She would cope, she knew that. But her mother and Kenny would probably freak out, saying that she was irresponsible. But she could get over that. Prove to them that they were wrong. And when they saw the baby . . .

But Paul was another prospect altogether. He was carefree. Just getting his life back together. He was getting more work as a jockey. He was grateful now for having been given another chance, working hard and conscientiously to prove that everyone was right to have faith in him. How would he react to the tie of having a baby around? Amber didn't expect that he would suddenly go down on one knee and propose to her. But she didn't want to lose him because he didn't want the responsibility of having a baby around in his relationship.

"What's up?" Della removed the wrapper from

another chocolate bar.

"Nothing," replied Amber. It was silly to even think about pregnancy and babies. She was only a few days late – she hadn't even done a test yet.

Even if she did feel rather sick.

It could have been the thought of going out to see Henry, thought Amber, as the buzzer sounded to announce that Paul had arrived. They were going out to Henry's cottage today. Paul was going to ride Princess Pushy for the last time before their big race next week. Amber had been dreading meeting Henry again after Stella had dumped him so cruelly.

"I guess that's Paul." Amber shoved her diary into her handbag and went to the intercom.

"Right," Della said her mouth full of chocolate.

"Hello," Amber said into the intercom.

"Hi, sexy," Paul's voice filled the apartment.

Amber felt herself go pink with embarrassment, but Della gave no indication that she had heard him.

"I'll be down in a minute." Amber grabbed her coat. "I'll see you later, Della."

"Right," Della chomped in reply, heaving her feet luxuriously onto the sofa and changing the channels on the television.

Of course it could have been the smell of all that chocolate that was making her feel sick, pondered Amber as she ran down the stairs to the front door.

Paul was sitting on the wall outside. He got up as Amber slammed the door, opening out his arms for her to leap into.

"God, I missed you," he mumbled, trying to kiss her at the same time. "Can't we just go inside and go to bed?" Paul turned Amber back towards the apartment. "I'd rather ride you than Princess Pushy!"

"No," laughed Amber. "Your horse needs you!" She shoved him in the direction of his car. "Besides which, we couldn't get to the bedroom for all of the chocolate wrappers that Della has littering the floor."

"Yack!" said Paul, opening the car door courteously for Amber.

"Yes, she does rather look like one," laughed Amber as he slammed the door shut.

The sick feeling returned as they sped out of the city. Amber wondered if it were possible to feel terrified and delighted all at the same time. Paul chattered as he drove, but Amber felt miles away, living in a world where she was breaking the most earth-shattering news to him.

The yard was deserted when they arrived at Henry's.

"Where is everyone?" asked Amber, straining to look through the car windscreen. "They'll all have gone home," explained Paul. "They work in the morning, doing the stables and stuff and then go away for the afternoon and come back to do the evening stables later on."

Amber nodded, but thought the whole place looked abandoned and uncared for. The old Labrador barked a greeting as Paul parked his car next to Henry's Jeep. He turned off the engine and an unearthly silence descended on the yard.

"Where's Henry?" Amber whispered. It was so quiet that it seemed wrong to even talk.

Paul shrugged. "Let's try inside," he said as they walked up the path to the cottage. The curtains were half closed, giving the cottage an eerie, deserted feeling. Paul hammered on the door. "Henry knows that we're coming," he frowned. "He can't be far away; his Jeep's here." He fished his phone out of his pocket and dialled Henry's number. They could hear the phone ringing inside the cottage, the noise echoing around the rooms.

Amber felt a surge of panic grip her insides like an iron fist. She darted a look at Paul and saw that he was as afraid as she was. Something must have happened to Henry. Something was very wrong. Paul tried the door and it swung open. The cottage felt damp and lonely.

"Maybe he's inside." Paul spoke as if things were normal, as if maybe Henry had overslept or had got engrossed in a pile of paperwork, but his calm voice betrayed the panic that they both felt.

Amber followed Paul inside the cottage. She was sure that they were going to find Henry dead. Losing Stella had unhinged him so much that he had taken his own life. The television was on in the lounge, the sound faint over the noise of their breathing. Paul pushed open the door. Amber gave a sigh of relief.

Henry was alive, sitting on the sofa watching the television.

"'Lo," he grinned foolishly in their direction, his eyes blinking slowly as he tried – and failed – to focus on them. On the floor beside him was a near-empty bottle of whiskey and a beautiful cutglass tumbler lying on its side, a small pool of liquid seeping slowly into the grubby-looking carpet. He looked terrible, his face pinched and grey, the clothes that he wore seeming to hang off his body as if they had been made for someone several sizes larger. He was very, very drunk.

"Henry?" Paul said, his voice filled with relief.

"She's l-left m-me, you know," Henry stumbled over the words. "Left me." He shook his head as if he couldn't believe what he had just said.

Amber brought her hand up to her mouth to stifle a sob. Stella had done this to Henry. She had left him and broken his heart. The smell of whiskey reached Amber's nostrils and suddenly she knew that she had to get out of the room. She dashed outside, retching miserably on her knees on the muddy patch of grass that served as a lawn.

After a while she felt better. She picked herself up, wiping the mud from her now damp knees and walked back inside, ignoring the curious glance that Paul shot in her direction.

"You OK?" he frowned.

"Mmmm," Amber said, trying hard not to breathe the whiskey fumes. She pulled out a chair from beneath the dining table and sat down.

"Where did you say the coffee was?" Paul asked as the kettle whistled on the gas cooker.

Henry said something unintelligible. Paul went into the kitchen where Amber could hear him opening cupboards as he looked for the coffee. After a moment he reappeared in the doorway, shrugging his shoulders at Amber helplessly.

Amber grinned. "Leave the domestic stuff to me!" She was glad of the excuse to get away from Henry – it was awful to see such a wonderful man so broken in spirit. "Make yourself one!" Henry shouted merrily.

Amber found the coffee jar, made three cups and took them back into the lounge.

"What the hell are you playing at?" Paul snapped at Henry, shoving the coffee cup into his shaking hand.

Henry shrugged. "Just thought that I'd give it a try," he laughed, fumbling for the whiskey bottle and shaking it gently. "Seemed to work for my father." He gazed at the liquid in the bottle for a moment before laying it down gingerly.

"Drink that coffee," ordered Paul. "You'll feel better. Whiskey isn't the answer." Henry did as he was told and sipped at the coffee. "My father was an alcoholic," he said suddenly. "I always vowed that I would never touch it. But after Stella . . ."

Paul seized the bottle and went into the kitchen. Amber could hear the sound of liquid glugging down the plughole.

"Don't touch it again, all right?" Paul said on his return.

They drank their coffee, then Amber collected their cups and took them to the kitchen.

"Come on. We need to work Princess Pushy." Paul hauled Henry to his feet.

"I just want Stella back," Henry said as he followed Paul unsteadily out into the yard.

"Well, drinking isn't going to get her back, now is it?" Paul said gently.

"I don't understand why she left me. I was crazy about her. Thought that she was crazy about me."

Amber wiped her hand across her eyes, furiously dashing away the tears. How could she tell Henry that Stella had indeed been crazy about him?

*   *   *

"I just need to nip into the chemist's on the way home," she told Paul as he drove along the driveway from Henry's cottage, a lot later. "Della used all my make-up remover. I'll have to buy some more."

Paul sat in the car, reading the racing newspaper, while Amber went into the shop. She bought a pregnancy testing kit, feeling as if everyone in the shop was staring at her, shoved it deep into her handbag and then, with a new bottle of make-up remover in a paper bag, went back to the car.

Back home, Amber went into the toilet and opened the packet. The kit was easy to use according to the instructions. Amber followed the steps on the instructions and then sat on the edge of the bath to wait. The moisture soaked through one square, lighting up a blue line and then as it soaked through into the other square the next blue line lit up immediately. Amber stared at the two boxes, each with a bright blue line.

The test was supposed to take a few minutes. This was too soon. There must be something wrong with it. But she knew that there was nothing wrong with the kit. There was something wrong with *her*. She was pregnant.

41

Amber decided that this was probably not a good time to tell Paul. He was writhing around on the ground clutching his thigh muscle where seconds earlier Princess Pushy has lashed out with a hind leg and kicked him.

"Fuck!" he yelped, his face contorted in pain.

Kathy grinned. "She's a bit tetchy this morning. I'd stay away from her back end if I were you."

"Thanks," Paul said bitterly, scrambling painfully to his feet. A long dirty mark scored the front of his jeans where the mare's iron-shod hoof had made contact with his leg.

"Lucky it wasn't a few inches higher!" Henry grinned, coming across the yard, his arms full of the brightly coloured silks that Paul would wear when he raced Princess Pushy later. "Amber would be *really* upset."

Amber met his eyes and grinned back. Henry looked a different man from the one that they had found reeling drunk. The sparkle that had been in his eyes when he was around Stella had gone, but the dead, lifeless look that had been there the last time had gone too. Now he looked rather lost and bewildered, but calm and almost resigned to the fact that Stella had left him.

Kathy led Princess Pushy into the horse lorry. Paul hobbled over to the ramp to help Henry push it closed.

"Fuck, fuck, that hurts," Paul complained, leaning against the side of the lorry, wiping away the beads of sweat from his forehead with the back of his hand.

"Come on, you can get loads of sympathy later," said Kathy. "You've got a race to win now." Kathy slapped Paul hard on the arm, making him yelp again.

Henry's Labrador, George, waddled across the yard and shoved his nose into Amber's hand, his dark eyes gazing at her imploringly, pleading for attention. Amber rubbed his wide, square head gently. She missed Teddy terribly. Paul had told her that she should get another dog, but Amber didn't want to, not yet. She would be busy enough in a few months' time without having the extra work of a dog as well. Amber gave George a final pat – she didn't even want to think about the baby. If she didn't think about it then it didn't seem to be real. She would have to tell Paul, sometime, but finding the right moment was hard.

Amber was sure he wouldn't be very happy to find out he was going to be a father. The responsibility of looking after a tiny human being wasn't part of his lifestyle. He was so full of life, carefree, just restarting his career as a jockey. He had all of his life in front of him now. While for Amber, she was starting to live her life with a new life, something that she was going to be responsible for forever. Amber was sure that she would lose him. He would freak out completely. Their relationship was too young for such a big change. How could she have been so stupid as to let herself get pregnant?

One time without a condom! She had told him that it was OK. No way could she get pregnant, she had said as she counted the days diligently. Except that somehow she had miscounted, or *something*. One thing was certain. Something had gone wrong and she was pregnant now. And she was going to lose Paul as soon as he found out. Sure, he would be delighted at first. He had proved that he was fertile, that he was doing *it* right. But then, once the weight of the responsibility had sunk onto his shoulders – he would be gone – quicker than a race commentator could say, "They're off!"

Amber scrambled into the lorry and settled herself into the passenger seat. Kathy lit up a cigarette behind her, making Amber want to heave. She wound down the window, fighting waves of nausea.

"I'll get someone to give you a massage on that –" As they reached the top of the drive, a small, white car like the one Stella drove came along the main road towards them and for a moment Henry froze, the words dying on his lips. "Leg," he finished lamely as he realised it wasn't Stella driving towards them.

Amber wished that there was something that she could do to ease the pain that he was feeling. It was a dreadful thing to lose someone you loved. She would probably be feeling the same way in a few weeks' time, once Paul found out about her being pregnant. It wasn't going to be possible to keep the news from him too much longer. Her waistline was expanding at an alarming rate. This would probably be the last time she'd be able to wear these jeans.

Paul and Henry went off to find the course physiotherapist when they arrived at the races, while Kathy got Princess Pushy ready for her race.

Amber wandered onto the racecourse alone. They were early and the tarmac concourse was deserted. Only a few stewards and early spectators wandered around, shivering in the bitter wind that drifted around the buildings. Amber went inside and got herself a cup of hot chocolate in one of the restaurants. She couldn't face coffee or tea any more, but somehow the sweetness of the chocolate was just what her body seemed to crave. While she dreamily stirred her chocolate she saw a couple come into the restaurant. She recognised the man instantly – Derry Blake. How on earth could Stella have thought that he was attractive when she had someone like Henry in love with her? Derry glanced in Amber's direction, his cold eyes flickering over her momentarily then sliding away as he dismissed her as of no consequence. His companion was a pretty redhead, whose china-blue eyes never left Derry's face – until another man joined them. The other man was tall and very thin, elegantly dressed in a smart black overcoat, with a smart Fedora hat tipped over his eyes. He put his arm possessively around the woman who now looked anywhere except at Derry. Amber curled her lip in distaste. Derry and the woman were obviously having an affair. She disliked him intensely. He had no respect for anyone.

Amber made the hot chocolate last for ages, enjoying the warmth of the restaurant, until it was time to go out and watch the horses parade at the start of the race. It was bitterly cold outside after the warmth of the restaurant. Amber pulled her overcoat further around her, drawing the collar together at her neck. There were more people now on the concourse, the atmosphere bright and cheery in spite of the cold wind that darted sly gusts around the corners of the buildings, sending abandoned race tickets and litter scooting across the tarmac. Amber found Henry in the saddling enclosure. Kathy was holding Princess Pushy in one of the saddling stalls, while Henry buckled the saddle into place. The mare, excited by the tense atmosphere, swished her tail and laid back her ears as Henry pulled the girth-straps tight.

"How's Paul feeling?" Amber asked, gingerly rubbing the velvet-soft hair on Princess Pushy's nose.

"A lot better now." Henry pushed the last strap into place. "The physio gave him a good massage on that leg – hopefully that will have unknotted the muscles."

Princess Pushy shot out of the saddling stall as Kathy jerked her lead rein.

"Come on, we'll go to the parade ring," Henry said, watching Princess Pushy capering as a sheet of newspaper, caught by the wind, skittered across the grass, frightening the highly strung mare. "You OK?" he shouted to Kathy as the tough wiry little woman hauled on the mare's bridle to bring her under control.

"No problem!" she yelled back between gritted teeth.

The parade ring was already full. Owners and trainers huddled in groups, watching their horses and surreptitiously eyeing up the competition. The twelve horses that were competing walked around a tarmac path that circled the edge of the parade ring, while the spectators crowded against the white guardrail around the edge, trying to pick out the winner.

Princess Pushy looked thoroughly upset by the noise and commotion that went with a big race. She jogged sideways, her tiny hooves beating a rapid tattoo on the tarmac, flecks of foam flying from her mouth as she champed restlessly on her bit.

Amber saw Derry Blake and the owners of the horse he was training standing close to herself and Henry. Derry was resting his hand gently on the red-headed woman's bottom, as he stood beside her husband. What a bastard he is, Amber thought, shooting him a glance full of hatred. Any woman who had anything to do with that creep needed to have her head examined. He was pure poison.

The jockeys trooped out of the Weigh Room. Paul looked like a stranger in his racing clothes, his body unfamiliar in the transparent breeches and dazzling purple and white silks, his face unrecognisable beneath his skull-cap. He dropped a gentle kiss onto Amber's lips.

"OK?" he asked, full of concern. "You look frozen." He hugged her to him for a moment, Amber let herself lean into him, soaking up the warmth from his body. Loving him was too painful, when she was bound to lose him when he found out about the baby.

The bell rang, loud above the hum of conversation in the parade ring, signalling that it was time for the jockeys to mount. Kathy led Princess Pushy towards them, bracing her elbow against the mare's shoulder to steady her. In one swift, graceful movement Henry threw Paul up into the saddle and the mare bounded forwards as he fumbled for his stirrups.

Then, with a suddenness that surprised Amber, the mare shot sideways, surprised by an innocuous piece of litter that blew along the ground from the edge of the parade ring. Amber glimpsed the movement out of the corner of her eye, but before she had time to react the mare's enormously powerful muscular quarters had hit her in the back, knocking the wind out of her body and sending her sprawling to the ground.

A second later Henry was helping Amber to her feet. "She's OK, aren't you, Amber?" she heard him say.

She saw Paul's concerned face looking down at her from the horse as she nodded in agreement.

"I'm OK. Go on. The horses are going onto the course," she said, struggling for breath. Then she bent over as a spasm of pain shot through her tummy and then was gone as quickly as it had come.

"Are you OK?" Henry put his arm gently around Amber's waist, his kind eyes full of concern.

"Just winded," Amber managed to gasp. She let out her breath slowly. "I'm OK," she said, straightening up slowly, kneading her side.

"Sure?" Henry was oblivious to the fact that the parade ring had emptied and that all of the spectators had gone off to watch the race.

"Yes, honestly," Amber lied. Henry needed to go and watch the race. They had spent so long preparing for it, she wasn't going to deny him the chance to see it. She followed Henry to the Owners' and Trainers' Stand and climbed high up the steps so that they had a good position to watch the race from.

The pain had subsided to a dull throb. She longed to sit down somewhere quiet. But there was no chance of that now. The horses were already racing. Amber could see a brown blur topped by a kaleidoscope of colour at the far side of the track. Amber swallowed hard – she was sure that she was going to be sick and beads of sweat had broken out on her forehead.

"She's in fourth place," Henry whispered beside her, his voice filled with wonderment.

Amber glanced up to see the horses thundering past the stands. She glimpsed Paul's face for a split second, filled with concentration and determination. Once the race was over she would find somewhere to sit down and wait until the pain had passed. The race seemed to go on forever as Amber fought the waves of pain and nausea. As if from far away, Amber could hear the voice of the announcer, echoed by Henry's voice, rising higher and higher with excitement: *"Second place, she's in second place!"* Then what seemed like an eternity later, Henry bellowed, *"She's going to win! She's going to . . . she's won!"*

"Come on!" Henry yelled. "Let's go and lead her in!" Dragging Amber by the arm, he shoved and barged through the crowds.

Paul rode Princess Pushy off the track, his red, mud-splattered face split into a broad grin. *"We did it!"* he yelled over the deafening thunder of noise, shaking his whip in the air. Henry grabbed Princess Pushy's bridle. The mare's bay coat was wet with sweat, plumes of breath came from her enormous nostrils. She was exhausted, but proudly tossed her head as if to acknowledge the cheers and clapping of the spectators.

A man shot out of the crowd and grabbed Henry's hand, pumping it furiously as he shouldered his way through the crowd in his desperate attempt to stay beside Henry. "I have five horses – I want you to train them for me – phone me! Here's my card!" He shoved a crumpled business card into Henry's pocket. "I'll come and talk to you in the Owners' and Trainers' Bar later." He let go of Henry's hand and was immediately swallowed up by the tide of spectators who all wanted to touch the mare, her jockey and trainer.

"This way! Look this way!" the photographers yelled from all directions around them, as a barrage of cameras clicked and whirled around them. Princess Pushy, her nervous energy expanded, stood quietly in the place reserved for the race winners, between a grinning Paul and Henry, her ears sharply pricked, as if she were showing the cameramen how beautiful she was.

"Brilliant!" grinned Henry above the roar of noise. "You rode an amazing race!"

"Brilliant!" Paul grinned back. "You did an amazing job of training her!"

Paul hugged Amber to him, kissing her on the cheek as the cameras clicked and whirled once again. And then, as quickly as they had arrived, the cameramen darted away back to the track to photograph the next race.

"Come on, I think we should go and celebrate after Paul has weighed in," Henry told them, giving Princess Pushy a final pat before Kathy took her back to the lorry.

Paul released his grip on Amber's shoulder and suddenly her legs crumpled and she slid to her knees.

"Paul!" Her voice was a strangled whisper as another dart of pain shot through her stomach.

42

"Where is Stella?" Amber croaked. She ran a tongue that felt as if it were three sizes too big over lips that felt cracked and dry. "I need Stella!" Amber wailed, vaguely aware beyond the waves of pain that tore at her stomach of Paul's pinched white face gazing at her. She could not read the expression in his eyes. "Stella," she whispered again, longing desperately for her friend's calm control. Stella would know what to do – she would be able to make the pain go away.

"It's all right," Paul's cool hand passed gently over Amber's sweat-dampened forehead, smoothing away the tendrils of wet hair that clung to her pale skin. "A nurse is coming."

Amber opened her eyes again, forcing herself to focus, trying desperately to ride the pain, rather than tense against it, but it was too strong for her, too frightening to control. The room was very bright, the powerful lights in the ceiling seeming to penetrate her eyes, making her head ache. She turned her head. She was surrounded by machinery; tubes and pipes, and red lights that winked. Hospital. But she had no memory of arriving, or the journey. A door opened. She could hear noise from outside her room, voices, someone yelling, someone else in pain. Amber closed her eyes again.

"This will stop the pain, Amber, and then we can have a look at what is going on," said a female voice.

Amber winced as a needle was thrust into the back of her hand and then smiled. The pain had miraculously gone, but then so had any sensation except a disconcerting feeling of floating. Tentatively Amber looked at Paul. He looked terrified. Amber groped for his hand and his fingers closed gently around hers, stroking her fingers distractedly as he watched the nurse work.

"Excuse me, Daddy," the nurse said, leaning over Paul to lift Amber's top.

Amber saw his eyes widen. His mouth dropped open as if he were about to speak, but then he closed it again, biting his bottom lip as if he were afraid of what he might say.

"I'm just going to do a scan," the nurse said. "See how the baby is."

She smeared an icy gel over the slight bulge of Amber's belly and then deftly began to work the scanner. A moment later the unmistakeable sound of a super-fast heartbeat filled the room.

"That's his heart!" Paul's voice was filled with awe.

"His!" laughed the nurse, switching off the machine and handing Amber a wad of tissue paper. "Typical man!" Then she became serious. "Well, the baby is OK at the moment. But I imagine the doctor will want to keep you in hospital for a few days, just in case there are any problems."

And then she swept from the room, leaving Paul and Amber alone.

"I'm sorry that I didn't tell you before," Amber whispered, when the silence between them grew to be an almost physical presence. "There never seemed to be a right moment to say 'I'm pregnant.'"

"Pregnant," Paul said slowly as if he were speaking a new language and he was having trouble getting his tongue around an unfamiliar word. "How the hell did it happen?"

Duh! Amber wanted to laugh out loud. How did he think it happened, she thought fleetingly, but somehow the atmosphere didn't seem right to make jokes.

"I suppose the night when we didn't use a condom," she said gently.

The whole scenario had an air of unreality about it. Only a short time ago she had been worried about paying her debts, now the whole landscape of her life had altered. Pregnant. A baby. The baby that was part of herself and Paul, created out of the love that they had felt for each other. But something that would alter Amber's life forever. Getting rid of the baby was never an option. And yet the thought of having it in her life was terrifying. Yet again Amber wished that Stella were there. She would tell Amber how easy it was to rear a baby – as if she knew! It will be just like having another puppy, Amber could almost hear her saying – it just needs love and feeding and changing. And at least we won't be mopping its puddles up off the floor – at least a baby does its business in a nappy. If Stella were here Amber wouldn't be feeling so desolate and afraid.

Paul looked grey-faced. He shook his head in disbelief, making Amber afraid. This was too much for him to take in. It had been a bad way for him to find out. To have her dropping to the floor, clutching at her belly, just when he had won the big race of the day and was looking forward to an evening celebrating his success. From the look on his face when she had moaned, "Get me to hospital – I think I'm having a miscarriage," he obviously had thought she was joking. Through the waves of pain that were rocketing through her body Amber had read his expression – he was thinking 'Stop messing around, Amber. Don't play jokes on me *now*'. And then Henry had scooped her off the floor and yelled at someone to bring them to hospital.

Now Amber clutched at his hand, trying to hold him physically, fighting the terrifying feeling that mentally he was a million miles away, lost in his own world. Maybe lost forever.

Exhausted by her ordeal Amber's eyelids became too heavy to hold up and she dozed, aware of Paul's presence beside her, aware that he was just sitting, looking at her, but looking at her as if he was not seeing her any longer. Each time she opened her eyes the fear she had felt over the possibility of losing the baby was replaced by some nameless fear about Paul. He did not seem angry, or delighted, or scared, or anything. Merely silent.

Amber was glad when a nurse came and told her that a bed had been made ready for her on one of the wards, she would have to stay in hospital for a few days, until they were sure that she was not going to lose the baby. Amber was not allowed to walk to the ward, instead Paul pushed her in a wheelchair, following the straight back of the nurse who guided them through the dim, deserted corridors. Even in the middle of the night there was activity on the ward. Nurses moved around the beds, their uniforms rustling, rubber soles squeaking against the lino floor, speaking in hushed tones to the patients as they administered medicines or a reassuring word. A bed had been found for Amber, beside the window. "I'll let you get into bed," the nurse told Amber before turning to Paul, "Amber needs to rest now. You can come back tomorrow." Paul nodded. Amber saw the relief at being told to go shining in his eyes; he was glad to be going away from the hospital, away from *her*. Amber could feel him sliding away from her, like sand on a beach. She could not hold him, she was losing him piece by piece. A pregnant girlfriend was too much to cope with.

"Do you want me to tell anyone that you are here?" Paul asked, kissing her chastely on the forehead as he prepared to leave. Amber wanted to grab his arm, cling to him, plead with him not to stop loving her. Instead she said, "No, I don't want anyone to know." It was hard enough to cope with her own feelings and Paul's without having to deal with the wrath of her mother or her smug pity.

Amber stayed in the hospital for two days, lying in the narrow bed, being poked and probed by a succession of doctors and nurses. Paul came dutifully every evening, bringing grapes and flowers, to sit beside her bed shuffling his feet and making stilted conversation about the weather. Had it not been so sad Amber would have found it funny that they were having such inane conversations when usually they discussed everything under the sun.

Eventually a nurse had come and told Amber that she could go home.

Paul came that evening. Amber was ready to go and had phoned the apartment to let Della know she was coming home. As if Della cared!

They walked out into the pale evening sunshine, two tense strangers talking about anything except reality. Paul found a taxi, gently guiding Amber into the back seat, before getting in himself, sitting slightly apart, gazing out of the window, while a black cloud of fear settled heavily on Amber's shoulders.

"Paul, are you OK?" Amber had asked, fearing that he was anything but OK.

"Just give me time to get my head around this," was all that he had said, in a tone that she could not read.

His voice sounded as if he were a stranger, discussing the weather.

Paul walked Amber to the apartment door in silence. Amber was terrified to speak, afraid of the demons that might be unleashed if she began to question Paul about his feelings. She just had to wait. Wait and let him come to terms with what had happened. He had been so delighted when he had seen the blob on the scanner screen and yet now he seemed so distant from her.

"Will you be OK now?" he asked gently as Amber pushed open the door.

"Yes," she answered tonelessly. She did not feel very OK. She was terrified, terrified of losing Paul, terrified of losing the baby, terrified of what the future might hold.

"Are you sure Della is there?" he asked.

Amber could hear the TV in the background. "Yes, she's there."

Paul wrung his hands together as if he were uncertain what to say or do. He hovered for a moment, as if deciding whether to come in with her or bolt.

"I'll talk to you soon," he said, choosing the latter. And then he was gone, running lightly down the steps and disappearing through the front door.

Amber listened as the door slammed shut and then wearily made her way into the apartment.

"Oh, you're back," Della sprawled in one of the armchairs surrounded by the debris of her life: chocolate bars, crisp packets and the television remote control.

"Yeah."

Amber suddenly had no energy to move. She slumped down in the other armchair and tried to lose herself in the mindless programme that Della was watching.

Della, humming tunelessly to the theme tune of her favourite television soap, unwrapped yet another chocolate bar. Amber gritted her teeth, her nerves stretched almost to breaking point as the cellophane rattled and then Della long teeth crunched down onto the chocolate, chomping loudly, still humming while she ate. The urge to rush over to the sofa and force the chocolate bars into Della's mouth until she choked was very strong. Amber wondered fleetingly how long she would get in prison for murder by chocolate bar. Probably not very long, considering the strain she was under.

"Do you want one of these?" Della rattled a chocolate bar.

"No." Amber almost heaved. It was strange the odd things that happened to your body when you were pregnant. All of the things that she had once loved to eat, she now hated. Chocolate was suddenly the most revolting substance in the world. As were Chinese takeaways, once almost her staple diet.

"Suit yourself," Della said, shoving the remains of the bar she was eating into her mouth. Amber's stomach lurched uncomfortably. She closed her eyes to block out the sight of Della chewing.

"Are you OK now?" Della stopped chewing and

turned to face Amber. As she spoke great waves of chocolate fumes made Amber want to cover her nose and mouth with her hand so that she could not smell the chocolate odour.

"I think so." Amber forced herself to smile.

"Good." Della gave Amber the thumbs-up signal. "I've no problem living with a baby in the apartment. Don't mind even baby-sitting."

"Thanks." It was hard to imagine life with a baby. There was so much to consider, so much responsibility. Amber had never imagined a scenario with her looking after the baby with Della. She had always pictured herself with Paul, the three of them as a family. Life as a single mother had never occurred to her as a possibility.

The clock slid at breathtaking speed around to midnight. Paul always telephoned at around ten o'clock if they were not together to say goodnight. Tonight, however, there was no telephone call. Ten sped around to eleven o'clock. Amber dialled Paul's number and got his message service. A leaden chunk of fear slowly sank to the pit of her stomach. Where was he?

Della heaved herself out of the armchair and said goodnight as she headed in the direction of her bedroom. Amber sat silently, watching the clock slide around, fingering her telephone, willing it to ring. Paul must not leave her. Not like this. Amber couldn't bear the thought of life without him. She would do anything to keep him. Get rid of the baby, if that was what it took. She would do that. Anything. Amber picked up her telephone again, checking to see if the battery and reception were working. They were fine. Everything was fine. The reason that Paul had not rung, the reason that Amber could not get him on the telephone was that he did not want to speak to her. He was gone. She had lost him. He was never coming back.

43

Stella clipped the chain back onto Teddy's collar. "You can come in later on," she whispered, gently rubbing his soft ears. "I'll bring you in when they've all gone to bed." Stella had taken to creeping downstairs once everyone had gone to bed and bringing Teddy inside to her room. She found it comforting to drift off to sleep with him curled in the small of her back. Most mornings she woke early to find her arm around his small, warm body, drawing much-needed reassurance from his presence. She stood up, biting her lip miserably as Teddy whimpered despondently.

"I don't think he likes being chained up," Henry's voice said suddenly, making Stella jump. Henry came out through the French windows and walked down the path towards her. "He had a better life when you lived with Amber."

Stella drew herself up to her full height. "He'll get

used to it," she said tensely, completely thrown by Henry's sudden appearance and at the way that her whole body quivered with delight at him being there.

"I doubt it," Henry said wryly, walking past Stella and crouching down beside Teddy who squirmed with delight, pawing at Henry, jumping up to lick his face.

"How did you know where I was? Did you want something?" Stella asked, stunned into confusion, her panic making her defensive.

Henry stood up slowly, one hand still dangling at his side for Teddy to lick. "Amber told me where you had moved to. I just wanted to tell you that . . ." He was silent for a moment, looking at Stella as if he wanted to absorb every particle of her.

Stella was silent too, gazing back at him, longing to take the two strides that separated them and fall into his arms. Then she dropped her eyes.

"I just wanted to tell you that Amber is in hospital."

Stella felt a jolt as if she had put her fingers into the electric socket. "What?" she exclaimed.

"She's had a threatened miscarriage."

"Miscarriage?" repeated Stella slowly. "Miscarriage? I didn't even know that she was pregnant!"

"Came as a bit of a surprise to Paul too." Henry smiled tightly. "He just found out he was going to be a father in the same moment he found out that Amber might lose the baby."

A tense silence fell between them. Stella longed to touch Henry, wished that he would come and take hold of her. She couldn't move, afraid of what would happen if she took a step forwards. She had to get over him – the pain was too great to go through all of that again.

"Just thought that you would like to know. She's in Saint Elizabeth's ward."

Stella nodded. "Thanks for letting me know – it was kind of you to come and tell me." Henry shrugged. "It gave me an excuse to come and see you," he said so quietly that Stella wondered if she were hearing things. "I miss you," he said.

Stella met his eyes and looked into their loving depths. One step was all that it would take and she would be back in his arms.

"I –" she began.

"Stella!" Xanthe shrieked from the open French windows. "Derry Blake on the phone for you!"

Stella watched myriad emotions flicker across Henry's face. His eyes grew hard, the love that she could see reflected there fading and being replaced by a coldness as he stared back at her. Stella couldn't move. It was as if she were rooted to the spot, hating to see the coldness in his eyes.

"Hadn't you better go and take that call?" Henry said coldly.

Stella moved towards the house, her limbs heavy as if she were fighting her way through treacle. The phone was out in the hall. Stella picked up the receiver, conscious of Henry walking past her, bitterness oozing from the straight line of his back and his tense, set jaw.

"Hello," her voice sounded flat and dead as she spoke into the receiver.

"Hello! I couldn't speak to you earlier. I was entertaining a client."

Stella watched Henry walk out of the front door. Xanthe stood beside it, holding it open for him, smiling flirtatiously at him.

"Mmmmm," she said closing the door softly behind him, "I fancy a bit of that."

Stella wanted to drop the phone as if it were red-hot. She wished that she had never phoned Derry Blake. She hadn't even really meant to phone him. It wasn't the kind of thing that she did, asking a man out. She had turned his business card over and over in her hands, just looking at it, wondering what it would be like to go out with someone as sleek and desirable as Derry, but she couldn't pluck up the courage to speak to him on the phone. She had picked up the receiver a few times and then replaced it, losing courage at the last moment.

Sorcha had come into her office, and that had stopped her trying to use the phone. Peter Shaughnessy, the chairman, wanted to see her, Sorcha told her. Stella had gone up to his office feeling sick. No one got to go to Peter's office unless it was really important. He must be going to sack her – maybe he'd found out that she was fiddling her expenses – maybe the Guards were with him waiting for her.

Peter's office was on the top floor of the building. It was enormous, taking up the same amount of room as the office that all of the journalists working for the magazine were crammed into. Peter asked her to sit down on a vast leather armchair, and told her that Kevin had suffered a nervous breakdown and was going to be off work indefinitely. And he wanted Stella to take over Kevin's role.

She had gone back down to her own office feeling as if her luck had turned. She was a powerful, independent woman . . . and she could ring Derry Blake if she wanted to. It had taken her long enough to pluck up the courage, until finally she had decided that she definitely needed to let her life move forwards. It was no use regretting the past. She had to forget about Henry; he wasn't what she wanted. And she had to forget about Amber – they had fallen out. There was no going back. And so finally she had reached across her desk at work and dialled his number. He had told her that he couldn't talk to her at the moment, but that he would ring her back, in the evening. And now he had. And at a very bad moment.

"But now you have my full attention, as someone as gorgeous as you deserves," Derry was saying, his voice smooth as warm chocolate and as sickly sweet. "Would you like to come to the races with me?"

He seemed oblivious to Stella's stunned silence on the end of the phone. Out of the window she could see Henry getting into his Jeep, his face cold and set.

"Er, yes, lovely." Stella was barely aware of what she was saying, listening to the familiar sound of the Jeep rattling and screeching as Henry started it up and drove slowly away.

"Right then, maybe you can meet me at the races?

You can park in the Trainers' carpark – I'll tell the steward there to expect you."

Stella heard herself agreeing as Derry gave her directions, while her throat constricted miserably and her heart pounded dully against her ribs.

Stella put down the phone. She should have been feeling delighted; she had just got an invitation to the races with Derry Blake. He was just the kind of man that she had always been searching for, wealthy, good-looking, powerful and yet . . . Stella sighed, remembering how she had felt standing in the garden when Henry looked at her.

* * *

Stella wasn't looking forward to going to the races. There was no feeling of nervousness about it, but there was no buzz of excitement. It should have been thrilling to go out with Derry, but she felt nothing. The spectre of Henry seemed to be looking over her shoulder. She thought of Amber often, wondering how many weeks pregnant she was or had been. Why had she never told her? But maybe she hadn't found out until after Stella had left. She wondered if the pregnancy had continued, or if she had miscarried. She longed to go and see her, but she was too afraid of the reception she might get. If things had gone wrong, Amber would accuse her of gloating. Stella buried herself in work and in creating a new life for herself. Anything to block out the memories of her old life.

*   *   *

Stella arrived at the races. As Derry had instructed, she drove into the Owners' and Trainers' carpark, her small car looking incongruous amongst the large cars and four-wheel drive vehicles. She walked across the carpark, into the racecourse and straight into Henry who was being interviewed by a television camera. A large crowd had gathered around him, jostling the cameraman and his sound assistant.

"How do you think Princess Pushy will do in the big race on Saturday," the interviewer was asking Henry.

Stella stopped, jerked to a halt like a dog reaching the limit of its leash. As if he knew she were there Henry turned to look at her, their eyes meeting over the crowd that had gathered around him.

"Henry?" the interviewer questioned him again.

Henry shot a cold glance at Stella and then dragged his eyes away. She could see him gathering his thoughts, forcing himself to concentrate on what the interviewer was saying.

"His Lordship is very important all of a sudden." Derry's voice dripped sarcasm. He took Stella's arm, spinning her around to face him, and then kissing her full on the mouth.

Out of the corner of her eye Stella could see Henry falter again as the interviewer asked him another question.

"Come on!" Derry took Stella's arm. "The owners of

the horse I've got running have a hospitality box. We'll go up there. Nicer than mixing with all the riff-raff." He smirked as Henry dashed by, trying to escape the horde of journalists that was pursuing him.

The hospitality box was hot and airless.

"JT and Olivia Burke," Derry introduced Stella to the owners of the horse that was running in the big race of the day.

JT was short and almost as wide as he was tall, with a shiny bald head and tiny eyes that reminded Stella of a pig that they once had in one of the sheds when she was a little girl. He slapped Stella's bottom as he was introduced to her. "Derry's a lucky man," he chuckled.

He had a laugh that reminded Stella of the noise that the pig made just before they fed it. His wife Olivia was a feisty-looking redhead, with so many freckles she looked as if she were tanned. She was slender and pretty, with a hard, sharp little face and cold eyes that never left Derry.

"Are you Derry's girlfriend?" she asked moodily, the moment she and Stella were alone.

"Just a friend," Stella replied.

Olivia visibly relaxed, becoming instantly more friendly towards Stella.

JT and Olivia's horse, Bamboozle, came third in the race. Afterwards JT and Olivia got steadily drunker. Olivia leaned provocatively forward to reveal the tops of her freckly breasts as often as she could. Stella sighed, wishing that she hadn't come. Derry had virtually ignored her all day.

"I think that we'll head off." Derry took Stella by the hand.

"Derry," murmured Olivia, huskily, pressing herself up against him and running her hand around the back of his neck. "I'll see you *very* soon. I hope."

"Of course." Derry put his hand on the small of her back and slowly let it slide downwards. "JT is a lucky man." Then releasing Olivia abruptly he turned, opened the door and guided Stella outside. "Silly tart!" he hissed nastily, as he led Stella across the racecourse. "I just need to check the horse and then I'm going to take you for a lovely dinner to make up for having to put up with JT and Olivia." Derry slid his arm around Stella's shoulder, suddenly attentive and tender. They headed out of the course and into the lorry park.

"No point in standing around in the cold." Derry stopped at the most enormous lorry that Stella had ever seen. "You can wait in the lorry while I go into the back to check the horse." He guided her up the steps of the sleek blue and gold lorry into the most sumptuous living accommodation that Stella had ever seen. It was like being inside a really plush miniature house, with a tiny but elaborate kitchen along one wall and an eating area opposite. A pair of silky curtains hung open to reveal a bedroom area with what looked like a shower beside it.

"Handy for the grooms to sleep in if they have to travel long distances," Derry explained airily. "Make yourself at home – I'll just go and check the horse." He disappeared through a door into the back of the lorry where the horses travelled.

Stella wandered around the living accommodation, fingering the pale wood of the kitchen units and the plush velvet of the seats.

"Come and see the amazing entertainment system in the bedroom," Derry said brightly as he returned.

Stella followed him through the curtains into the bedroom.

"Sit down," he said, gesturing to the bed.

She sat, feeling a little apprehensive.

"Watch this." Derry grabbed the remote control from a small recess above the bed and flicked a switch. Immediately the living accommodation filled with soft music. Then he sank onto the bed beside Stella. "What's your favourite kind of entertainment?" Before she had the time to answer, Derry cupped her chin in his hand and covered her lips with his, kissing her gently. "I wanted to do that all day," he whispered, beginning to slowly unfasten the buttons on her shirt.

"I'm sorry, but I . . ." Stella gently pulled his hand away from her shirt. "This is a bit soon for me." Derry was gorgeous, infinitely sexy, but every time Stella closed her eyes she saw Henry's hurt face as he looked at her from the centre of the crowd of journalists. She couldn't sleep with Derry until that memory had been erased.

"Just relax." Derry's hand was persistent, travelling now up her leg, sliding up her skirt, his lips strong against hers.

Stella turned her head away from his lips. "Please,

Derry, not now . . . not so soon."

His lips moved to her neck and his hand moved upwards.

"Derry! Please! You're rushing me!"

He didn't seem to hear her, his hand moving between her legs and his weight forcing her backwards onto the soft plush bedcover.

"Stop it!" hissed Stella. Finding a strength she didn't know she possessed she shoved Derry away and scrambled to her feet.

"You don't know what you're missing," Derry drawled and the sound of his cruel laughter followed her as she fled through the living accommodation, bumping into the kitchen units in her haste to escape.

She shot hastily down the steps out of the lorry, her face on fire with fury and indignation. Her skirt was wrinkled around her thighs, her shirt hanging loose and her hair flying in wild disorder around her face. Hastily she tucked in her shirt, trying to pull down her skirt and tidy her hair all at the same time.

Then, out of the corner of her eye, she glimpsed a familiar pair of shoes. She stopped and slowly straightened up.

Henry's eyes met hers impassively. "I hope that you had a good time with Derry Blake," he said coldly.

44

Stella glanced up from her magazine as the doorbell rang, expecting one of the other girls to leap to their feet to go and answer it.

"Not for me," October shrugged.

"Nor me," said Julia, raising her eyebrows expectantly at Stella.

Xanthe merely continued to apply another layer of glossy pink lipstick, pursing her lips and blowing a kiss at herself in the mirror that she held in her hand.

"I'll go then," Stella sighed, putting down her magazine and levering herself to her feet.

She walked to the front door, her bare feet padding softly on the wooden floor. It was probably yet another politician canvassing for votes. The girls had taken to sending Stella out to answer the door as a joke, letting her stand for hours listening to the boring political speeches. Stella grabbed a sweatshirt from the bottom of the stairs, pulling it over her head as she turned the door lock. Her flimsy pyjamas were not suitable for standing in the cold listening to speeches.

"Hel –" she swung open the door to see Henry on the doorstep, "– lo," she finished lamely, feeling her cheeks flame with colour.

"Not out with Derry tonight?" he asked, his lips curling with distaste.

"Is Amber OK?" Stella asked, a dart of fear shooting through her once she'd got over the initial shock of seeing him. There must be terrible news for him to come to the house again. Maybe she had lost the baby or maybe she had . . .

"She's fine, and so is the baby. Don't know why you're asking me – you don't seem to have any interest in her. You never even went near her when she was in hospital."

"I wanted to," Stella mumbled guiltily. It was just that she hadn't been able to pluck up the courage.

"Too busy shagging Derry Blake?" he asked coldly.

"Is that all you wanted? To come here and be nasty to me?" she said miserably.

"No, actually, I didn't want *you* at all."

Stella glanced up at him but he was looking beyond her, down the hall. Stella spun around to see what he was looking at.

Xanthe sashayed down the hall, her blonde hair swinging in time to her strides, her impossibly high heels tapping a tattoo on the wooden floor. Stella felt her mouth drop open. Xanthe wore the shortest skirt that she had ever seen, revealing a gorgeous pair of tanned, toned legs and the best part of her knickers.

"Hi, Henry," Xanthe breathed sexily, pouting her full glossy pink lips towards Henry. Stella saw him swallow hard before he puckered up to kiss her.

"OK then, gorgeous, let's go!" Xanthe grabbed Henry's arm, swinging him around with careless grace, and marched him off down the drive.

Stella leant against the door – she didn't dare move for fear that her legs wouldn't support her. Open-mouthed, she watched Xanthe grab Henry's bottom and squeeze it playfully.

"My car, I think!" Xanthe steered Henry towards her Mercedes.

Stella could watch no longer. She shut the door and leant against it, breathing hard. What a bitch Xanthe was! She had no right to go out with Henry, even if Stella didn't want him.

Stella went back to the living room. She stood in the doorway, looking at the other two girls. "Did you know that Xanthe was going out with Henry?"

Julia looked up, her hand continuing to stroke Gucci the cat rhythmically. "Is there a problem? I thought you had finished with him?"

Stella nodded slowly. "I have," she said pensively. She looked from one girl to the other. "I'm going to go out for a while," she said suddenly. She could hardly bear to be in the house. She *had* ended her relationship with Henry, but it wasn't right for Xanthe to go straight out with him. That wasn't right, surely. She had really thought that Henry had cared about her, but he had replaced her so quickly. And with someone as awful as Xanthe. She couldn't understand it.

"Don't be long," October said. "Don't forget that we're having some friends around later."

"Should be lots of lovely men for you to meet," Julia added, her plummy voice grating on Stella's nerves.

Stella closed the door. They treated men and relationships as if they were of no importance, moving from one to the other with no thought for anyone's feelings. Stella went upstairs to her room and looked in her wardrobe for something to change into. Her new room had a wardrobe that stretched the whole length of one wall, with rails set at different heights for hanging coats and dresses and skirts all separately. Beside these were the shelves where she had put her shoes and sweaters and underwear, each neatly organised, instead of crammed together like they'd been at the apartment. Stella fingered the row of dresses, each seeming to symbolise a fond memory of her past life. On impulse she pulled out a red dress, smiling as she drew it towards her. It smelt vaguely of her old apartment – the joss sticks that Amber burned when she'd been smoking and didn't want Stella to know.

Stella slipped the dress off its hanger, held it up to herself and looked at herself in the mirror. The red dress was beautiful, the colour fabulous against her skin, making her hair look as if it were alive with a thousand different colours. She stroked the front of the dress, moving slightly. The fabric was still slightly marked with the stain, if you looked really hard. Stella smiled at the memory. Amber had thought she'd got away with it but eventually Stella had noticed the faint blemish on the dress, had remembered seeing an identical dress at the dry cleaner's and had drawn her own conclusions. Stella gave a small laugh out loud at the memory of how Amber had tried to conceal the damage from her. Stella slipped out of her jog-pants and pulled the sweatshirt over her head. The red dress would be perfect for tonight, and somehow it comforted her, bringing back happy memories of a life now lost to her.

She got her coat and headed outside to her little car. She would go and see Amber, make things up with her, before the girl's party. Amber at least had a grip on reality – *she* would never have gone out with Henry just after Stella had finished with him. That would have been an unwritten rule between them. The girls at the house seemed to have their own rules for everything – basically, they didn't care about anyone except themselves.

The city streets were quiet and Stella was soon parking her car outside the apartment. How familiar everything looked, the square brick building slumbering beneath its mantle of ivy and Virginia creeper. Stella got out of her car and stood outside the building, suddenly afraid. What would she say to Amber? She leant against her car, the cold metal chilling her skin. What *would* she say to Amber? She didn't know. She stood looking up at the building, mulling over the things that she should say – and the replies that Amber might give her. How easy it would be to march up to the doorway and press the buzzer of the intercom and talk! How they would laugh when Amber saw her wearing the red dress! They would joke about how Amber had tried to conceal the damage from her. Maybe Amber would even tell her how the damage happened. It was bound to be a long and funny story. Amber was brilliant at telling a funny tale. But maybe Amber wouldn't want to talk to her. The row would start up again. Maybe things wouldn't be good with Amber being pregnant. Maybe Stella should leave. Just put this stage of her life behind her and move on. Forget Amber and her pregnancy.

Stella got back into her car and put her head into her hands. They had been such good friends. She missed the easy companionship, missed the love and trust that they had felt between them. But that was all wrecked. Amber wouldn't want her around. She had her own life to lead.

Stella started her car and headed back to her new home. The beautiful building lay elegantly before her, the drive and road outside crowded with expensive cars. This was what she had wanted, to move in elegant, wealthy circles, meet a lovely millionaire. Stella took a deep breath, smoothed back her hair, applied a fresh coat of lipstick and then went into the house to join the party.

"Stella!" cried Julia as Stella walked back into the house. "Come and meet some *lovely* people!"

Stella followed Julia into the lounge. It buzzed with

noise and music – people filled every space, crowding together and spilling out onto the lawn through the open French windows.

"I sent your dog over to one of the neighbours, couldn't bear that yapping while we were having our party," Julia said over her shoulder. "And I've shut my cat into your room – Gucci can't *bear* parties. I hope you don't mind." She handed Stella a tall blue-coloured drink that a girl, dressed in a very short waitress's outfit, was carrying on a tray. "Drink that and you won't mind about anything."

October threaded her way through the crowded room to Stella. "We have *loads* of people who are just *dying* to meet you!" She seized Stella's arm and led her to a group of people. "This is our new housemate, Stella." October thrust Stella into the centre of the crowd of people.

"Hello," Stella said, knowing what it must feel like to be a specimen in a zoo.

"Hell-ooo!" A tall, red-haired man grabbed Stella's hand and held it up to his fleshy mouth. His face was the same colour as his hair and his eyes were almost transparent behind thick round glasses. "My name is Rupert." Stella's hand felt wet where Rupert's thick lips had suctioned onto the skin. "I'm in property. Let me introduce you to everyone." Rupert slid his hand into the small of Stella's back possessively as he introduced the circle of faces. "Liam," he indicated a foxy-faced man, "he's into hotels. And this is Miranda."

A horsey-faced woman glared at Stella. "His wife!"

she spat, in a warning tone.

"Lovely." Stella shook hands with her. She had a grip like a vice, probably from hauling her horses around on the hunting field.

"Devon," Rupert continued, spinning Stella around the circle of people, "he's an investment banker." Stella smiled at the short, dumpy man, his head topped by a mass of grey curls like a judge's wig, hardly daring to shake his hand for fear that another possessive wife was going to leap at her. "He's not married," Rupert said as if he could read her thoughts.

Devon let out a loud bray of laughter. "No point in taking your own sandwiches to a picnic, eh? Never got married, still testing the girls out. Amazing how quickly a fat wallet will open a girl's legs!" Devon let out another bray of laughter, his piggy eyes looking Stella slowly up and down.

Stella felt as if he were undressing her with his eyes. And it wasn't a pleasant feeling. She took another swig of her drink – the blue liquid tasted of cranberries and something sour that she couldn't identify.

"And what do you do?" asked Miranda, gripping her husband's arm as if to remind Stella that he belonged to her.

"I work for a magazine."

"Oh," exclaimed Rupert, his piggy eyes lighting up momentarily, "you're a publisher."

"No," Stella shook her head, "I just work there."

"Ohhh . . ." The light of interest in Rupert's eyes flickered and died.

The hum of conversation started again, talking about people and places that Stella had never heard of. They all seemed to be trying to outdo each other with tales of the wealth and houses that they possessed and the amazing faraway places that they had visited. Stella felt completely left out of the conversation. It was as if they had examined her, discovered her to be someone of no consequence whatsoever and now were not interested in her. She finished her drink, excused herself and went in search of the waitress with the tray of glasses. She hated this party. These people were dreadful, completely self-obsessed, full of their own self-importance. Not caring about anyone for themselves – it was all about possessions and wealth. Had she really wanted to be part of this? Wanted to belong to people like this?

Stella groped her way outside. The whole house seemed to be moving as if its foundations were shaking. There were people crowding into the hall. Stella was aware of blurry shapes, their faces merging into a mass of colour and eyes that all seemed to be watching her. The front door had two locks. It took Stella quite a while to locate the right one – her fingers kept slipping off the round knob and then she wasn't quite sure which way to turn it to open it. Was it left to open? Which way *was* left? Then slowly she pulled open the door. It was very difficult – she needed the support of something solid to help her to stand up which made it almost impossible to manoeuvre the door open and actually step through it. Eventually she managed to get through the door and grope her way out into the front garden.

The fresh air felt icy on her skin. She gulped in huge breaths, feeling the coldness tingle on her tongue, sucking it into her lungs. She took wavering steps out onto the lawn, feeling her shoes fall off as she walked onto the grass. Each blade of grass seemed to prickle beneath her feet, the dampness soaking into her skin, each sense intensely alive. There were car headlights, swinging into the drive, their beam bouncing off her brain and hitting the bone at the back of her skull. In that moment Stella knew without doubt that she was going to be sick. The feeling of nausea grew in her belly, becoming more and more fierce with every passing moment. The trees at the edge of the garden spun wildly, the sky and trees merging into a continuous blur of colour as if she were on a roundabout that was going too fast. Stella sank slowly to her knees, retching violently onto the grass.

The garden stopped spinning so wildly. Stella blinked, trying to focus her eyes. A pair of shoes appeared at the edge of her vision, brown shabby-looking brogues, a pair that she was sure that she recognised, but somehow couldn't place. A second pair appeared – sandals with long, narrow feet inside them – the toes wriggled, the bright pink nail varnish on their tips dancing as Stella tried to focus.

Slowly she raised her head, bringing her hand to her mouth, which suddenly felt damp. It took an immense effort to raise her head, past the two pairs of shoes, on upwards as she scrambled clumsily to her feet, past trousers and a pair of brown legs, a shirt and a tanned tummy and then on upwards, straight into Henry's amused, yet horrified face.

45

Ruby's reaction to the pregnancy hadn't come as a surprise to Amber. She had gone ballistic. Incredible really for someone who had dragged up her children in the wake of her affair with a married man. But, as Amber had suspected, she didn't expect her children to live their lives by her example.

"What!" Her mother had been lying in the newly built Jacuzzi enjoying her new luxurious life in Sycamore Avenue. "You fucking idiot!" Ruby scrambled out of the Jacuzzi, splattering water all over Kenny in her haste. The glass of champagne that she had been drinking went flying, rolling across the pale blue tiles, the champagne swirling and then dripping into the swirling water of the Jacuzzi. She had a great body for a middle-aged woman – her legs were toned and her bottom and belly still taut. Kenny watched her go, naked lust written all over his face.

"How could you be so *stupid!*" Ruby shrieked, wrapping a fluffy towelling dressing-gown over her leopard-print swimming suit. "Just when things are going right for you! Kenny's given you a job, sorted out your debts, and *this* is what you do!" She stamped over to the bar beside the pool, poured another glass of champagne and handed it to Amber, the irony of the gesture lost on her. Champagne was usually for celebrations, not to be drunk while getting yelled at. "What about the baby's father? Is he still around? Is he standing by you?"

Amber shrugged, miserably. "I don't know. Probably not."

"Are you going to get an abortion?" her mother demanded.

"Of course not," Amber said sullenly. Her mother had managed three pregnancies on her own. How dare she suddenly start expecting Amber to live her life differently!

"Calm down." Kenny heaved himself out of the pool and padded over to the bar.

"Thank you," Amber said gratefully, trying not to stare at the large fleshy man that her mother lived with.

Kenny poured himself a glass of champagne. "It's no big deal." He raised his glass at Amber, who wasn't sure if he was mocking her or not. "Amber could do worse – it's not like she's on drugs or anything. Anyway, Ruby," he ducked as he spoke, "it's about time you became a granny."

"Get lost!" grinned her mother, swinging a badly

aimed punch in Kenny's direction.

"Seriously though," Kenny said, seizing Ruby and pulling her into his arms so that she couldn't pommel him any more, "Amber can still work. I'll give her maternity leave and then she can find a crèche for the kid."

Amber nodded. Everyone was making plans for her, automatically assuming that she was going to be alone.

*   *   *

Amber woke on the morning of Georgina's wedding feeling absolutely dreadful. She had woken feeling dreadful ever since the pregnancy was confirmed, spending the first moments when she first opened her eyes waiting for the terrible waves of nausea to subside enough for her to make the dash from her bedroom to the bathroom. But this morning it was worse. It wasn't just the nausea, but a dreadful feeling of loneliness and despair. The novelty of discovering that she was pregnant had sunk in. Now the realisation that she was going to go through this alone was beginning to sink in. At first she had thought she'd lost him forever, then comforted herself with the thought that maybe he had just wanted to think about what had happened, come to terms with it on his own. That's what he had said, after all. Then, after she had given him a few days alone, Amber had tried to phone him and found that the phone was still switched off. She had left messages, humorous at first, gradually becoming more panicky and desperate, until she had realised that he wasn't going to contact her again. She was alone.

"Time that we got up, Baby," Amber said, gingerly inching herself off the mattress. She had discovered that if she moved slowly enough the nausea was not as bad as it would have been if she'd just got out of bed normally.

"Bloody wedding! We haven't got a thing to wear." Amber had taken to talking to herself as if the baby was actually with her. Somehow it made her loneliness seem less daunting. She moved her hands slowly over her body, feeling the unmistakeable changes that were happening to her. She had never had any breasts to speak of – now they were sizable assets. It was a shame that Paul was not around any more to enjoy them, thought Amber, wrenching open her wardrobe door with a vicious tug. Even thinking about Paul made Amber miserable. Amber tried desperately not to think about him, but relentlessly he filled her thoughts, day after day, however hard she tried. It was hard to be without him – all of the fun seemed to have been drained out of her life. She had felt so sure that they would always be together. He had been her soul mate; there would never be anyone else that she would love as much. If she had not become pregnant they would still have been together.

But somehow Amber could not resent the tiny new life that grew within her. The baby was part of Paul, part of the special time that they had shared together. If she did not have Paul, at least she would have his child.

At first, after she had almost lost the baby and when she had lost Paul, she had been afraid. The thought of being alone was terrifying. Her heart felt as if it would break with misery. She had ached physically for Paul, spending days just sitting, hoping that he would come back, waiting to hear the sound of his footsteps, her heart lurching with hope each time the telephone rang, hoping, longing that he would come back. The pain had gradually lessened to a dull ache. Being without him was still dreadful, but at least she had the energy to eat and go to work.

And it was dreadful to be without Stella. Amber missed her terribly. And Teddy. Stella would have known how to help her get over the loss of Paul. She would have made everything seem OK again. What's more, her constantly expanding wardrobe of gorgeous clothes would have been the perfect place to find a suitable outfit for the wedding! Now all of her clothes were gone, along with her fabulous selection of shoes, handbags and scrumptious accessories. Instead Della's clothes were piled into Stella's once tidy wardrobe. Amber doubted very much, judging by the outfits that she had seen Della in, that there would be anything suitable for her to wear even if she could find something to fit her. Della's clothes would have swamped Amber even now that her body had expanded with her pregnancy. Finding something to wear was an impossible task, nothing felt right any more. Or if it did it was too scruffy, too dressy, too tarty, too anything other than suitable for the wedding of your younger sister to a man old enough to be her father who also happened to once have been her schoolteacher.

Eventually Amber resurrected a rose-pink dress in a floaty kind of fabric that swirled around her when she walked. It skimmed her body rather than clung to it, so that she looked voluptuous rather than pregnant – she hoped. Her old grey overcoat didn't really look right with the dress, but Amber couldn't do anything about that. She added an enormous vibrant silk pink rose that she had once borrowed off Stella and forgotten to give back, pinning it to the lapel of her coat to give it an air of festivity and then wrapping a double row of silvery necklaces around her neck Amber finally stood back to admire her handiwork in the mirror.

"OK, Baby." Amber gently stroked the slight swell of her belly. "That is as good as it is going to get."

Della was sprawled in her favourite armchair, the TV, tuned in to a Saturday morning children's programme, blared with laughter and inane chatter.

"Switch on the kettle before you go, will you?" Della said, in between mouthfuls of toast from the pile on the plate that rested on her knee.

"Sure," Amber walked across and turned on the kettle. "Can I get you anything else?" she added sarcastically. "More toast?" Then she added under her breath, "Arsenic, powdered glass?"

"Yeah, throw some more bread in the toaster for me, will you?" Della's eyes didn't move from the television screen, where a bunch of children were throwing water-filled sponges at a giggling young blonde presenter. Amber's sarcasm was totally lost on her.

Amber viciously shoved more bread into the toaster. "I hope that it chokes her, don't you, Baby?" she muttered under her breath.

Ronnie's car horn sounded outside. It was time to go.

She collected her handbag, thinking longingly of Stella. If she had been there she would have been examining Amber's outfit, adjusting the way the rose was pinned onto her coat, adding another necklace, stepping back to admire her handiwork, while all the time keeping up a steady stream of conversation. Instead, Della was just a dull lump who only thought of herself and where her next mouthful of junk food was going to come from.

"I've got to go now," she said to Della. "Can you manage to butter the toast and make the tea yourself?"

"I'll be OK," Della said through a mouthful of toast.

"I'll be off then."

Silence but for the chomping of toast.

"Bye, Amber, bye, Baby," Amber muttered through clenched teeth.

Amber slipped a packet of mints into her pocket to take away the dreadful taste that seemed to permanently linger in her mouth at the moment and went down to the car. Ronnie looked unrecognisable, his hair cut short, clean-shaven and wearing a new-looking suit. Even his shirt was new – it still had the creases from where it had been folded into the packet. Amber didn't recognise the car.

"Borrowed it, from a mate in Galway," he had told her in a surly voice, adding quickly, "It's not stolen."

Amber shot him a quick smile. "I never asked if it was, did I?" For once she wouldn't have to have a heart attack every time that a Garda patrol car glided past.

But Ronnie was gaping at her. "You look pr– preg –" He stumbled over the word like a pubescent schoolboy.

"I am," Amber said quietly, hoping that he wouldn't launch into a "I'll kill the father of the baby for leaving you" type of tirade.

"Congratulations," Ronnie said uncertainly, unsure if it was a good thing or not. Amber didn't mention her condition again. The pain of Paul leaving was too raw.

The crowd outside the church looked an odd mixture of people, the couple's respective friends and family standing as far apart as possible, eyeing each other warily. Georgina's friends, young and trendily dressed in bright colours, giggled in small groups, while Martin's friends were an older, sedate, nerdy bunch in grey suits who looked nervously at the youngsters.

Georgina walked slowly up the aisle on Kenny's arm. Kenny, who looked enormous and very handsome in a diamond-in-the-rough kind of way, grinned with delight. Ruby leant out from her pew at the front of the church to watch their progress. She spotted Amber and waved brightly, looking unrecognisable in a smart pale blue, very expensive-looking suit, smiling happily beneath the most enormous hat that Amber had ever seen. No one would ever think that there had been any trouble between mother and daughter. Georgina winked delightedly at Amber as she glided past, her figure voluptuously curvy in a tightly fitting cream silk dress. Amber felt bitter tears of loneliness prickle at the back of her eyes. She would never make this same journey on Kenny's arm to marry the man of her dreams. No one would want her now that she was going to be a single mother. She was destined for a life of loneliness. She would die a bitter old maid. She would never find anyone to love again, she thought melodramatically.

At the end of the aisle the schoolteacher turned to look at his bride, his face softening as he smiled tenderly at her. The priest walked out in front of the altar, clearing his throat in readiness for the service. Behind them the door clanked shut, the huge handle banging heavily on the enormous wooden door. Amber saw the priest look up as someone came in late.

"You're all very welcome," the priest began his service.

"Move up. Let me sit down!" whispered a familiar voice beside Amber. She stifled a cry of surprise as Paul shoved her with his hip as he pushed into the pew. "Sorry I'm late," he whispered, reaching for Amber's hand.

"Are you staying?" Amber said, unable to believe that he was truly here.

"Yes. Definitely. I promise," he whispered.

"Thank you," Amber whispered back, slipping her hand into his.

46

Stella thought that she was going to cry when Xanthe told them all. It made it worse that everyone else was so excited. They had all forgotten that she had ever had anything to do with Henry. Or that she could still not forget him.

"You've actually got *engaged*!" shrieked October, jumping to her feet and dashing across the lounge to throw herself dramatically at Xanthe, kissing her theatrically on both cheeks.

"It's only taken six months to wear him down!" Xanthe flicked back her long blonde hair and gave an enormous self-satisfied smirk.

"Well done," Julia said in her husky voice. "Can't believe that you've beaten me. I was sure that Clifden was going to propose to me before you got round to it!"

Xanthe plonked herself on the sofa. "Well, I had to kind of guide him into it," she smirked.

"How did you manage it?" October clapped her hands together in delight, as if obtaining a marriage proposal was a huge game.

"Actually Daddy took him out to lunch and pointed out to him what a huge asset I was."

"And what huge assets Daddy has," chortled Julia, pushing her wide mouth into a pout.

"Quite!" Xanthe roared with laughter.

"Absolutely," agreed October, examining her long fingernails and flicking an imaginary piece of dirt from beneath one of her red talons.

"That is wonderful news," Stella forced herself to say. As long as she concentrated hard on the pile of press releases that she had been flicking through, then she wouldn't cry.

It was hard to imagine that Henry and Xanthe were going to be married. She couldn't imagine how the kind, gentle, impoverished Henry could find anything to love about the thoughtless, brash, affluent Xanthe. But it seemed that once Xanthe, like a cat with a mouse, got her claws into Henry she wasn't going to let him go. He was very good-looking and so nice that Xanthe was probably congratulating herself on finding a man she could manipulate and boss around. And he was so poor that the promise of Xanthe's father's money had no doubt been too much for him to turn down. After all, his stables were his priority – he had to keep his business afloat.

Or perhaps he had just been steamrollered by Xanthe, dazzled by her glamour.

Stella hated Xanthe's attitude to Henry, for instance the way she liked to refer to him mockingly as "His Lordship". It sounded like the kind of nickname that you would give to someone that was arrogant and cocksure of themselves, like Derry, or Rory. Henry was too gentle to be mocked like that.

"Look at this," Xanthe got up and flounced over to where Stella was sitting. She waved her hand at Stella. "Isn't this just the most gorgeous ring that you have ever seen?"

"Very nice," Stella said, glancing at the ring.

"Here!" Xanthe wrenched the ring from her finger. "Try it on!" She thrust the ring in Stella's direction.

"Thanks." Stella took the ring from Xanthe and slipped it onto her finger. She twisted her hand, watching how the ring reflected the light into a thousand shimmering shafts of colour.

"So," Julia said, holding out her hand for the ring as Stella pulled it off her finger, "where is the wedding going to be?"

Xanthe leant forwards, delighted to be holding court as her ring was passed around.

"Well, I thought that abbey in Mayo where Pierce Brosnan got married, and then the reception in Ashford Castle."

Stella somehow couldn't see Henry being very comfortable with all the swanky arrangements Xanthe was describing.

Stella felt a pang of regret and she tried very hard not to think about Henry. In the months that Xanthe had been going out with him, she had tried to avoid seeing them together. On the rare occasions that Xanthe brought him into the house for coffee after they'd been out, Stella always made sure that she kept upstairs, in her room, to avoid seeing him. She had once gone into the lounge by mistake, not realising that he was there, when she had come back from an evening out. She had opened the lounge door to find him sitting on the sofa on his own. She had felt herself go pink, a hot flush spreading slowly all over her body. Henry's face had lit up. The meeting had been very painful and she had vowed to make sure that their paths didn't cross again.

She'd worked hard to rid herself of his memory. She had thrown herself into a busy schedule of evening classes, riding lessons, anywhere that she thought there might be the possibility of meeting someone suitable for a relationship.

She had plenty of dates, with some lovely, wealthy men, but somehow she had lost the determination to find someone. Everyone got compared to Henry whether she liked it or not. No one yet had matched up to him. No one had made her heart sing like he had when they were together.

"I'm going to get Tamara Brennan to organise *everything*," Xanthe was saying. "Only the best for me!"

"Tamara Brennan!" October and Julia gasped in unison,

"She's *the* wedding planner," October added enviously.

Xanthe didn't deserve someone like Henry – he was

too kind, far too nice for someone like her. Stella wondered again what he saw in her.

"Have you set a date yet?" Julia asked again.

"I thought in a couple of months' time. No point in waiting."

There was a ripple of laughter from the girls.

"You'll give Tamara an ulcer getting everything organised in that short time," said October.

Xanthe shrugged diffidently. "She'll be earning bloody good money from my father, so she'll just have to work hard for it."

"Quite," agreed Julia, and the conversation drifted on to the silk dress that Xanthe was having designed for her and the absolute fortune that it was going to cost to fly in the special flowers from Thailand that she had already picked out for her bouquet.

Stella only half listened to the conversation. Two months. Two months, she wanted to shriek in bewilderment. Two months and then Henry would be lost to her forever. She was horrified at how the finality of his wedding distressed her.

"I'm going to be late for the gym," she said, getting slowly to her feet. She wanted to rush from the room, and throw herself onto her bed and cry and cry and cry, but she couldn't let herself do that. She had given Henry up and he was Xanthe's husband-to-be now.

She collected her bag and headed off to the gym. She had started going as an antidote to wanting to comfort-eat. She had to keep busy, keep moving, not let herself have the chance to sit down and eat. She knew that however bad she felt at the moment, if she ate to cheer herself up then she would feel worse again. The whole terrible cycle of eating and then feeling miserable because she had eaten and then eating because she felt miserable would begin again. And she had worked too hard in the past to let that happen again. She was never going to end up looking like her sister, with her squashy middle and enormous backside. The gym had taken her mind of eating – and off Henry. There she could exercise away the hurt that ending the relationship had caused.

After a couple of hours in the gym, Stella had walked, pedalled, rowed, pushed and pulled on every machine available. She was starving, exhausted, purple in the face and drenched with sweat. She felt calmer, the desperate sadness that she had felt had settled into an aching numbness in the pit of her stomach.

She showered and then went out into the changing room, finally stopping the incessant movement that she had used to escape from the pain of thinking about Henry. Sighing, she leant her forehead against the mirror, feeling the cold glass against the aching heat of her skin. Then slowly she straightened up and looked at herself. She had to stop thinking about him all of the time. Just had to.

There was little that she could do to repair the ravages made on her looks by the gym. Her complexion would take a while to calm down from the fiery red to its normal pale pink and her hair, in spite of her ministrations with the hairdrier and brush, still somehow managed to look as if she had been dragged through a hedge backwards. Quickly she dressed, shivering now in the cool air of the changing room, and then hurried outside to her car.

"You look awful," said a voice as she left the gym and headed across the carpark towards her car.

Stella felt her heart start its familiar pounding.

Henry looked gorgeous as ever. He'd got his hair cut since she'd last seen him, probably due to Xanthe's cajoling. The style suited him, showing off the neat shape of his skull.

"Thanks," she smiled faintly, wondering if Henry was aware of the feelings that seeing him wrought in her.

He stood just a few feet away from her, his eyes flickering incessantly over her face. Stella longed to move into his arms, to feel the warmth of his body against hers.

"Have you been to the gym?" he asked unnecessarily since she was dressed in trainers and jogging bottoms.

"Yes." Stella took a stride backwards, not trusting herself to be so close to him. She found that she could not tear her eyes away from him. Even the shabby clothes that he wore could not detract from what a handsome man he was. She wanted to burn the image of him on her memory, hold him there forever.

"You look too thin," he said, suddenly.

"As if that is any of your business," Stella snapped, suddenly hostile. She wanted to get away from him.

Being so close to him was too painful – she loved him too much, even now.

"You made that very clear," Henry snapped back coldly, shoving his hands into the pockets of his baggy cord trousers.

"I have to go." Stella could feel the panic rising in her – she had to get away from him, before her emotions betrayed her.

"Me too." Henry glanced towards the hospital at the edge of the carpark. "My father is sick. We haven't spoken for years. He wants me now he is dying."

"Oh," said Stella, thoughts of her own father tumbling through her mind. She groped for words, for the right thing to say.

But before she could respond Henry spoke again.

"Maybe I'll see you at the wedding," he said and began to walk away, his lips clamped in a tight, hard line as he looked back over his shoulder at her.

She turned and broke into a run, wanting to get to her car before the turmoil of her emotions exploded and she began to cry.

After all that had happened between them, he still expected that she would go to his bloody wedding.

*　　*　　*

A week later Stella was sitting in an editorial meeting. She had thrown herself into her work with a frenzied enthusiasm in order to block out the dreadful feelings of pain and regret that plagued her. From now on she was going to concentrate on her career, forget Henry, and eventually meet someone suitable to marry.

"So, ideas for the special money issue?" Shaughnessey said looking at the feature editors that were sitting around the vast boardroom table.

Stella fingered the brochures that she held, waiting for an opportunity to speak.

"I'd like to do a piece on this." Fleur Lombard, editor of the social diary, held up a large glossy mock-up of a magazine page. "The Thornhill Estate."

Stella felt her eyes widen in disbelief. There, in Fleur's hand, was a picture of the gorgeous house next door to Henry's cottage. The house that she loved so much. The photograph on the glossy mock-up was taken from a distance and showed the whole of the house, surrounded by its fantastic gardens and the parkland around it.

"Lord Thornhill, the owner, died a few days ago. He was an alcoholic, damaged all of his liver and everything with his drinking. He was hugely wealthy – old money, you know." Fleur glanced at Peter to judge his reaction to her idea. Peter pulled an interested face and she continued. "The estate and the title has passed on to his son, a horse-trainer – they'd been estranged for years. Seems like the old man didn't like his son wanting to train racehorses."

Stella closed her eyes, gripping the edge of the table as the room swayed uncomfortably. She could hear Fleur shuffling more mock-up pages.

"I thought that we could do a piece on the estate and

the new owner."

Stella opened her eyes and looked desolately at the new mock-up page that Fleur held. The page showed her gorgeous house, and superimposed in front of the house was the new owner of the house. Henry.

47

Stella walked unsteadily back to her office. The corridor seemed to stretch for an eternity, the cream carpet and walls blurring with the swirling mass of brightly painted modern art that her boss collected. Every step seemed an immense effort as if she were struggling uphill. Her breath sounded loud in her ears, each intake roaring as she gasped to suck it in. Finally she reached the door to her office, fumbled desperately to turn the handle and then almost fell into the cool silence. Slowly she closed the door behind her and sank to her knees, with her back against the cool wood.

Henry. The Henry that she had loved so desperately and given up because she was afraid of living in poverty for the rest of her life, had just inherited a fortune. Henry, the man she had given up because he wasn't the man she had wanted – *was* the man she wanted. No wonder those old portraits in Murtaghs'

House looked so familiar! His ancestors were local aristocrats! How could she have been so blind? Stella threw back her head and let out a mournful wail of desperation.

She could remember very little of the meeting after the social editor had put up the mock-up page with Henry on it, standing in front of Thornhill House. Just immense pain. She had wanted to run from the boardroom, hide somewhere dark to come to terms with what had happened. She had survived the meeting though.

Now as she crouched on the floor trying to compose herself, she marvelled at her own powers of endurance. As if from afar she had watched herself sitting at the boardroom table, surrounded by the other editors and journalists, nodding her head at the required moment, making the appropriate noises to make everyone else in the room believe that she was totally engrossed in her job, instead of dying inside. At some stage too she remembered suggesting a feature on the perfect wedding day make-up for all skin tones, for her own pages, which had been approved by the boss. Now it was over and she finally faced the devastation of her life.

"Fuck, fuck, fuck," groaned Stella, clambering to her feet an interminable time later. Every muscle ached with the enormous tension that cramped her body. She had loved Henry so, so, so much. She had given him up because she couldn't have borne seeing that love die as they struggled to make a living, as she began to resent him for not being able to provide for her and probably their children's needs. Now he had Xanthe. They were going to live together in the gorgeous house that Stella had loved so much. Henry was lost to her forever. All because of her own stupidity.

Stella straightened herself, smoothing down her skirt that had wrinkled up around her thighs as she crouched on the ground. Tilting her chin, she walked slowly to her desk, sat down and took a deep breath. Life had to go on. She had fucked up – big time – now she had to get on with life – and forget Henry.

Stella's day seemed to go on forever. She was exhausted by an all-pervading sadness that seemed to soak into her very bones, making every task an immense effort. Finally, though, the end of the day arrived. She waited another half an hour, making sure that her boss would realise that his faith in her was justified. That he had promoted the right person, that she was conscientious and dedicated to her job. The extra half an hour that Stella put in at her desk dragged slowly, the clock hands seeming to be determined to linger for as long as possible on the numbers.

At last she closed down her computer, listening with relief as the final notes of the shut-down sequence sounded.

*　　*　　*

She hadn't expected to find any peace at the house, but the level of excitement was far greater than she had ever imagined, or could stand. Xanthe had returned from spending a few days at her father's villa on Lanzarote, where she had been topping up her tan and relaxing before the onslaught of having to hassle the wedding planner over the trivia of her wedding.

"Hey, come and listen to what Xanthe has just found out!" October greeted Stella at the front door.

Shrieks of excitement could be heard coming from the lounge. Gucci, the fat cat, slunk past along the hall, glanced disdainfully at Stella, and then headed upstairs out of the way of the noise. Stella followed October towards the source of the commotion.

"Listen to this!" October pinched Stella's arm in her excitement. "Tell Stella, Xanthe!" she begged, pulling Stella towards the sofa.

"This really *has* to be the most exciting thing ever!" Julia was crouched on the floor at Xanthe's feet, clapping and exclaiming with delight. "Henry has just inherited his father's mansion!"

"Really?" Stella feigned delight. She sat down on the sofa, looking out through the French windows at Teddy, who seeing the girls in the lounge was straining at the end of his lead, yapping sporadically.

Xanthe leant forward. "Henry fell out with his father years ago. Seems like the old man didn't like his idea of training racehorses. Threw him out without a penny, but he let him live in the old cottage, hoping that he would soon get fed up of earning his living. But he didn't and they never spoke until just before the old man died."

Stella stared fixedly at Teddy, straining against his

chain, wanting to get into the house. She began to feel very sick. It really was all true. Henry really had just inherited the gorgeous Thornhill House.

"Henry's father was an alcoholic, seems like he had some very fixed ideas and Henry was as stubborn as he was." Xanthe twisted her enormous ring, examining the white line in her tan where the ring had protected her skin from the sunlight. "Anyway, girls," she went on, obviously tiring of talking about Henry, "I'm going to get Tamara to organise the most fantastic hen night!" October and Julia's eyes widened in anticipation. "I want all of my very best friends there – about two hundred and fifty of them – and you can come too Stella if you like," Xanthe added quickly, remembering that Stella was there. "I want to take over Neo's for dinner and then a VIP night of partying."

Stella felt her own eyes widen enviously. Neo's was the most fabulous nightclub, and the most exclusive. Its membership list was said to read like an edition of the *Irish Who's Who*. The nightclub had only opened recently and was reputed to be an exact replica of a street in Pompei, complete with slave girls serving the drinks. Peter, Stella's boss, had been invited to the grand opening a few months ago and had returned to work wearing a real gold slave bangle that the owners were giving out as souvenirs.

"Fabulous!" Julia and October's voices echoed each other.

"Unfortunately," Xanthe began again, "Daddy's got a horse running on the same day, so I'll have to suffer that first before I can enjoy myself." She raised her eyebrows skywards in annoyance, tutting in disgust. "You'll all have to come with me for moral support."

Stella felt herself nodding in agreement, wondering why on earth she had complied with Xanthe's order.

*   *   *

"I *hate* this," complained Xanthe as they trooped into the racecourse. "It's so *cold* and *boring*," she moaned, dramatically pulling the fur collar of her full-length mink coat together at her neck and shivering theatrically.

"I don't," Stella said quietly, her words lost in the bitter wind that seemed to blow straight from Siberia. "It's the best fun ever." She looked eagerly around her, letting Xanthe and the other girls hurry off to the hospitality box that Xanthe had persuaded her father to hire for them. She had actually missed coming to the races.

She strode purposefully off towards a programme seller, eager to see which horses were running today. She had become fascinated by racing while she had been with Henry and it would be interesting to see if any of the horses that she had seen before were running. She bought herself a programme and flicked through the pages, recognising many of the names of the horses and their trainers and jockeys. She really ought to come to the races, Stella decided, even if she wasn't involved with Henry any longer – it was still a brilliant day out.

The thought of being with Xanthe and all of her braying friends didn't hold much excitement so she wandered off towards the parade ring to watch the horses. As she crossed the tarmac towards the parade ring she caught sight of a familiar figure in the centre of the ring, watching the horses go around. She felt her stride falter, uncertain if she could bear to see Henry. But it was too late. As if he could sense her presence from a great distance, Henry looked up and caught her eye. Stella felt her mouth split as if of its own accord in a wide grin, her hand raised in greeting.

"Hi," Henry mouthed.

Stella smiled back. She leant against the parade ring, watching the horses go around. "Come in," Henry beckoned Stella into the grassy centre of the ring.

Uncertainly Stella ducked under the rail and went across the grass towards him. Henry introduced her to the elderly couple who were standing with him. "Rosie and Connor Flanaghan."

Stella smiled politely at the couple who were dressed in identical tweed jackets and felt hats. Rosie wore a tweed skirt that revealed calves knotted with varicose veins, while Connor wore tweed trousers in the same fabric.

"What's the competition like in the race?" Connor boomed.

"Let's go and watch them parade over here," Rosie suggested tactfully, noticing the way that Henry was looking at Stella.

"What?" Connor roared, scowling at his wife, his long moustache bristling as she led him away. "I pay good money to talk to Henry about my horse. Where are you taking me to, woman?"

"Come along!" Rosie boomed back.

Stella caught Henry's eye and smiled.

"You can talk to him anytime. Henry's busy now."

"Good to see you." Henry's voice was deep and sincere, his eyes roving over her face as if he were afraid that she would disappear if he looked away.

"And you," Stella said sadly. She missed him terribly. And whatever chance she could have ever had of restarting their relationship was lost now.

"I'm sorry about your father," she said, dragging her eyes away from his face and turning to look at the horses as they walked around the ring, heads bowed against the wind. Out of the corner of her eye she could see the jockeys beginning to come into the parade ring – the race would begin soon.

"Thanks," Henry said sadly, looking at the churned turf beneath his heavy boots. "We kind of made up before he died. Two stubborn fools, that was the trouble."

"I heard that you inherited the house," Stella said quietly. It seemed weird to call the magnificent mansion merely 'a house'.

Henry nodded, looking sideways at Stella. "I'm a lot better proposition now, aren't I?" he said bitterly.

Stella opened her mouth to speak but no words came out. She didn't know what to say. It was impossible to explain to Henry how she felt.

"Is Amber ... Paul . . .?" she blurted out.

"Amber's fine," Henry said, a cold edge in his voice. "Not long now until she has the baby. Paul's not riding today. He won't leave her." Stella bit her lip and looked away. Lucky Amber. How wonderful it must be to have someone with her like that.

"I was wrong about him, wasn't I?" Stella whispered.

"You were wrong about a lot of things," Henry said bitterly.

The steward rang his bell for the jockeys to mount. Kathy pulled Henry's horse towards them. "This is I Agree, isn't it?" Stella said, remembering the horse from one that she had seen at Henry's before.

"That's right," Henry said, obviously impressed that she had recognised the horse.

"What's the competition like?" Connor Flanaghan had returned to stand beside Henry.

"Good luck," Stella said. She had no business being with Henry now – he needed to talk to his clients.

Stella made her way out of the parade ring, dodging easily between the horses as they were led around. Funny, she thought, how afraid of the horses she had been when she had first started to come to the races. Now she moved amongst them as easily as if she had grown up with horses. She made her way up to the hospitality box. The girls were already partying in earnest, completely immune to the racing that was going on outside.

"Tamara!" Stella heard Xanthe yell, as she shoved her way through the heaving throng that was packed into the gaudily decorated room. "Tamara! I ordered Lanson champagne. This is Moet!" Stella cringed inwardly for the poor Tamara. Having to be at Xanthe's beck and call couldn't be pleasant, no matter how much she was charging.

"There you are!" Xanthe screeched, catching sight of Stella. "What *have* you been doing?"

Stella took a glass of champagne from one of the flustered-looking waitresses. "Outside. Watching the racing."

"Ohhh!" Xanthe gave her a look as if she thought that actually watching the racing was the most bizarre thing to do.

"I'm going out onto the balcony," Stella said, walking past Xanthe. "Your father's horse is running."

"Ohhhh, yeah, I'd better watch then." And she screwed up her face in distaste.

Stella opened the balcony door, letting in a blast of icy cold air.

"*Eweuch!*" Xanthe grimaced. "It's cold out there!"

Stella shrugged. "Stay inside then."

"No," Xanthe said with the affected air of a martyr. "I had better come out and watch." She bellowed back over her shoulder, "Tamara! Bring my coat, will you?"

Stella leant against the balcony wall, immune to the bitter cold, soaking up the atmosphere of the racecourse. Below them the spectators yelled and roared encouragement at their respective horses, while far away on the course the horses sped over the jumps.

"Fuck," complained Xanthe, "it's like waiting for nail varnish to dry. How bloody boring!" She leant over the guardrail, tipping her champagne glass slightly so that a drop of the golden liquid spilled out, falling and splashing on the top of a flat cap. Xanthe stepped back, giggling gleefully. Then, to Stella's intense embarrassment, she did it again. Eventually tiring of this game she leant over the balcony again, scanning the crowd.

"*Goodness, who* is *that?*" she shrieked, in such a loud voice that the man below them turned and looked up. "*Coooeeee!*" Xanthe yelled, waving wildly. "I wouldn't mind a bit of *that!*" She pointed at the man.

Stella looked at the people milling below them. The man that Xanthe had waved at had stopped and was looking up at them, a broad grin splitting his far too handsome face.

Stella looked. Straight into the highly amused eyes of Derry Blake.

48

Stella whooped in delight as Henry's horse I Agree charged past the winning post seven lengths ahead of the other runners.

"What a horse!" she exclaimed in delight, remembering watching him when she had first known Henry. Then he had barely wanted to canter around his gallops after the other horses. Henry had worked a miracle training I Agree to win a race in such style.

"Oh super!" Xanthe mumbled sarcastically, craning her neck to look through the crowds at the ramrod straight back of Derry Blake as he walked through the spectators. His horse, Stressed Up, had come second.

"You had better go and be with Henry," Stella said, trying to catch Xanthe's eye and get her attention. "He'll be being awarded his trophy." Then she added, "And getting his photograph taken. I saw that the *Irish Tatler* were taking pictures of all of the winners."

The words were hardly out of Stella's mouth before Xanthe wheeled away from the balcony rail and yelled "Open the door! Now!" at Tamara who was inside. "Quickly!" she yelled, her voice rising in temper as Tamara fumbled with the catch of the sliding door. "I have to go to the winning post . . . enclosure ... thing!" she squawked.

She barged her way through the hospitality box in her rush to get to Henry and get her photograph taken. "Drink more champagne everyone!" she yelled, rushing out the door with Tamara hurrying in her wake.

Stella shook her head as Xanthe's strident shrieks faded into the hum of noise from her party friends. The fact that they were at the races seemed to have passed most of them by. Not one person had gone out onto the balcony to watch the races, or had even glanced at the overhead television that was relaying each event live. All that they seemed to be interested in was chomping their way through the canapés and champagne like a horde of hungry locusts and trying to outdo each other with the tales of how they were spending their money. Stella looked around the room. There was no one here that she wanted to be with. But she longed to be beside Henry, sharing his victory, proud of the brilliant job that he had done on the horse.

"I'm going to congratulate Henry," Stella said, touching October gently on the arm.

"Really?" October smiled.

Not bothering to reply, Stella walked through the

hospitality box, down the stairs and into the fresh air. Outside on the tarmac all of the spectators were hurrying towards the Winners' Enclosure to see the winning horse.

The crowd around the outside of the enclosure was like an impenetrable wall, everyone wedged in together, shoving good-naturedly to try to get a glimpse of the winning horse and his trainer.

Stella shoved her shoulder into the crowd. "Excuse me," she said firmly and to her surprise the crowd parted, letting her through. Suddenly she found herself at the edge of the enclosure. Inside, beneath a tented awning that flapped listlessly in the wind, were the winning horses and those connected with them. I Agree stood proudly in between Henry and the jockey. Xanthe stood beside Henry trying to elbow Rosie and Connor Flanaghan out of the way and posing for the cameras, grinning broadly and pouting as they clicked and whirled wildly.

Henry caught Stella's eye.

"Well done," she mouthed, giving him a thumbs-up signal, genuinely delighted that he had been so successful, for a moment all of their past problems forgotten as she shared his delight in the success of the horse. Then Stella's delight turned to revulsion as she glanced past Henry and saw Xanthe flicking her long eyelashes at Derry Blake, who shot her a seductive smile, full of invitation.

Kathy finally led the horse away as the Winners' Enclosure began to empty.

Stella felt the full blast of the wind again as the crowd around her dispersed as everyone headed back to watch the next race.

"We'll head off to the Owners' and Trainers' Bar," Henry said as he put an arm around Rosie and Connor Flanaghan's shoulders and led them away.

Stella felt her heart sink, realising in that moment that she had grown to love being part of the racing scene. Now she was an outsider, that world was lost to her forever.

"Would you like to come with us?" Rosie shot back over her shoulder at Stella, who nodded gladly and jogged after them.

Xanthe hurried up to join Stella. "Who is *that?*" she said as she pointed discreetly at Derry who was walking ahead of them in the direction of the bar, chattering to the owners of the horse that he had trained.

"Derry Blake, he's a trainer too," Stella told her, adding "just like Henry." It might be a good idea to remind Xanthe who Henry was – she seemed to be completely enthralled with Derry.

"Daddy should put his horses with him," Xanthe said wistfully.

God, thought Stella, Xanthe was incorrigible!

They reached the bar and Xanthe ordered Tamara to get some drinks, shoving a fistful of money in her direction. She seemed to have forgotten that Tamara was supposed to be organising her wedding and was using her as a maid instead.

"Congratulations," Rosie smiled as she stood beside Xanthe. "I hear you're getting married."

"Yes," said Xanthe, in a tone cold enough to freeze water, looking down her nose at Rosie.

Stella cringed. She knew it was part of a trainer's wife's job to chat to the owners of the horses. A little bit of politeness cost nothing. Rosie was a lovely old lady and here was Xanthe treating her like dirt.

"Have you set a date yet?" Rosie persisted.

"Yes, we have," said Xanthe and turned her back rudely on Rosie. "Tamara, I must insist that the priest wears black shoes, otherwise the colour co-ordination will be ruined."

Rosie glared at Xanthe as if she couldn't believe that someone could be so rude.

Stella stood uncertainly on the edge of the group of people. She didn't want to talk to Xanthe, and felt that she couldn't talk to Henry.

"Who is your friend?" said a silky voice at her side.

"Hello, Derry." Stella didn't turn to acknowledge him. ""That's Xanthe. I share a house with her. She has just got engaged."

"Ahhhh!" Derry's voice was devilish, filled with the promise of mischief.

Stella saw Xanthe glance in her direction, watched her spin around, Tamara still talking to her as she stalked across the room towards Derry.

"Hello," Xanthe preened, holding her hand out seductively for Derry to kiss.

"Well," Derry took her hand in his and brought it

slowly to his lips, never once taking his eyes off her face. He kissed her hand, his lips lingering on her skin. It was a gesture filled with erotic promise. "Where have you been hiding all of my life?"

I should think that she was at school most of your life, Stella itched to say.

"I'm here now," Xanthe said, making no effort to remove her hand from Derry's.

"What are you doing getting engaged? What a terrible waste! Especially when I have just found you."

Xanthe giggled flirtatiously.

Stella began to feel very uncomfortable as the sexual tension buzzed between Xanthe and Derry. What the hell was Xanthe playing at? Derry Blake was pure poison – he didn't give a damn about anyone or anything. And Xanthe didn't give a damn about Henry or she would never mess around with someone as evil as Derry. Stella swallowed hard and took a step backwards, gazing fearfully towards Henry. He felt her looking at him, glanced up from his conversation and looked from Stella to Xanthe, his handsome face falling as he saw Derry Blake.

"It's time that we left for Neo's," said Tamara, touching Xanthe's hand.

"I'm busy," she shot back nastily, jerking her hand out of Tamara's reach.

"Neo's?" Derry mocked, putting on an impressed face.

"Xanthe's having a party there," Tamara smiled, politely professional.

"Ahh," Derry said silkily. "Maybe I will see you later then." His eyes locked onto Xanthe's again, filled with forbidden promise.

"It's a private party," Tamara said. "Xanthe's hen night."

Derry gently brought Xanthe's hand to his lips again and kissed it once more, his eyes roving seductively on to Tamara. "Hen night? Girls only? Sounds perfect. I love hen nights." His voice held a challenge that Tamara couldn't stop him going to Neo's. "I'll see you later." He smiled at Xanthe, before spinning on his heel and walking away.

Stella glared after Derry – he even had the audacity to stop and talk to Henry. She was filled with anger as she saw Derry congratulate Henry, shaking his hand and nodding in Xanthe's direction. No doubt telling Henry what a lovely girl she was.

* * *

The dinner at Neo's was an exclusive affair for fifty of Xanthe's closest friends before the party afterwards to which everyone else had been invited. Stella had been surprised to find that she had been invited to the dinner, but then realised afterwards that October and Julia had probably arranged it so that Stella could drive them home afterwards.

"Isn't this gorgeous?" October said, looking around the room.

Stella nodded. Neo's was truly fantastic – acres of

white marble seemed to stretch in every direction, tall columns stretched up to a ceiling that had been painted to look like a scene from an orgy, naked bodies entwined and intermeshed into each other. They were handed glasses of pink champagne by a near-naked waiter – Stella almost choked as he turned away – his bottom was barely covered by a fig leaf.

"Isn't he gorgeous?" October squeaked in excitement, gazing lustfully after the waiter, whose body gleamed with the oil that he had slicked all over his skin.

Stella nodded in agreement, hardly glancing at the young man. Somehow no one seemed to interest her any more, not even the gleaming, toned bodies of the waiters that all of the girls seemed to be gazing at in open admiration.

Stella began to wish that she hadn't come. She had spent so long wanting to belong to this kind of set. Once she would have donated one of her limbs to have been invited to a party at one of the city's most exclusive nightclubs, attended by some of the wealthiest people around. But it wasn't as much fun as she had thought it would be. Having a quiet dinner in a small restaurant with Henry, tired and satisfied after a day at the races, was far more fun. She hadn't realised how much she had enjoyed discussing the other horses and the trainers. She had always been longing for a different, better life. And now she had discovered that it wasn't as glamorous as she had anticipated.

"I was in Monte last week," the identikit blonde

beside her was saying, "New York next week – I've got my name down for one of the new Marwari dresses, got to go for a fitting."

"Yah," droned an identical blonde, swishing her long hair back over her shoulder, "I got my Marwari *last* week. Gorgeous. Amazing how each piece is handwoven by children in India."

Stella wandered away, sipping her drink, half listening to bits of conversations as she mooched around, looking at the enormous lewd oil paintings on the walls, running her fingers along the cold stone carved faces of the marble statues.

A youth dressed in a toga blew a single note on a long gold horn. "Dinner is served."

Stella followed everyone into the dining room. Long tables had been laid out with golden plates and cutlery, with huge bowls of fresh fruit in the middle of the table, huge bunches of grapes spilling out from amongst fresh peaches and oranges.

"The table plan is on the wall," Tamara repeated, standing in the doorway, guiding everyone to the seating arrangement.

Stella found herself sitting on the end of one of the tables, beside two of Xanthe's cousins who had obviously been invited to smooth family feelings. The two girls were definitely non-identikit blondes, both very plump and very dark, and had no manners whatsoever. Stella quickly gave up trying to talk to them after her attempts at conversation were barely acknowledged.

Stella picked at her food, nervousness making her feel nauseous. Halfway along the other side of the table Xanthe was holding court, ordering poor Tamara around as if she were a servant. Tamara, wearing a fixed smile, grimly fetched and carried, tending to Xanthe's every whim. A movement in the shadows between the tall columns caught Stella's eye and she glanced up, horrified to see Derry walking across the room. He reached Xanthe, slid his arms around her from behind and seductively kissed the side of her neck.

"Derry," giggled Xanthe, rubbing her head against his where it nestled against her neck. "This is supposed to be a hen night! Ladies only,"

"Perfect," Derry said standing up straight again and surveying the girls who were looking at him open-mouthed. "Hens should always have one good cock in with them."

"Can I offer you anything?" Xanthe said huskily, turning her head to look at Derry over her shoulder.

"Yes, I think you can," Derry said, ignoring the amazed stares of the rest of the girls. "But I'll let you eat now – you'll need the energy," he said, blatantly dropping a kiss onto Xanthe's bare shoulder.

Derry moved away, snapping his fingers in the air, and one of the waiters darted forwards.

"Yes, Mr Blake, sir?"

Derry was obviously well known.

"Get me a whiskey." He walked away out of the dining area.

A shocked silence fell over the party and Xanthe glanced around the table as if she had only just realised what a tart she had made of herself.

"Isn't he awful?" she said feigning shock, gazing up and down the table. "Tamara, how *could* you let him in?"

"I'll get rid of him," Tamara said between gritted teeth. She looked as if working for Xanthe was the worst experience of her whole life.

"Don't bother!" snapped Xanthe. "I'll do it myself."

Once the dinner was over Xanthe got to her feet, her eyes glowing with mischief.

"You all head into the disco – I'll just go and get rid of our unwanted visitor," she said, heading towards the bar, walking unsteadily on her high heels.

Stella followed everyone into the disco. Loud music boomed from every corner of the room, making the floor and walls seem as if they flexed with the bass beat. The near-naked waiters slunk onto the dance floor as the girls began to dance, grinning as the drunken women groped at their slippery bodies.

Stella endured an hour of the booming music. Her head ached horribly and the thought of lying in her comfortable bed was very appealing. October and Julia didn't look as if they were too worried about leaving yet. Stella grabbed her handbag. She would go home alone, leave them all to it.

Her high heels clicked on the marble corridor as she headed out of the nightclub, then as she felt the strap dig into her toes she pulled off her shoes. They had been hurting all night. She crossed the deserted reception area where they had originally had a drink, her aching feet padding silently on the cool marble.

Then she stopped, spinning around, alerted by a soft murmur.

Tucked away in a recessed alcove amongst the columns and statues, was a sofa, and lying on the sofa, entwined, oblivious to her presence, were Derry and Xanthe.

49

Stella itched to punch Xanthe as she flicked through a magazine, looking for ideas for her wedding. Xanthe had betrayed Henry, dear sweet kind Henry, with someone as sly and rotten as Derry Blake. How the two of them suited each other! Stella glared at Xanthe's immaculate mask of make-up and the body that was kept toned by the personal trainer that she met at the gym every other day. Everything about her was false. There was nothing real about her. Or rather, the real Xanthe, the one hiding behind the make-up and expensive clothes, was rotten to the core, just like Derry. Neither of them cared a jot about anyone else or their feelings as long as they were satisfied.

"You don't care about anything very much, do you?" Stella snapped, unable to restrain herself.

"I beg your pardon?" Xanthe stopped flicking pages and stared coolly at Stella.

Tamara who was sitting at the table behind Xanthe, jotting down her ideas, stopped writing, her pen poised over the page while she listened eagerly to the row that was brewing up.

"I said," Stella said coldly, "you don't care about anything very much."

"And just what is that supposed to mean?"

"You went off with Derry Blake on your *hen* night!"

Xanthe shrugged her shoulders, opening her hands in a complacent gesture.

"Your *hen* night!" Stella longed to launch herself at the sofa and pound her fists into Xanthe's smug face.

"Oh Stella," Xanthe sighed, "that was just a last little fling before I get married. My fiancé won't ever know. While the cat's away and all that."

Stella narrowed her eyes, unable to believe Xanthe's words. She shook her head, "But where does love come into it?" The hot anger she had felt had vanished, to be replaced by a deep despair. Henry deserved something better than this.

"I *do* love my fiancé," Xanthe said smugly, "actually." With that she stood up, ending the argument, and flounced out of the room, with Tamara trailing in her wake.

She paused in the doorway, looking back at them with a grin.

"I am glad that Derry Blake is around, though." She raised her eyebrows and smirked before turning away.

* * *

Stella slept badly, turning over and over in bed unable to get comfortable, or switch off from the myriad thoughts that swirled around in her mind. Teddy, disturbed by the constant movement, slunk miserably off the bed and finally curled in Stella's discarded clothes on the floor. It was hard to bear the thought that Xanthe was marrying Henry purely for who he was – she didn't give a damn about him, just that marrying him would give her some social standing while she carried on as if she were still single. Henry would be devastated when he found out what an evil bitch he had married. He deserved better. Stella longed to get up out of bed and go and tell him immediately. Twice she sat up and turned on the bedside light, ready to get up. But then she had turned off the light again and lain back down. If she went to see Henry it would just look as if she wanted to damage his and Xanthe's relationship. It would look as if she wanted him back now that she had found out that he was rich. And she did want him back, but not just because of his new-found wealth. She wanted him back because she loved him. She had loved him from the first moment that they had gone out together and had fought against that love because she didn't think he was right for her.

Stella seemed to have only just dropped off to sleep when her alarm clock buzzed. There was no sign of the other girls when she went downstairs – none of them went off to a job like she did and so kept very different hours. In fact, she saw very little of them on the whole. Xanthe had once laughed snidely that the only eight o'clock that she ever saw was the one when it was time to go out for the night.

Stella was glad to get to work. At least there she could find solace from the thoughts that swirled through her mind.

"Morning, darling," Peter Shaughnessy air-kissed beside her head. "How are things with you? How is that new feature on stress-free weekends coming along?"

"Great." Stella was glad to have something to focus on. "I've been contacting all of the spa hotels that I could think of, Delphi, Inchydoney, to see –"

"Darling!" Her boss turned away abruptly, cutting her off in mid-sentence as the head of advertising, Hazel Brown, walked down the corridor. "I wanted to talk to you about some new contracts." Peter walked away with his hand resting on Hazel's back, without even glancing back in Stella's direction.

Stella sighed bitterly. The moment that someone more important had come along her boss hadn't even wanted to know her. What a false, artificial world she worked in, where everyone was nice to each other to their faces and then stabbed each other in the back!

Stella walked up to her office, noticing as if for the first time the smarmy fake chumminess that everyone seemed to exhibit. Ian McGowan, one of the designers, cut his friend dead in mid-conversation as Stella walked in, dashing up to tell her about some photographs he had been sent. Stella was more important than his friend in the hierarchy of the magazine. Stella suddenly loathed every second she was in the building. She loved what she did for a job, she was brilliant at it, but all of the fake intimacy was awful. She didn't want any part of it. If only people could just accept others for what they were. And she had been part of that awful chain of artificial friends, wanting to be with people who were wealthy, looking down on those who were poor and humble. And now she could see all that sham world for the fake it was.

Just before lunch-time she made a phone call to another of the spas that she wanted to visit as part of the feature that she was writing. At first the owner wouldn't come to the phone to talk to her, but once Stella had explained to her secretary that she was an editor on one of the biggest social magazines in Ireland suddenly the owner was on the other end of the receiver, dripping sweetness. Stella ended the call and put the receiver down.

Slowly she got to her feet and walked out of her office, shutting the door quietly behind her.

"Can I come in?" she knocked on Peter Shaughnessy's office door which was ajar.

He was on the phone. "Well, I –"

"This is important." Stella stood in the doorway.

"I'll call you back," he said, putting the receiver down and raising his eyebrows quizzically at Stella.

"I'm quitting." Stella surprised herself as the words tumbled from her mouth. She had intended to tell him that she was going to take some time off, but now it was done. She had ended her career.

"Why?" Peter asked simply.

Stella crossed the floor and sat down on the leather sofa opposite his desk.

"I've just had enough of . . ." Stella fumbled for the words. What had she had enough of? Everything. The whole circuit that she had become mixed up in, the whole game of striving to become and longing to be someone that she could never be.

Peter smiled suddenly, leaning forwards, meshing his fingers together and resting his chin on them. "Take some time out," he said quietly. "Go home to the country for a bit. Recharge your batteries and then see how you feel. You can work freelance for me for a while and I'll keep your job open for a few months."

Stella looked at him in surprised gratitude.

*　　*　　*

Stella headed back to the house. The drive was full of cars, so she parked out on the road and went inside. The lounge was full of wedding-dress samples – they were draped over the sofa, on the table, all over the floor, spilling out of the boxes and suitcases that were stacked all over the room. Amongst the masses of pale silk fabric and glitter sat October, Julia and Tamara scribbling on her ubiquitous pad while Xanthe paraded through the room in a gorgeous cream silk halter-neck dress that clung to the contours of her body like a second skin.

"What do you think?" Xanthe asked, spinning

around to give Stella the full benefit of her dress, her huge engagement ring catching the light as she turned, sending shafts of light across the room that reflected on the glittery dresses. She seemed to have completely forgotten their earlier argument – she was so thick-skinned that nothing seemed to bother her.

"Lovely," Stella said, her voice filled with awe. Xanthe really did look stunning in the dress. Henry would be truly dazzled.

Then something inside Stella snapped. Like floodgates giving way when the weight of water becomes too strong, the emotion within her surged out. "You don't give a damn about Henry! You'll just break his heart, you bitch!"

Xanthe stopped waltzing around the room and turned to face Stella, hands on hips. "Excuse *me!* What *are* you talking about? *You're* the one who broke Henry's heart! If anyone is a bitch it's *you.*"

Stella felt as if she had been hurled into a brick wall. Slowly she backed away. It was true.

"I have to go," Stella said slowly and every word seemed to be an immense effort. She had to get away. It was impossible to stay here and watch Xanthe and Henry get married.

She shot upstairs, threw some stuff into a couple of bags and pounded back down the stairs, Teddy at her heels.

October was standing at the bottom of the stairs. "Stella, wait," she said. "I need to talk to you."

But Stella ignored her, hurrying by and slamming

the front door in her face. She ran down the drive to her car with Teddy hurtling after her as fast as his short legs would carry him.

Behind her, Stella could hear the door open.

"Stella! Stella!" October called, running down the drive after her. "Wait!"

"Just leave me alone," Stella snapped. Throwing her bags into the back seat of the car, she picked up Teddy, shoved him into the passenger seat and then scrambled into the driver's seat and slammed the door shut.

"Stella, talk to me!" October mouthed, hammering on the side window. "Don't rush off like this! I think you're making a mistake!"

Since when was October so concerned with her? Stella fired up the engine and drove away, the car tyres screeching in protest. Getting away from here was certainly no mistake.

*   *   *

A short time later she was heading out of the city, the back seat filled with her bags and Teddy on the front seat, looking eagerly out of the windscreen to see where they were going.

"Right then, Teddy," Stella mused aloud as she drove, "where shall we go?" She wanted to escape from the city, find somewhere where there was peace and quiet, somewhere where she could put all thoughts of Henry behind her and start her life afresh. "Wexford, maybe?" She looked across at him as if she expected him to reply. "You'd like it there. We could rent a cottage somewhere. Just me and you. Make a new life for ourselves." Teddy gazed solemnly at Stella as if he understood every word. "Somewhere you can live inside. None of that being chained up outside for you."

Teddy cocked his head on one side, his small pink tongue lolling out of the side of the mouth as if he were grinning in agreement.

"And I think that I would like to meet a nice racehorse trainer," Stella told Teddy. "I think that I like racehorse trainers." Then she laughed. "But I'm not going to turn anyone down who is nice just because they aren't a racehorse trainer!"

She steered through the traffic, not really driving with any purpose.

"My boss said that I should go home, sort out my life." Stella gave a snort of derision. Home was in Dublin, with those two-faced bitches, who thought of nothing but money and social standing.

Just as she had always done.

She had resented her parents because they were poor; she had rejected Henry because she thought he was poor; she had fought with Amber because she thought Paul wasn't good enough. What a shallow, nasty bitch she'd been! She didn't deserve forgiveness; she didn't deserve friends; she didn't deserve her parents' love. She certainly hadn't deserved Henry's love.

"Oh Teddy," the tarmac blurred as tears suddenly began to flow, "what a mess I've made of everything!"

Stella couldn't see to drive any more. She stopped the car at the side of the road and laid her head against the steering wheel, weeping bitterly. She felt Teddy licking her face. "Oh, I'm OK. I'm OK, Teddy. Don't worry . . ." She sat up, searching for a tissue in her handbag to wipe her tear-stained face. Teddy gazed at her anxiously and she smiled to reassure him. "You know what, Teddy? You'd like Mayo even more than Wexford. Do you think we should go home? I have a lot of making up to do there." Teddy licked her in agreement.

She started up the engine and eased out into the traffic again. At that, Teddy turned around on the front seat, curling himself up into a ball as he settled down to sleep with a contented sigh.

"That's it," Stella smiled, stroking his soft hair. "Go to sleep just when I need you to navigate."

*   *   *

Teddy sat up with a yawn and put his front paws onto the dashboard, wagging his tail gently.

"I bet you need a pee." Stella indicated and pulled over to the side of the road.

She was halfway to Mayo.

"East, west, home is best," she recited softly, letting Teddy out onto the grass verge.

Further west the road narrowed, becoming gradually more bumpy, winding through wild, untamed countryside, banks and tangled hedges and lines of stone walls, the mountains brooding in the background. Stella pulled into a lay-by to watch the sunset. The sun began to slowly slide down behind the hills, casting pink and orange light over the rust-coloured land, making everything glow an unearthly pink. The night sky began to encroach as a mosaic of tiny black clouds drifted across the pink and orange, making the trees on the skyline look a deep inky black against the glow from the sky. Down at the bottom of the hillside that Stella was on was a lake, still and silent. The sunset was reflected on the glass-like surface, magnifying the beauty of the sky. Stella felt an immense peace drift over her. She was going to get through this awful time. Life was going to go on.

50

Stella put down her sketchpad and looked at the picture that she had created. The seascape that she had done in pastels was quite good.

"Not too bad, Teddy, what do you think?" Stella held up her sketchpad in Teddy's direction. The dog continued to dig in the sand, pulling at a half-buried piece of driftwood.

"I think that it's lovely!" Stella's mother reached across and picked up the picture.

Stella smiled at her mother. "You have to say that!"

"Well, it's true." Her mother lay back on the tartan rug, shielding her eyes from the bright sunlight.

Stella sighed deeply. "This is lovely though," she said softly. "Spending time just doing nothing." She lay on her back and closed her eyes, letting the warmth of the sun soak into her body. It was wonderful to be home. For the first time ever she felt truly relaxed here.

This was where she belonged amongst people who loved her for herself.

"What are you going to do now?" her mother asked gently, for the first time since Stella had arrived on the doorstep.

Stella sat up, hugging her knees to her chest, gazing out at the sea.

"I've spent my whole life hating this place," she said quietly, biting her lip to stop the sudden tears from falling. "I've spent years searching for something, pushing away the people who loved me because I thought that they weren't good enough. And being attracted to shallow worthless people. All that glitters isn't gold, isn't that what they say?" She glanced across at Irene, who lay on the rug, looking at her, her eyes gentle. "I've messed everything up."

"You haven't," her mother said gently, "Give yourself a bit of time. Think about what you're going to do with your life now." Teddy dropped a small branch onto the rug beside Irene and she threw it across the sand. "Just relax for now."

Stella rolled onto her belly and looked across at Irene, trailing her hand in the warm sand, digging her fingers down beneath the top layer until she reached the cool dampness beneath.

She nodded slowly. She didn't have a clue what she wanted to do, now that she had left Dublin. Coming home had been the best thing she could have done. Her heart, frozen with loathing for her childhood and her parents' humble life, had finally thawed and at last she was able to return their love.

Paddy's treatment was working, the consultant had told them – they were 'reasonably optimistic' about the outcome. And so, to her immense relief, she and her father had a second chance at a relationship.

Stella felt calm and relaxed. Here there was no striving to be more wealthy, no relentless networking to build up more influential contacts. Life in the countryside had a peace and gentleness to it that soothed her.

She smiled at her mother. "I don't ever remember *you* doing nothing. Just sitting to relax," she said.

"I couldn't. Not for a long time. Not since your father had his accident," replied her mother.

Stella gazed out across the deserted stretch of golden sand to the beautiful sea, glorious today, each gentle wave a deep turquoise blue topped by a breaker of pure white. Gorgeous today, but deadly just the same. This same peaceful-looking ocean had almost claimed the life of her father, allowing him to live, but live a ruined half-life.

"After that I spent all of my time looking after him, and you lot." Her mother smiled at the memory.

"Didn't you ever resent it all?" Stella asked, gazing out at a boat far away on the horizon.

"No," her mother replied, surprising Stella with the strength in her voice, "I never resented one moment that I spent looking after your father. I loved him just as much when he was injured as before." Her voice became softer, her eyes distant as she continued, "I believe that for every person there is one love, one person that you truly belong with. That person is your father, for me. I could never love anyone else."

Stella nodded slowly. It was true. And she had rejected the one person that she belonged with: Henry.

She had come to a decision: she couldn't put right the damage that she had done to their relationship, but she had to tell him the truth about Xanthe. He might not believe her. But she couldn't let him go down the aisle without at least trying to save him from that fate.

And there was Amber . . .

"Mammy," she said slowly, "I have to go back for a few days. There are a few things that I have to sort out."

* * *

There was no sign of anyone at the apartment. Stella pushed her finger onto the buzzer again, but no one came to answer it. Amber must have gone out.

"Shit," Stella sighed. She had been all fired up for apologising to Amber, had got all of her words organised in her mind and now she wasn't in.

On impulse Stella jogged across to the small corner shop opposite the apartment and brought a small card, with a picture of a dog on it that didn't look unlike Teddy. Rummaging in her handbag she unearthed a pen and scrawled *'I'm so sorry for everything. I'll call back later'* on the card and shoved it into the envelope.

She went back to the apartment. There was no point

in pushing the card into the letter- box. Sometimes Amber didn't check her mail for days on end – she always seemed to think that if she didn't receive her credit-card bills then they didn't actually exist. Stella still had her key – she would go up and just shove the card under the door. That way she would be sure that Amber had received it.

She locked up her car, winding down an inch of the passenger-seat window so that Teddy could get some fresh air. As she walked away the small dog pressed his nose to the gap, whimpering crossly at being left. Stella opened the main door, breathing in the familiar scent of the scented candles that one of her ex-neighbours always burnt overlaid with the faintly musty smell of the hallway. Everything was so familiar, as if she had never been away – even the bicycle that belonged to the man who lived in the bottom apartment was still resting in the same position she had last seen it against the wall. She went upstairs feeling as is she were trespassing, expecting at any second that one of the residents would come rushing out and yell at her to clear off. But no one did.

She reached the door to her old apartment and crouched down to shove the envelope through the gap between the door and the carpet.

A low moan of pain came from inside the apartment. "Amber?" Stella gasped. "Amber!"

There was a silence for a moment, followed by another moan and then Amber shrieked, "Stella, is that you? Come and fucking help me! Quickly!"

"Amber!" Stella could hear the panic rising in her own voice as she rummaged frenziedly in her handbag for the door key that she had thrown in after she opened the bottom door. "I'm coming! What's the matter? Are you hurt?" A thousand images flashed through Stella's mind, each one more horrific than the one before it: Amber being attacked by burglars, Amber suffering a heart attack, falling on a knife.

"For fuck's sake, Stella," growled Amber, "I'm having the bloody baby!"

Stella found the key and hastily fumbled to get it into the lock, frenziedly turning the key, unable to remember which way to turn it to open the door.

"Turn it to the fucking left," snarled Amber from inside the apartment.

"Yes, yes!" gasped Stella, finally shoving the door open and exploding into the apartment.

Amber lay on the sofa, her back arched with pain. Stella felt her mouth drop open. Amber's belly was enormous, her sweatshirt straining across the huge mound.

"Help me, will you!" Amber gasped, pushing a sweat-dampened strand of hair from her grey forehead.

"What do I do?" Stella turned around, took a stride towards the kitchen, memories of demands for hot water, soap and towels in the movies flooding back. She turned again – what *did* they do with them when they had them?

"What do I do?" she gasped again.

"Ring –" Amber puffed, her face contorted with

pain, "For –" puff, "A –" puff "Fucking –" puff *"Ambulance!"*

"Right," Stella replied, turning around twice until her shock-befuddled brain remembered where the phone was.

Stella found the phone and punched in the number for the emergency services. It seemed to take forever to direct her call to the ambulance service.

"I need an ambulance," Stella gasped, feeling as if she were some character in a television hospital drama.

"What is the problem?" asked the super-calm voice on the end of the phone.

"My friend," Stella glanced across at Amber who arched her back, writhing with the pain, "she's in an awful lot of pain!"

"Tell them I'm having a fucking baby, you stupid cow!" roared Amber, clutching at the back of the sofa, sweat pouring from her forehead.

"Oh," Stella couldn't get her brain to co-operate with her mouth. This wasn't the scene that she had imagined. She had imagined herself and Amber meeting and quietly discussing their argument over a cup of coffee. If she had stopped to think, she would have known that the baby had to be due around now, but as usual she had been selfishly obsessed with her own affairs, her own big gesture of 'doing the right thing' world.

"Tell them I'm in fucking labour!" Amber yelled, sinking back onto the sofa as the vicious wave of pain subsided.

"She's in labour!" Stella yelled into the phone.

"How often is she getting contractions?"

"She says how often are you getting contractions?" Stella put her hand over the receiver to ask Amber, as she clawed in agony at the back of the sofa.

"Just pain!" Amber hissed, her legs writhing as she tried to escape from the dreadful agony that was trying to rip her body apart.

"Is she dilated?" asked the woman on the phone.

"No, I think she's Catholic." Stella could feel the panic rising within herself. It was terrible to see Amber in such pain and to be able to do nothing about it.

"Right," said the woman patiently. "Listen, you have to try to keep her calm. We'll have an ambulance there as soon as possible. Give me the address." Stella gave the woman the address, watching Amber fearfully. She was silent now, lying flat on the sofa, still, her eyes wide open, reflecting only pure terror.

"She's dying!" Stella shrieked into the mouthpiece.

"Calm down!" snapped the operator. "You have to keep calm. Go and have a look at your friend and then come back to me. Try to get her to breathe deeply."

Stella took a deep breath and walked over to the sofa. Amber turned her head fretfully, as if she had only just realised that Stella was there.

"She says you must breathe deeply," she said.

"I know!"

"Go on then," Stella said encouragingly.

"I'm going to die," Amber wailed fretfully, as she began to shiver.

"No, you're not! You have to breathe, like they do on TV. Just breathe deeply – like this," and she puffed out her cheeks and blew deep breaths through her lips.

Amber shook her head, a faint smile twisting her pale lips.

"See how easy it is to fucking breathe!" said Stella.

Amber copied Stella's puffing, laughing and then yelping with pain at the same time.

Stella, remembering the phone operator, got up.

"Don't leave me," growled Amber.

Stella hovered between Amber and the phone and then dashed to pick up the receiver.

"She's breathing – puffing – you know."

"Brilliant, you're doing really well," said the operator. She sounded so calm that she could have been nonchalantly painting her nails or something on the other end of the phone. "The ambulance will be there any minute now. Go back to your friend."

Stella went back to Amber.

"Why didn't you get help before?" she asked gently, perching on the edge of the sofa and lifting a damp strand of hair off Amber's grey forehead.

"Paul's coming. He's just gone to see a house he wants to buy for us, out in the country." She flexed her legs, twisting in anticipation of another pain. "The pain started and I thought that he would be back in time to bring me to the hospital, but they got so bad I couldn't move and then you came."

"Hold my hand. Grip onto me when the pain starts." Stella slipped her hand into Amber's damp, hot one.

"Don't you dare say anything about him being unreliable," Amber gasped, tensing her body as another pain wracked through her.

Stella felt every bone and fibre within her hand being crushed beyond endurance. "I wouldn't dare," she said, gingerly easing her hand out of Amber's grip – maybe the hand-holding wasn't a good idea – it was just that they always seemed to do that on the TV.

"It's coming," Amber writhed again, puffing furiously. She half clambered and half fell off the sofa.

"Ha, ha," Stella felt her mouth open in panic, "don't be silly. It's too soon! This is no time to joke."

Amber strained, her face screwing up with the effort. "No – joke."

Stella dashed to the phone. "She's having the baby!" she roared, quivering all over with panic.

"Can you see anything?"

Stella glanced out of the window. "No, there's no sign of the ambulance!"

"Can you see the baby?" the operator said. Her voice was calm, but there was an edge of tension in it suddenly.

Stella looked back at Amber as if she expected to see a baby suddenly in her arms. Then it dawned on her what the operator wanted.

"Ohhhhh!"

She put the phone down and went back to Amber. Leaning down, she peeked. "Oh fuck!"

"Help me!" Amber whimpered.

Stella dashed back to the phone. "I can see

something!" she hissed into the receiver.

"*Stella!*" shrieked Amber.

Stella threw down the receiver and dashed to Amber.

A few minutes later the door banged open and Paul, followed by two burly ambulance men, shot into the room.

"You've got a little boy," Stella said proudly, holding up the towelling bundle that she had in her arms, so that Paul could see the crumpled, angry-looking red face of his son.

Paul reeled in shock. His face was suddenly so white Stella thought he was going to faint. She changed her mind about handing him the baby and handed it to an ambulance man instead.

"We need to get you to hospital – get you and the baby checked out," said one of the ambulance men to Amber.

They helped Amber into a wheelchair.

"Can I come and visit you again?" Stella asked.

"Yes, please," Amber grinned, lifting her hand to wipe a smear of blood off Stella's pale face. "Bring Teddy with you next time. I'll take him for a walk and you can play with Junior."

The ambulance man put the baby gently into Amber's arms.

"What did you want anyway?" Amber grinned at Stella over the top of the baby's head.

Stella grinned back. "Just to say that I was sorry."

51

Stella drove slowly up the hill, feeling a sense of tremendous peace wash over her. She could never fail to love the beauty of this place. The road curved gently upwards, winding through the dappled green woodland that bordered it. One day, Stella thought, she would love to come back and paint this place. The trees made a canopy of green above the road, dappling the road with the shadows of the leaves. At either side of the road the forest was a multitude of greens, the pale undersides of the bracken mingling with the waxy darkness of the rhododendrons and the glowing shades of the grasses. Stella reached the top of the hill, slowed the car and pulled over to the lay-by where she had found Teddy what seemed like a lifetime ago.

She got out of the car, and looked through the canopy of the leaves, across the parkland to Thornhill House, Henry's new home. Soon to be the one that he would share with Xanthe.

Stella took a deep breath. She had to see Henry. To try to make him understand why he couldn't marry Xanthe. Stella clipped the lead onto Teddy's collar and started to walk back down the hill towards the entrance to Thornhill House. She wanted to walk down the drive, just for once to savour the house and the parkland. Driving would have made it all happen too quickly. She wanted to try to imprint the memory of it deep within her, so that she could draw on it sometime in the future when the pain of losing Henry had receded.

The entrance to Thornhill House was at the bottom of the hill. The stone wall that marked the border of the parkland curved in to form an imposing entrance. Stella felt her steps begin to falter, nervously. What if Henry told her to clear off? What if he wouldn't listen to what she had to say to him? That was a chance that she had to take.

"Come on, Teddy," Stella said in a voice that sounded a lot more positive than she actually felt and she strode past the towering iron gates and tall stone pillars that marked the entrance to Henry's home, a slim but no longer too-thin figure in jeans and a simple T-shirt.

A long straight avenue stretched in front of her, running through grassland as smooth as a garden lawn. Sheep grazed at either side of the avenue and lay beneath the shaded shelter of sprawling oak trees. Teddy strained at his lead, eager to be let off to run free.

Every stride brought Stella closer and closer to the house. And the closer that she got, the more nervous she felt. It was so quiet, only the occasional bleating of a sheep and the nervous sound of her breathing broke the silence.

The avenue ended in a curved forecourt in front of the house. Stella felt tiny and very conspicuous as her footsteps crunched across the greys and creams of the gravel. Close up, the house was even more beautiful than it was from a distance.

Henry's Jeep stood beside the stone steps that led up to the front door.

Stella smiled, shaking her head. Henry really didn't care what anyone thought of him. He had no need to exchange his battered Jeep for something new and flashy, just because he was now the owner of a magnificent house and had just inherited a fortune. Stella and Teddy walked up the stone steps. Beside the door was a huge recessed alcove where a chain with a fancy handle was hanging. Stella pulled the chain, turning back to look out at the magnificent view from the front door as the resounding note of a bell rang in the depths of the house.

A moment later Teddy whined, cocking his head to one side as footsteps that he recognised echoed within the house. The enormous blue door swung back and Henry stood in front of them.

While Teddy went wild with delight, Stella looked first at Henry and then gazed past him into the depths of the house. A magnificent chandelier, at least five feet long, hung from the ceiling behind him and beyond a vast hallway stretched so far ahead that she couldn't see where it ended. Teddy was going crazy on his lead, rearing on his back legs to jump up at Henry, whining for attention.

"Hi, Teddy!" Henry crouched down beside the little dog, rubbing his ears and his muzzle. "Great to see you." He stood up slowly and looked at Stella. "Hello, Stella." His voice was cool, with none of the easy affection that he had greeted Teddy with. "You had better come in." He stood back to let Stella walk into the house. "You can let Teddy off the lead."

She did so with fumbling fingers.

"Paul rang me and said that you delivered Amber's baby," Henry was saying as he closed the enormous door behind her. "That was very brave of you. I'm glad that you two have made up."

He led the way along the hallway and through a door into a vast room. Light flooded in from the tall windows that looked out onto the gardens that Stella had seen when she and Henry had walked in the woods above his cottage.

"Sit down," Henry said coolly. Stella glanced around, there were three enormous sofas arranged around a huge fireplace and two more pushed back against the walls of the room. Henry perched himself on the edge of one of the sofas by the fireplace Stella, following his cue, took a place opposite him. Teddy made straight for the rug in front of the empty fireplace and settled down as if he had lived there all of his life.

"How are you?" Henry said, his voice politely cool as if she were a stranger who had just come to call at the house.

Stella quailed at the thought of talking to him – he was so cold, hard, as if hatred oozed from his every pore. He didn't want her here. He was always courteous when they met at the races, but this was his territory now. He was a different person from the one that she had once known. And he was making it very clear that he didn't want Stella around.

"Henry, I . . ." Stella faltered. The words wouldn't form on her lips. She loved him so much that the pain of being close to him was too much to bear. The weight of her stupidity for dumping him when she had truly loved him was total agony. Stella wished that she hadn't come. She should have stayed away, let the pain of missing him gradually recede with the passing of time. But she couldn't go away until she had said what she needed to.

"Henry, you can't marry Xanthe!" The words tumbled out of her mouth.

Henry looked shocked at her outburst. Then he recovered his composure. He lay back against the cushions on the sofa, folded his arms and stared at Stella for a long time, silently.

"What gives you the right to tell me that?" he asked at last.

Stella swallowed hard. This was the most awful thing that she had ever done. "I *know* Xanthe – I *lived* with her – and she's not right for you."

"Why is that then?" Henry raised his eyebrows sardonically.

"Because she doesn't love you for yourself," Stella said quietly. How could she tell him that Xanthe had betrayed him with Derry Blake? It would be too cruel; it would break his heart.

"And who does?" Henry said coldly. "You certainly didn't."

"I did," Stella said quietly. "I was just afraid of . . ."

"Being with someone poor – a nobody," Henry finished the sentence for her.

Stella nodded bleakly. He must despise her for being so shallow.

"And now you want me back because you think I'm rich."

Stella shook her head, violently. "No. No. I realised what a mistake I'd made before you got all . . . this . . ." Stella gazed around the room. "But then, when I heard you'd inherited the house I felt that I couldn't come because you'd think that I just wanted you for what you were. Not who you were."

"I don't believe you," said Henry, his eyes icy cold when Stella looked up to meet them. "You're shallow and greedy and you've come here try to disrupt my plans to marry."

Stella shook her head again, unable to speak because of the huge lump that constricted her throat. "No," she whispered. "I knew that you wouldn't have me back because you would think that. I just wanted to . . . warn you about Xanthe . . . and say goodbye. I'm going away, back to Mayo."

"I see," Henry said coldly.

Stella buried her face in her hands, unable to bear his impenetrable coldness.

There was a long silence, broken only by the sound of Teddy sighing as he turned around on the rug before settling back down to snooze.

"You can't marry Xanthe," Stella tried again.

"What the fuck makes you think you have the right to tell me who I can or cannot marry?" Henry exploded. He got up and paced in front of the fireplace as if he could barely control his anger.

"Because I love you. And, Henry . . ." Stella whispered, "Xanthe's having an affair with Derry Blake."

"No, she's not." Henry shook his head vehemently. He picked up one of the ornaments from above the fireplace and examined it as if he had never seen it before.

"Well, she's had a fling with him then – I saw them, Henry. She doesn't love you – she'll ruin your life – I know she will. It will be a marriage based on lies and infidelity. A terrible mistake."

Henry swung round from the fireplace. "My only mistake was to fall in love with you!" he said and crossed the room with three quick strides. "You stupid, stupid woman!" He pulled her to her feet and entwined his fingers in the hair at the back of her head, tugging it downwards to tilt her face up towards his. "I'm not marrying Xanthe," he said.

"Oh!" she breathed. "Thank God! What happened? Did you find out about Derry Blake?"

"No. I was never marrying Xanthe." He let her go, then flung himself down on the settee, chuckling softly.

"What?" Stella frowned. "But you – you – do you mean you got engaged to her without ever intending to marry her?" How could he? The Henry she had known wouldn't do such a thing. "Wasn't that a cruel thing to do?"

She crossed the room unsteadily and sat down beside him.

"I was never engaged to her."

"But – but –"

Henry's lips twisted in sardonic amusement. "Stella, I've known Xanthe for years – her father keeps a few horses with me. The first time you saw us together her father had asked me to give her a lift to the Jockey of the Year Award ceremony. He didn't want her drinking and driving."

Horrified, Stella thought back to that occasion and the assumptions she had made. "It can't be true!"

"The girls knew I was in love with you and that you had turned me down. So October had the idea that if I started taking Xanthe out it would make you jealous and you might come back to me."

"October?" And she had thought October and the others didn't give a damn about her.

"I tried it!" said Henry. "I'd have tried anything!" He shook his head at the memory. "But that didn't work the way she had planned!"

"But the wedding . . . so that was all an elaborate practical joke as well?" This was horrible. How could he do such a thing to her? Suddenly she felt angry tears welling at the corners of her eyes.

"No, of course not!" He looked outraged at the suggestion. "What do you think I am? It was – is – no joke. Xanthe really is getting married. Her fiancé works abroad – he arrived back to Dublin for the wedding a few days ago."

"But she told me she was marrying you –" And then Stella stopped short, realising that Xanthe had told her no such thing. She had simply said she was getting married and, fired by jealousy, Stella had drawn her own conclusions.

"No," said Henry, "I'm sure she didn't tell you that. From what you've said, you seem to have managed to make that blunder all by yourself."

She felt such a fool.

And now she mustn't make another huge stupid blunder. Like, for example, throwing herself into Henry's arms now, wildly begging him to take her back. She must move slowly, carefully, keeping her hard-won balance. And she needed to get away from Henry now before she lost her fragile control of her emotions.

She got up abruptly and walked away from him to one of the huge windows, where she stood trailing her fingers over the long silk curtains. She gazed out at the parkland beyond the gardens, the timeless scenery that had seen generations of Henry's ancestors live and die.

"I made such a mess of everything," she said,

closing her eyes to fight back the tears that threatened to spill down her face. "I hurt you. I hurt Amber. Everyone who was important to me. I spent my childhood hating my family for what they were. Now I can see how wrong I was. Happiness has nothing to do with money or possessions."

She turned to Henry, summoning up her strength.

"I must go now. I'm going back to Mayo. Maybe soon . . . or some time in the future . . . we can meet and talk . . . about all the mess I created."

And then, before he could react, she was walking hastily out of the room and out of Henry's house, half blinded by the tears that flowed down her cheeks.

Wiping her eyes on a crumpled tissue that she found in her jeans' pocket, she tilted her chin upwards and walked swiftly down the long drive, Teddy trotting obediently beside her, his warm body nudging at her calves as if he wanted to reassure her of his presence.

This time she knew she had done the right thing. She had regained a little bit of dignity and had allowed Henry retain his.

Back at the car, she was about to open the door to let Teddy in when his sharp ears picked up a sound and he turned to 'point' back towards the house. A rhythmic sound came faintly to Stella's ears and a movement caught her eye. In the parkland in front of the house, half-hidden from view by the canopy of leaves, a horse was galloping, its rider crouched low in the saddle. Stella watched until they disappeared from view. Then, with a sigh, she turned away. That was all in the past now.

She settled Teddy in his seat and had gone to open the driver's door when a clattering sound startled her.

The horse and rider were coming up the road towards her. It was Henry on I Agree.

Stella closed the car door on a wildly excited and barking Teddy, and moved to the front of the car as Henry vaulted from the horse.

He stood before her, his eyes full of love.

"I don't want you to go," he said gently.

Stella took a stride forwards into his arms.

"I don't want to go either," she whispered, raising her face to be kissed.

They came up for air, and stood there smiling in each other's eyes.

And I Agree, shaking his head, gave a snort of disgust at being ignored for so long, and splattered Stella's T-shirt with froth from his mouth.

"Oh, hell!" said Henry.

Stella looked down at her spattered T-shirt. The marks were spreading slowly as the moisture soaked into the fabric.

And one of the stains looked distinctly like a love heart.

The End

Published by poolbeg.com

Winners

JACQUI BRODERICK

Redwood Stables is a hive of activity as fearless female jockey Paris O'Shea and her groom Merrianne Ryan get ready to put tetchy thoroughbred mare Destiny through her paces at the Limerick races.

Paris is a real winner in life and has little time for other people's errors. She and horse-trainer Derry Blake make a dynamic couple as they announce their engagement. If only her father Paddy would stop drinking and get over the past, everything in Paris's life would be perfect.

Merrianne is fed up with being ordered about and dreams of being a lady who lunches with a stunning wardrobe. But can she really turn her back on her hippie mother Shula and string of toyboys?

Neither of them can know that one event during the following day's racing will change both their lives forever, and test their inner strength beyond their limits.

ISBN 1-84223-168-5

Published by poolbeg.com

Trainers

JACQUI BRODERICK

'She loved them both desperately but now they were forcing her to choose'

Betrayed in love yet again, Tara Blake returns to Ireland to the loving protection of her older brother Derry, a ruthless playboy who is one of Ireland's top racehorse trainers.

Back home Tara is drawn to Morgan Flynn. Flynn was once a top jockey but following the death of one of his horses he was branded as reckless and is now struggling to keep his dilapidated stables alive.

Torn between loyalty to her brother and the man she loves, Tara looks on helplessly as Derry and Morgan embark on a dangerous game of rivalry and vengeance.

Against the backdrop of Ireland's fiercely competitive and glamorous world of horse-racing, the two men will stop at nothing in their battle to win the ultimate prize.

ISBN 1-84223-169-3